*Dark Reaction*

**JODY SWANNELL**

Copyright © 2023 by Jody Swannell

All rights reserved. This book or any portion thereof may not be reproduced or used in any manner whatsoever without the express written permission of the publisher except for the use of brief quotations in a book review.

Publisher's note: This is a work of fiction. Names, characters, places, and incidents either are the product of the author's imagination or are used fictitiously. Any resemblance to actual events, locales, or persons, living or dead, is entirely coincidental.

Edited by Kristen Corrects, Inc.

First edition published 2023

## Contents

1. The Nightmare — 1
2. Decisions — 11
3. Road Trip — 19
4. Companions — 29
5. Jacob — 40
6. Dad — 50
7. Nekxus — 60
8. DMRM — 71
9. Protocols — 81
10. Cult — 92
11. Animals — 103
12. Pyramid — 114
13. The Hatch — 125
14. Imperial Jade — 136
15. Funeral — 147
16. Vaccine — 158
17. Youth — 169
18. The News — 180
19. The Restaurant — 190
20. Apnea — 200
21. Scarab — 211
22. Debate — 222
23. Broadcast — 233
24. Feast — 243
25. Anchor — 254

Acknowledgments — 265
About the Author — 267
Also by Jody Swannell — 269

# CHAPTER 1
## *The Nightmare*

"I WOKE UP TERRIFIED, gasping for air, my heart racing." I quivered, remembering the dream.

"You used to do that when we were roommates," Jacob said, his voice distant.

When I'd roused from the nightmare, I called my best friend immediately. The resulting panic attack freaked me out. He put me on the speaker.

"This was different," I insisted. "I tried to tell myself, *Calm down. It's only a dream.*"

I brushed my long curls off my cheek. I was still underneath the soft down duvet, soaked in a cold sweat, trying to relax. Controlling my breathing proved difficult, and I wondered again if I had sleep apnea.

"Tell me about your dream," he said.

"It began at work," I started. The buffet-style Chinese restaurant Jade Castle was affectionately known by most customers and staff as just The Castle. "I was standing near the salad bar, and despite the place being empty, I felt a strong sense of urgency to get out of there."

"Mhmm," he said.

"After searching the room for my car keys, I saw a glimmer of light reflecting off the quartz crystal charm on my keychain. It struck me as strange because my keys would usually be in my purse, not sitting on the table. Out of nowhere, I heard a familiar voice order me sternly: *Run.*"

"Creepy. Then what?" Jacob asked, yawning.

"I turned my head to see that Andrei was now standing there. His eyes were wild," I said. Andrei was generally soft-spoken. His thick Russian accent made him sound a little more severe than the tone his voice usually portrayed. In this situation, there was no mistake. He was commanding me to run. I didn't know why, but it frightened me. "Then I looked around and saw Di." Di was my boss and friend, The Castle's owner. "He was standing beside Andrei with a large knife. There was a perplexed look on his face as he stared down at the huge blade. It was as if he had never seen one before."

"Oh, dreaming of knives is a bad omen," Jacob said pointedly.

"I panicked. I scanned the room, looking for an explanation. Out of the corner of my eye, I saw an insect. The thing looked like an oversized earwig with large pincers on its rear end that curled up threateningly. It didn't have any eyes or antennae, but it did have teeth—*too many teeth*. I backed up slowly, then it morphed into a faceless man; he wasn't alone either. Two other men joined him on either side."

"No shit," he mumbled with a mouthful of toothpaste; I could hear him brushing his teeth.

"The guy in the middle leaned in towards me and spoke sinisterly: *You're dead!* Then I woke up."

"Christ, Kim, that's absurd," Jacob said.

"It was insane," I agreed. "Thanks for listening; I'll see you before I leave for Mexico, have a great day."

"You too, crazy girl," Jacob said, chuckling.

I stretched out, trying not to disturb my dog Loki, who was blissfully sleeping on top of the duvet at the foot of my bed.

Today was going to be my last day of work for a while. I was getting four weeks off while the restaurant underwent renovations. I'd been looking forward to this holiday for quite a while now and hoped everything would go smoothly. Working as a restaurant manager was challenging, with so many moving parts that I spent most of my time just trying to keep things organized.

Di and I met at a local gym years ago. He used his intelligence and charm to persuade me to help him run his business. I had no problem resigning from my previous workplace. The only thing lower than my former boss's standards was the pay.

The Castle was a busy place, and because business was so good, this afforded Di some extra cash flow he was using to revamp the dining and buffet area decor. He planned to replace the out-of-date flooring, install a small waterfall with a beautiful stream, and add a garden that would run around the dining area.

At my recommendation, Di hired my neighbour Andrei to do the renovations. After my divorce, I'd become close friends with his wife, Anastasia, who preferred to be called Ana. When Di started to discuss his makeover plans for the establishment, I made the introduction because Andrei owned a small construction company. I was delighted with the prospect of having my friends work together and thrilled when they hit it off fabulously. They collaborated and came up with a beautiful design.

Yet I couldn't stop worrying about the nightmare's meaning. *Will things not go according to plan?* Loki straightened out and yawned but didn't attempt to get up, so I had a few minutes before I needed to take him out for a pee. I searched a couple of my favourite websites about dream definitions, hoping for some help interpreting the nightmare's meaning.

Unsuccessful, I put my phone back and looked down at my adorable fur baby, sleeping peacefully. Oh, how I wished to be in his position. Before I got Loki as a puppy, I thought the endearing term *fur baby* was stupid. I adopted him after going through a somewhat messy divorce, and thanks to Loki, I saw how quickly a pet could take someone's heart and fill it with love and joy.

Di, Andrei, and I had plans to get together after the dinner rush to discuss the next couple of weeks. I didn't have much input in this situation, but as the manager, I was included in the planning—the fact that I was friends with both parties didn't hurt.

"Loki," I called softly, "hey, baby."

My dog opened his eyes, and his tail started to wag as he looked up at me. *Bless his heart; he's so cute.* He trotted up to my face and started licking my chin. I rubbed his ears and told him, "Yes, you are a good, beautiful boy." He got more excited, and the face-licking started to tickle. "Okay, get off me. I'm getting up."

Loki patiently waited for me to throw on a T-shirt and sweatpants to take him for a short walk to relieve himself. We found Ana standing on her porch tending to her herb garden, and I waved to her.

"Morning Ana, how are you?" I said.

"I'm great. It's another beautiful day—we could use a little rain. My grass is turning to shit," Ana replied, looking up at the sky.

The word *shit* hung in the air longer than expected because she extended the vowel in her pronunciation. Her Russian accent made her sound so cute when she swore. Whenever I swore, I sounded like a pissed-off truck driver.

Ana tossed a treat to Loki, who anticipated it and caught it mid-air. Loki adored her because she was always spoiling him with bits of dehydrated liver. She claimed it was good for him. Ana had her own set of keys to my place because she enjoyed taking Loki for walks. Fortunately, we worked different schedules so he wouldn't be stuck alone in the house for very long.

"I'll see you tomorrow," I told her.

"Yes—we will drink coffee and complain about people," she said and laughed. "Best of luck tonight." Ana winked at me and waved.

"Thanks, enjoy the sunshine." I followed Loki, who was pulling the leash in the direction of his favourite route towards the nearby park.

My morning routine included walking my miniature Doberman around the neighbourhood and to the playground. I often saw Ana sitting on her porch, enjoying her morning coffee. We'd bump into each other often in the warmer months—winter was a different story. Hamilton, situated beside Lake Ontario in Canada, made it a windy and icy place to live during the colder season.

After the walk, I took a long shower before preparing bacon and eggs on my countertop grill. I fed Loki his meal and, of course, shared mine with him. He was trained to sit like the sphinx in Egypt, and it melted my heart as I watched him hold the statue-like position until I flicked some bacon at him. He popped up and snapped it out of mid-air like a professional.

As I dressed for work, I couldn't shake the lingering apprehension. I could still hear those terrifying words—*You're dead.* I could also hear Andrei's urgent command—*Run.* It seemed simple enough, but of course, I didn't run. I just stood there like an idiot, wondering what was going on. The more I tried to ignore the bad feeling, the more it persisted.

After finishing my breakfast dishes, I poured myself a second cup of coffee and started to feel better. The anticipation of meeting with Di and Andrei cheered me up. Ensuring there were no loose ends before the upgrades and...*vacation time.* I kissed Loki and headed off to work.

The Castle parking lot was vacant when I arrived. Sitting in my car, I tried to ignore the wave of paranoia. I'd been coming here for almost five years to open the restaurant; why did I feel so apprehensive now? *One silly dream?* I wondered. Eventually, I gathered my wits and got out of my little black compact.

After a brisk walk to the front door, I locked it behind me until one of the chefs showed up. Once the staff started arriving, I began to relax. The Castle became alive with familiar faces, and my negativity faded, replaced with excitement.

The day went by quickly, and we worked through a busy lunch and supper. The staff cleaned up and put away as much as possible. I helped a couple of servers load their cars with perishables to take home; there was no reason to see good cuisine go to waste just because we were closing for a few weeks. I made a mental note to call the food bank in the morning to pick up the rest before it spoiled.

Di was in the back going over the blueprints. He was looking forward to *refreshing the environment,* as he liked to put it. When he bought the building, it came with all the existing kitchenware. Although it was good enough, Di was anxious to upgrade to more modern equipment.

I watched the parking lot for Andrei. It had been weeks since I'd seen him because he often worked out of town. A white work van pulled into the parking lot.

"Andrei's here!" I called out to Di.

"Fantastic! He's right on time," Di said.

"I'll pour the drinks," I said.

I knew Andrei would drink vodka, and Di wasn't too fussy, so I prepared three glasses of the hard spirit with lime and ice. No one would get corked, but it would be nice to take the edge off.

Andrei dressed casually, just as I'd expected he would. Clean blue jeans, a white collared cotton T-shirt, and pristinely shined black shoes. Di wore a full suit, which was typical for him. I wasn't sure if it was because his parents were wealthy back in China and he was accustomed to expensive tastes, or if it was just how he preferred to carry himself. His wife Jing had far simpler tastes and liked to tease her husband for his fondness for formal clothing.

The front door featured tinted glass, and as I placed the beverages on a table, I watched Andrei walk up to it. I considered him handsome, like Captain Picard, since he didn't have much hair. Jacob was so fond of *Star Trek* that he forced me to watch it with him when we lived together. Andrei's infectious smile made me happy when he opened the door and made eye contact with me.

"Ah, Kim! So nice to see you. I've missed you!" Andrei said.

"I've missed you too!" I said as I strolled over to give him a hug. "I saw Ana this morning and told her how much I was looking forward to seeing you tonight."

Andrei laughed. "Yes, I know. She told me I must bring these for you." He handed me a plastic container filled with freshly baked buns.

*Oh sweet*, I thought, smiling. I was a sucker for bread, especially Ana's baking. Going to the bakery and purchasing fresh rye, rolls, croissants, and bagels was something I indulged in a little too often. It was starting to show on my hips and thighs.

"Thank you. We can enjoy these baked goods with a glass of some of the best vodka." I motioned to the table where I had set the drinks.

"Nice to see you, Andrei." Di approached the table and shook hands with Andrei before sitting down. "I couldn't wait for Kim to chase out the last customers so we could spend this time together before you come with your guys tomorrow and rip the place up." He pointed at the dining room.

Andrei laughed. "Yes, we're ready to get started. I was worried the flooring wouldn't ship on time, but my supplier came through. Everything is ready to go."

"Excellent!" Di said. He picked up one of the glasses I'd prepared. "Cheers to you, my friend," he said, raising his glass towards Andrei, "and to you, Kim. I don't know what I would do without you." Di smiled at me.

I mused that statement was an exaggeration, but I appreciated the compliment anyway.

"Cheers," Andrei said and raised his glass.

"Cheers," I repeated.

We clinked glasses and took healthy swigs of vodka. Di smiled broadly, and Andrei relaxed back into his chair as he took another sip.

Someone barged into the front entrance, and I stood up immediately.

"Sorry, we're closed," I said, then my eyes widened.

The intruder wasn't alone—another guy followed him. They were both wearing black surgical masks, the kind abundantly available since the global pandemic.

My breath caught in my throat, and horror set in. I realized that the first guy was holding a shotgun or rifle and pointing it toward us. Even if I knew the difference between the two, I couldn't have figured it out. I was filled with fear and had trouble focusing, feeling like I might collapse.

Andrei stood and held his hands in the air. Di just sat still in his chair. The first guy yelled at Andrei, "Don't move!"

"Nobody is going to move. Just calm down," Andrei replied, his voice calm.

"Shut up," the first intruder barked as he poked the gun's barrel into Andrei's chest.

That guy stood there holding the gun toward Andrei while the bigger guy walked purposefully over to the counter. He thrust out his arm and shoved the cash register. Obediently, it crashed and broke open, spilling money onto the floor.

"Where's the safe?" the second guy snarled, pointing a large knife toward Di.

Di's voice shook when he replied, "It's in the office, but it's empty."

"Oh really? It looks like this idiot wants to play games! Hey Jimmy, we like games, don't we?" The tone of his voice suggested that he did not.

*How stupid is this guy?* I thought to myself, *Calling the other guy by his first name.* Jimmy didn't seem to care that his name was revealed, as he responded with creepy laughter.

"It's no joke," Di said. "We're closing for construction, and I took the money to the bank yesterday. Just take whatever you want and leave us, please. Here, you can take my wallet too."

Di reached into his pocket but stopped when the guy with the gun snapped at him.

"I told you, don't fucking move, or I'm going to shoot your buddy here!" Jimmy dug the gun in Andrei's ribs.

I'd never felt fear like this before. I thought I might faint. At the pounding of my heart, my smartwatch buzzed on my wrist, the health app warning me to calm down. The big guy, Jimmy's buddy, walked towards me with the knife, waving it in a circle at my head.

"I think you can show me where the safe is, can't you, honey?" he said.

Inside, I felt what I assumed were my bones vibrating. *Oh God, this is how it ends.* I'd seen too many movies and figured I'd be beaten, raped, and left for dead. Jimmy's buddy walked around and positioned himself behind me. *Help!* I thought, desperate. I looked into Andrei's eyes and saw the cold expression on his face. We locked gazes for what seemed like an eternity but was probably more like half a second. Eerily, I heard his voice echoing inside my head—*Run.*

I moved instinctively because I had no idea what I was doing. It was like how my body reacted when I tripped on something. I stumbled forward. This intruder was close enough to me that I could hear him breathing, even with the mask covering his face. I looked down and raised my right leg, then I stomped his foot and twirled away from him.

"Ah, you bitch!"

Andrei brought his arm down on Jimmy's gun. Or was it up? I

couldn't tell—things were happening so fast. Andrei had outmaneuvered the guy and now possessed the firearm. He swung the butt end of the gun and whacked the guy in the head so hard he dropped to the floor like a stone.

I didn't see what happened next because Jimmy's buddy threw me aside violently. A sharp pain flared in my shoulder and hip when I slammed into the floor.

The gun went off, so loud that I felt like it burst my eardrums. I was stunned and confused but made an effort to stand anyway.

I looked down at Jimmy's buddy; he was lying on his back with his chest blown wide open. Blood was everywhere. I looked across the dreadful scene to see Di standing beside Andrei. They were both looking at the floor where Jimmy lay unconscious. Andrei held the gun at his side but looked ready to handle it.

Andrei used to be a sniper in the Russian army, but it hadn't crossed my mind how skilled he was. Undoubtedly, this wasn't his first experience with violence. His reaction was professional during the attempted robbery. I believed wholeheartedly that he shot the intruder out of necessity and I felt an immense sense of gratitude that he was there. I could only imagine what would have happened if he wasn't.

Other than feeling a little dizzy, I didn't perceive pain anymore. Di rushed over and put his hands on my shoulders. He squared himself in front of me and looked into my eyes.

"Kim? Are you okay?"

"Yeah, I think so," I replied, surprised at the sound of my voice. My ears were still ringing from the sound of the gunshot. "Are they both dead?"

"No." Di nodded his head towards the animal Jimmy, who was lying there without moving. "He's out of it."

Knocked out was what he meant. Andrei had clocked the guy hard. I turned back and eyeballed the big guy bleeding all over the floor, and a wave of nausea washed over me. I sat in the nearest chair. I couldn't take my eyes off the dead guy.

"*Govno*," Andrei said with disdain and spat on the body.

I didn't have to be Russian to understand that he said *shit*. I'd been hanging around with Ana enough to have picked up that word, along with a few other choice phrases. I stood there for a moment, waiting for someone to say something else, but the room remained unbelievably quiet.

The Jade Castle was a fair-sized building that stood alone just away from downtown, near the mountain and not too close to the residential area, which allowed for an ample parking lot. I hadn't heard any sirens yet. Had anyone heard the shot go off? I didn't sense any immediate danger anymore, so I was unconcerned. If Andrei had the gun in his hands, I felt safe enough.

Then, I began to wonder if these guys were alone. Were more criminals waiting outside? I dropped the thought, assuming there weren't, or they would have burst in through the front door by now.

"Now what?"

Di and Andrei both looked at each other before turning to face me.

"I don't know," Andrei answered.

# CHAPTER 2
## *Decisions*

I FELT RESPONSIBLE. Maybe none of this would've happened if I'd been more cautious and locked the front door after Andrei came in. Now that the restrictions from the pandemic had relaxed, one only had to look at the headlines to know that violent crime and vandalism had skyrocketed. We were in a severe predicament, and even though he was a scumbag, a man was dead.

Jimmy started to moan, calling our attention back toward him. He was regaining consciousness and attempting to sit up.

"Just sit still," Andrei snapped as he aimed the gun at Jimmy.

Jimmy looked around the room sluggishly until his eyes rested on the floor where his partner lay sprawled out in a bloody mess, dead. "You killed Ryan!" He started to laugh.

Without his mask, which had fallen off during the struggle with Andrei, I saw his teeth were rotten and dirty. How could he laugh at his dead friend? I found it disturbing and reckoned he was insane. I looked at Di to see his eyes had narrowed and his jaw clenched.

"You guys are so dead!" Jimmy said as he shook his head in disbelief. "I'm going to tell his brother. He and his buddies will come in here and tear this place apart! I wouldn't want to be in your shoes. Ryan's brother's got a mean temper. He *likes* to hurt people." Jimmy's eyes lit up as he continued. "When the cops get here and arrest you, you won't be safe in jail either. He's got friends in the joint too. I'm going to put the word out. You're going to get it big time, asshole!" He directed this last part at Andrei.

Andrei didn't seem to be fazed by his words, but Di was getting increasingly upset. His face beet red, he turned and marched into the kitchen. I guessed he had decided to make a call to the authorities.

When Di came back, he'd taken off his jacket, rolled up his sleeves and was now wearing one of the cooks' aprons. His pallor returned to normal, and he had a determined look. I tried to identify Di's intentions but failed. He looked like he was ready to prepare a meal. *Maybe he's in shock*, I speculated.

Jimmy, on the other hand, didn't seem to share my logic. He started to get agitated.

"Hey man, what do you think you're doing? You can't hurt me," he said, but his words were without confidence. "The cops are on their way." Jimmy looked around the room, perplexed. Then his voice started to sound manic. "The cops are coming, right? What the hell are you thinking? You're not going to get away with this. Come on, man, just let me go," he pleaded.

Perhaps Di was playing mind games to intimidate the guy. Jimmy's threats made it clear he would ensure the outcome would devastate my friends and me. *Does Di think he can negotiate a truce or something?*

Jimmy made an effort to get up and run, but Di moved like lightning and snapped up the knife lying on the floor beside Ryan's corpse. Double-quick, Di grabbed him from behind and cut his throat broad and deep. Jimmy's scream was cut short.

I gasped, my hand flying to my mouth in shock. I looked up at Andrei, who put the gun down, picked up his glass of vodka, and chugged the rest of it. The gravity of the situation set in thoroughly. My mind raced as I assessed options until I settled on an image.

"I know where to bury the bodies!" I exclaimed. How odd the words sounded as they flew out of my mouth.

Di and Andrei turned and looked at me in a way that made me think they'd briefly forgotten I was there.

"It's a long drive up north, but no one's going to find them," I assured.

"Good," Andrei said after a moment.

Di wiped the blade on his apron and said something in Chinese. He took the apron off, threw it over Jimmy, and stood still for a few seconds before speaking. "Thank you, Kim. I will clean this up by morning." He motioned to the bodies on the floor and looked at Andrei. "The Jade Castle will be ready for renovations. Andrei, what do you need from me?"

"I need garbage bags, and I will need your help loading this filth into my truck." Andrei jutted his chin out towards the dead men. "Kim and I will take care of the disposal. I'll ensure my crew will be here in the morning and inform them that I won't join them until tomorrow. Are you okay with meeting up with them at eight o' clock?"

"Yes," Di said, nodding confidently.

Di went into the kitchen again, where I could hear the water running. He was probably washing his hands. I walked to the bar and helped myself to a water bottle. After drinking more than half of the bottle in one big swallow, I took a deep breath and let out a long sigh. Andrei joined me, and I offered him a bottle. He shook his head no, so I grabbed the vodka and poured him a healthy glass. He sipped the alcohol appreciatively.

"Listen to me—I know this is serious, but it's all going to be okay. If you're not up to this, Di and I will take care of it."

"No, I'm fine," I said, trying to sound unruffled.

Strangely enough, I was telling the truth. Maybe this would all hit me hard later on, but the mortal fear I'd experienced had passed, and now I was eager to get this over with and put it behind me. Without discussion, all three of us had agreed: *This never happened.*

"My older sister lives in Timmins," I started. "Derek and I used to drive up there when he went hunting. I would stay with Julia and her family while Derek met up with his party, and they continued to travel north to moose country. On our drive up, we would sometimes take one of the side roads to…well, you know." I blushed.

"I see. Are you sure Derek won't visit one of these so-called side roads in the future?" Andrei asked.

"Oh, I'm positive. He travels with Fred now. I was the one who found all of the secluded spots. My ex-husband may think he's a hotshot lawyer, but when it comes to directions, he couldn't navigate his way around the mall. It was practically a disability for him," I said sarcastically.

"Okay, we should leave soon. Do you need anything?"

"What about Ana?"

"Ana will be fine. I'll talk to her, don't worry." Andrei offered a half-hearted smile. "We'll have Loki stay with her tonight."

I wondered what Andrei would say to his wife. Would he spin some story? I hoped Ana wouldn't worry too much. It was going to look suspicious with Andrei and me driving off into the night. I had little insight into their marriage, but it looked like they trusted each other. I figured they would cross that bridge when they got to it.

"Okay, that makes sense, since she's babysitting Loki anyway. While you talk to her, I'll drop off my car and run into the house so I can change out of these clothes," I said.

"I'll only need a couple of minutes with Ana, then we should leave right away," he said.

"Agreed. I'll be ready," I promised.

Andrei patted Di on the shoulder and said, "Let's get this over with. I'll bring my truck around back. Kim, can you go open the door? I'm going to back up as close as possible."

Grateful to be distancing myself from the bloody remains in the dining room, I went to the back door and opened it wide. Di followed into the kitchen and started gathering towels, a fresh apron, rubber dish gloves, and various cleaning products. Ironically, the floor he was about to scour was going to be ripped up and replaced in a few days.

Andrei backed up to the rear entrance in his van—a large cargo van with no stickers advertising the name of his business, thankfully. Carrying a load of dead bodies into the woods, it would be better to be unremarkable. When he opened the back doors and brought out a sizeable upright dolly with all-terrain tires, I marvelled at the equipment in it. There was everything we needed, including an old tarp and a few assorted shovels.

Seeing the shovels made me wonder exactly how long it would take to dig a grave. I pushed the concern away as a problem we would deal with later and kept busy helping Andrei untangle some tough-looking adjustable straps.

It took some time for Di and Andrei to roll up and duct tape the tarp around the bodies before loading them into the van. Andrei cycled the action until the shotgun chamber was emptied, then wrapped the firearm, ammo, and knife in a towel before putting them into a garbage bag. He tossed the bag on top of the dead men.

"I think I'll call Jing now," Di interrupted. "I'll tell her we hit a few roadblocks and are working on redesigning a few things. I must ensure she doesn't wonder why I don't come home soon." Di explained, "She will wait for me, but at least this way, she doesn't worry and call—or even worse—come looking for me." Di rubbed his head to soothe himself as he imagined the dreaded scenario.

Jing was six months pregnant. They had tried but failed for years before conceiving; it had not been easy. They'd gone through a couple of miscarriages, and this made Di anxious when it came to Jing's health. Her obstetrician had advised Jing to take early maternity leave and avoid stress. She was experiencing a difficult pregnancy, which bothered Di quite a bit.

"I'll tell her it had something to do with the fountain and we had to make some minor adjustments to avoid complications," he said. "If she does call after you two leave, I'll just say you're gone, Kim, and I'm still here finishing up with the contractor."

"Yeah, for sure, that makes sense. How long do you think you are going to be?" I asked.

"I don't know, a couple of hours, I guess." Di scratched at his chin thoughtfully.

It was getting dark, and I felt we were utterly exposed whenever I saw headlights off in the distance. We kept on as few lights as possible. Prying eyes could still make out people moving inside if anyone paid enough attention.

Di called his wife from his cell phone and spoke to her in their native Mandarin. Andrei and I waited for him to finish his conversation. I felt a little better now that the brutes weren't laid bare on the floor anymore. I looked at Andrei, who made eye contact with me and gave me a little smile. His confidence was comforting.

Di ended the call and came over to join us. "Okay, you two better get going, but first, I want to apologize. It's my fault this escalated and got too far out of hand. Generally, I don't condone violence, and I'm sorry you had to see that." Di looked into my eyes as he spoke. "I'm not sure how you feel, but I don't regret what I did. I can't quite explain it to you, but I know in my heart there would've been more trouble for all of us. We would have lived to regret letting them escape this hideousness."

"Today, we're not victims. We are survivors," Andrei said firmly.

I advanced toward Di and gave him a warm hug. He embraced me and kissed me on the forehead. *Are you going to be okay?* I thought silently towards Di. Weirdly enough, I watched him as he nodded as if to say yes. I perceived the head-nodding response to my silent question as a coincidence, but something inside nagged me nonetheless.

Di and Andrei shook hands. *This whole predicament is so outrageous.* We were supposed to have had a pleasant evening. Instead, it turned out to be a massacre, and we were all behaving as if it was business as usual. I shuddered to think about what could've happened on top of this catastrophe if things had transpired differently.

There was still quite a journey before I could put all of this behind me. The drive up north alone would take seven or eight hours. Add to that digging a hole then the drive home. I looked at my watch and noted it was almost nine already, not that it mattered much. I was wide awake.

"I'll wait for you to knock on my door, okay?" I said to Andrei. "If Loki sees me, it's going to be harder for Ana to settle him down for the night." I felt a pang of sadness that I wouldn't be able to see my best friend. I wanted to cuddle my fur baby more than ever, but these were extreme circumstances, and every minute counted. It would be better to push through and finish it.

"All right, see you soon," Andrei replied.

Di locked the back door behind Andrei and walked me to my car. "Don't worry, life is precious; we must take the bad with the good."

"Yeah, I guess that's true. Take care," I said.

"Thank you, same to you, Kim," Di said.

I got into my car and turned on the radio. As I drove out of the parking lot, the radio started to play "Missionary Man" by the Eurythmics, so I cranked up the volume. Music was my go-to for everything from sadness to celebration. I rationalized that it helped make life feel more pleasant or less painful. Either way, I needed the distraction.

On the drive home, I felt hyper-alert and shaky. I was glad Andrei would be driving to the woods, and I doubted my ability to concentrate. Everything felt a little surreal now that I was away from The Castle. How quickly things could change.

*Swim or drown*, I thought to myself. Those words have been in my head since I was a child. Before developing Alzheimer's disease, my dad was a chief warrant officer in the Canadian Armed Forces, and he had little oddball things he used to say to my sister and me. Anyone who grew up with a parent in the service—an army brat—knew they wouldn't get much sympathy for a weak character.

Dad was constantly driving us to test our limits, much to our mother's distress. *GT—good training—*was one of the other things he liked to tell us. Our father would remind our mother that she should let us girls run free and expected us to learn *pain or balance,* as if those were the only two options. Sometimes he treated life as if it were an army exercise, and although I loathed it when I was young, his *good training* advice was eerily helpful right now.

It took me more than fifteen minutes to get home. When I pulled into my driveway, I glanced next door. Andrei hadn't arrived yet. I got out of my car and heard a vehicle nearby, and I saw it was his van coming down the road. *Good.* I rushed into my house before Ana or Loki could notice I was home; I wasn't ready to face them yet.

Once inside the house, I kicked off my shoes and cast aside my purse. I wasn't sure where to start, so I went straight to the bathroom and stood with my hands resting on the vanity, looking at myself in the mirror. *Who are you?* I asked myself. The stranger in the reflection was a doppelgänger looking back at me with the same question. I had the ominous feeling that someone was watching me. It was similar to the weird sensation I felt when—on the rare occasion—I smoked a joint with too much THC. For me, what was excessive was perfect for my best buddy Jacob, who enjoyed high quantities of it.

I washed my hands, removed my makeup, and braided my hair so it wouldn't get in my way during the oncoming task. *Just keep going*, I told myself. I went into my bedroom to get changed. I turned on the light and peeked towards my bed; it looked inviting. I would crawl into that soft heaven of pillows and blankets with my sweet pup and begin putting this all behind me soon enough.

I found a pair of old jeans and a lightweight, long-sleeve shirt I could trash after the nastiness ahead. I planned on burning the clothes as soon as I got back—maybe after a nap. While changing, I noticed a good-sized bruise starting to form on my hip, and my shoulder was red and sore. I tried to ignore it. *GT*, I told myself.

Would anyone come looking for those slime balls? If they didn't advertise their deplorable plans, their associates might think they were hiding out. It wouldn't be much of a stretch of the imagination to believe that jerks like those had met with some misadventure.

I looked out my window to see if Andrei was waiting for me. My porch light had a motion sensor and his truck wasn't running, so he wasn't ready yet. *What was he telling Ana?* I knew he would have to say something crazy to her; I couldn't imagine what it would be. There was no sense in me dwelling on it at the moment, so I sat on the edge of my bed and tried to think about what I might need for the trip.

I sat looking at the canvass on my wall; I'd painted it a couple of years ago. When I hung it up facing the foot of the bed, Derek complained it was *too busy* for the bedroom. By then, I was indifferent to his opinion and kept it there despite his statement. He was a liar and a cheat; I kept it there out of spite.

I loved the colours—soft, with hazy clouds of the seven chakras in the body, but I painted them upside down and without a body. I spent a long time mixing the colours to blend into a swirling circle around the middle. It reminded me of a vortex, and I felt like I was falling into it.

The doorbell rang, which startled me out of my daydreaming. When I tried to jump up, the pain shooting from my hip down my leg shocked me, so I nearly lost my balance. I hurried to switch off the bedroom light then bee-lined it to my entrance.

# CHAPTER 3
## Road Trip

I OPENED the front door to find Andrei standing there in black clothing and work boots. He was around six inches taller than me, so as he stood on my porch on the lower step, we were almost the same height. I looked at his face, directly into his eyes, for any sign of distress. I wanted to know how it went with Ana.

"Are you ready to go?" he asked.

"Yes," I replied and bent down to put on a pair of old blue sneakers.

He waited for me to lock up, and we walked to his van. I couldn't stop glancing at his living room window to see if Ana was looking at us. The light was on, but she wasn't in view. I slipped into the vehicle and buckled up.

"So, what did you tell her?" I asked hesitantly.

"The truth," he said.

"No way," I exclaimed, unable to hide my surprise. "What did she say? Oh my God, she must be freaking out, right?"

"She *is* worried about you, but she isn't freaking out. Once we get back and you get some rest, she'll come over to talk with you." He patted me on the shoulder to reassure me everything would be fine.

I wasn't sure what to think about the casualness of his behaviour.

*How could he be so coolheaded?* It was hard to believe that he told Ana the truth and even harder to conceive that she accepted it. We were driving north to the woods to bury a couple of dead guys we were transporting in the back of his work vehicle. There was nothing ordinary about what was happening here. How could he be so poised?

"We have to stop for gas, and I'll grab us something to eat," he said.

My stomach growled as if in agreement. "I think there's a gas station near the coffee shop just before we get onto the highway. I could go for a coffee too. It's going to be a long night," I said.

Andrei nodded. "Yes, I was thinking the same thing."

He pulled into the gas station, and I kept thinking about the tarp behind me while he filled the tank. I didn't like being near the bodies and couldn't wait to bury them somewhere. *Wow, how insensitive.* So much for taking the moral high ground. Here I was, committing a felony, and all I could think about was how inconvenient it was for me. If I could have foreseen these events, I would never have predicted my reaction in a million years.

After fuelling up, we pulled over to the drive-through menu.

"Hi, what can I get you?" a youthful voice asked through the speaker.

Andrei looked at me.

"I'll take a medium regular, a plain bagel toasted with butter, and two peanut butter cookies," I ordered.

"And I will have a large black coffee, a roast beef sandwich, and half a dozen assorted donuts," Andrei said while he raised his eyebrow at me.

I nodded at him because I knew he wouldn't eat them all. I reached for my purse, and he scowled at me and shook his head.

"No, I'm paying," he objected.

"Thank you." I knew better than to argue with him. "Do you mind if I turn the radio on?"

"Please, go ahead," he said.

I flipped through the stations until I heard the classic rock station playing "Strange Animal" by Gowan. I left it there, respectfully keeping the volume low; I just wanted a little background noise. I unlocked my cell phone and looked at my GPS to find the history of previous routes I'd taken. I pinpointed a location very close to where I thought we should go and estimated about seven hours to get there.

"A little over seven hours to go," I said.

---

After a couple of hours, I spoke up. "Sky is clear, and the moon is shining bright. That should help us find our way around in the dark woods."

"Mhmm, we should keep the flashlights from our cell phones to a minimum once we get out there; we don't want to attract any attention." He paused. "I'm proud of you, by the way." He looked at me for a second then directed his eyes back to the road. "When you crushed that monster's foot and circled away from him, your action helped save us."

I replayed the incident and thought about what to say to Andrei. *Should I tell him I heard his voice?* I asked myself. *He might think I'm nuts —or worse, lying.* I wouldn't lie about something like that, but it felt strange to talk about it. I wasn't sure if he would believe me.

"To be honest with you...I could swear I heard your voice speak to me. It was in my head very clearly. You said, *Run.* I was looking right at you when I heard it, but your lips didn't move, so I'm not sure how that's possible." I wanted to explain more. I knew it sounded crazy, but I was positive it had happened.

"That's very interesting because I did say that to you—*in my mind*. The fact that you heard my voice say the word is incredible," Andrei said, looking sideways at me.

I let out a small chuckle. "Wow, I thought you would write me off as insane."

"No, I don't think that. Ana can explain it best, but it's your Companion. Your life force must be extremely balanced," Andrei said.

"My Companion? What does that mean?" I asked, wondering if perhaps he was the one who was crazy.

"You know we moved here from Russia because of Ana's expertise in microbiome research?"

I nodded for him to continue.

"To put it simply, her understanding of the microbiome has put her in a position where she now specializes in studying Companions. The folks at her company gave them that name. It's a kind of acronym, the way she explained it to me. COMP Anion—collective of microbiome partners and the word *anion*, a negatively charged particle. The anion is an inside joke I don't understand; perhaps when Ana explains everything to you, it will make more sense," he said.

I wasn't a hundred percent sure what he was saying or how it connected to the experience I had of hearing his voice in my head. I saw a pair of headlights behind us and waited for the car to pass us before pushing him to elaborate.

"Okay...so Ana works as an expert in Companions, which sounds fascinating, but what does that have to do with me hearing your voice in my head?" I asked.

"The Companion is an entity that exists within you but is separate from you. Your DNA is less than fifty percent of your body. The rest of your cells are microscopic colonists with a single collective consciousness. There is a symbiotic relationship between your body and a self-aware entity made up of these microscopic residents," he said. He let out a little laugh. "Ana would be pleased. If you only knew how long it took her to help me understand this."

"Like a soul?" I prodded.

"In my opinion, not really. But the existence of some religions could have resulted from misunderstandings in the communication between the minds of historical individuals and the entity within them. The Companions create a magnetic field around their human partner similar to how the atmosphere envelops the Earth," Andrei said. "These two consciousnesses communicate with each other on their distinct frequency. We talk and use body language while Companions communicate through energy exchange."

"Like a gut feeling?" I asked. The memories of sitting on the couch with Jacob and watching reruns of *X-Files* flooded my mind.

"Your gut feeling is one example of your Companion ascertaining an interaction." Andrei tilted his head sideways and continued. "It's more complicated. I thought the words—*run*—directly towards you, and your Companion received it, then it echoed my voice for your mind to hear. It resembles radio waves, and you are the receiver creating the sound in your head." He pointed at the stereo system.

Everything Andrei said made perfect sense to me. I'd graduated from university with a degree in philosophy, but they never taught us this. As I imagined my relationship with this microscopic collective appropriately named *Companion*, a couple of memories hit me, and I started to laugh.

"What is it?" Andrei asked.

"My older sister Julia used to sit in her room talking to herself out loud. I used to spy and make fun of her. She said she was talking to her special friend that lived inside her. I guess the joke is on me."

I felt a little enlightened by this revelation, and as captivated as I was, the coffee had gone through me, and my bladder was screaming. Unfortunately, there wouldn't be a washroom for quite some time. I weighed my options and stared out the window. The stars were so beautiful away from the lights of the city. Even with the moon shining, I could still make out Orion's Belt and a few other minor constellations. As I admired the vast starry sky, I imagined the universe brimming with life.

"I'll have to get you to pull over for a second. I need to pee," I said.

"No problem." He slowed the van down as he pulled onto the shoulder of the highway.

We were nearing Sudbury, and the traffic was light at night. I planned on slipping behind one of the trees so passing vehicles couldn't see me with my pants around my ankles while I squatted. After he came to a complete stop, I hurried to a secluded spot and relieved myself. I wasn't there for long, and I saw another car slow down and pull up behind Andrei's van. *What the hell?*

I pulled up my jeans and stood up but remained behind the pine tree where no one could see me and watched. *Oh, no!* I saw a black car with a white front door, which meant it was a provincial police car. My heart beat faster, and my knees felt weak. I watched the officer leave his car and walk to the driver's door to talk to Andrei. I was scared that we were busted.

"Is everything all right here?" he asked Andrei.

"Yes, sir, I'm just waiting for my girlfriend. She couldn't wait until the next gas station," Andrei responded in a friendly tone.

"Is that right?" The officer sounded suspicious.

That was my cue. I came trotting out with the friendliest smile I could muster. I jumped into the passenger seat, leaned toward the driver's side window, and looked up at the officer.

"I'm so sorry about that. I really couldn't hold it any longer; too much coffee." I smiled sweetly. I could feel my face flushing red as my blood pressure went through the roof. I hoped he would see it as embarrassment from being caught peeing in the woods and prayed he wouldn't ask to see what was in the back. I attempted to be cool like Andrei.

"Where are you heading?" the officer asked.

"Timmins to visit my sister," I said before Andrei could speak. "I'm off for the holidays, so we figured we'd get on the road after work to take advantage of the light traffic. I'll get more time to spend with my niece." I smiled at him again and held eye contact.

"Well, drive safe," he said. "There may not be much traffic at this time of night, but the deer will run out of the woods and stop on the road to stare at the lights. If that happens, honk while you brake; the sound might scare them off." He squinted at the road ahead of us as if he could picture the animal.

"Thank you, sir," Andrei said.

"Have a good night!" I waved to him.

"You too," he said as he walked back to get into his cruiser.

Andrei started the van, pulled out onto the highway, and continued to the daunting task ahead of us.

"That felt like a close call," I said.

Andrei nodded. "It was."

I kept glancing in the rear mirror to see if the OPP would follow us. He did for a while, so we drove without saying anything; evidently, we were both nervous. After half an hour, the police cruiser pulled out and passed us. I felt better when his red taillights faded off in the distance ahead of us.

For the moment, I was glad we weren't going to drive to my

sister's. That would be awkward, and Julia would think I was out of my mind.

---

We finally arrived close to our destination; I looked up and down the highway to ensure there were no headlights. I directed Andrei to slow down, and he peered at the side road I had picked out. It was less of a side road than two parallel pathways running into a dense canopy of trees.

"Perfect," he said.

He pulled onto the trail and drove for approximately fifty metres. His van was bulky compared to the road; we wouldn't get much farther anyway. It was so narrow that we'd have to back out as it was, so I prayed we were far enough in that we wouldn't be visible to passing traffic. Derek and I used to drive deeper into the forest, and I already knew it was a dead end.

Andrei turned off the ignition and looked at me. "Are you ready?"

"Ready as I'm going to be."

We got out of the vehicle and searched the area for a couple of minutes, carefully keeping our phone lights low to the ground and listening for any traffic. We came to a small clearing where the trees didn't cover the sky. The moonlight reached the earth, making it easy to see in the dark without the flashlights.

"This will do," he said.

We returned to the truck, and a nervous feeling washed over me. *Get it together, Kim*, I scolded myself. I looked up at the sky again and wondered how long we had before the sun would rise. The sky's deep black colour had already faded into a dark blue, and the stars were disappearing fast.

I helped him grab the shovels, and he carried the wrapped-up package with the weapons. I didn't bother asking him which shovel was better to use. I followed his lead to the spot he'd picked, obediently took the shovel he handed me, and started digging beside him.

We didn't talk; we just kept digging and listening for cars. Whenever we heard one approaching, we would stop and look at each other, patiently waiting for it to pass before we resumed. I was soaked with sweat and getting eaten alive by black flies. It was late June, the prime season for those little bloodsuckers, and I cursed myself for not grabbing bug repellent when we stopped for gas. I didn't think of it at the time. Andrei was his usual proficient self and didn't flinch at the buzzing pests around his ears.

We had been digging for almost two hours, and he stopped to survey the ground.

"Okay, it's good enough," he murmured.

I looked at my watch. It was a quarter to seven, and the sun shone brightly through the leaves. As we climbed out, I observed that the oval hole was slightly over three feet deep, unlike the rectangular graves in a cemetery. Andrei picked up the wrap with weapons and tossed it into the pit. I followed him to his truck, and we sat on the back bumper for a minute listening to the road.

The burden of getting the bodies out of the van and into the makeshift grave we dug for them was next. Andrei got in and stepped over the covered corpses to get the dolly. I had a strong appreciation for that equipment and doubted my ability to help him carry the dead, although I would have tried.

We wrangled the bigger guy Ryan onto the dolly and used the straps to hold his body in place. I grabbed the handle while Andrei hefted the bottom, bearing the brunt of the weight to lift it down out of the van. He wheeled it through the light brush as I followed, ready to help if he lost his balance. At the pit, he directed me to unsnap the ratchet strap while he held the considerably heavy dolly at a thirty-degree angle. After I got it open, he flipped the dolly cart forward while bracing the bottom with his foot, and the sack of shit flopped into the pit.

We repeated the process with Jimmy. Because of their size difference, it was a lot easier.

Once they were both in the trench, we unceremoniously started to pile the dirt over them. That was incredibly less strenuous, and we finished in no time.

"Let's get a few sticks and leaves to make it look like the ground here wasn't disturbed," Andrei said. He grabbed some brush.

Afterward, we returned to the van, and I watched near the edge of the tree line for a clear road before waving to Andrei that it was safe to back out. I jumped in the passenger seat, and we were on our way home.

My hip and shoulder were aching from all the action they had experienced within the last twelve hours. I worked out at the gym regularly, but that didn't prepare me for this kind of effort.

"Tell me more about the Companions?" I asked.

"I'm sure you have many questions—as I said before, Ana will fill you in on everything, but I can tell you about my experience." He tilted his head thoughtfully. "When I was in the military, I worked with many men who had a conscious connection with their Companions, which made them excellent soldiers. Of course, we didn't have a name for it at the time. It's beneficial to coordinate your actions with another soldier by focusing your thoughts. Unfortunately, many men couldn't understand what was happening, and they grew paranoid, which caused many fights and dismissals," he said.

"How so?"

"People talk in their heads," he stated. "Then they start to talk to each other with their inner voice. Trouble starts when they become aware of the physical responses caused by the Companions' cooperation. It turns their reality sideways. A confused soldier may direct his thoughts toward another soldier, for example—*Are you trying to destroy me?* The second guy opens and closes his mouth or licks his lips. The questioner perceives it as a *yes*. Maybe the second guy scratches his nose, blinks, or crosses his arms. The reaction happens directly after the soldier poses the question in his mind. Well, all of a sudden, the first soldier suspects he's in a world that is conspiring to destroy him," Andrei said as he rolled his eyes. "Nobody wants their mind read."

"So the Companions help us read each other's minds?" I asked, seeing how this could be a big problem for everybody.

"No," he scoffed.

I looked out the window in the distance. "Thank God for that."

"It's rare for someone to hear the words another individual is thinking. Tests with animals indicated that they use pictures and strong emotions to communicate, not verbal cues. Most Companions are damaged, and I suspect if they weren't, we might have more success with directly transmitting the information. For you to hear my words in your head means your Companion must be healthy, as is mine, but I get treatment," he said.

"Treatment?" I asked, suspecting he was holding something back.

"Ana will speak with you. Your body must be stressed and tired. We can discuss these things later, and you can process this information after you've rested."

He closed the door on the subject for now. I stared at the passing trees, watching dozily as the landscape changed to rocky cliffs and a few sporadic lakes. Finally, we were on the familiar highway series near Hamilton. When Andrei dropped me off, I was disappointed Ana's car was gone. That meant Loki was with her, and I longed to see him.

Andrei looked at me and said, "Get rest. Ana will bring Loki home to you later tonight." He gave me a weary smile; he also needed sleep.

"Okay, goodnight Andrei," I said and hugged him.

"Goodnight, Kim," he said.

It didn't take me long to throw my clothes in the trash, jump into the shower, and crawl under my bedsheets.

## CHAPTER 4
## *Companions*

I WOKE DISORIENTED, but it didn't take long for the memories to come flooding back. My phone showed it was six p.m., and I'd missed three calls from Jacob. *I'll call him later.* Jacob would lose his mind when he discovered what I'd been up to.

Loki was on my mind, and desperately wanting to see him, I dressed rapidly. After brushing my teeth and twisting my hair into a large clip, I carefully descended the hardwood stairs because my bruises from the previous day were throbbing. I checked the fridge for orange juice and drank from the jug; aside from Loki, I lived alone, and no one would complain.

Slipping into my sandals and anxious about seeing Ana, I paused for a moment before leaving the house. Perhaps she wasn't even home yet. *Just go*, I admonished myself for procrastinating.

As I opened the door and stepped outside, the humidity hit me like a ton of bricks. My appreciation for air conditioning was reinforced as I closed the door.

"Kim, you're up!" Ana called out from her porch.

I felt overjoyed at the sight of them; she struggled to hold the dog leash because Loki was choking himself, trying to run to me. She offered a warm smile and unclipped the collar to release him.

"Hello, baby!" I said to him while he ran to greet me. "Thank you so much for watching him, Ana."

"Don't mention it; he was the one who took care of me," she joked while walking across the yard to join us.

He was so excited he almost knocked me over while I was squatted down to pet him.

"Do you mind if I come in for a little visit?" she asked.

"By all means, come on in."

I picked up the wriggling bundle of joy that licked me as if I had just returned from a journey across the galaxy. We went into my house, and I turned on the radio because I liked the ambience. I put on the coffee maker and brought a plastic container out of the fridge; it had sliced meat, cheese, and pickles previously prepared in anticipation of my holidays. After grabbing a box of crackers from the cupboard and pouring them on a plate, I tossed a piece of salami to Loki, who was waiting patiently.

"I already fed him his meal," Ana said as I placed the comfort food on the table.

"You're wonderful; Loki and I are very grateful. I'm brewing gourmet coffee for us."

"That sounds nice." Ana sighed.

*My goodness, she seems cheerful*, I thought, a little confused. Ana was a beautiful woman; with striking blue eyes, she stood about five foot eight and possessed a lean build. She reminded me of a volleyball player. Her long pale blonde hair rested just above her waist, and although she was in her early forties, she looked like a model. I somewhat envied her.

After pouring the coffee, I sat on the sofa, and Loki decided to curl up on my lap.

"So…" I grappled with where to start the conversation we were about to have.

Ana took a sip of her coffee and looked at me as she placed the mug back on the coaster. "Where would you like me to start?"

"You?" I scoffed. "I thought I was going to have to start. Andrei said he told you what happened last night?" I paused to see her reaction.

"Yes, he did," she said carefully. "You might experience symptoms of post-traumatic stress from the violence. Andrei has been trained, and he informed me that Di told him he was in the Chinese militia, so I'm not worried about either of them. If you need professional help, let me know, and I'll take you to our company psychologist. We have the best," she assured.

"Thank you. I appreciate it, Ana, but working in the food service industry, I've been mugged twice. I won't be losing sleep over witnessing the death of two thugs. My father told my sister and me countless stories of violence he saw in the Middle East. We weren't sheltered. Life can end in the blink of an eye for anyone. I'll be okay," I said.

"You should know that your life *was* in danger. Something happening in our world has people doing monstrous things to each other. Partially because their Companions are sick," she said.

I almost forgot about Andrei's details on Companions and Ana's expertise on the subject. Perhaps I was a little shaken after all. Although we were friends, we didn't usually discuss our jobs. I vaguely knew she worked for a big company involved in state-of-the-art research in biology—or so I thought. When we got together, we often gossiped about the other neighbours or talked about television shows we liked to binge watch.

"Oh, that's right, you're supposed to tell me more about the Companions. You aren't concerned about what happened at the restaurant last night?" I asked speculatively.

"No, what's done is done. There are much bigger issues at stake," she said.

"Well, I guess you should start at the beginning."

She tucked her hair behind her ears and folded her hands together while leaning toward me. I grabbed a piece of cheese, bit half and gave the rest to Loki. I was looking forward to this story.

"It started for me years ago when I studied the human microbiome at the state university I attended in Russia. Nekxus approached a few of us to work on a project investigating how the microbiome influenced human health. I agreed, of course, and it wasn't long before I dropped out of the university to work permanently for Nekxus," she said.

She stopped to take another sip of her coffee. *Nekxus*, the name of the company she worked at—I had completely forgotten—was a massive complex in the industrial area in Hamilton near Lake Ontario. Our neighbourhood was in the upper part of the city, which the locals referred to as *the mountain*, on the top side of the world's longest escarpment. There was rarely a reason for me to drive near the industrial section. Nekxus was so enormous that when you drove by it on the QEW highway, you could see that several buildings took up a large portion of the harbour.

"I realized how critical our research was early on. Many departments have diverse projects, but all have one common goal."

"What's the goal?"

"To heal humanity," she said.

I nodded thoughtfully. "People *are* pretty screwed up."

"You don't know the half of it." She rolled her eyes and proceeded to explain. "The relationship between the human cells in your body—*the ones with your DNA*—and the microbiome collective—*which behaves like a single entity*—are beyond symbiotic. They are dependent on each other for survival. This may seem obvious when I say it to you, but remember, most people don't know or understand their dual nature. People have difficulty accepting that they are not the only life form occupying their bodies."

"It is a little far-fetched sounding," I admitted.

"More than that, they aren't even the primary occupant. The Companions seem to be *behind the wheel*, to put it simply, and we are the co-pilots. When you think of the inner child, the human is the inner child, not their Companion." She chuckled. "We aren't sure if it was always this way or an evolutionary process."

"Holy shit, eh, it's hard to believe. What an amazing job you have," I exclaimed. "How do you talk to it—or should I say yourself?" My brain kicked into overdrive with questions.

"There is a reciprocating interchange between both organisms. One is usually subordinate. Our Companion tends to influence the human aspect of ourselves more often than not." She ate a piece of cheese. "It seems the Companions can manipulate all sorts of things on a fundamental level; we are still analyzing data collected worldwide from various departments performing experiments. We've tried biofield and electromagnetic therapies, but success in regulating homeodynamics has proven elusive."

I listened in awe as Ana described the world in a way that seemed alien to me. *Aliens*—I thought about Jacob and how he loved fantastic ideas and anything that could be interpreted as a conspiracy. It wasn't about extraterrestrials or UFO abduction, but this stuff was right up his alley. Jacob ended his relationship with his last partner because Frank was *too narrow-minded*, as Jacob put it. Frank disregarded Jacob's beliefs and maintained that no aliens, gods, or ghosts existed. He took it a step further to say there was no such thing as love, maintaining it was all just chemicals.

"Would you like a glass of wine? My coffee's gone, and I think I'm going to switch drinks," I asked.

"That would be nice, thank you." She stacked a cracker with cheese, salami, and a pickle. I was impressed when she popped the whole thing in her mouth.

"Red or white?" I gathered the coffee mugs and put them in the sink.

"Red, and don't be shy—fill it up," she said.

I stretched to reach the top shelf of my china cabinet and brought out the giant wine glasses I used for guests. I opened a new bottle because the half-full one sitting on the counter was a cheap bottle. I would drink it later while cooking some other time. Loki started to whimper and sat at my feet, looking up with a request in his eyes.

"Why don't we let this aerate for a few minutes and take Loki for a quick spin around the block?" I asked.

"Sounds like a plan." She stood and stretched.

I grabbed his leash. He jumped and danced around when he knew he was going for a walk. The three of us strolled casually around the neighbourhood, stopping here and there while Loki sniffed the ground or other dogs. A few people greeted Loki and commented, "What a good boy." He seemed to prance as if he was aware of his popularity.

When we returned and settled into the living room with our drinks,

Ana continued illuminating me about the complicated subject of our fellow life force.

"Theta waves produced by our brains are essential for communication crossover. Communication manifests in several ways. Our imaginations, dreams, gut reaction, feeling of being watched, and artistic abilities would often be riddled with underlying messages that the Companions were trying to convey. Our subconscious intermingles with the Companions' collective, which can also be manipulated by it. Companions don't speak as we do; lacking vocal cords makes it problematic."

"No doubt," I said.

"On an intuitive level, we have an inner dialogue. What surprised me at first was how the whole world turned into a—how should I put it—magic eight ball," she laughed. "I would look around for signals and evidence of these secret messages, and my god, did I find them." She looked into her glass, remembering her strange experiences.

My phone chirped, and I saw Jacob had sent me a message—*If you don't respond in the next five minutes, I'm coming.* I picked up the phone and started typing that Ana was visiting and he should come tomorrow around lunch, adding a winky emoji so he wouldn't panic.

"Sorry, I want to let Jacob know I'm not dead. I've been ignoring his calls," I said, my tone guilty.

"I understand," Ana said and sipped her wine.

When I finished typing to Jacob, I ordered a large Hawaiian pizza from the food delivery app. "Pizza should be here in forty-five minutes."

"Thank you. I was just about to suggest something because Andrei is at the restaurant working, and Aleksander is out with his girlfriend." She grinned. "Now, where was I?"

"You were explaining how the Companions interact," I said.

"It's not cut and dry, unfortunately. When the anatomy and physiology of an individual are healthy, there is a harmonious existence between the two life forces. You can look into another person's eyes and pose a clear question in your mind, and *you will get an answer.* You may not like or understand it, but the response is inevitable once energy is activated."

She gave me a stern look and held it until I suspected she was doing exactly what she had just described. I started to feel pressure, and I couldn't help myself from blinking and swallowing.

"Good," she said.

"Did you just ask me something?"

"Yes," she replied.

"What did you ask? Did you hear my voice?"

"No, I can't do that. That's extraordinarily rare. I asked you if you wanted me to continue the conversation. Why don't you try? Think of a simple question and watch me. I can't predict what my Companion will do, but if you look hard enough, you will catch something," she said.

"All right." I shrugged.

I thought about what kind of question I should ask her. *What did I want to know?* I might have been apprehensive if it wasn't for the red wine, but I felt pretty good. A request that could persuade me to believe her information came to me.

*What time is it?* I asked her with the voice in my head. I looked at her face and watched her, waiting for something to show me she understood my thoughts.

Ana sat motionless for a second, and I wondered if everything she told me was just a fantasy. Suddenly, she turned her head sharply to the right and lifted her chin to look up at the wall. I gasped, and she turned to face me with a puzzled look.

"Did it work?" she asked.

"Yeah, I think so. Wow, Ana, that's crazy," I said.

"What did you ask me?"

"You don't know?" I was perplexed. "I mean, it looked like you answered," I said, clearly missing something.

"Right, I should have explained it better. My Companion likely used the energy field to manipulate me like a puppet to respond to you and your Companion. I was relaxed and receptive. If I were stressed, it wouldn't necessarily work," she said.

"I see. I asked you, *What time is it?* A second later, you looked up at the clock on my wall like a Terminator; it was delightfully creepy," I said.

We both smiled and played questions back and forth with each other for a while before she stopped, saying we should break. It can get exhausting and stressful for the Companion, she explained. The energy field that the microbiome creates must reach out into the surrounding environment like invisible tentacles and interact on a microscopic and subatomic level. It needs to rest.

"I'm surprised how sensitive you are, Kim. Sadly, most of the population has an unhealthy and damaged life force. Their Companions are weak, and their bodies are full of sickness." Ana faltered. "In Russia, I've witnessed many terrible experiments designed to restore the balance between an individual and their Companion. They tested on animals—most of the time. Sometimes, they used prisoners," she said, her expression mournful.

"All animals have Companions?" I asked.

Ana smiled at Loki. "Yes."

The doorbell rang, which set him off. He jumped off the couch and ran to the front door barking like a tiny demon.

"Hush, it's *pizza*. You want some pizza, don't you?" I asked my furry friend.

He shut up and wagged his tail. I grabbed my purse and opened the front door. The pizza delivery guy was standing there with the bag and a debit machine in one hand. He handed me the pizza, and after entering a tip and tapping to pay, I looked at him and thought, *Hey, cutie.*

"'Night, miss," he said and winked at me.

I giggled inside at the thought of this fascinating new superpower. It didn't take us long to polish off the pizza, and I poured the rest of the smooth Cabernet Sauvignon into our glasses.

"I want to tell you about Nekxus. The company quickly exposed me to a ton of information, which was all right for me, so I hope you don't feel overwhelmed. Nekxus has offices around the globe, with infinite financial resources and technology decades ahead of what the general population is aware of." Ana paused and looked off into the distance.

"I'm all ears," I said.

"With your permission, I'd like to ask my superior if I can bring you into the headquarters with a visitor pass," she said.

"Absolutely," I said without hesitation.

After listening to Ana tell me about Companions and their microbial signatures, I was thrilled to see Nekxus with my own eyes. I pictured a bunch of laboratories and brilliant scientists in white lab coats.

"You see..." Ana leaned in and spoke deliberately. "Humanity's infested."

"With what?" I asked.

"Something is feeding on us, and that's not the worst part. A monumental amount of the world's problems—especially the violence—directly correlates to being infected with this parasite. Crimes like murder, rape, assaults of all kinds, negligence, robbery, forceable confinement, and drug abuse can all be traced back to parasitic infestations. Unfortunately, these awful behaviours are becoming more common in today's society. This parasite is polluting our world, and in its wake, it is leaving a jungle of psychopaths. It goes beyond antisocial behaviour; the general population is becoming prone to criminal and violent behaviour with no regard for the feelings of others," she said.

Ana could tell I was getting rattled by her words because she reached across the table and took my hand.

"I know it's hard to hear, don't worry; I don't think you're a psychopath for what happened at the restaurant. There's a difference between criminal actions and protecting yourself. We only get one life. Bad things happen, especially today," she whispered and squeezed my hand.

"So, our species is digressing? I don't understand; how is this *parasite* causing this awful behaviour?" I asked.

"Well, it is siphoning specific chemicals from our glands. Namely oxytocin, endorphins, serotonin, and dopamine," she said.

"No shit. The feel-good chemicals?"

"Yes, shit. It's a slow process, but eventually, it changes the glands, so they can't produce these chemicals properly. The individual starts to become restless with erratic sleep habits, odd impulses, stress, anger, and aggression. Many people, especially very intelligent ones, become truly sociopathic and focus their energies on dominating others at any cost. Governments and large corporations are riddled with these individuals whose success results from their total disregard for humanity." Ana's face contorted in anger.

"Okay, now you're going to tell me why we can't just rid ourselves of this parasite. I'm going to guess we can't remove it for some reason?"

"That's right; we're trying. Nekxus dedicates to this goal. Its mission statement is *heal humanity*. One of the biggest problems is that these creatures feeding on us aren't exactly in our dimension." She looked at me as if weighing my reaction.

I stared blankly at her until I felt my head start to bob up and down as if to tell her to keep going. It was weird to be aware of my Companion moving me to agree silently. I was determined to hear everything she had to say, no matter how outlandish it sounded.

"You've heard of dark matter?" she asked.

I nodded again as I searched my memories for any information I could remember on the subject, which wasn't much.

"Good—there's a hidden fourth dimension in our universe where the darkest matter exists. I'm not an expert on this subject, but I can tell you that these creatures originate from this mysterious dimension. Somehow, they are feeding off of exotic particles that we produce. Our Companion has a parallel existence between our dimension and this dark matter dimension.

"These parasites latch on to our bodies via our Companion to devour these particles. They seem to be able to alter our glands' production of the chemicals when they feed to the point where the *feel-good* chemicals disappear into this dark matter parallel world." Ana waved her arms in the air to demonstrate the hidden dimensions. "They feast and reproduce while our humanity slips into despair."

We sat in silence for a while until we heard a car coming up the road. Loki popped his head up, and I saw headlights pulling into the driveway next door. Andrei was home.

"I guess you better get going," I said.

"Yes, Andrei will be wondering how you are coping. Shall I tell him you are accepting everything just fine?" she asked.

"Yes, please let Andrei know I am doing well. What will you say to your boss? Do you think I'll get a visitor pass?" I asked. I was intrigued by the opportunity of getting a tour of the infamous Nekxus complex. I was eager to learn more about my Companion and how better to communicate with it.

"I do. I'll tell my supervisor you heard Andrei's voice. He will be very interested in you and your Companion's connection. That ability is rare, and we need as much information as possible to fight off this plague."

"Great, I have one more question, if you don't mind," I said.

"Sure, what is it?"

"What does this parasite look like?" I asked.

Ana took a moment to think before answering me. She seemed to remember an image as her face changed into a look of disgust. Then she looked into my eyes.

"It's classified, but the best way for me to describe it to you is to say they resemble a swarm of tics," she whispered.

## CHAPTER 5

*Jacob*

I SLEPT IN LATE, rushed to walk Loki, and gave him his meal before Jacob showed up. At eleven a.m. sharp, he knocked. He had bagels and coffee in his hands. Immediately, I took them and put them aside, then I almost toppled the poor guy over when I threw myself at him to get a big hug.

Jacob wore athletic shorts, sneakers, and a T-shirt representing his favourite soccer team. He wasn't athletic, but he liked to look the part, maintaining it was a European style, making him look more attractive. I smelled his favourite cologne, the fragrance he wore when single because—according to him—it gave him confidence. I also noticed a fresh haircut.

"I am so happy to see you. The last couple of days were absolute chaos!" I grinned.

"I can see that, Kim; you almost *spilled* the coffee. I spared no expense and picked us up the good stuff." He wiggled his eyebrows.

It was specialty coffee from our favourite coffee shop, Bean Island Café. When the weather was nice, we would sit on the patio, drink coffee, and chat with Loki at our feet because it was a pet-friendly small business.

"Hey buddy, don't worry; I didn't forget you." Jacob tossed Loki a gourmet biscuit the café sold to pet lovers. Loki caught it and jumped on Jacob's leg until he kneeled to offer a belly rub. "Now, don't make me beg, Kim. What is going on?"

"Let's sit in the living room to talk," I suggested.

"Girl, how serious is it? You don't even want to sit back on the patio and enjoy your holidays in this beautiful weather?" he asked.

"Not today; we need privacy. I have some things to tell you. It's going to be tough for you to believe, but—"

Jacob interrupted. "You're going to tell me *every detail*, don't even start that shit with me, Kim. We tell each other everything—spill it right now."

Although he had a no-nonsense tone, I knew it came from a loving place. Jacob and I met in the philosophy class we took at the university. We shared an apartment until I married Derek. He was never a big fan of Derek and warned me the guy was a two-timer but supported me anyway by being my man of honour at our wedding. He liked to joke that I came out on top in the divorce because I got the house. As philosophy graduates, neither of us had considered how little the field had to offer regarding financially stable employment opportunities.

"Okay, okay. Remember I told you about the restaurant get-together I had the other night?"

Jacob nodded for me to continue.

"Two masked criminals barged into the restaurant when Andrei, Di, and I were having a drink."

"Shut up," Jacob exclaimed. "I'm just hearing about this now? Are you okay? I can't believe you didn't call me! Where have you been? The police station? The hospital? Are the guys okay?" He was getting emotional and stood up to start pacing around the room as he threw his questions at me.

"Sit down and let me finish; it gets worse," I said.

His eyebrows climbed far up his forehead in shock at that statement. *Sit down, please*—I focused the thought on him, and he obliged by sitting on the sofa and crossing his legs. I could see he was impatiently waiting for me to continue as his toes kept flipping back and forth.

"One was carrying a shotgun and the other a knife. The degenerates demanded money, and things went south fast. Long story short—they're both dead. Andrei shot one, and Di cut the other's throat open."

I waited a moment for him to start breathing again. All the colour had left his face, and he had both hands on both cheeks. I thought he looked like the kid on the cover of the *Home Alone* movie.

"Then Andrei and I drove the corpses up north and buried them in the woods while Di cleaned the crime scene." I sighed.

Jacob sat still and gave me a long, hard look. He tilted his head sideways then started to laugh. He didn't believe a word I said.

"Whatever, Kim. Will you tell me what you've been up to? You met someone, didn't you? One-night stand? Don't be ashamed—I've had my share." He grinned.

"I wish I'd met someone. I'm serious, Jacob. I wouldn't lie or joke about this shit. It's been a rough couple of days," I said.

He stared at me, this time with a concerned expression. I stood up and pulled my pants down a little on one side to show him the gigantic bruise that had formed on my hip. He gulped and covered his mouth when I pulled my shirt off my shoulder to show him the other bruise from the assault. Jacob got up, rushed to my side, and put his arm around me. The gesture made me emotional; I sat down and started crying. Loki stood on his hind legs, put his paws on my lap, and licked my hand.

It didn't take me long to calm down, but Jacob was still upset. I drank my coffee and listened to him complain about the pathetic state of the city and how the authorities were *too soft on criminals*. He carried on for a while until being interrupted by the phone that had started ringing in his pocket.

"Oh, just let me get rid of this," he said.

"Go ahead."

I helped myself to a bagel and listened to him talk on the phone.

"Hi Matt, can I call you later? I'm with Kim attending to a serious situation. Yes, she's good, thanks. Okay, yes, bye." Jacob hung up.

I raised an eyebrow at him; his cheeks flushed. "Matt?"

"He's a regular at the bar. I was faithful to Frank, but now that I'm single, I've always had a bit of a crush on Matt. He would frequently come to the bar, chat me up and leave huge tips." He smirked. "We've been on a couple of dates, but I feel we're hitting it off."

"I'm happy to hear you are moving on," I said.

"Enough about me; what about you? I can't imagine what I can say to you to reassure you that everything will be okay. I hope you buried those bodies deep, Kim. I couldn't take it if you get in trouble for those lousy pieces of shit. What about Andre and Di?"

"I believe they're good. Andrei is a military man, so there's that." I flipped my hand's palm side up as if that explained everything. "I haven't spoken with Di since the incident, and I assume he's all right. I hope so, anyway. I know it goes without saying; you can't tell anyone what I'm saying to you," I said.

"You know me better than that. I can't believe you didn't call me to help you with the digging," he scolded. "I could have made it easier on you."

"You were at work," I said defensively.

He rolled his eyes. "Like the bar couldn't survive without me. Seriously, Kim, neither of us has significant jobs in the grand scheme. What about Mexico? Are you still going to go?"

I'd completely put off the thoughts about the trip planned with my sister and her family. Her husband Jeffery had discounted timeshares through his work, and we planned to spend two weeks on the beachfront property enjoying the ocean, but now I wasn't feeling it. Jacob was going to stay at my house with Loki while I was away, but I couldn't imagine going on a trip anymore.

"Umm, I don't know. I think I'm going to cancel."

"You need to go now more than ever. Get away. I'll make sure the pooch is spoiled." He rubbed Loki's ears affectionately. "You've been through the divorce from that psychopath Derek and now this trauma. Come on. You need to go away and clear your head," he insisted.

"I think it might be better if I stick around here for now. I have some things I need to think about, and I don't want to ruin Julia's holiday because I'll be too distracted to enjoy myself. It's all too fresh." I faltered for a second.

"Is there something else, Kim? I feel like there is more going on—

not that what happened wasn't enough. Maybe you need to seek out some professional help?" he suggested.

"No, I'm okay, don't worry. You're right, Jacob. There is more to the story, but it's harder for me to explain." I sat back to consider my words.

"Let's hear it. It can't be worse than what you've already told me."

"Oh, it's not. Give me a second to use the bathroom," I said.

After using the toilet and washing up, I looked at myself in the mirror to see if I looked as crazy as I was about to sound. My reflection seemed self-assured. I thought about how I would begin explaining things and decided that because Jacob was uncommonly open-minded, I'd start with the nightmare.

"All right," I sat back down on the couch. "Remember I called you about the nightmare?"

Jacob used his index finger to circle forward in the air motioning for me to continue.

"All day, I couldn't shake the ominous feeling it left me. Then, of course, we got robbed," I said.

"I'm not surprised," Jacob said as he finished his last coffee sip. "I believe there is much more going on when it comes to our dreams; they aren't just a product of imagination."

"It was more than that. When the one scumbag came behind me with the knife, I heard Andrei's voice loud and clear in my head—he said, *Run*—but I was looking at him, and his mouth didn't move; he didn't say anything," I said, shaking my head in bewilderment.

"During a crisis, all sorts of strange things can happen. This one time, I could have sworn I saw people laughing at me when I was choking on a cherry tomato in a restaurant. I looked around for help, and it seemed like everyone was mocking me. It was my imagination getting the best of me while I was in a panic," he said.

"I see your point, but it felt so real that I told Andrei about it when we drove to the woods to bury the bodies."

Jacob still wasn't convinced and speculated, "It was a coincidence. Naturally, he would think for you to do something to provide a distraction so he could pull some fancy Russian army moves on the lowlife. I'm sure you read his body language and facial expressions."

"That is a reasonable explanation, except, in this case, he *thought* the words towards me and I *heard* them. Not only did he admit it, but he explained that we have Companions. A life form created and controlled by the conscious collective of microscopic colonists known as the microbiome. Ana's specialty at Nekxus is the microbiome—Companion. She told me all about it."

"What in the blue hell are you talking about, Kim? *Companions?*" he interrupted.

"Yes, Companions—a combination of bacteria, viruses, fungi, and an assortment of other microscopic creatures that exist in time and space differently than we do. Our bodies contain more foreign DNA than they do human DNA. The big surprise here is that these microscopic colonists' collective consciousness seems to *co-exist with ours*. At least that's how I understood it," I said.

"That's deliciously fabulous! I love it! Nekxus, eh? I knew they were a big deal—I've seen the enormous complex near the harbour—but I've never investigated their actual purpose." Jacob beamed.

I laughed because I suspected he would react this way. Jacob loved fringe sciences and fantastic ideas; he was broad-minded. I filled him in on all the particulars that Ana had told me the day before. He sat listening practically on the edge of his seat, concentrating on every tiny detail.

Once I informed him of as much information as possible, we took a break to let Loki out into the backyard while we sat on the deck chairs. I didn't want to talk about the subject outside. I feared the neighbours would hear, especially Ana, because I knew she had divulged confidential information.

"Now I see why you don't want to go to Mexico. I hope Ana can get you that visitor's pass. I'm dying to hear what it looks like inside the Nekxus buildings. Don't worry. I won't breathe a word of any of this, but you must keep me in the loop." He looked positively vibrant as he seemed engrossed with the new revelation. "I wonder if the Companion is our soul? I would've loved to have done my dissertation on this instead of existentialism." He suppressed a laugh.

After returning to the living room, Jacob and I practised asking questions silently in our minds and watched each other for reactions.

Answers would always be forthcoming one way or another, but sometimes it seemed our understanding of the response needed to be made more explicit.

Asking a yes or no question seemed practical. I would ask Jacob something like, *Do you love mushrooms?* Within a second, he would blink and wrinkle his nose. I knew he didn't like them, so I saw what I expected. But later, I asked him the same question, and this time he opened and closed his mouth in what I'd call a silent *yup* because that's what it looked like to me. So we speculated that we were missing crucial information in translating these reactions. I wasn't clear on who was pulling the strings either.

I remembered how Ana described the world as a magic eight ball, and we deliberated on all possible ways to understand messages that Companions would try to tell us. As a couple of philosophy graduates, that conversation took more than an hour.

"I wonder why more people aren't aware of this?" Jacob rubbed his chin. "It seems too fucking obvious to me now that we've had this chat. Come to think of it, I think some people do know!" He clenched his fists. "Working at the bar, I thought I had an instinct for people. For example, I could feel it when someone was watching me, but now I realize that chances are they were focusing their energy on me. My Companion was on high alert." Jacob squinted with suspicion as he reflected. He sat back, folded his arms, and crossed his legs.

"I don't doubt it; it's a real eye-opener. Everyone knows a lot is going on at a subconscious level. Our connection with another life form is something else to wrap our heads around. I found it easy to understand the microbiome by searching on the internet. It doesn't say anything about the collective consciousness nor, of course, how to communicate with it. Philosophically speaking, it would probably offend many religions to know their Companion—or shall I say their *soul*—is a sentient field composed of bacteria and viruses, among other things," I said.

Jacob started to laugh so hard that his eyes teared up. His laugh was contagious, high-pitched, and squawky, which also caused me to laugh. I pictured a bunch of religious zealots scratching their heads in confusion while standing around a scientific journal, reading about the microscopic origins of their souls.

"By the way, I have all the ingredients we will need for your famous spaghetti sauce," I said, coyly changing the subject.

"Excellent! Let's get started. I'm famished." He got up, and Loki followed him into the kitchen.

Jacob cut the vegetables and fried them into the ground turkey without draining the grease; he told me the turkey was lean enough. I grated garlic and parmesan for the French bread, set the table, and fed the dog. The sauce smelled delicious. I had a ravenous appetite for his spaghetti and was looking forward to enjoying my favourite dinner.

As we sat in the dining room to appreciate a fine home-cooked meal, I noticed Jacob kept looking at my newest painting that I'd hung on the dining room wall a week earlier. I expected him to comment and waited patiently, trying not to slop red tomato sauce all over my yellow summer blouse.

The painting was shades of blue, from almost black to a pale blue. It was slightly different from my usual pictures because it only had one colour. I usually loved mixing various hues and drawing abstract versions of things that brought out strong emotions in me.

"Well, that one's different. Let me guess." Jacob looked at the floor for a moment as if searching for something. "It's a beetle?" he asked as he stroked the back of his head.

"A beetle?" I sat back in my chair to look at the picture.

At first, I was puzzled by his guess, but I saw what he meant. It surprised me because I wasn't thinking of an insect when I painted it. I imagined a cloudy sky near the end of the twilight before darkness took over. *Fascinating*, I thought. The darkest blue portion of the painting, which was supposed to be a cloud, resembled a beetle; I was shocked I hadn't noticed it before.

"Yeah, it looks like a bug coming from behind a shower curtain." Jacob laughed. "I was surprised to see it beside the dinner table, not your usual colourful landscape pictures. This one is kind of creepy and monochromatic."

"Jeez, Jacob, don't hold back." I rolled my eyes.

"Sorry, don't get me wrong, it's lovely—in its way. It's just so *different* from your usual work. On that note, it would suit my décor, so please feel free to give this one to me when you get bored looking at it. Don't you dare paint over it; I will buy you a new canvas. I want to keep this one."

"In that case, I forgive you," I said.

We finished eating and cleaned up together. It was reminiscent of the time we were roommates. I had a wonderful experience at university—thanks to Jacob. I may not have extracted a great career from my program, but I was grateful to have gained a best friend.

My phone beeped; I glanced at it to see that Ana had sent me a text message: *Visitor pass is a go. Be ready Friday morning at 7.*

"Awesome."

Jacob tilted his head. "What is?"

"Ana sent me a text saying she got my visitor pass. I'm going to see Nekxus on Friday morning," I wiggled a little dance, delighted; Loki jumped up and down, responding to my excitement.

"I'm so jealous—I can't wait to hear everything. I doubt it's possible to take pictures, but I expect full details on the weekend," he said.

"For sure," I agreed.

We enjoyed a glass of wine before he left. I poured the sweet Riesling I purchased while visiting a nearby winery in Niagara-on-the-Lake. I had yet to tell him about the parasites because I wanted to wait until after dinner.

"I have one more piece of insight to add to the clusterfuck of information I've already dumped on you," I said.

"Oh really? What, pray tell, would that be?" he asked.

"This will probably blow your mind or confirm your worst suspicions." I sighed as Jacob leaned forward in anticipation of what was to come. "Ana explained that there's a hidden fourth dimension and that the elusive dark matter resides in it. She said it rarely interacts with our matter and is exotic by comparison. Unfortunately, a parasitic life form from that dimension is feeding off us." I waited for Jacob to sit still before continuing, giving him a chance to readjust as he appeared to be hugging himself.

"Monsters from the fourth dimension—good God, it sounds like a horror movie!" he said. "Are they vampires or what?" he asked glumly, as he thought better than to question the validity of my story.

"From what Ana said, they are more like tics. It seems they must be interdimensional somehow because they latch on to us and consume certain chemicals our glands produce. Namely, oxytocin, endorphins, serotonin, and dopamine," I said.

"That's just fucking great," Jacob said, annoyed. "So, if they *latch on*, we become miserable wretches?"

"We already are. Ana said humanity is infested with them, which is why our relationship with our Companions has malfunctioned. They deplete us of feel-good chemicals, causing increased psychopathic, violent, antisocial and sociopathic behaviours."

"That explains a lot," Jacob grunted. "If I wasn't dying to know what was going on at Nekxus before today—I am now. You better message me on Friday as soon as it's convenient. It doesn't matter that I'll be working the bar; I want to arrange the next update. Fourth-dimensional bugs," he said, shaking his head in disbelief. "Maybe that's what you painted, eh Kim?" He pointed toward where my blue twilight painting hung.

"I don't know."

We finished our wine in a darker mood, feeling helpless and wondering what we were supposed to do with the knowledge of a freeloader that we couldn't sense. Jacob joined me for a quick walk around the block with Loki before going home.

"So, what will you do tomorrow? I bet you can't wait until Friday; I'm anxious."

"I have to call Julia and tell her I won't be meeting her at the airport on Saturday. I'll think of some excuse; then I'll visit my dad."

"Tell her you have tested positive for COVID. That way, she can't argue with you," he suggested.

"Good idea; I'll talk to you soon," I promised.

"Damn right you will," he said and kissed me on the cheek before leaving.

## CHAPTER 6
### *Dad*

**ONCE AGAIN**, I woke up struggling to breathe. No horrible dream this time, but it was frightening to jolt awake gasping for air. I'd put off getting checked out for sleep apnea, but it was happening more often, so I figured I should call soon. I left Loki on the bed to sleep, quietly slipped into the bathroom, and turned on the shower. Adjusting the water to lukewarm, I closed my eyes and let the water stream at my face to wash away any negativity.

After breakfast, I considered calling Julia to tell her I wouldn't be going on the trip to Mexico with them, but I decided to phone her after I visited my dad. It would look suspicious if I told her I had COVID before I saw him. I called the dog sitter for Loki to ensure they could take him for the day so he wouldn't be bored.

"Loki, you're going to daycare today," I teased him. He wagged his tail and ran in circles before anxiously jumping up and down at the front door handle.

"Oh really? So eager to get rid of me?" I joked. He couldn't understand every word but was excited when I said *daycare*.

Much to his pleasure, I put on his harness so he could be buckled in the seatbelt for the ride to the dog centre. Once we arrived, I handed the leash to the young girl behind the counter. He was ripping to enter the play area, where the noise of dogs barking and playing filled the building.

"Bye, buddy," I told him unnecessarily—he ignored me anyway. "Thank you. I'll be back this afternoon to pick him up," I said to the attendant.

"We'll take good care of him, Miss Hart, see ya later," she said, smiling.

Hearing my maiden name Hart filled me with joy. Even before the finalization of the divorce, I changed it back promptly. I had no intention of keeping Derek's surname, Lynch.

I drove to the best bakery in town and picked up a dozen chocolate chip cookies for my dad. He preferred peanut butter chocolate chip, but his nursing home had a policy restricting peanut butter in case of allergies, so these would have to suffice. The Doon Care Centre, where he was staying, was a decent place.

A receptionist at the entrance greeted the visitors. "Good morning," he said behind the surgical mask.

"My name is Kim Hart. I'm here to see my dad Doug Hart in room 602," I said, donning a mask per the nursing home regulations.

He clicked a few buttons on the keyboard. "Would you mind having a seat for a moment? There's a note in the file here. I think one of the nurses would like to speak with you before you go to his room."

"Sure," I said. I sat down in the chair he pointed to and waited for five minutes, worrying about what the nurse would say.

Finally, the head nurse Janet came out to talk. "Hi Kim, how are you?" I could see her eyes creased with concern.

"Very well, thank you, and yourself?"

"Good, come with me to my office; I know you're probably looking forward to seeing your father." She led me down the hall where we could have privacy. "Please, have a seat." Janet motioned to the couch.

I sat obediently. "Thank you."

"I just wanted to connect with you in person about Doug. Our records show that your sister lives out of town and doesn't often visit, so I trust you will reach out to her in person. Doug's Alzheimer's substantially worsened and has interfered with some of his daily tasks. He has hallucinated some peculiar delusions—seeing and hearing things that are not there. I just wanted to warn you before your visit. Hopefully, today is a good day, but if you have trouble, press the call button. There have been a couple of times we've had no choice but to sedate him." Janet spoke softly with kindness.

"Thank you for the heads up," I said. "I will put extra effort into communicating clearly and slowly. I don't want to add to Dad's stress."

I left Janet's office feeling sad after learning of my dad's deteriorating condition. When I got to his room, his door was wide open, and he was sitting in his armchair watching television.

"Hi, Dad," I said. He turned to look at me, and his face broke into a big smile.

"Kimmy! I was thinking about you." He stood up and came to get a hug.

"Look what I brought you. Chocolate chips," I said and closed the door behind me, and removed my mask.

"Awe, thank you, Kimmy, you are a sweetheart." Dad beamed as he opened the cardboard box and devoured a cookie. "Where's Jules?" He reached for a second cookie.

Julia lived eight hours away and didn't come to see our dad very often. She had excuses like work, distance, and my young niece Sherry was in soccer and softball. Truthfully, I suspected she didn't care to see Dad. Watching his condition go downhill was hard, especially since he was a proud military man.

"She's at soccer practice with Sherry," I lied.

"Who is Sherry?" He had a puzzled expression on his face.

"Sherry is your granddaughter, Jules's daughter," I said gently and held his hand.

"Oh, that's right," he said. He seemed embarrassed as he struggled to remember, so I changed the subject.

"What are you watching? It looks interesting," I asked. I recognized the show as *Planet Earth*.

"I don't know. It's some nature show. It reminds me of when I was in the Falkland Islands."

"Is that right? I don't remember you going there," I said.

He laughed for a moment before elaborating. "I probably didn't tell you. No one knew we were there. It was back in 1982 when I was in the Airborne Regiment before the government disbanded it. An American soldier, two British soldiers, and I were in the back of a transport helicopter when the Argentines managed to sink the container ship and a destroyer. Oh boy—that was a venture." He rubbed his head as he remembered.

I sat listening intently. Alzheimer's affected my father's short-term memory and made it difficult for him to create new ones. He had good long-term memory, though, and it wasn't his character to lie, so I had no reason to doubt the truth of his story, no matter how far-fetched it seemed.

"We were called in without warning; my superior officer Captain Howler told me to gear up and say goodbye to your mother for a few weeks. I couldn't talk about it afterwards because neither the Americans nor us Canadians were supposed to be there. But we *were* there; the British didn't capture over ten thousand Argentine prisoners alone," he said.

"Wow, Dad, seriously?"

"Damn right! Airborne boys were involved in more than a few asinine situations. The Falkland War was almost as bad as the Middle East." He looked towards the television but not at it.

He was living in the past, and I could only listen. When I looked it up on the search engine, I figured he was probably around twenty-two years old during this war. I know he travelled on more than one *exercise* he didn't discuss. These were war games that my father assured me a few times in the past weren't games.

Sitting in the chair, he looked vulnerable, rocking while reliving some traumatic memory. I wondered how healthy his Companion was and tried to focus my thoughts on a question for him. I couldn't think of anything in particular, so I just reached out with my mind and asked —*Dad, can you hear me?*

He turned and looked me in the eye. "I hear you, Kimmy," he said.

"You *heard* me?" I almost yelled but checked my volume before continuing. "I mean, what did you hear, Dad?"

"I hear you in my head."

"No way, I can't believe you know about the Companions. I just found out about them," I said excitedly. "Why didn't you tell me?"

"Tell you what? I don't know what you're talking about." He wore a puzzled look.

I wanted to know more from him. I felt so angry with the disease that afflicted him. I calmed myself down and spoke slowly. "Tell me you know about the Companions," I said carefully. "You said you heard my voice in your head, right?"

"Oh, that," he said. "I learned that little trick from the Americans. Our captain brought one of their officers to the base one day. He selected half a dozen guys from our unit, had us line up against the wall in one of the large buildings, and gave us each a manilla envelope with a room number written on it. He told us to go to the room, but under no circumstance were we to look inside the pouch, and once we got there, a waiting officer would give further instructions. All the envelopes had different numbers on them. I went into the stairwell on my way to the room, and as soon as I knew I was alone, I unravelled the red string from the button on the envelope to see what was inside. I was so compelled to open it. A single piece of paper inside said in big black marker, *If you are reading this, go to the basement.*"

"What was in the basement?"

Dad laughed. "The American captain was in the basement waiting. All envelopes had the same paper inside, but I was the only one who opened mine. At first, I thought I was in trouble, but he told me he selected me because of my actions to join their efforts in Project Stargate."

"Project Stargate?"

"Yeah, yeah, that mind-reading stuff. The government shut it down because it wasn't very reliable. The remote viewing was too subjective. We collected a bunch of data, but it must have been ineffective. They taught us how to handle each other by talking in our heads. Anyone can do it, but most people who are aware keep it a closely guarded secret because they're usually manipulating each other." He shrugged. "Ask your mother; she's very talented. She always figured out what you girls got up to without saying a word." He smiled, thinking about my mother.

Mom had passed away in a car accident eight years earlier. I didn't have the heart to remind him that she had died, so I nodded. I was relieved when there was a knock at the door. I flipped my mask back on and let one of the personal support workers in with Dad's lunch.

"Hi Doug, how are you doing? I hope you're hungry." He put the food tray on the TV stand beside Dad's chair.

"Thank you. Meet my youngest daughter Kim." He motioned toward me. I doubted he knew the orderly's name.

"Nice to meet you," I said.

"You too. Enjoy your lunch, Doug." The worker pushed open the door and rolled off with the lunch trolley.

I watched Dad eat his lunch and thought about my childhood with him. I could pull out a few memories where I was confident he could see right through me. Especially when I lied to him, he always knew. *How stupid did I look to my mind-reading military dad when I lied to him about doing my homework?* I had to give him credit; he went pretty easy on me.

Out of the corner of my eye, I could see his desk had a small stack of papers, meaning he was drawing again. I moved across the room to check out his work, pleased that the pens I purchased for him for Christmas were finally getting some use. I lifted the pile and leafed through it admirably. His pen and ink drawings weren't as colourful as my paintings, but the photo-realistic artwork was inspiring and beautiful. Looking at the pictures made me realize that although his disease was getting worse, there was still so much I didn't know about my dad.

"I see you've drawn pictures of the pyramids, Dad; you must have enjoyed your time in Egypt," I said.

"I spent six months in the Middle East; the UN had us staying in Damascus most of the time, beautiful grapefruit trees right at the hotel. A few US soldiers were staying at the same place. We had to lend them our Canadian uniforms to go shopping because the locals were dangerous and conditioned to despise the Americans," he said.

"The pyramids in your drawings have so much detail. They must have been stunning to lay eyes on." I held up one drawing of the grand pyramid to inspect it.

He got out of his chair and came to the desk to see which drawing I had. He took another one from the pile that showed a long hallway with spheres lined up on either side and held it beside the one in my hands.

"This one is a machine," he said.

I knew his mental condition was fragile, so I didn't argue; I just smiled and nodded for him to continue like a child telling a story. I figured this was one of the delusions the nurse informed me about earlier.

"I sat inside that chamber for about an hour, and let me tell you, I may not have believed in God before that experience, but I have ever since," he whispered.

"I've never known you to be religious."

"Oh, I'm not. I believe in God—not much else. I'm not sure what the other pyramids do, but the big one exterminates bugs." He shuddered.

My skin prickled, and goosebumps started to form when he said that. I told myself that his brain was compromised. It was a little too close to the current subject of my life, and I couldn't help myself from entertaining the idea that my dad was aware of the hidden dimension.

"Bugs?"

He looked scared suddenly as his eyes opened wide and his gaze darted around the room, searching. He walked to his bed and sat down at the foot of it with his arms crossed and hands gripping his upper arms. I decided to change the subject, scolding myself for upsetting him.

"Come here, Dad; let's see if there are any game shows on TV." I picked up the remote control and flipped through the channels, searching for something to distract him.

Finding one with a big wheel, a bunch of bright colours, and the noise of an audience clapping, I left it on the channel, hoping to cheer him up. I turned my head from the television to find he hadn't moved. I felt sad seeing him look so vulnerable.

"I want to give you something, Mary." He had me confused with my mother.

"Dad, come over and watch TV with your *daughter*," I said, trying to trick him out of his confused state. I watched him open his nightstand drawer and pull out the familiar wooden box he kept beside his bed. It contained his army medals and other personal mementos like Mom's wedding ring. He'd had the box for as long as I could remember. "Dad?"

He stood up, opened the box, and dumped all his sentimental possessions onto his bed. Before I could interrupt, he twisted the box and the bottom popped off, revealing a hidden compartment. I watched in awe as he gently held up a relatively large stone. It looked like an emerald. *No wonder you hid that! It must be valuable*, I thought. He responded by looking back at me and nodding in affirmation.

"What is it?"

"It's an extraordinary stone. Mostly imperial jade, but this one keeps the bloodsuckers at bay. I snuck it back here from Egypt."

I stopped myself from rolling my eyes at his statement because, as silly as he sounded, he believed himself.

"It's beautiful," I said.

I pretended not to hear the *bloodsucker* comment and took it out of his hand when he passed it to me. I held it up and inspected the semi-precious stone. Imperial jade was worth more than regular jade because it was rare and transparent, like an emerald, but less expensive.

"You can keep it," he insisted as he put the box back together, returned the items, and placed it back in the nightstand drawer. He then parked himself unceremoniously in his armchair.

"No way," I protested.

I didn't want to take away something so important to him that he'd kept hidden beside his bed all this time. I tried to hand it back to him, and he turned and looked me in the eyes. They were starting to get red and filled with tears. In all my twenty-six years, I had never seen my dad cry, not even when Mom died. It scared me. I felt him in my head; he was pleading with me to keep the stone. I didn't hear his words like the time with Andrei, but there was no mistake; he pushed the thought —*keep it*. I felt like something else controlled my body as I opened my purse, emptied my pink makeup bag into the bottom of it, put the stone carefully inside, and zipped it shut.

I sat with him for another hour, watching the television and enjoying the moments when he would laugh at the contestants whenever he caught them making mistakes. Like most people who watched these shows, he seemed to take pleasure in feeling superior to the average folks on game shows. The second show ended, and I figured it was an appropriate time to head off and pick Loki up from the dog sitters.

"Well, Dad, I think I'll get going. I've got to pick my dog up from the daycare." I sighed; it was always hard to leave him.

"Okay, Jules, but your mother won't be happy you're bringing a dog home. I'm not taking care of it, either. It's your responsibility," he said.

I didn't mind that he thought I was my sister, but it was hard to listen to him talk about Mom like she was still with us. I tried to send him warm thoughts—*I love you, Dad!* I projected the words to him.

"Get *out* of my head," he screamed at me so suddenly that I let out a whimper.

"It's okay, Dad, relax." I regretted my decision to push our Companions to converse with each other.

"No, *you* relax!"

He seemed to be looking through me, not at me. It filled me with anxiety to witness his tantrum. An orderly came barging in and guided me to stand aside while he attempted to calm my father.

"Hello, Doug, you're safe, don't worry," the orderly said.

"Safe? Safe? No one is safe—*wake up* and smell the coffee, kid. The world is at war. There is a goddamn invasion, and our weapons are *useless*," he screamed at the guy.

Another orderly showed up, and I was so worried about my dad that I stepped toward him and tried to calm him.

"It's me—Kim. It's okay. I'll stay until you feel better," I said.

He reached out and grabbed my arm. I stood still but heard the first orderly tell the second one he needed a shot. I gasped, horrified that this was happening but tried to remain calm. I tried to take a step back, but my father pulled me close to him.

"Remember, the triangle is the strongest geometric shape. Remember that, Kimmy. Use the meteor to save yourself," he yelled at me while the orderlies gave him a shot in the ass then put him into his bed.

"Are you okay, ma'am?" One of the guys patted me on the shoulder.

"Yes, I'm fine. I'm just worried about my dad. Is he going to be okay?"

"Oh yes, he's going to sleep it off, and chances are he won't remember this. Usually, with this disease, they forget these little outbursts," he said.

I nodded slightly, suspecting he was lying or at least exaggerating. I gathered up my purse and left the building. I sat in my car for a few minutes, shaken. After a couple of deep breaths, I started the engine and drove to pick up Loki.

Once we got home and ate dinner, I gathered the nerve to open my purse and look at the stone Dad gave me. I held it up to the light to examine it. The gem was beautiful and heavy; I looked deep into the transparent green hue to see black imperfections that looked like a web. Suddenly the stone felt ice cold. I put it down quickly, shocked by the change in temperature. Loki whimpered; I sighed and prepared to take him for his neighbourhood stroll.

# CHAPTER 7
## *Nekxus*

**THE RADIO PLAYED** 3 Doors Down, and I sang along with the music while preparing to visit Nekxus with Ana. It was already six thirty, and I hadn't gotten any sleep. Instead, I stayed up all night worrying about my dad, wondering what to wear, and keeping Loki awake so he would sleep while I was gone. It was going to be a long day.

My phone dinged; it was Ana.

*I hope you are awake.* Her message ended with a winky emoji.

*Ready whenever you are,* I typed in response. I had settled on wearing my black work pants, black shoes, and a formal navy-blue blouse without any print that might look too loud. I kept peering out the window, eyeing for Ana so she wouldn't have to knock. She came out a few minutes before seven; I knew she was the kind of person who wouldn't be late. My shoes were on, so I only had to grab my purse and kiss Loki before exiting.

"Good morning." I dashed across the lawn to get into her SUV.

"Hi, Kim. Ready for a big day?"

"Absolutely," I said.

"Good. When we get there, don't be overwhelmed by the security protocols," Ana said. "I go through it every day. It might seem excessive to you, but I can assure you it's necessary. My boss Samuel will be waiting for us with a visitor's pass. He's very interested in meeting you."

"Is he? Why is that?" I asked, curious.

"Well, you must understand that we operate with a great deal of confidential information and technology. I told Samuel about what happened at the restaurant, leaving out some details. He knows enough to understand your Companion reproduced Andrei's voice for you to hear. That was enough for Samuel. We haven't had many subjects whose Companions demonstrated the ability to echo a voice for their human counterparts to perceive. He wants to run a couple of tests on you..." She hesitated. "First and foremost, no one will push you into anything. You will volunteer, or I promise *no one will perform any tests*. Once you see the agency from the inside, I'll wager you will be interested in helping us."

My mind wandered as I tried to picture what kind of tests they had waiting for me. I had assumed Ana was bringing me as a guest or a tourist; I didn't realize I would participate in anything.

"I don't see why not." I paused for a second. "Unless it's going to hurt or something." I looked at Ana and thought, *Is it going to hurt?*

She laughed and replied, "Don't be afraid. They may take blood and urine samples, but our technology is advanced and not physically invasive. You'll see."

When we arrived at the facility, it was even more impressive than I'd imagined. As far as I could see, all of the buildings belonged to Nekxus, each branded with their company logo—a blue triangle with NEKXUS written in black letters surrounded by yellow shading. We passed an occupied guard station to get into the maze of parking lots, and Ana drove around different-styled towers for a few minutes. One area looked like a giant crown with large metal domes and spheres arranged in a semi-circle. We parked in front of what seemed to be the main building, judging by its beautiful garden and fountain.

I marvelled at it all. "It's so pretty. You can tell it is a privately owned company."

"That's true, but many governments globally are invested in this company. We have public officials employed in each location representing their prospective countries. Canada has the best international policies, and its neutrality makes it the prime location for Nekxus's main headquarters," Ana said.

"That makes sense." I was distracted by the colourful tulips and their lovely floral scent.

We walked into the main entrance, which I half expected to be like a mall or stadium. Instead, it looked like the airport security gates before boarding.

"Follow me," Ana directed.

We put our purses in the bins and walked through a high-tech metal detector.

A man who wore a nice suit with expensive shoes spoke. "Good morning, ladies."

"Good morning," Ana replied. "Kim, I would like to introduce you to Samuel. He's the chief operating officer for Nekxus," she said.

Samuel appeared to be around fifty years old, with sharp eyes and the impressive physique of someone who worked out regularly.

"Nice to meet you," I said while offering to shake his hand.

"Pleasure is mine. Welcome to Nekxus," he said. He had a firm handshake but soft hands, I observed.

We walked through a grand complex where escalators and hallways led away in every direction. We went up the middle escalator, the longest I'd ever seen, to a beautiful common area where people were eating, reading, and chatting casually. The ceiling had a fantastic skylight, allowing the sunshine to light up an assortment of lush greenery.

"This is one of sixteen lounges in this complex for our staff to socialize and relax." Samuel gestured with his arm towards the sitting room. "There are twenty-one buildings here in the Hamilton division. We have scientists from around the world working on many vital projects. We employ the world's leading experts like Ana here, who studies the microbiome, as you know." He smiled at Ana. "Scientists from numerous fields work in their specialized departments. We have an astrophysics lab, a full wing for the mathematicians, an entomology building, a computer science complex full of brilliant software engineers and programmers, and one of the lower levels boasts the world's leading scatology division."

I listened in awe as Samuel described the different sciences that Nekxus studied and their experiments. We stood beside a panel on the wall that lit up when he tapped it. A map of the complex appeared; he touched a building, and a directory of staff with their titles appeared. It was overwhelming to see how many people worked there. Ana remained quiet and let Samuel do all of the talking.

We entered a large office on the upper floor and sat in comfortable yellow armchairs.

"Our mission statement is simple: *Heal Humanity*," Samuel said.

"No small feat," I remarked.

A young man in casual clothing walked in. "Would anyone like a refreshment?"

"Coffee would be lovely, Anthony," Ana replied.

"Yes, please," I said.

"Thank you, Anthony," Samuel said without taking his eyes off me.

I felt at ease despite his attention and envisioned that it must be an excellent workplace. I had a similar sensation when I visited the casino, where the atmosphere was so welcoming it was hard to notice the time passing.

Samuel leaned forward in his chair, put his elbows on his knees, and folded his fingers. I suspected that things were about to get serious. His facial expression had changed from friendly to one of stress.

"Ana told you all about the Companions. Before we get started, do you have any questions for me?" he asked.

"I have many questions." I laughed nervously. "I guess what comes to mind is how can I understand my Companion. I get confused when I try; sometimes, when I ask the same question more than once, I get a different answer."

Samuel nodded knowingly. "Yes, of course; remember that your Companion might behave like an entity, but it's a collective of microscopic lifeforms functioning together *like* a single organism. This collective exists in a symbiotic relationship with you. The complexities are hurdles you will overcome with practice. Have patience and pay attention to yourself; things will make sense in time," he said.

I nodded and took a sip of the coffee Anthony had brought; it was delicious.

"I told Kim we were interested in testing her and scanning her Companion. I want to put her in the Pyramid too—if I have your permission, Samuel," Ana said.

Samuel scratched his goatee thoughtfully before responding. "Yes, Ana, we should get started if Kim is willing." He looked at me. "There are some documents for you to sign, stating that you agree to submit to a few tests and a non-disclosure agreement."

"Sure," I said. "I have to ask, what is the Pyramid?"

"It's a machine designed by engineers who have spent decades studying different ancient pyramids globally and their purpose. The popular Giza pyramid in Egypt functions as a giant transmitter of extraordinary energy that repels the Darachnids that plague us from the fourth dimension."

"Darachnids," I repeated the word.

"It's a lot to wrap your head around, Kim. It will make more sense when you see it," Ana said.

"I'll be back, ladies," Samuel said and walked into an adjoining room.

I sipped my coffee and felt uneasy. Ana must have noticed because she put her hand on my knee.

"Darachnids, Ana? The swarm of mites you told me about?"

"That's what we call them, yes. An enemy inside our bodies but outside our dimension—sounds like a paradox," she said conspiratorially.

"Companions and Darachnids—any other foreign lifeforms I should be aware of?"

"I don't think so," Ana snorted. "We have our hands full trying to understand these two."

Samuel returned, carrying a large tablet. "This is for you, Kim. Please read it over; when you finish, it will prompt for a thumbprint which will be your signature." He turned to Ana. "I have a project I need you to look over; if you would come with me, we can give Kim a few minutes of privacy to look over the document," he said.

"Certainly. I'll return soon, Kim. If you have questions, press the intercom; we'll be next door." Ana gestured to an oval electronic gadget on the coffee table and left me alone to review the agreement.

It was uncommonly straightforward, only taking about ten minutes to skim through. As my signature, I placed my right thumb in the block provided at the end. After it clicked in approval, I set it on the table and looked out the window. It was a phenomenal view, considering we weren't too high up—perhaps eight floors—but I could see ships out on Lake Ontario.

Ana returned a couple of minutes later with a file folder. I saw my name on it. *That was quick*, I mused.

"You can leave the tablet on the table; Anthony will grab it later. Let's go to the medical centre so they can collect a couple of samples, then we'll head to the lab where I work. Unfortunately, we'll have to drive there," she groaned. "This place is so big that some days I spend more time travelling between buildings than getting any research done." She clicked her tongue.

"I can see that," I said.

"I've spent quite a bit of time in the technology wing. They have some nanotechnology that will provide advanced treatment to eliminate archaic antibiotics. The damn drugs have detrimentally injured our Companions to the point that they seem to have lost the ability to protect themselves and prevent the Darachnids from utterly polluting our bodies."

"How bad is it?"

"It's bad." She looked toward the window. "You've seen the tents downtown, and I know you've been on the receiving end of violence from thugs."

I nodded for her to continue while we exited the building and headed for her car.

"We gathered several volunteers from the encampment by offering them some money to participate. We scanned them in our DMRM— dark matter resonance machine. We have an AI program capable of replicating images of the matter detected from the fourth dimension into pictures on our monitors. The dark matter looks like poorly recorded black and white video."

"Amazing," I commented as she unlocked the vehicle.

"It is, considering it's from a hidden dimension overlapping ours." We got in, and she backed out of the parking space. "The volunteers were infested from top to bottom with the nasty critters. The ability to see the Darachnids with our technology has been possible for decades, and we are witnessing an increase in the number of parasites in individuals. Our studies show that, in most cases, shitty behaviour directly correlates with the size of the infestation. More dark matter Darachnids equal more severe violent and anti-social behaviour. We took blood samples to confirm that the necessary hormones in their bodies were too low and their glands weren't functioning properly." Ana ran her fingers through her long hair absentmindedly.

"Damn," I said.

"We could also see that their Companions had so much damage that they behaved in an almost schizophrenic manner. Aggressive behaviour is becoming the norm because of the increased infestation," she said sadly.

"It sounds like a plague."

"Mhmm, they have been wreaking havoc on our society for centuries." She pulled into a parking space in front of another Nekxus building with a sign above the entrance that said MEDICORIUM.

We arrived at the medical centre. Inside, the appearance was similar to most medical clinics. Technicians were wearing blue scrubs and bustling around like an emergency was happening. The atmosphere here differed significantly from the one at the main office building. I placed my thumbprint on another tablet for verification, and a kind young lady took blood, urine, and saliva samples from me. We left that building, and Ana drove us across a small bridge to the third building with strange architecture.

"That's a neat-looking structure."

"Isn't it? This is where I spend most of my time." She parked and we passed another walk-through body scanner inside the entrance. Ana led me to a set of elevators, and once we entered, she placed her hand on a console that scanned her palm.

"Lower level 83," she said.

"Level 83," a disembodied voice from the elevator spoke, much to my surprise.

"That's Zeevax, the AI that runs almost everything around here."

"Are we going eighty-three levels down?" I searched for a panel with numbers, doubting that we were going that far down.

"Not exactly. We are going deep, but some levels take up more than one floor, so the engineers have labelled floors according to different schematics. Zeevax has voice recognition, so even if I knew all the floors, the AI wouldn't allow me to go anywhere I don't have clearance for," she said.

I didn't get a straight answer on how deep we went, but we were in the elevator for almost a minute, and it felt like we were going fast. When the doors opened, Ana motioned for me to go ahead. I stepped out to find myself in a laboratory populated with dozens of people. She wasn't kidding about the floors either; the ceiling was high. I saw a vast open area ahead with some complicated machinery and was in awe of the fantastic instruments and equipment.

"It's overwhelming at first." Ana smiled.

A handsome young man strode across the lobby towards me. "Welcome. You must be Kim. I'm Ramesh; I've been looking forward to meeting you."

I felt myself blushing uncontrollably. *Get a grip*, I admonished myself. "Hi, nice to meet you." I took his outstretched hand and shook it.

He squeezed my hand politely and turned to Ana. "I've run the CS through a few practice tests and had Zeevax examine the software and backups. We are good to go," Ramesh said.

His Indian cadence was endearing. I was a sucker for accents.

"There is no time to waste then, is there? Let's get started. Kim, come with us," Ana said.

I followed them down metal stairs to a massive machine with a square glass chamber in the centre. I looked at Ana. *Am I going in there?* I questioned her in my mind. She blinked once and nodded affirmatively.

"That's the CS," Ana said, pointing at the glass cube. "It stands for Companion Scanner. It'll show us the health and status of your microbiometric field—your Companion."

"All right, are you going to be able to see how many Darachnids are in me...on me? I don't know how to say that," I said, puzzled.

"No, not here; the DMRM is in yet another lakeside building; one-third of the buildings are in that section of the complex, which is completely devoted to the fourth dimension, in one way or another," Ana said.

"DMRM and CS; some departments are more inventive in naming their equipment than others in Nekxus." Ramesh laughed.

"Like the Pyramid?" I said.

"Precisely."

"What is the Pyramid?" I asked, looking back and forth between Ana and Ramesh, not concerned with who answered. I was curious for an explanation because pyramids seemed to have been a common theme the last couple of days.

Ana tilted her head towards Ramesh, and he responded. "That's where we get cleared of the Darachnids. I will explain more in detail when we go there later; for now, let's look at your Companion." He pointed to the glass cube.

Ana took me to a changing room, and I slipped out of my clothes and put on the thin white jumpsuit and disposable slippers. The material was feather-light with no buttons or zippers. It had little strings to tie up at the side made from the same material. I rubbed the sleeve; it felt like cotton but was softer.

"It's a custom fabric for the CS, created so it doesn't interfere with the scanner," Ana said, answering my thoughts.

"It feels quite nice."

We came out, and about a dozen more scientists stood on the upper level, with Ramesh looking down at us. I felt self-conscious. My reality had been dreamlike since the horrible incident at The Castle. I thought about how my dad described some military assignments as unnerving. He remarked that sometimes when they boarded a plane and parachuted into an unknown country for a mission, he felt like he was on another planet. Lately, what he described was making more sense to me.

"You're not claustrophobic?" Ana asked.

"No, I'll be okay," I said.

"Okay, great. You see that scanner up there?" Ana pointed to the ceiling.

I looked up to see a sizeable claw-shaped object big enough to cover the glass cube at the bottom. It had a dull metal appearance, and I could see pulleys and gears, so I gathered it would get lowered once I was in the box.

"Yes, I see it."

We stepped onto the platform, Ana put her hand on another panel just outside the cube, and one of the glass panels slid open. She motioned for me to step inside.

"Okay, Kim, now you are just going to stand in the middle of the CS. It doesn't matter which way you face, but try to be very still. Try to take slow deep breaths; it helps to keep you from moving. The scan will take about five minutes, so if your nose is itchy, scratch now."

"I'm ready," I said, wanting to get it over with; I could feel the scientists on the upper level watching me with anticipation.

"Zeevax, please prepare the scanner," Ana commanded.

The glass door closed, and she walked away. I stood with my back to the scientists because seeing them made me nervous. While maintaining my posture, I listened to the upper scanner lower over the top of the cube. It clamped shut when it settled into place, and the room was considerably darker. It started to make a humming noise, and I tried to imagine I was an actor in a carnival pretending to be a statue.

Years ago, I watched a man painted gold standing motionless like a trophy. I stared at him for a few minutes, and he didn't blink. If it weren't for the slight rising of his chest from breathing, I wouldn't have known he was alive. The discipline required to be motionless was intense, and it felt like twenty minutes passed, not five, before the machinery clicked open and stopped humming. I continued to stand still—just in case—until Ramesh appeared before me.

"It's okay, Kim. You can move now," he said.

He looked a little eager to me, so I thought, *Is everything okay?* He immediately looked into my eyes and tilted his head to the left like a dog responding to a whistle. I didn't know what to make of that, so I searched the room for Ana. She was up at the control station with the other scientists looking at a screen and talking excitedly. I could make out a few words like *bizarre* and *more tests*. Ramesh touched my elbow to guide me toward the room where my belongings were.

"What's wrong?"

"Nothing," Ramesh replied. "You can change into your clothes. Ana will be with you shortly." He smiled at me reassuringly.

"I can hear them talking. Something's wrong. Tell me, please," I said.

Ramesh squared himself in front of me and gave me a sober look. "Nothing is wrong—that is what they are discussing. Ana will explain it to you in more detail, but they are fascinated because your Companion is *perfectly healthy*. We've never seen a Companion like yours. Every scan we've completed has had either a weakened or damaged microbiome, except yours."

# CHAPTER 8

*Dream*

AFTER OPENING the locker and changing my clothing, I noticed a JUMPER DISPOSAL sign over a plastic bin, so I tossed the white suit in it. While sitting on the bench to put my shoes on, my thoughts about what Ramesh had said felt like good news. *My Companion's healthy.* I was looking forward to seeing the picture. Ramesh leaned against the railing, watching for me when I came out of the restroom.

"Ana wants to show you the results of your scan." He swept his hand for me to go ahead of him.

"I'm dying to see it," I said.

Just being at Nekxus Corp was exhilarating, and my curiosity to see my Companion was growing by the second. I followed Ramesh up the stairs; Ana was tapping at the terminal where five scientists crowded around her. She wore an intense expression on her face until she looked up, and we made eye contact, then her expression softened as she waved me to come closer.

"Come and see, Kim. It's amazing."

I positioned myself in front of the other scientists between her and Ramesh at the station. It was like nothing I'd ever seen. The board responded to Ana's touch as she moved images around by dragging her fingertips above the glass. She touched a purple box that lit up in the centre; then, she fanned her fingers wide and slid her hands to either side; instantly, the beautiful image of my Companion — a luminous celestial orb — appeared.

"That's you," she said.

It was stunning. Goosebumps formed on my skin, and I felt on the verge of a religious experience looking at the glowing microbiome field. Unlike the rainbow chakras of the Vedics or the radiant yellow souls in Christianity, my Companion's image sparkled in dozens of spirals alternating between vibrant purple and fiery orange.

"Can my Companion see what I see?" I asked.

"Interesting question, Kim," Ramesh said. "No, we don't think so—but we don't know for sure. The emotions you feel will reverberate to your Companion and vice versa. If you have strong emotions toward something you *see*, it will be perceived on some level by your Companion."

"It's wonderful; I didn't realize it would shimmer like that," I said.

"They usually don't," Ana said. "Yours is much brighter than any others we've seen before. Let me show you."

Ana touched the corner of the screen then made a few taps and swoops until ten smaller images of Companions popped up on display in two rows of five. They were dull, hazy orbs that glowed in hues of red and green. Two of them were just soft red. Seeing the substantial difference between mine and the examples in front of me was astonishing. Ana tapped the screen again and selected yet another image of a Companion similar to mine but green with hints of purple; it sparkled almost imperceptibly.

"This one belongs to a Tibetan monk who has been meditating for long hours since childhood and had minimal contact with others. He has the healthiest Companion we've ever scanned—until yours." She tucked her hair behind her ears and closed the screen.

"I don't know what to say; I try to eat healthily and go to the gym," I shrugged, feeling a little ridiculous at my feeble explanation.

"There's something *different* about you, and we must learn what it is because there's so much at stake," Ramesh said.

I felt the panic in his voice, and it concerned me. "I'm happy to help. What else do you folks need from me?"

"Thank you," he said, putting his hand on my shoulder. It gave me butterflies, and my face flushed in embarrassment.

"Are we going to the Pyramid?" I asked abruptly, anxious for a diversion.

"Not yet; we're taking you to the DMRM. I suspect that somehow you and your Companion have managed to avoid being overwhelmed by the Darachnids from the fourth dimension. We want to analyze the degree of contamination before visiting the Pyramid," Ana said. "Samuel will meet us there."

"Samuel? Oh, he's waiting for us?" I asked.

"Zeevax will have alerted Samuel already with your extraordinary CS results," Ana answered. "He will be at DMRM before us, anticipating your arrival. Time is critical right now. The Darachnids went through a breeding cycle about two years ago, and the eggs are due to hatch. Soon, the larvae will begin a feeding frenzy that will exponentially affect society and the animal kingdom. We are about to see the plague of dark matter infiltration multiply by at least five, and we don't have a viable weapon or the means to liberate the population of this pestilence." Ana shivered.

"Shit," I said, too nervous to ask how many eggs were hatching.

I understood that humanity had already been suffering from this parasite, and Ana hadn't told me how many, on average, populated each individual.

"I'll meet you both there. I want to go over the data briefly." Ramesh waved at us as he joined a group of scientists still gathered around the terminal, going over the results from my scan.

Ana and I left the same way we entered, back to the elevator and her car to drive to the colossal superstructure where Nekxus studied the exotic substances from an invisible dimension. Admiring the scenery as Ana navigated the labyrinth, I wondered absentmindedly about the cost of hydro.

"The hydro company must be making a killing from Nekxus. How much power do you think this entire complex uses, Ana?" I gazed out the window at the mammoth architecture, especially the domes and towers that looked like giant machines.

"None," she said. "We have a nuclear fusion reactor underground.

Hamilton was selected strategically as the base location for this technology because its proximity to Lake Ontario is ideal for keeping the reactor cool—it generates a magnitude of energy, which causes tons of heat as an aftereffect."

"I thought fusion reactors were theoretical," I said.

"There are many things Nekxus has patented that are *theoretical* to the general public." She winked at me.

"If you told me that last week, I would have laughed, but after all that has happened and all that I've seen in such a short period, I'm not surprised," I said. "I feel like Alice in Wonderland right now."

"I know the feeling." Ana nodded.

We parked in front of a small building with a set of revolving doors that looked heavy and whose dull metallic finish didn't reflect much light. They were unremarkable compared to the rest of the complex; therefore, logic dictated that we were going underground again. Before entering the building, the door spun open, and Samuel stepped out to greet us.

"I trust you ladies are holding up. I promise a mouth-watering lunch after the dark matter resonance machine finishes its evaluation. I'm confident Ana reassured you there is no reason to be frightened, Kim. Exposure to any traces of radiation is fractional compared to what your cell phone transmits. We've both been in the DMRM plenty of times." He looked toward Ana.

"I haven't had the chance to explain much to her, Samuel; it's a substantial amount of information to digest all at once." She looked at me apologetically before continuing. "You see, not many people get to view our diverse classified sectors. Many of our staff are restricted to work in their specific departments without stepping foot in another building. We've been dragging you around the complex, but it isn't without a purpose. As I've mentioned earlier, time is running out." Ana trembled slightly.

I followed them to the elevator. There were two; the second one was three times the size of the one we entered. It was so large that I speculated it must be the service elevator for equipment and supplies.

"So, these Darachnids—do they look like regular tics?" I asked.

Samuel looked at me before responding. "Zeevax, display the

Darachnids," he commanded to the air. The side of the elevator's ordinary metal appearance suddenly displayed a hologram of a dreadful little beast that looked more like a creepy spider than a mite. I felt my heart rate pick up; I wasn't expecting a picture to pop out of nowhere.

"That's how I'd pictured it," I said cynically.

The elevator didn't appear to have a screen, but that didn't stop their AI from creating one. I wasn't the biggest fan of bugs—they gave me the creeps—but they were fascinating, and I had a healthy respect for them. This Darachnid slightly resembled other mites in our world. It had a globular body, eight legs like a spider, and no antennae. On the feet was a cluster of spike-like appendages. A web of pure energy extended from its back end, and its mouth hid a protuberance that extended a slim tube with a donut on the end of it. I wanted no part of it.

"You see the stylet here on this adult male?" Samuel pointed at the hollow mouthpart of the bug. "The torus tip will lengthen and bloat three times this size and shrink to about half when feeding. Somehow the Darachnids can syphon and convert matter from our dimension into sustenance for themselves in theirs," he said.

"No thanks." I laughed nervously.

The elevator stopped, and the doors opened to a chamber that boasted so much electronic equipment that it was almost dizzying. The advanced construction was spectacular in appearance. We walked into the spacious oval room surrounded by tiers and pillars that ran from the top of the ceiling—which I estimated to be at least four floors high—and dropped to an unseen lower level. Not far from the elevator, a steel railing overlooked a profoundly deep cavern that resembled an upside-down tower that went into the earth.

"The fourth dimension is very cold and only fractionally interacts with matter in ours. It also moves immensely slower. These Darachnids are blind and larger than the tics you're familiar with, but their movements are barely perceptible. Although we can't *purposefully* interact with matter from the fourth dimension—not easily, anyway—our life force radiates into it somehow. The combination of our complex energy, human and otherwise, crosses the barrier on a quantum level between our worlds."

Samuel's explanation sounded majestic, and he strode purposefully to the railing in front of us. I marched to the edge to observe that the shaft was filled with thick tubes. Wires tunnelled down and curved to the left. I guessed a generator or transformer was running by the humming sound. I realized we were *inside* a giant, powerful machine and gazed down to see that the abyss kept going. Spirals of glowing hollow tubes lit up the deep cavity.

"I present to you...the DMRM." Samuel held out his arms dramatically.

"Awesome," I said.

"In the adjacent edifice is where the laser beams are oscillating... I won't bore you with quantum mechanics for atomic physics," Samuel said; he probably read the confusion on my face.

"Let's get you into the WIMP pod." Samuel led us across a small truss bridge onto a platform with an egg-shaped pod.

"You won't have to change your clothes this time, Kim," Ana pointed out.

"The DMRM uses the pod to scan the hidden dimension, not you. It will reveal clearly where the insects are and how many are infiltrating our dimension and feeding off you," Samuel said.

"WIMP?" I asked uncertainly.

"Weakly Interacting Massive Particle, that's one of the names for the matter from the fourth dimension—or the dark dimension," Samuel answered.

I was trying to keep my cool, but the flood of information nauseated me. I looked at Ana, who seemed to be keeping a close eye on me, and wondered how she felt. Knowing our world was unthinkably overlayed with another, abundant with organisms consuming us, disturbed me. Hearing my father's words echo in my head—*You need an attitude adjustment*—I set my mind to push forward.

"Ready when you are," I said.

"You will wear these over your eyes once inside the pod." Anna handed me a pair of pitch-black goggles.

"It won't take long. The DMRM will examine the dark dimension inside the pod. You will experience very bright flashes of light at regular intervals that will increase quickly. The strobing will stop after ten seconds. Try to relax and stand still," Samuel said.

Ramesh entered the room from the elevator and joined us; he looked at me and smiled. I didn't blush this time, but my heart rate increased. He was around the same height as me, with voluminous almost-black hair that was perhaps a little too long as it feathered past his ears. I smiled back at him and turned to face Ana, dumbfounded by this young scientist's allure. Ana seemed to be reading me as she cocked her head to one side, and a slight grin escaped her.

Samuel offered his arm and walked me to the pod; it was spacious enough to fit my compact car. I walked to the centre and looked around briefly to notice that the inside walls resembled a solar panel; they were slightly reflective, all black, with metal wiring inside.

"That's good, Kim; put these goggles on. Like I said, relax and stand still; it won't take long." Samuel nodded and stepped out of the capsule.

I put the goggles on and heard Samuel command Zeevax to "Proceed with Dark Scan."

The opening hissed shut, and I stood in the pitch dark for a moment, anticipating the examination. The goggles were exceptionally effective; as the strobing began, I could see the light flash faintly through them. The intervals started slow and increased in speed until it seemed to shine continuously, then it went dark. A moment later, the door hissed open.

"You can take the goggles off now," Ana said.

"That was fast."

"Indeed," Ana said. "Are you ready for lunch? I'm starving."

"Lunch? Are we going to look at how bad my *infestation* is?" I asked, impatient to see the invaders with my own eyes.

"Zeevax needs time to process the information from the DMRM and rebuild an accurate model of the findings. We have time." She steered me back to the elevator.

Ana and I returned to the common area in the main building to eat in the lounge. We chatted about the adjustments she'd made coming to live in Canada eighteen years ago. She told me funny stories about some of the challenges she faced with Andrei—especially regarding language barriers. They were happy living here and proud to raise their son Aleksander in this country. She described the Russian complex as adequate but small compared to Hamilton's main headquarters.

"Samuel wasn't kidding when he described the food here; this is the best poutine I've ever eaten." I stuffed my mouth with another forkful of the decadent cheese-covered fries dripping with velvety gravy.

Ana gave a little smile, barely picking at her Caesar salad; it was unusual for her not to have an appetite. I'd come to know her as a plentiful eater.

"Are you all right?"

She glanced up at me and gave a weak smile. "I'm nervous. The Pyramid requires enormous power; it's good for mitigating an individual's infestation, but even with the nuclear fusion reactor, it's impossible to treat everyone." She folded her hands and leaned forward on the table, and elaborated. "You see, Kim, it takes the Pyramid about three hours per person to predominately terminate an average infestation. The power supply is adequate, but the required crystals burn out each time, and we must continuously replenish them. We synthesize them, so that's not the issue either. The problem is time."

Without doing the math, I understood. "You can't treat everyone because there are too many people."

"That's right, and reinfestation is inevitable. People come close to one another, these fucking buggers can sense it, and they will detach and latch on to another host." She took a sip of her tea before continuing. "Like osmosis, the Darachnids will transfer from an overcrowded infestation to a host with a low concentration."

"Damn, Ana, there must be something we can do," I said. "How could it be possible, out of all the knowledge and technology the Nekxus Corp has accumulated, that nothing could stop this pest? What about all of the children? Couldn't the company at least treat the young first?"

"The children aren't infected. I must have forgotten to mention it. Until puberty, the children seem to repel Darachnids. Unfortunately, right around the teen years, the kids are fair game." Ana sighed. "Our division in China theorizes that it's a survival tactic. They believe that Darachnids don't infect the young as a form of self-preservation. If a host has lost too much of their life force to the dark dimension, they're dangerous to others and themselves. It's a good theory, but I don't buy it. Once this next cluster of hatchlings are born, we will see how bleak human nature can get," she said.

I took a sip of the vanilla milkshake I'd ordered and sat back in the plush chair. "I'm relieved to hear the kids aren't affected. I had assumed it was every creature, no matter what age, since the Companions are so unwell."

"Responsibility for the injuries to our Companions belongs to us humans. We have harboured dark matter parasites for centuries, which explains disproportionate violence in the past despite healthy Companions mitigating infection. The advent of modern-day antibiotics has been wreaking havoc on our microbiome since the 1940s. We didn't foresee modern medicine's damage to our Companions until 1992. We just discovered the correlation between *excessive* infestation by Darachnids and our weakened microbiome field. We don't understand the link or how they interact, but a definite pattern has emerged," Ana said.

"Antibiotics? Really?"

Ana paused to chew a bite of her salad before continuing. "The global resistance to antibiotics has been exacerbated by the Companions' attempts to defend themselves against them. Antibiotics have increased life expectancy while decreasing homeostasis in the body, meaning we live longer but are more miserable. By protecting ourselves from some diseases, we have exposed ourselves to another more sinister threat."

It made sense. Often pharmaceutical companies treated one disease only to find out too late that the treatment caused an unpleasant side effect. It reminded me of the Thalidomide disaster in the 1950s. I looked around the room at the Nekxus staff enjoying their lunches as if nothing were wrong. *Aren't you all scared?* I scanned the room to find people responding by gulping or distractedly scratching at themselves. It made me wonder how many of them knew our danger. The way I understood it, the hatchlings were going to suck us dry of the molecules responsible for the positive effects our hormones gave us and leave us in a pitiful state of violence and misery.

"How often do the bugs breed?" I recoiled at the thought.

"Roughly every thirty years, they go through a breeding cycle."

"Thirty?"

"Yes, well, twenty-nine and a bit," she said. "Imagine the fourth dimension as a world where time moves painstakingly slow—it probably has something to do with the temperature difference. Anyway, their breeding cycles are closely in sync with Saturn's orbit. The universe isn't without her mysteries." Ana rolled her eyes and sipped her water.

"Isn't that the truth," I said.

I could see across the room that Ramesh was stepping off the escalator. I looked at Ana, and she turned to see what I'd caught sight of. Seeing Ramesh, she waved her arm to draw his attention toward us. He spotted her and crossed the elegant lounge to join us.

"I'm here to collect you two ladies," Ramesh said charmingly. "Samuel, Mia, Chung, and Fischer are waiting in the boardroom."

"Tell me," Ana said.

"Tell you what?" I said, interrupting even though she was questioning Ramesh, not me.

"Zero," Ramesh replied.

"I knew it. Come on, Kim, let's go." She jumped up, grabbed both of our purses and handed my bag to me. She ushered me down a hallway to a small elevator on the opposite side of the lounge.

I guessed what had them so worked up. "I have no Darachnids, right?"

"Exactly," he said.

# CHAPTER 9
## *Protocols*

THANKFULLY, the short ride in the elevator was chilly from the air conditioning because standing so close to Ramesh made me feel inappropriately warm and giddy. We exited the elevator to step out directly into a conference room. *This place takes ostentatious to a new level.* Egyptian statues, artifacts from all over the world housed in cases, and ancient papyrus decorated the walls under the protection of more glass coverings. I recognized some Mayan relics, Chinese scrolls, Mesopotamian tablets, and Egyptian antiquities. There were other antiques I wasn't familiar with; I wondered what kind of treasures Nekxus didn't exhibit.

"Great, you're all here. We can get started," Samuel said.

"Kim, I'd like to introduce you to some of our senior staff. Meet Beth; she's my right hand." Samuel held his arm out towards Beth, a plump lady with short brown hair, glasses, and a severe expression that made me not want to mess with her. She strode across the room and shook my hand firmly.

"Nice to meet you," she said.

"Nice to meet you too." I tried to let go, and she crushed my knuckles, exhibiting her strength before she released my hand.

"Chung coordinates activities and communication between all the Nekxus locations here and abroad."

Chung nodded politely.

"Hi, Chung."

"Fischer is our CTO, or chief technological officer." Samuel elaborated as he probably saw my face contort in confusion at the abbreviation.

"Good afternoon, Kim," Fischer spoke in a very thick German accent.

"Nice to meet you," I repeated, feeling like a parrot.

"Also joining remotely from a few other satellite divisions is Grant from the US, Navjot from India, Mei from China, Diego from Mexico, Oliver from Britain, and finally Reed from Scotland," Samuel said.

I gave a little wave to the faces on the drop-down screen above the conference table. There were at least twenty leather chairs, but I counted seven glasses of water waiting for us. Ramesh stepped to the nearest chair and pulled it out for me.

"After you," he said.

"Thank you."

"Before we start, I want to be clear regarding Kim's presence here. We've thrown *all* protocols out the window. We don't have anything to lose by keeping knowledge from her and everything to gain if we can learn how she's successfully defended herself from the foreign entity. Even if she doesn't understand what's happening, I want her in the loop as we advance. Some details may seem abstract, but we might conceptualize some rationale for her capability. Does anyone object?" Samuel asked.

The room was deadly quiet. I contemplated the VIPs in the room, impressed by their devoutness to this project. I was clearly out of my league and had no business sitting at the table with these hotshot intellectuals.

Ana was seated beside me, and she reached over to touch me on the arm lightly. "Try not to panic."

"Zeevax, reveal Kim's digital history," Samuel commanded.

"Completed," Zeevax's neutral robotic voice responded.

Square sections of the conference table in front of each person seated lit up. I was surprised to see the separate terminals, like a giant tablet. People started tapping at the screens and moving things around, opening files with information about me. I gasped out loud when I saw the details.

"What the..." I shut my mouth and started tapping open files with my pictures at different ages to see how much they had on me. I shouldn't have been surprised after experiencing the Nekxus technology already—it was astounding. My baby pictures, school marks from all grades, social media, videos from random security cameras in shopping malls, and GPS mapped a trail from everywhere I'd ever travelled since owning a cell phone. I would have felt less exposed after seeing Zeevax's records on me if I were standing in the centre of the room buck naked.

On the side of the screen, I noticed a contact list of people I knew. I scrolled to find it freakishly thorough. My family members, friends, close associates, and people I hadn't thought of in years. Not only were they listed, but the panel displayed their information when I tapped their pictures. I even found a complete history of my heart rate that my watch tracked on a graph from the entire time I wore it, only showing gaps when I put it on the charger at night.

"What do you make of it, Zeevax?" Fischer asked.

"Minimal anomalies," Zeevax replied.

The screen in front of me changed as Zeevax took over. A short list of seven dates, photos of me at the time, and a brief title. They looked like news articles. At the bottom, I saw the date from a few days ago, when Andrei and I buried the corpses from the horrible incident at the restaurant. I felt panicky and tapped it to see that the GPS tracked the whole trip, including a recording of our time in the woods and my heart rate during the entire incident. I felt the blood leaving my head as I experienced shock and fear. How would I explain this? I looked at Ana—*Oh my God, Ana! Do they know?* I practically screamed the words in my head. She looked at me silently and slowly nodded.

*They know.* Nekxus knew about the crime Andrei, Di, and I committed. My mind raced, but Ana seemed calm; therefore, I surmised that they weren't concerned with the deaths of two criminals under the circumstances.

"This is interesting," Chung said, breaking the silence.

I prayed he wasn't talking about the road trip. Chung took control, and we reviewed a folder about my dad, not the trip to northern Ontario in the middle of the night. He opened a file, and we all read the information on the display. Two sub-folders opened side by side—one dated before I was born in 1982; the other was 1998 when I was two years old. My sister Julia would have been eight.

Strangely enough, the older record was a military record about my dad and a few other soldiers on a classified mission to the Falkland Islands. That was interesting; he'd just brought that up to me. I read through the description of the events. A Nekxus complex was on one of the smaller islands there; from what I read, it was there at the same time as my dad was.

Oliver's voice from the monitor hanging down above us spoke up. "In the Falklands, on an uninhabited island, Nekxus built a subsidiary compound. The British overseas territory was perfect for studying cosmic microwave background, gravitational lensing, and astronomical events. Far enough to keep away from prying eyes and unoccupied by the locals. The Argentine government was not pleased with the British complex and sent their military to invade the islands and claim them as their own. Nekxus brought a few expert soldiers from Canada and the United States to work beside the British troops to protect its interests. This wouldn't be common knowledge as foreign involvement went against the sanctions at the time."

"Doug Hart must have learned of another war in the Falklands—the war with the fourth dimension. Soldiers wouldn't be privy to highly classified information, but we can't control conversations between individuals and gossip," Beth said pointedly while looking at me.

I felt myself swallow and suspected she was using her Companion to interrogate me. *You know I told Jacob*, I said in my head, looking back at Beth. Her eyebrows rose, and she pursed her lips. It didn't bother me much; I was ashamed of a few things in my life but telling my best friend all my secrets wasn't one of them. Plus, I told him before signing their agreement.

"Doug, Mary, and Kim have never been prescribed antibiotics. Julia has on multiple occasions," Mei said.

She was soft-spoken, but her voice held an authoritative pitch, and everyone in the room looked at the monitor respectfully while she talked. "I wonder, Kim, did your father have any strong opinions against modern medicine, or is this just a coincidence? I can see that medical records from your grandparents indicate that they weren't prescribed any antibiotics either," Mei inquired.

"He didn't like doctors. I don't remember him bringing me to visit one. When I was ten, I fell and cut my chin open—he was on the base working, and my mother wasn't home. A lady took me to the hospital, where they gave me eight stitches; my dad was furious when he came home."

I thought it was because he was embarrassed. After all, he was a proud man, and someone else had taken care of me. I scratched my head, wondering if that was indeed the case.

"So Kim hasn't taken antibiotics, which helps, but doesn't fully explain why Kim's Companion is so healthy. Your father's involvement in the Falklands and the American remote viewing project would've had him working cooperatively with his Companion whether he understood it or not," Chung said.

"When I saw Dad yesterday at the nursing home, he was confused and threw a tantrum. He told me the pyramids were machines that exterminated bugs—he called them *bloodsuckers*. I looked through his drawings... There were pyramids, and he talked about God, Project Stargate, and the Falklands. I don't know what he knows or remembers because of his Alzheimer's," I said.

"We'll have a couple of agents go to the nursing home and examine Doug's drawings." Samuel may have sensed my concern as he turned to me. "Don't worry, Kim, they will be discreet; he won't know they were there. I'll ensure they go into his room when he's outside in the common garden during daytime hours."

"Okay." I didn't see the harm or think I had a choice.

"I'm also going to reach out to our connections in the Canadian military to acquire more details on Doug's involvement in the described projects. Zeevax is thorough, but the record-keeping wasn't digital during most of his time served," Samuel said.

Navjot spoke up from the video call. "I find his comments about the pyramids interesting and will investigate further into the Egyptian connection. Doug seems to know a little too much for it to be a coincidence. Is there anything else you want to add about Egypt and the pyramids, Kim?"

"Nothing else comes to mind. Dad ranted a little about the triangle being the strongest geometric shape. Everyone knows that, but other than the Nekxus logo, I don't see the significance," I commented.

"We don't know precisely what we're looking for, so right now, nothing is considered insignificant," Samuel said.

"I see you've been to Mexico a few times, Kim. On your visit to the Mayan temples, did you encounter anything strange?" Diego asked.

"No. Julia's husband has timeshares on a property there, so we go on vacation together, except for the last couple of years because of COVID."

*Dammit, I forgot to call Julia to cancel.* I would have to call her tonight and explain something to her. She'd be disappointed, and my niece would be very upset because I rarely saw her.

"If you think of anything at all, let us know. The crystals we synthesize used in the DMRM were designed from a similar specimen discovered inside a small chamber in a Mayan temple in Chichén Itzá," Diego said. "They have a unique molecular arrangement that creates a frequency which causes minuscule gravitational waves that penetrate the fourth dimension. Zeevax uses these in the DMRM to record and recreate the images of the Darachnids latched on to us. The creatures are just dense enough to be registered by our equipment, plus they have some matter inside them that they've consumed from our dimension."

"Okay, I will try," I said.

"I recommend Kim submit to all procedures at our disposal; there is no time to waste. We should start examining the variables in Sector F and put her in the tank," Beth said. "Then we can compare the data before and after maximum exposure."

"I disagree," Ramesh snapped. "It could unnecessarily compromise her disposition and ruin any chance we have at understanding what's special about her. We have no reason to suspect she could ward off a forced infestation, and it might forfeit any opportunity to observe her potential."

I looked at Ana, a little concerned by the terminology, especially the words *forced* and *maximum exposure*. She didn't return my glance, but her jaw was tight, which didn't reassure me.

"I agree with Beth," Fischer weighed in.

"Ramesh is right. We have only one example of immunity, and we certainly don't want to reduce any potential to learn from Kim. Time is limited, but our resources aren't. We have the greatest minds and Zeevax at our disposal. There are many techniques to use that aren't invasive. I believe the tank should be a last resort," Grant said.

I listened for a few minutes as the committee debated back and forth on the tests they wanted to do. I peeked at my phone to see if Jacob had messaged me, but there was no signal. I wondered why while ignoring the increasingly heated discussion around me. Maybe the machines interfered with the cell signal, but that wouldn't make sense because Zeevax had internet access. I suspected Nekxus was blocking it for security reasons.

"What do you think, Kim?" Ana interrupted my daydreaming.

"Well," I stammered. "What's in Section F and what is the tank?" I asked. I had pictured a tank full of Darachnids crawling around sinisterly, waiting to feed on me, and I wasn't too keen on that particular plan.

"Section F is where we keep the animals. You saw the larger elevator that led to the DMRM?" Ramesh asked me.

"Yeah," I said, nodding. It wasn't a maintenance elevator like I had suspected; it was sizeable enough to fit a big cage. My thoughts flashed to my baby Loki, and my skin got hot with disgust. I was not a fan of animal testing. That explained why the DMRM pod was so big too. They could fit a cage with a large mammal in there. Ramesh didn't seem to be a fan of it either, from the angry expression on his face.

"The tank is simply a chamber surrounded by containment units that house the animals with the highest concentration of Darachnids infestation that Nekxus could induce," Ramesh said sadly. "The results of that experiment are always the same. Darachnids from an over-infested host will detach and—with some unforeseen magnetic force that we don't yet understand—float directly towards the host with little to no infestation."

"I don't believe we'll learn enough before the hatch to make a difference. We're in the final hours. In light of this, let us approach cautiously and perform the least invasive testing first. Only after exhausting all other possibilities do we ask Kim's permission to go inside the tank," Ana recommended.

"I understand your point, Ana, but what if her bizarre ability reverses and we can't treat her?" Ramesh argued. "Remember what happened with the Gamma Project. The Pyramid was ineffective, and none of the participants could be treated." Ramesh loosened his collar, looking agitated.

"It comes down to what Kim decides." Mei's soft voice had a calming effect on the room.

Ramesh sat back in his chair with his arms folded. I looked at him for a moment, and he looked into my eyes with a sad expression. He shook his head as if to signal me to refuse to participate with Beth's original recommendation. I looked around the room and up at the monitor to find the rest of the participants reading and studying their screens, searching for answers that weren't readily forthcoming.

I took the opportunity to consider my options. On the one hand, I wanted to do everything I could to help. This outside force was threatening the lifeforms on our planet. As unnatural as it seemed, the universe might not be without its sense of irony—danger from a parasite that made us want to kill each other. Jacob always tried to tell me that aliens would invade eventually—if they weren't already here. He hoped they'd be friendly and help us advance our civilization. Instead, we had this mindless insect attached to us from a place we couldn't easily remove it.

"I have a couple of requests," I said.

"What would you like?" Samuel asked.

I figured it couldn't hurt to ask. The worst thing Nekxus could do is refuse. I wanted to give the people I cared about the best shot at defending themselves from this grim-sounding future. I made some obvious assumptions and wished to exploit the same privilege for myself.

"I assume Andrei has been in the Pyramid?" I asked, looking at Anna.

"He has," she confirmed and folded her hands on her lap, as I suspect she knew where I was going.

"I would like you to grant permission for my loved ones to go into the Pyramid—my sister and her family, my dad, Jacob and my dog Loki."

Although I hadn't even seen the Pyramid, I wanted them treated. It was a colossal request, I knew. The company didn't even employ me, but I gave it a shot anyway. Before anyone could respond, I made my counteroffer. "I will submit to Ana's suggestion. Whatever it takes, starting with the less invasive tests."

"That's very brave of you, Kim," Mei said.

"I'm one hundred percent against Kim subjecting herself to the tank. Whether she's willing or not," Ramesh fumed and walked out of the room briskly.

I was surprised by his reaction, and the air in the room instantly felt cooler. Ana grabbed my attention by turning my chair toward her. The others were busy discussing my request as another debate ensued regarding privacy and the dangers of bringing outsiders into the complex.

"You don't have to do anything you don't want to, Kim. Please don't feel pressured by our friendship to subject yourself to something as dangerous as the tank. My recommendation as a scientist is not the same as it would be as your friend. I'll tell you honestly that if it were my son Aleksander, I would've refused and walked out like Ramesh. I am scared for your well-being, but I am also afraid of what will happen to us if we don't find a way to protect ourselves from the next wave of hatchlings."

I thought about what she said before responding. We all had our priorities, and of that, I was soberly aware. I couldn't blame her for emphasizing her son's well-being more than mine. I was trying to secure treatment for a few of my loved ones under the premise that I could negotiate with my cooperation. My shortlist didn't include all the people I cared about—I wanted to have Di and Jing—but first, I would see how the group reacted to my original proposition.

"I understand, Ana. The stakes are so high that I won't be able to forgive myself if I don't help in any way possible. Plus, it's not like I'm sacrificing myself on an altar."

Ana tilted her head sideways, and her eyes popped at my comment. The look on her face told me she wasn't sure about that.

"I think it would be wise to have a specialist speak with your father before he comes to the corporation. We certainly want to meet with him. No one seems to have a problem bringing your dog in. We've tentatively agreed to allow your friend Jacob to get treated in the Pyramid—if that is what he wants—he would have to sign off on the same documentation you did, of course," Samuel said. "Your niece hasn't reached the age where the Darachnids will have afflicted her. As for your sister Julia and her husband Jeffery—we are still considering."

What Samuel said wasn't what I wanted to hear, but I wasn't about to argue just yet. I was grateful for Nekxus allowing my dad, Loki, and Jacob to have the Darachnids removed. I was also pissed off, but I didn't want to show it because I had hope for my sister and her husband.

"I wish you'd reconsider my sister and brother-in-law. Julia and Jeffery are good people, and they're trustworthy. I know they'll behave with discretion; you can trust them," I said.

I could see that Ana's screen differed from mine, so they must've had a vote. I would ask her about my sister's chances later. Suddenly all of our screens changed to display a group of protesters. From the time stamp on the upper corner, I could see it was a live feed from the main entrance in front of the security gate.

"The organizers have reassembled at the entrance," Zeevax declared.

There were groans in the room, and Beth stood up and excused herself from the meeting.

"Thank you for your participation; I'll be in touch soon. Zeevax will prepare a package for you all to review and organize a time for us to reconvene. We have a domestic issue to handle," Samuel said to the monitor.

The participants expressed their gratitude, and the monitor was turned off.

"What are they protesting, Ana?" I asked.

She put her palm to her forehead. "The end of the world."

# CHAPTER 10
## *Cult*

ON THE SCREEN, we could see that demonstrators held signs and gathered around the guard shack while they attempted to block vehicles from entering the property.

"So they know about the threat to our survival?" I asked Ana.

"Not quite; the protesters believe Nekxus is the threat," she scoffed.

"I have notified the authorities," Zeevax announced.

"Ana, please take Kim to the biometrics office and register her for security clearance level 3 with a parking pass. Make sure she knows how to use the Nekxus and NexChat apps. I will speak with the director and have Zeevax prepare a schedule and a liaison," Samuel said.

"Come with me, Kim. Let's get you set up." Ana stood up, grabbed her purse, and gestured for me to do the same.

We entered the elevator and left Samuel, Chung, and Fischer to finish their discussion. Once we were alone, I breathed a sigh of relief, not realizing how tense I was until we were away from the others and the conference room. Ana seemed uneasy; I could hear the tension in her voice as she directed Zeevax to take us to the lounge.

"I'm so worried—Andrei keeps telling me to relax, but how can I? Aleksander knows everything. I told him when he was old enough to understand what was happening in our world. That's the reason he is going to university to become a doctor. He wants to work for Nekxus and help with the war against this invisible enemy. I believe in this company and its mission statement, but when it comes down to it, Nekxus will always put the interest of the masses over the individual."

"I feel like you are giving me a warning," I said.

"In a way, you're right, Kim. I *am* warning you. I want you to be safe, but the scientist in me wants to dissect you and your life to discover its secrets. I'm apprehensive about how far the company will go before we learn something from you." She twirled her long blonde ponytail around her fingers.

"I'm not thrilled about the risks, but I'm not stupid—you wouldn't bring me in here and show me all these highly classified projects and technology if the company weren't desperate. I can see that much. If something about me can benefit in some bizarre way, who wouldn't want help?" I flipped my palms upward and opened my arms. "I've already been on the receiving end of the effects of the Darachnids doing their dirty work. I bet the shitheads I've had to deal with were covered in them, making those brutes violent."

The elevator opened, and I checked my volume so the Nekxus staff wouldn't hear my panicked, foul words. We passed through the lounge and down the escalator to an office near the exit. Inside the room, I saw sophisticated security identification and authentication equipment.

"Kim, this is Carla. She will establish your clearance; if you'll excuse me, I have to step out for a couple of minutes to make a phone call," Ana said.

Carla, a middle-aged woman with a friendly voice, pointed out a brown leather chair in front of a camera. "Hello, Kim; have a seat, and let's get you set up."

"Thank you." I sat and put my purse on the side table.

Everyone here was very polite, and I could see that the company spared no expense with the decor, which made me confident that the wages had something to do with friendly attitudes—or perhaps it was visiting the mysterious Pyramid. Carla scanned my face, fingerprints, voice, and iris. Once she finished collecting my biometric data, she handed me a tablet with yet another non-disclosure agreement; I glanced through it briefly and signed it. I seriously doubted that many people read the fine print. It was longer than the one for my credit card, and I didn't read that one either.

"May I see your cell phone?" Carla asked.

"Sure, here you go." I pulled out my phone, unlocked it, and handed it to her.

"I'm going to put the company's Wi-Fi password in here and download the Nekxus and NexChat apps. Then we'll go over the tutorial together, so you know how to navigate the apps and use the map. It's easy to get lost around here." She laughed.

"Oh, I believe it; this complex is enormous."

Ana came back into the office and sat with us; she typed on her phone, messaging someone while patiently waiting. Carla taught me how to use the company directory in NexChat and gave me a few pointers for the Nekxus app. The messaging app was straightforward, with over eighty thousand employees on the index. She showed me how to toggle an individual's title, name, country, city, or building as search options.

"Finally, here is your parking fob. You won't have to do anything with it, the transmitter will send a code, and the receiver at the security entrance will automatically open the gate. You only need to remember to leave it in your car," Carla said.

She handed me a little metal blue triangle with the Nekxus logo on it.

"Mine just sits in my glove box," Ana said.

"Same," Carla said.

"Ready to go? Let's wrap it up for today. Samuel and the committee want you to come early tomorrow morning to get started," Ana said. "Thank you, Carla, have a great afternoon."

"My pleasure, see you." Carla smiled and shut the door behind us as we left for Ana's car.

"Wow, that was something," I said as we walked through the parking lot.

"This is only the beginning; the next few days will be absolute chaos. You're going to want to get some rest tonight." Ana unlocked her car and got behind the wheel.

As we approached the main security gate, I saw past the guard shack where the protesters had situated themselves. They flanked the entrance and the exit so they could harass cars going both directions. One of the security guards flagged Ana to pull over in front of the booth.

"Hello, ma'am; the police are working on clearing a path for traffic. If you want to hold up here for a couple of minutes—it shouldn't take long," the guard said, his tone apologetic.

"No worries," Ana said.

I saw two police cruisers with their lights on from where we were temporarily parked. A couple of officers stood around, speaking with some individuals I suspected were the organizers. We could read a few of the placards that people held up: *The end is near*, *Jesus is the way*, *Nekxus is Satan*, *Save yourselves*, and *Pray for salvation*.

"I take it this is this group has rallied here before?" I asked.

"Mhmm, they've been coming here for years. It started at the Nekxus location in the United States. After being involved in the Gamma Project, a couple of the participants started a religious cult. They organized marches around the property periodically until the state police removed them," she said.

"A religious cult?" I exclaimed. "You must explain to me the Gamma Project and how it resulted in a cult."

"The Gamma Project was the brainchild of a couple of scientists in the American division. In all their supposed wisdom, they tried to learn something from repeatedly exposing young student volunteers to the tank and Pyramid, alternating back and forth to see if they could build immunity to ward off the Darachnids." Ana rolled her eyes. "They built up an immunity all right—*to the Pyramid*." She let out an exasperated groan.

"Oh, no," I said, seeing where that was going.

"Two men got it in their heads that Nekxus was employed by demons trying to steal their souls. They weren't privy to information about the fourth dimension or the Darachnids. The subjects were told the experiment was to see if they could rehabilitate the animals."

"Rehabilitate them from what?" I asked.

"They were trying to readapt them from being excessively violent towards humans. Scientists from Nekxus told the subjects to sit close to the caged animals and focus positive energy on them. The animals had a high concentration of Darachnids. The participants were told the Pyramid enhanced their ability to direct positive vibes." Ana groaned in disgust.

"They believed that?" I exclaimed, shocked.

"It was as close to the truth as the company was willing to admit. After the Pyramid stopped being effective in ridding the participants of the parasites, the Gamma Project subjects grew increasingly paranoid and violent. No amount of time in the Pyramid could reduce the number of parasites. Nobody anticipated that the Darachnids would be the ones to become immune to the effects of the Pyramid bath," she said.

"That's horrible. What if that ability gets passed to others?" I gasped.

"That is still a concern for Nekxus; they scrapped that project instantly. Two of the experiment's victims were distraught and became suspicious of the breakneck speed with which the program ended. They started investigating the company."

"How did their investigations result in a cult?" I asked.

"They found Nekxus had connections with the Vatican by following news articles and pictures of scientists they had worked with and concluded that demons were trying to infiltrate the church. They believed God chose them to stop the evil legion of demons that worked for Nekxus." Ana shivered as if from a sudden chill.

"You said they're a cult now. What do the organizers call themselves?" I asked.

Ana sniffed. "They call themselves Cosmic Saviours. It's ridiculous. Andrei and I raised Aleksander to be Orthodox, and after everything I've seen working for Nekxus, I truly believe in a higher power. We have agents working and cooperating with many religious sects. Catholic, Islam, Buddhism, and Hinduism all have rich histories full of lost knowledge regarding our origins. In India, the Nekxus branch specializes in studying ancient scripture and artifacts from over two hundred religions. We have no shortage of faith in the company, but the Cosmic Saviours is a *misinformed*, dangerous cult." Ana's grip on her steering wheel tightened.

I felt myself self-consciously hugging my purse when the guard motioned us to drive out the exit. As we passed the mob, I could hear angry shouts at Ana's car. A young woman with a long braid down her back, wearing a golden sundress with black stars printed all over it, was shaking her fist like a club and screaming hysterically at the car.

"You will burn in hell, demon bitches," she swore at us.

I counted about fifty people in the group, more than half holding signs. As we passed them, I read more signs with drawings of crosses on fire—*Cosmic Saviours Unite!* More radical doomsayers chanted on the other side of the entrance over and over—*Nekxus caused COVID.* Others held signs of various predictions of catastrophic futures that claim Nekxus was bringing on the apocalypse.

"Brutal. Do these alarmists often show up on the property?" I asked.

"That only started again recently. Five years ago, after the Gamma Project shut down. The demonstrations stopped during the lockdowns from the COVID pandemic. They've become more aggressive and are showing up in larger numbers lately." She pulled out of the complex onto the highway to head back home.

The increase in excessive violent behaviour was about to get a lot worse. When these eggs hatched, the number of Darachnids would multiply. I was afraid the world might look like the Cosmic Saviours' catastrophic predictions. *People vulnerable to manipulation might follow a cult led by individuals corrupted by a scourge of Darachnids ingesting their mood-improving hormones from the hidden dimension.* Additionally, I feared weakened Companions would increase anti-social behaviours, attracting more troublemakers.

"Nekxus should beef up security. If things are about to get as bad as I've been led to believe, waiting for police to show up to disperse the crowd might be too little too late," I said.

"This fanatical behaviour is typical of hosts who are badly contaminated. Ironically, their accusations of the Nekxus starting the COVID flu pandemic are true. Fortunately, no one of great importance takes the group seriously," Ana said.

"*Excuse me?*" I blurted, feeling my jaw drop. I didn't think I heard her correctly. "Did you say Nekxus *caused* the COVID pandemic?"

"Yes, that's what I said." Ana turned off the highway; we were in upper Hamilton, just about to arrive home.

"So, the Cosmic Saviours are right about the corruption in Nekxus?"

"I wouldn't say that, no. The intentions were good. Remember I told you the Darachnids have a breeding cycle that's in sync with the orbit of Saturn?" she asked.

"Yeah," I said.

My brain was scrambling, trying to figure out what the company could have gained from a global pandemic.

"In 2019, the breeding cycle commenced. Nekxus was attempting to control the process by keeping people apart. Whenever a group of people or animals gather in clusters, whether at a concert, sporting event, election rally, family picnic, or you name it, the Darachnids cross over to other hosts. The male-to-female ratio is one in four. We hoped to keep people apart long enough so the males wouldn't have the chance to jump to another host and spawn with the females. It was a global attempt to cull the herd. Once a female's eggs hatch, the young will consume the mother. The males die off after breeding, and females unable to produce eggs should theoretically die off," Ana explained.

"Did it work?"

Ana gave a dismissive wave of her hand. "It was effective but not nearly as much as we'd hoped."

"So, the virus was fake?" I asked, trying to understand a highly complex scheme before she dropped me off.

I was excited to get home to Loki and also couldn't get enough information on the actual predicament we were in. It was like waking *into* a nightmare instead of from one.

"No, the virus is real, but the conspiracy theorists were correct in that it was not zoonotic. The Sars virus was engineered in our Nekxus laboratory in China and released in Wuhan because it was the optimal location for it to spread," she said.

"My God," I said.

Many people died from the virus. As fascinating as it was to learn about the company's mission to heal humanity, it hit home that they were a dangerous force to be reckoned with.

"Understand, Kim, we are at war for our lives," Ana said.

I remembered hearing that from my father only yesterday. I rubbed my temples, feeling ill-prepared for what was to come. *I should have joined the military instead of going to school for philosophy.*

"The variants?" I asked.

"Yes, that was all Nekxus. People were becoming immune and not taking it seriously. The company struggled to get the world panicked enough to shut down and not come close to one another long enough for the breeding cycle to end." She sighed.

We were pulling onto our street now; I looked at Ana to see her shoulders had slumped. It was hard to admit all this to me even though we were friends. I worried she thought I might be judging her. Her lips tightened the moment I had the thought. I reached over, put my hand on her shoulder, and squeezed it.

I tried to reassure her. "I'm sure you've been doing your best to help. I know you carry great weight with this secret war that most people don't even know about."

"Thank you. Some days are harder than others. There were times I wanted to tell you, but until now, I didn't have permission, and the risk was too high."

"What about Loki and Jacob?" I asked, changing the subject as she pulled into her driveway between our houses.

"Tomorrow, you can bring Loki," she said with a small smile.

I knew how much she loved him. "Great."

"Talk to Jacob when you have the chance. He will have to be a willing participant and sign the non-disclosure agreement." She turned off the engine. "The company will send a doctor to speak with your father and get the proper permission from the nursing home he's staying at."

"I've already told some things to Jacob," I said tentatively. "I should also send the contact info for the Doon Care Centre where Dad's staying."

She turned to face me. "Zeevax has all the information regarding your father."

I stiffened. "Oh, I forgot about Zeevax."

"We know you've spoken with Jacob already. Samuel investigated his background and feels that Jacob's awareness is only a minor breach considering the circumstances. He's much more concerned with what we can learn from you." Ana opened the car door and stood stretching.

"I don't have any secrets, do I?" I got out of her car and shut the door.

"Oh, you do." Ana tilted her head, studying me. "There is something about you we don't know, but believe me when I tell you: The company will find out."

"Well, I pray it helps," I said and came around the car to hug her. It was a big day for me, and I needed it more than she did.

"I'll touch base with you tomorrow. Your liaison will reach out soon," Ana said.

"Thank you, see you later." I waved.

―――

At my front entrance, as I fumbled in my purse for my keys, I could hear Loki whimpering with excitement on the other side. When I walked into the foyer, my heart leaped with joy as my little pup jumped and wriggled around, wagging his tail so boisterously that I had difficulty picking him up. Once I did, he gave me slurpy kisses all over my face. I carried him without taking my shoes off to the back sliding patio door and opened it to let him out to the yard. He still hovered around me, determined to get a few rubs in before he went to pee.

"That's my good boy," I praised.

Loki was play-driven and brought me his frisbee. I obligingly threw it across the yard a few times for him to release some of the pent-up energy he had from being in the house all day. My watch showed it was quarter after four, so I had time to prepare a nice dinner and take Loki for a walk.

"Come on, Loki, let's go get a treat. You've been such a good boy, haven't you?" I gushed.

He responded by zooming past me to the house, waiting eagerly to go inside. I removed my shoes finally, changed into sweats, and put rice in the cooker. Standing in front of the opened fridge, trying to decide what I would fry to put on top of my rice, I heard an odd noise from my phone that chimed like a musical triangle. I closed the fridge door and reached into my pocket to see what kind of notification I'd received. Unlocking my phone with my face, I noticed that the NexChat app, which had a cute little blue image of an atom on a black background, showed a red badge count with a one displayed. I tapped the app to see my first notification. A message opened with a picture of Ramesh. I felt giddy suddenly. *How immature!* I chastised myself.

It read, *Good day, Kim; I will be your liaison tomorrow. Can you meet me at the lounge at 7:30 a.m. for breakfast? Then we'll get started.*

"Breakfast," I breathed out loud. Loki, now food-driven, looked up from his relaxed position with his ears perked at the word.

I typed back to Ramesh, *Sounds good. See you tomorrow!* I hesitated before sending the message, thinking of putting a smiley emoji at the end. That might seem too flirty, especially since he probably had a significant other or spouse. I hit send without the emoji and tried not to feel disappointed at the thought of this guy I had just met in a relationship with someone else. Before putting the phone back in my pocket, it chimed again. I looked at the banner to see that Ramesh had sent a smiley face. I grinned like an idiot and opened the fridge again to find something to cook.

I ate my stir-fry with a glass of red wine and some grungy nineties music playing in the background. Loki had finished his meal cheerfully and had perched himself at my foot, patiently anticipating the morsels of my dinner. After cleaning up, we walked around the neighbourhood so he could potty, and we returned to cuddle up in front of the television. I pulled out my phone and placed it on my couch's arm, tapping Jacob's name and the speaker button. It didn't get the chance to ring twice before he picked up.

"Sweet Jesus, Kim, I've been waiting all day for you to call. What's going on? How'd it go?" Jacob asked impatiently.

"Oh well, you know."

"Don't be a bitch, Kim! Talk to me," he said.

I giggled evilly, knowing I was torturing him.

"Okay, okay. Sorry, I'm trying to keep the situation light. I will tell you everything I know. What are you doing?" I asked.

"I'm putting my fucking shoes on," he said good-humouredly. "I'll be there soon."

# CHAPTER 11
## *Animals*

**TWENTY MINUTES PASSED** before Loki jumped up and ran for the entrance. His ears were superior to mine, so I didn't hear Jacob's car pull up. I left the front door unlocked because I expected him to come flying through the front door without knocking. Loki whined when that didn't happen, so I went to the kitchen to see what the hold-up was.

At first, I couldn't see Jacob, only his green sedan parked in my driveway. My window was open, and I could hear his voice—he was talking to Ana. I leaned close to the screen to listen and saw he was standing in her yard. She was on her front porch, leaning over the rail, speaking in a low voice to him. Curiosity was almost getting the best of me, but I decided to wait a few minutes. Spying wasn't an option, though, because Loki started to bark, eager to see his buddy. Jacob looked at the front door, then I watched Ana hand him something; he smiled and waved as he strode across the property to my place.

Jacob walked right in and immediately picked up the wiggly fur ball. "Hey buddy, did you miss me?"

"*So?* What did Ana say to you?" I asked impatiently.

"*I can't believe it*, Kim. You got me in there too!" Jacob put Loki down and pulled out a dog treat from his pocket. The pooch obediently sat still until Jacob flipped it up in the air, then he jumped up and snatched it. "When I got out of my car, Ana called me over and told me that Nekxus is engrossed in your interesting results. She asked if I would volunteer to perform a couple of non-invasive tests to help them determine whether your readings were an anomaly or if the findings were similar with people close to you."

"What did you say?" I could hear the excitement in his voice and watched him shift his weight from one foot to the other. *You said yes*, I thought directly at him. A huge smile spread on his face, showing his pearly whites. He triumphantly held up the Nekxus business card Ana had given him.

"What do you think I said? It's like a dream come true! I can't wait to get in there and see this futuristic Nekxus company for myself." Jacob ran his hands through his short hair. "Remember when my ex and I vacationed in Belgium, and I sent you that postcard with the picture of the Atomium?" He took off his shoes.

"Yes, I still have it in my photo album."

"That was the coolest landmark I've ever seen, and it was built in the '50s." Jacob went into my kitchen and helped himself to the fridge, grabbing a bottle of Chardonnay. I opened my cupboard door and stretched to reach a bag of chips. We'd spent countless nights like this talking, drinking, and pigging out on snacks.

"You won't be disappointed; one of the buildings *is* a machine."

"Fantastic," he said as he uncorked the bottle.

We sat in the living room, and I recounted my day to Jacob, trying to replicate every detail. In all the years we'd known each other, I'd never seen him so quiet. He sipped his wine and munched the chips, but otherwise, he just stared at me, barely blinking. After I told him about the Cosmic Saviours cult protesting at the gate, I sat back and finished my wine. His odd expression caused me to suspect he was using his Companion to query me.

"Are you getting your Companion to interrogate me?" I asked, amused.

"You *could* tell," he replied. "I wondered. I was trying to see if Nekxus was the bad guy. I kept asking you if you considered the company dangerous."

"To answer your question—I don't doubt that the company is dangerous. The Canadian government doesn't have as much power as they do. I bet since they operate globally, Nekxus has more power than *most* governments."

Now that Jacob and I understood the jeopardy humankind was in, we spent the next few hours discussing the possible reasons for my startling results and hypothesized potential futures.

"It's a war," Jacob said flatly.

"Damn, that's the third time I've heard that in the last two days. I read that the COVID pandemic was the war of our generation." I shuddered. "It seems the disease was only a battle in the true war. The Cosmic Saviours should make a sign that says, *Save us from the WIMP War.*" I snorted with laughter, and Jacob stared at me with his mouth agape like I was off my rocker.

"The Wimp War, Kim? Really? What the hell are you talking about now?"

"You know WIMP—weakly interactive massive particles. That's what they told me. The molecules of dark matter are called WIMPs; they even have a WIMP pod." I giggled. It was a long day; I'd had no sleep and felt more than a little drunk from the second bottle of wine we polished off.

"Okay, you're done. Let's take Loki for a walk and watch a movie. I'll stay the night and see you off early before you go eat breakfast with this Ramesh fellow you have a crush on," he said, lifting one eyebrow at me.

"What the hell are *you* talking about?" I repeated his words back to him while feigning ignorance. He knew me too well. He tapped his temple with his index finger, then woke Loki up, and we took him outside.

After a short walk and some fresh air, we put on one of Jacob's favourite movies, *The Fifth Element*. I must have passed out because the last thing I remembered was laying on the couch with my feet on his lap, watching Bruce Willis negotiate with aliens. Then out of nowhere, Jacob was shaking me.

"Kim, *wake up*," he shouted in my face.

"What's going on?" I jumped up, my focus cleared, and I got scared when I saw the look on his face. His pupils were dilated, his eyebrows pulled up, and he was pale like he'd seen a ghost. I glanced around the room, searching for the phantom or whatever had him so scared. The television was still on and the credits were playing, but I didn't see anything else.

"God dammit, Kim, you had me scared. Don't do that to me," he said and sighed deeply.

"What?" I rubbed my eyes then pet Loki's chin, who had jumped on the couch, wagging his tail because of the commotion.

"You were snoring, then stopped; I looked to see if you'd woken up and noticed you weren't breathing. I watched your chest, but it didn't move, and I couldn't wake you up—I swear to you."

"I knew it." I tried to stifle a yawn.

"You did?"

"I suspected that I've had sleep apnea for years. I've never bothered to get checked out, but I've woken up gasping for air periodically throughout my life. Sometimes with vivid nightmares about drowning, and other times I just struggled to breathe as if paralyzed," I said.

"You should go to a sleep clinic and get checked out. Maybe Nekxus has something like that. From what you described, it sounds like they have everything." Jacob rubbed the nape of his neck and pressed the remote to turn off the television. "Go to bed. I'll be in the spare room if you need me."

I kissed him on the cheek and went upstairs to wash my face and brush my teeth. I set the alarm for five in the morning; that way, I'd have plenty of time to shower and dress before meeting Ramesh for breakfast.

Crawling under my sheets, I heard a familiar pitapat up the stairs. Loki jumped onto the mattress and parked himself at the foot of the bed. He probably had a mind to sleep with Jacob, but my bed was the softest.

---

I woke to The Cars playing "You Might Think." To give my fur baby and house guest another hour of sleep, I turned off my phone. My alarm was a shuffled playlist; I'd hear a different song each morning to begin my day. I thought of it like a horoscope, a fun little game I made up where my day's mood would be predicted by whatever music the alarm played.

I walked into the kitchen to find Jacob pouring water into the coffee maker. "You're up already?" I said, surprised.

"As if I could sleep." He threw his hands in the air. "I've been on the internet all night googling bugs, dark matter, bacteria, nuclear fusion, and anything I could find on Nekxus. I even searched for that cult you told me about—Cosmic Saviours. Their leader looks like a real whack job. I don't know if I'm ever going to sleep again." He clucked and started the coffee maker.

"I'm freaking out, too."

"You wouldn't know it to look at you. You're the most composed chick I've ever met," he said.

"Nonsense, I'm always nervous." I grabbed a couple of coffee mugs and the creamer from the fridge.

"Maybe on the *inside*, but outwardly you have a poised disposition. Probably from having a drill sergeant for a father," he said.

"Warrant officer," I corrected. "I don't know, maybe. I know Julia holds it together pretty well, even when Mom died—*shit*, Julia!" I'd completely forgotten to call her to cancel Mexico.

"What is it? Never mind, I bet you didn't call her yet," he said, shaking his head.

"I'll call now; she's an early bird."

"I'll take Loki for a pee." Jacob took his coffee to the back patio, where Loki was already waiting at the door to go outside.

I called my sister and explained I wouldn't be joining them for a vacation this year. I lied to her by saying I tested positive for COVID and was experiencing terrible symptoms. She was disappointed but didn't put up much of a fuss. She advised me to get some rest and promised to send my apologies to my niece.

Ana told me I should bring Loki to the company, so Jacob helped me pack his doggy travel bag with everything he'd need. She indicated to Jacob that she might call him to meet her at the front gate of Nekxus in the afternoon, so he planned a breakfast date with Matt to be available the rest of the day in case she did.

Jacob walked me to my car. "Do you have everything?" He buckled Loki's harness to the seatbelt in the back seat.

"Yes, Mom," I teased.

"I'll talk to you later tonight." He winked and got into his sedan. He waited for me to pull out of the driveway to leave.

"Ready for an adventure?" I asked my pooch. He didn't care what I said; his head was stretched toward the partially opened window, enjoying the smells. Thankfully, the protesters weren't there when we arrived at the main security gate. The fob Carla gave me worked, and the metal bar lifted when I pulled up to it. The guard in the Nekxus uniform nodded at me then returned his attention to his monitor. I left the transmitter in the glove box as Carla suggested, resisting the urge to pull it out and show the guard.

After parking, I walked to the front entrance with Loki leading the way, wondering if anyone would give me flak for bringing my dog. Ramesh was waiting on the other side of the metal detectors waving at me with a big smile.

"Hello, little fellow; what's your name?" Ramesh leaned down to pet Loki, who was wagging his tail vigorously.

"Loki," I said.

"I must apologize for storming out on the meeting yesterday. Please believe me when I tell you I am not usually so rude," Ramesh said.

"That's okay; I saw the protesters, and Ana told me what happened to their leaders in the Gamma Project, so I have a small inkling of where you were coming from," I said.

"I appreciate that, thank you. Are you hungry?"

"Famished. Will people be annoyed that my dog is here?"

Ramesh scoffed. "Absolutely not."

He was right. Not only did no one seem to mind Loki being in the lounge, but they were also happy to see him. He was elated to be on the receiving end of so much affection and praise. Loki must have heard the words *good boy* from at least thirty people. Breakfast was delicious, and since my dog garnished so much attention, Ramesh and I weren't alone, so I didn't feel awkward and nervous.

"I want to show you the Pyramid before we start with some other tests for you today." Ramesh stood up. "I'll get a shuttle so Loki can ride in the open air here."

"A shuttle? Nice. Ana and I drove around yesterday. I didn't know there were shuttles."

"Let me show you." Ramesh opened his Nekxus app and pointed to a little icon of a car. He tapped it open and chose a building from the list. "You see, it already knows where I am. You choose where you want it to take you from the list of buildings on the screen."

"Amazing," I said.

We went to the front and waited on a bench on the left side of the entrance. I laughed when the self-driving vehicle pulled in front of us at the main entrance.

"I should have known there wouldn't be a driver," I said as we got in. "I'm so impressed by how automated everything is here."

"It takes a little getting used to."

Before arriving at our destination, Ramesh explained his role in the company as a bioelectromagnetic specialist. He worked at Nekxus in India before transferring to Canada, studying how electromagnetic fields interact with biological entities and their Companions. He talked about how molecular physics and crystals go hand in hand with his work.

"I am always learning. This company has amazing opportunities. Once they recruit a person, the company takes over their education. Nekxus has its own university in Germany; that's where I was acquainted with the up-to-date scientific discoveries and technology that the company uses." Ramesh reached down and scratched Loki's ear before continuing. "There, I learned what we know about the fourth dimension and the history collected about humanity's interactions with it. We've known about the Companions for a long time but didn't recognize them as symbiotic entities with consciousness until the last thirty years. Now we're going back and rifling through our historical data to make connections and learn how to heal the Companions. We believe they have a quasi-existence between the two dimensions."

The shuttle pulled up to the building with the revolving doors.

"I'm going to take Loki to that patch of grass first, in case he needs to pee." I didn't want a puddle in the building. "So, the Darachnids can attach to us because of our Companions and this dual existence between the two dimensions?" I asked.

"That's the working theory right now." Ramesh walked over to the grass with us. "Life forms here can penetrate the dark dimension and vice versa. Interestingly, tests in Russia proved that nuclear bombs had zero effect. The animals wandering around the Chernobyl disaster area were also tested, and their radiation exposure didn't affect the Darachnid infection ratio. It was the same for animals that weren't exposed."

"Yikes, splitting an atom doesn't affect the dark dimension, but life does—it's almost theological," I said.

"Life forms emanate exotic matter that crosses to the hidden dimension, which attracts the bugs like a magnet, to put it simply," he said.

Loki finally found a spot he liked and urinated on a lovely purple flower. *Figures; you had to mark the garden*—I focused the thought on him. He looked up at me and wagged his tail, trotting proudly with us to the revolving door that led underground.

"So, do they bring the animals in that one?" I asked, pointing at the massive elevator door beside the regular one we entered.

Ramesh sighed deeply before responding. "Sometimes. There is also a back entrance that exists for the larger animals to enter level 161. Zeevax, take us to the Pyramid," Ramesh instructed.

"These numbers seem random. Unless there are many levels."

"You are right. They are random—Zeevax selects them. I'll introduce you to Zeevax's tech team later. The programmers and computer specialists are one of the nicest groups here," he said.

"That's saying a lot—people here are friendly."

"They don't last if they aren't," he said pointedly.

"Can we see the animals?"

"No, you don't have clearance for that, but I can show you this. Zeevax, display video alpha-ram-thirty," Ramesh said.

This time I was prepared for the screen to appear on the elevator wall. Once again, the video displayed was in three dimensions.

"Is this now?" I asked.

"No, I don't have access to real-time. This is one of my files from eight months ago."

I saw rows of clear cages that must have been made out of some super-strength polymer because if they were glass, they would have shattered. Animals of all types and sizes were screaming, roaring, and foaming at the mouth. The sounds were bone-chilling. I shivered in fear and disgust. Even Loki had his tail tucked between his legs and started to whimper.

"Zeevax, display time-frame index six-two-four." Ramesh crossed his arms and shook his head disapprovingly.

The recording fast-forwarded to a great gymnasium-sized room with steel walls and doors. It looked like a modern-day gladiator stadium. The viewing area on the upper floor was transparent enough to make out people in lab coats and military uniforms. The doors opened, and different animals came flying out at breakneck speeds. It was a blood bath.

"*Holy shit,*" I gasped.

It didn't seem to matter what the species was; every creature that came out of an enclosure attacked. A puny little house cat darted to the left when the door opened and threw itself at a goat. The goat ripped the cat to shreds in time to have its head torn off by a gorilla. I saw a wolf, bear, dog, beaver, and an eagle moving around the room, struggling with a rabid ferret. They killed each so fast that, except for a badly wounded lion, they were all dead before our elevator door opened.

"That's fucked up." I stepped out, holding tight to the leash Loki was yanking in his attempt to escape the elevator of horror.

"You see why I don't want you exposing yourself to those poor creatures?" Ramesh put his hand on my arm and looked at me with a hint of sadness. "What you saw was the result of severe infection by the Darachnids."

I looked down at Loki and felt sick to my stomach. It was clear how motivated the company was to find a solution to this plague, especially once the hatchlings started feeding. On the one hand, what they did to those animals in the name of science and saving lives was…inconceivable. On the other hand, although humans possess higher reason, it wouldn't protect them from the savage behaviour I witnessed if they became grossly infected.

We stood in an empty lounge area that felt out of place for what I was expecting to see, especially after the DMRM level. There was a sign for a washroom and a clear fridge filled with water bottles and vitamin water. Earlier I learned that Nekxus provided all food and beverages on the premises at no charge.

"I recognized military uniforms," I said.

"Yes, you did. We are at war for our lives. The military is partnered with Nekxus," he said.

"Where do the animals come from?" I asked.

"They come from zoos, sanctuaries. Many wild animals already behaving violently. Treatment in the Pyramid is limited, so the company studied the effects of the *opposite* of treatment," he said.

"How did they get more Darachnids to infect the animals? Don't they always move from high to low concentrations?" I grabbed a bottle of vitamin water from the fridge.

"They would put two animals together—one drugged to stimulate the pineal, pituitary, adrenal, and hypothalamus glands. The overproduction of the glands caused increased secretion of the hormones, which would draw the Darachnids from one animal toward the drugged animal. Then we would separate them," he explained.

"After observing them in isolation, the drugged animals were pitted against each other?"

"Unfortunately," Ramesh said and walked over to a control panel and tapped the screen. "In about five minutes, the Pyramid will be available. We are booked in for eight thirty; it's occupied right now. It's constantly running, and we have eighteen of them worldwide."

"Am I going inside with Loki?"

"First, I will go inside the Pyramid, and you will observe. We know you aren't infected, so there's no need for you to enter it yet. There is an observation room for you and Loki. We put a pillow and chew toys for Loki. While observing me, Zeevax has prepared a barrage of questions for you to answer, and you'll have the opportunity to ask Zeevax anything you want. The AI may or may not answer them depending on classification," he said.

"How long will it take?"

"Almost three hours," he answered.

A woman came walking down the long hallway beside the washroom. She nodded at Ramesh, grabbed a water bottle, and went into the bathroom.

"Let's go see the Pyramid," Ramesh said, and the three of us walked down a long hallway.

## CHAPTER 12
### *Pyramid*

THERE WAS no door handle at the end of the hallway. Ramesh placed his hand flat on the screen to the right, scanning his palm. The door buzzed, slid sideways, and disappeared into a compartment inside the wall. Loki scampered into the open chamber ahead of us. It was a magnificent room with transparent windows that overlooked a great chasm where five coil-shaped towers shot sparks of electricity. The lightning jumped from one tower to another in a spiral pattern that worked its way down to a black dome at the bottom.

I whistled. "It's beautiful."

Loki looked up at me, tilted his head sideways, then sniffed at an odd chair in the room's centre. The electricity was so pretty that I kept staring at it, amazed by the raw energy. Ramesh walked across the room and opened an adjacent door, which caught Loki's attention, and he pulled on the leash to follow.

"This is the waiting room where you two can hang out with Zeevax while I get purified in the Pyramid bath," Ramesh said.

"Wow, this is a nice setup," I said, exiting the chamber.

The waiting room possessed two comfy couches, four armchairs, and a round black coffee table. I could see why Loki was so eager to come in here. A fluffy pillow was on the floor with some balls, a bone, and a stuffed fox. A bowl of water was nearby, and a small dish with treats. A marble counter that looked like a bar had a coffee dispenser, and I could see a vending machine with snacks.

"Help yourself to whatever you like; there is a bathroom around the other side of the bar." Ramesh pointed.

I leaned over to see the opening and felt grateful for the thoughtfulness as he placed a little faux grass puppy pad for Loki outside the bathroom entrance.

"Thank you," I said.

"Don't mention it."

"Where's the Pyramid anyway?" I asked.

Ramesh laughed. "You walked through it. If you need anything, Zeevax will assist you—Zeevax, display my Pyramid bath for Kim to watch," Ramesh commanded.

"Displayed," Zeevax responded.

The coffee table projected a holograph image of the room we had just walked through and the chair in it.

"I'll see you soon." Ramesh walked back into the adjacent room and sat in the chair.

The door closed behind him, and I turned my attention to the coffee table that now projected a mini Ramesh sitting in the chair. To my astonishment, the whole room descended and disappeared into a lower level.

"What's happening with Ramesh, Zeevax?" I asked shyly, looking around for a microphone.

"Decontamination of the parasite is commencing. Ramesh is in the bath compartment, which has lowered into an alternator. There the turbine generates a field to warp the space around it, cutting the Darachnid off from its local environment and essentially suffocating it. The process takes approximately 160 minutes to ensure total eradication."

Loki jumped up on the couch with the toy fox in his mouth, dropped it beside me, and curled up with it.

"I haven't seen anything resembling a triangle here. Why is it called a Pyramid, Zeevax?" I scratched Loki's head and sat back.

"The Pyramid is named after its predecessor, the Great Pyramid of

Giza. The largest pyramid in Egypt was engineered to concentrate the Earth's electromagnetic energy field. The repulsive force would purge fourth-dimension Darachnids from anyone who spent two days in the red granite bath box," Zeevax said.

"How did they know about the fourth dimension?" I asked.

"Unknown—the hieroglyphics described the purpose of the ancient generator; there was no information on where the knowledge came from," Zeevax responded. "Are you prepared for test number 352?"

"Sure, what is it?"

"Please watch the console and describe what you think the image looks like. There is no wrong answer. Are you ready?"

"Yes," I replied.

The console, which I had mistakenly thought was a coffee table, showed dozens of patterns that reminded me of animals. I named what came to mind, and the image would change. Zeevax administered psychological, emotional, visual, and verbal tests. At one point, the AI instructed me to play a video game that examined my reflexes.

"How are my results so far, Zeevax?" I asked.

"Unremarkable."

*Good thing my ego isn't fragile,* I thought to myself. "I have a couple of questions I'd like to ask."

"You may ask," Zeevax said.

"I was told that the Darachnids in the other dimension move exceptionally slow. How can they move from one host to another so quickly?"

"They have claws that attach to a host. When vertebrates come close to each other, some of the parasites from the host with a higher infection rate will soften their claws. When this happens, an unknown magnetic force takes over, and the insects float directly toward the other host. They extend their claws, attach to the new host, and feed." Zeevax displayed a hologram.

I watched the movie demonstrate Zeevax's description. Two transparent human cartoon characters walked up to each other and shook hands. One was overcrowded with Darachnids. As the two stood next to each other, the image zoomed in on the Darachnids' feet so I could see what had happened. What resembled spikes changed into thin hairlike strands that loosened whatever invisible grip they had. Then, almost comically, the Darachnids floated through the space between the two individuals. They tumbled and wobbled as if an invisible current guided them. It reminded me of a video showing the birth of seahorses, flipping all around nonsensically.

"It looks like they are in fluid similar to water."

"Unknown," Zeevax responded.

"Is every creature on the planet infected?"

"Vertebrates all appear to be plagued by Darachnids," Zeevax said.

"Interesting. What will happen when the eggs hatch?" I asked.

"Displaying," Zeevax responded matter-of-factly.

The hologram switched to an impressive-sized planet Earth. It showed an epidemiology map similar to one I'd seen on television when the world was obsessed with the COVID pandemic. In this case, the hot spots were yellow and orange.

"Present day," Zeevax said.

"After the eggs hatch, how bad will it get?" I asked.

"Displaying three-month projection," Zeevax said.

"Whoa," I gasped. In three months, it looked like we were going to be in a doomsday scenario. All the yellow areas had turned red, and the orange areas went dark purple.

"It is predicted that there will be outbreaks of violence worldwide, and martial law will be invoked in the first-world countries, causing a chain reaction of fighting until the entire world is at war. Humanity will plummet into an apocalyptic wasteland within five years."

"I don't understand why it's so bad now. The parasites occupied our dimension before the pyramids were built, right?"

Loki took his fox, jumped onto one of the chairs, and curled up, looking at me with sleepy eyes.

"It is theorized that they have been feeding off creatures in the third dimension long before humans evolved. The postulation is that vertebrates with healthy Companions can mitigate the occupation of Darachnids," Zeevax said.

"I'm the only one with a healthy Companion?" I asked.

"You and or your Companion may not be palatable to the Darachnids. More data is required," Zeevax said.

Leave it to the Nekxus artificial intelligence to make me feel like my strength at keeping a life-threatening parasite at bay is simply because *I taste shitty*. I wasn't offended; I'd been called worse things than bug-repellant.

"Shall I commence testing?" Zeevax asked.

"Sure."

I leaned forward and listened carefully as Zeevax explained that the next test was for my Companion. Zeevax instructed me to relax and let my Companion guide me to predict which number a computer algorithm would show. I tried to focus my attention and started guessing numbers. I went slow initially then sped up to see if it made a difference. As I predicted the numbers faster, my accuracy increased.

"Very good," Zeevax said. "Now, you will use the same technique to predict colours."

Zeevax gave me a few more tests with animals, countries, people's names, and constellations. I failed the constellation test. I didn't even recognize half the words; I couldn't have guessed them. It felt like I was playing a game; I would have been having fun if things weren't so critical.

"The scheduled tests and examinations prepared for you are now complete and uploaded into the archive," Zeevax said.

"How much longer until Ramesh comes out of the Pyramid bath?"

"Twenty-two minutes," Zeevax replied.

"Is it possible for you to summarize a twenty-minute overview of information, highlighting the important facts about the fourth dimension and Companions and tell me about it before Ramesh returns?" I asked.

"Yes."

Zeevax gave me a thorough rendition of Companions, dark matter, Darachnids, and the theory that the universe was proliferating with lifeforms. Some of it was over my head. I asked Zeevax to simplify information when describing the different spatial oscillation frequencies overlapping and interacting. Zeevax changed tactics and displayed more diagrams and maps. I was fascinated with the breeding cycle synchronizing with Saturn's orbit. There were strange ancient Mayan codices that described abominable child sacrifice rituals connected to appeasing the Darachnids.

"How did they know about the fourth dimension?"

Translations of the forgotten ancient language were within Zeevax's database.

"The Companions told them. Your ancestors had a superior understanding of symbolic communication. In those times—Companions were not weakened or damaged by antibiotics, contaminated food, and poor nutrition. The food your ancestors ate was rich in vitamins and minerals. Now the soil on Earth is depleted from agricultural methods that strip away nutrients. Pest resistance, speeding up the growth process to produce a greater yield, genetically modified organisms increasing the size of vegetables, and contaminated fertilizer has resulted in humans eating food that is, at most, one-tenth as nutritious as their ancestors consumed," Zeevax explained.

"So the Mayans and their Companions decided sacrificing children would rid them of the affliction?" I snapped. "I thought children didn't even have Darachnids?"

"The Darachnids seem to avoid the young, and records show that the Mayans thought that sacrificing children before they were infected would appease their gods to protect the other children from becoming cursed with the parasite," Zeevax said.

The door to the Pyramid opened, and Loki shot off the chair he was nestled in and ran straight to Ramesh, tail wagging. Ramesh looked the same; I expected him to look refreshed. He entertained Loki by bending down to rub his belly. *At least he likes dogs*, I thought to myself.

"How did it go here with Zeevax?"

"Enlightening," I said.

I got up and stretched; my foot had fallen asleep from sitting on the couch cross-legged while conversing with Zeevax. "How do you feel?"

"Fine, it's just a bit boring in there," Ramesh said.

"You ready to go to the DMRM?" Ramesh said to Loki. "He can come in with me, and we will see if he needs to go into the Pyramid. Hopefully not—eh buddy?" He looked at me. "We should get going; someone will be waiting to use the Pyramid."

"Oh right, Loki, drop the fox. Let's go," I commanded.

He was trying to sneak out the door with the stuffy toy in his mouth. He obediently dropped it, and Ramesh picked it up and handed it back. "It's okay, that's yours. You can keep it."

Ramesh led the way to the exit. Two soldiers stood in the waiting area in full military uniforms. They looked past us and went down the hallway to the Pyramid. We got into the elevator, and I thought about asking Ramesh about the soldiers, but the door opened quickly. He stepped out to the DMRM, where a couple of staff wearing lab coats greeted us.

"Oh, you're a precious little thing! Is that your baby?" A young woman with bleached blonde hair cut so short I could see her scalp was on her knees petting Loki. He had dropped the fox at her feet in exchange for affection.

"Hi Ramesh, you taking him in with you?" she asked.

"Hey Jennifer, yes I am. Do you have the hood?" he asked.

"I've got it." A heavyset man with very little white hair strode over, carrying a black cotton bag.

"We thought you might go into the machine with us and hold Loki. He will have to wear the hood. Otherwise, Benjamin here is a veterinarian who will give him an injection. Loki would be unconscious, so he doesn't panic," Ramesh said.

"No need, I'll hold him." I tensed at the thought of Loki getting a needle. I didn't realize how difficult it might be for scientists to elicit cooperation from animals.

"Wonderful," Ramesh said.

Jennifer gave Ramesh and me a pair of goggles each, and Benjamin handed me the cotton hood to put over Loki's head. They said it was all right for him to hold the fox. The bag was large enough to fit overtop his whole body, so I wrapped him like a baby. The black cover was practical because Loki didn't seem to mind the scan or to be unable to see anything. When the door opened, I took it off him and put him down, and we exited the DMRM to see a crowd of scientists peering at the upper-level panel.

"Unbelievable," Benjamin said.

"Let's go see." Ramesh took the hood that I handed him. "After you."

"I thought it took some time for the results?" I asked.

"Normally, it does. Zeevax is slowed down by monitoring many projects. Samuel has reassigned some of those as a lesser priority, and Zeevax has been given more computation power right now to speed up results," Ramesh said.

"It's amazing." Jennifer stepped away from the crowd towards us. "Nothing." She clapped her hands. Smiling brightly, she patted me on the back as if I'd accomplished something great.

"Even the dog is clear," someone said in disbelief.

A couple of men had deadpan stares as they looked at the monitor. And others were rushing back to their stations to investigate the results.

"Come with me, Kim; I want you to meet the Zeevax squad." Ramesh smiled.

"The computer programmers you mentioned earlier?" I asked.

"That's right; you'll love the people there." He picked up Loki's doggy bag off a table where I'd placed it, put it over his shoulder, and guided me back to the elevator.

"Computer lab," Ramesh said, and the elevator started moving downward.

"Does the military have many soldiers that come here?" I asked. Making conversation made me feel less awkward being in a small space with a man I found attractive.

"Mostly commanding officers. Nekxus is very particular about who receives a bath in the Pyramid. There are only so many pyramids built, and it's a real struggle to determine how to rank who gets to benefit from them. Priority is to individuals in superior positions in the government, military, medicine, and science—for obvious reasons. Dark matter corrupts, and we don't want leaders in important positions motivated by psychopathic and sociopathic dispositions."

"That makes sense," I said.

The elevator stopped, but the door didn't open. I looked down at Loki, sitting with his fox at his feet, staring at the door. Ramesh was smiling at me, and I felt my face turn red when the elevator suddenly started to move forward. I jerked in surprise, and Ramesh laughed.

"It's disconcerting the first time, don't worry. If you'd lost your balance, I would have caught you." He winked.

"Oh, my God," I said, feeling my face warm and flushed. "That wasn't what I was expecting. For a second, I thought the elevator was stuck." I giggled.

The elevator stopped again, and as I waited for the elevator to either switch directions or the door to open, I stared at Ramesh and thought—*Are you single?* I figured it couldn't hurt to probe a little. He stared back at me without moving. I could see his pupils dilate as I looked into his deep brown eyes. The elevator descended again for a few floors, and finally, the door opened.

We stepped out at the end of a hallway. The lighting here was pleasant; it was softer than the rest of the areas I'd seen at Nekxus. Old-fashioned lamps lit up both sides of the hallway, reminding me of torches in a tomb. The walls had designs that were almost pagan— spirals and geometric shapes with knots and braids.

"This is pretty," I said, admiring the artwork.

"Yes, the squad had Zeevax design it. It was a wonderful and curious choice for the AI."

"I love it," I said.

"Thank you," Zeevax said out of nowhere.

I jumped, surprised to hear the AI's neutral voice. I looked at Ramesh, who smiled knowingly and opened the door at the end of the hallway. We entered a room teeming with personnel. There were rows of cubicles and people rushing around focused on their tasks. No one noticed our entrance. Behind the rows of booths, I could see a transparent wall that contained a vast field of computer hardware devices. The data centre was impressive.

A burly fellow that looked like a motorcycle gang member walked towards us. "Hey, sweetie." He was hefty, with long hair pulled back into a braid and a beard that would make most men envious. His arms were covered in tattoos, and he had a big hoop pierced through his septum. "What's your name?" He leaned down to rub Loki's chin.

"That's Loki," I said.

"Kim, I'd like you to meet Billy," Ramesh said.

"Hi, Billy; it's nice to meet you." I waited for him to finish acquainting himself with my dog.

"It's wonderful to meet you both. Zeevax tells us you and your canine are free from the freeloading little buggers from the dark world." Billy dragged his eyes from admiring Loki to look at me with pursed lips.

"Billy's the best cyberneticist in the world. He and the brilliant folks in this department run the database and are responsible for Zeevax's creation, maintenance, and machine learning," Ramesh said.

"I'm a fan. I spent three hours with Zeevax and felt very comfortable with our interaction. You must be proud."

"Right on, I'm glad you like Zeevax. Working with a super-intelligent computer can be daunting. We are working with Zeevax on wicked technology to give the AI an avatar." Billy stroked his beard thoughtfully.

"Really?" Ramesh asked.

"Yes, Zeevax is developing a personality, and we're creating a face with physical characteristics to reflect that," Billy said.

"Nice," I said.

I thought about one of the projects I worked on in school. Our teacher assigned each class member to make an analytical report on a 1980s television series. I reported on a show about a funny artificial intelligence called Max Headroom.

The room was gridded out in cubes, and we walked through it in a zigzag manner to a room on the far side that looked like a control centre. There were quite a few greetings and praises for Loki, who pranced proudly, and was used to being treated like royalty. Sometimes I thought he was acutely aware of his environment and enjoyed playing it like a show pony.

"This is the nerve centre for our system. Zeevax runs the show here, and we are working around the clock to ensure that systems function optimally for our super-intelligence. Zeevax, please show us Kim's evaluation," Billy said.

A holographic sphere suspended mid-air in the centre of the room. It was a pie chart but more complicated because it was three-dimensional, making it look like an oddly coloured beachball.

"Interesting," Ramesh said.

A tall, lanky kid pointed at the chart. "Whoa, her Companion scores are off the chart!"

"That's Ken; he's talking about the yellow area of your profile right here." Ramesh motioned to the area.

The yellow section was by far the dominating colour. It had layers of yellow, some lighter and others darker, compared to the other colours. I could see the explanation for the colours on a desk and was just about to read them when my phone buzzed. I realized it wasn't just my phone; everyone's phone started buzzing. I looked at it to see that the whole front screen had an alert. *Report to assigned supervisor – Code Zero*, it read.

"Shit—it's started," Billy muttered.

Ramesh and Billy looked at each other warily.

"We have to go now, Kim," Ramesh said with urgency. "It looks like the eggs are hatching."

## CHAPTER 13

*The Hatch*

WE SAID goodbye to Billy and walked back through the maze of cubicles; I was keenly aware of a change in the atmosphere. Bustling around turned to frantic voices and exaggerated body language indicating stress. Ramesh appeared troubled and ordered a shuttle so we could return to the main building.

"How bad is it?" I asked.

"We knew it was coming. Zeevax predicted the hatchlings would arrive anywhere from five weeks ago to next month sometime. I don't have any previous experience with an event like this one. It'll be the first hatch in my lifetime. From what we've learned from the past, in a couple of days, we will witness the first wave of aggressive behaviour." He swallowed and looked at me.

The shuttle hadn't arrived yet, so I took Loki to the green space again to relieve himself before the ride back to the main building. "Does Nekxus have a game plan?"

"There are a few strategies they've begun to employ. Nekxus is in the process of building six more pyramids and has purchased properties in fifteen countries so we can build more. That will enable more people to get treated with our dark matter purification therapy," he said.

Loki started to wag his tail as the shuttle pulled up.

"The trajectory is not good, though." Ramesh motioned for me to enter the shuttle ahead of him. "It will take years for the engineers to build the pyramids. The technology is so advanced that the materials needed for sophisticated equipment are rare. Nekxus has been cooperating with a few government agencies to expropriate land to mine the rare substances necessary for the machine."

"From what Zeevax showed me, it's going to be a shitshow, isn't it?"

"That's correct." He frowned.

We rode the shuttle in silence back to the main building, which I discovered from looking at the Nekxus app, was called Commune A. Cars were piling into the parking lot, and there was a line at the metal detectors inside the main entrance. I assumed people were being called into Nekxus now that the notification went out and alerted staff of the situation. I picked Loki up because I didn't want anyone accidentally stepping on his paws in the increasingly crowded lobby.

"Did everyone get the alert?" I asked Ramesh quietly while we stood in line.

"Just level 3 and up; service staff don't have the same clearance for classified projects," he said.

We passed through the detectors and made our way to the familiar boardroom. Upon entering, we found it was already full of people. I counted more than a dozen others accompanied by Ana, Samuel, Beth, Chung, and Fischer. The monitor had a list of names, but there were so many that it only displayed whoever was speaking at the time. Ramesh put his hand on my back and motioned me to stand beside Ana in an open area. I felt uncomfortably out of place.

"Zeevax has confirmed through multiple tests that hosts whose infections are level red have eggs that are starting to hatch in all locations except Antarctica." Samuel was speaking from the head of the conference table to the group. "China recorded the first larvae, and they've begun to feed across the globe primarily from the densest populations."

A room full of the world's brightest minds was discussing our dire situation while Loki struggled against my hold on him because he was desperately trying to lick Ana. She took him out of my arms and cooed softly in his ear; I was grateful when he calmed down.

"Suggestions?" Samuel asked.

"I recommend we focus on the Bishop Project," a man with white hair, large circular glasses, and a thick accent spoke. I saw a flag on the screen's top right corner with *Bolivia* underneath it. I heard a few scoffs and groans in the room before another face appeared on the monitor.

This time I noticed the flag and country belonged to Peru. The top left side of the screen showed a name, Alfredo Diaz. "We don't need another disaster on our hands. That project should have been scrapped back in the 1940s after the Philadelphia catastrophe. The number of casualties Zeevax has predicted from amplifying a trans-dimensional field to encompass more than one life form at a time is unacceptable," Alfredo said.

Several voices commented in agreement.

A woman named Maria from Namibia spoke up. "We've theorized that we could use micro black holes to create controlled gravitational waves strong enough to stun the creatures, which could buy us more time."

"Black holes, even microscopic ones, are unpredictable," Oliver said in his cut-glass accent—I recognized him from the previous day. "What about Kim Hart and her dog? Zeevax has reported some promising conclusions from the examinations."

I felt self-conscious as all eyes turned to Loki and me. He was still relaxing in Ana's arms. Ana handed Loki back to me, pulled her phone out, and tapped on it before replying.

"Kim's friend Jacob is on his way," Ana said to the attendees. "Security at the front gate will escort him through the scanners. I'll meet with him in about twenty minutes."

"What about her sister and father?" Oliver asked.

"Dr. Jones is on her way to the Doon Care Centre to collect Doug Hart. We'll reach out to Kim's sister after our experts investigate the geographic possibilities," Samuel replied.

Another delegate took Oliver's place on the monitor and reported that they'd notified the military and that border security was tightening in all European countries. They were going to treat it like a plague and started to debate releasing another virus to keep civilians in their homes. I listened to government officials who opposed additional outbreak protocols due to economic collapse. They eventually conceded that the systems in place were doomed to fail against the effects of the Darachnid infestation either way.

"Why can't we tell people the truth?" I whispered to Ana.

"If history has taught us anything, widespread panic is the defaulting human condition. In Egypt, a breeding cycle hit and infested the civilization. Insurrections by the masses overcame the pharaoh and his court through jealousy of the Pyramid bath. You see, only royalty received treatment in the Pyramid at that time. You can imagine how that turned out," she said quietly.

"Zeevax has played the outcome of full disclosure to the populace a thousand different ways and comes to the same conclusion every time. Calamity is the result. People will turn their backs on authorities and flee their homes, looting and pillaging. Casualties through stampedes, traffic accidents, and violence of all kinds," Ramesh said in a hushed tone.

"Isn't that going to happen anyway?" I asked.

"Not as quick, and every minute counts. We will save some people," Ana whispered.

"We could move to human trials with the drug polyoxynylophil," a man named Geoff from the United States offered.

"The opioid epidemic has already demonstrated how devastatingly ineffective narcotics are at solving any problem," Ramesh said.

"I disagree; the increase in production of the endorphins could keep people from being overcome by the amount the Darachnids consume from people," Geoff argued. "Not only that, but the new pharmaceutical has concentrated synthetic hormones that are time-released so it can mitigate the overall drain from the insect."

"Have you taken a look at the drug crisis at all? If anything, it provides a fertile environment for the Darachnids to feed. It is a perfect breeding ground where infestations have been rampant because individuals gather close to each other in encampments. On top of that, the people on drugs are victims of two plagues instead of one. The addiction accompanying the feel-good stimulants puts vulnerable people in high-risk crime-ridden environments. I won't entertain any suggestions that include pushing more drugs," Samuel declared.

"Polluting people more than they already are is not a solution," Navjot weighed in.

"We must find a way to heal our Companions," Ana said. "There is a correlation between Kim's healthy Companion and her absence of Darachnid swarm."

"Correlation may imply causation, but we must prove it and replicate the results. How long will that take?" Geoff countered. "We have something tangible in the meantime and should use *all* tools at our disposal. Time has run out." His voice was borderline manic.

"Electro-acupuncture has had fractional positive effects on healing Companions," Mei's soft voice captured the room. "Our research here in Hong Kong has indicated that if we administer the therapy to children just before the age of maturity with a robust series of treatments, their Companions are healthier. On average, they seem to host smaller numbers of Darachnids."

"We created a synthesized version of the rare mineral we found to construct the Pyramid field. It repels pollution from dark matter. If we could discover the missing element from the rare meteorite, we might be able to build a mutated protein to put in a vaccine to repel the Darachnids. We've had minimal success, but without a sample of the exotic matter, it is short-lived," Diego said.

"Come with me, Kim; Jacob's arriving," Ana said.

We weaved our way through the crowd of debaters to the exit. I looked over my shoulder and made eye contact with Ramesh. He nodded once at me before turning his attention back to Samuel.

I was relieved to leave and see Jacob. That conference room may have had the best ventilation money could buy, but you could have cut the tension in the air with a knife. I felt myself expand like I could breathe better after we were away from the world's decision makers. The fate of all humankind rested on their shoulders, and I didn't envy them.

"Did you tell Andrei about the hatching?" I asked Ana.

"Not yet; we'll talk tonight. We knew it would be any day now." She sighed.

We stepped onto the giant escalator, and from our vantage point, we could see Jacob walking through the metal detector among a crowd of people lined up to get in. It looked like he was getting odd glances for being bumped to the front of the line by the guard escorting him. He grabbed his phone off the conveyer belt and looked around. *Jacob, look up here!*—I directed my thoughts toward him. At that moment, he looked up, his face lit with a huge smile. He waved at us, unaware of the frightful news everyone had just received. Onlookers gaped at his cheerful entrance.

"He has no idea," I said to Ana as we rode the elevator down to meet him.

At the bottom of the escalator, Loki caught sight of Jacob gliding toward us through the crowd and started whimpering. I put him down but held the leash tight. Jacob shamelessly got down on his knees and let Loki lick his face while he rubbed the belly of the pup, who'd flipped on his back. I couldn't help but smile at the two of them. They attracted the attention of people passing by; it was ridiculous, but I could see a few half-hearted smiles.

"Hi, ladies. Did you see the first-class treatment they gave me?" Jacob wiggled his eyebrows.

"Hi, Jacob," Ana said.

"Yeah, I saw it." I handed the leash to Jacob because Loki had decided Jacob would carry him up the escalator.

"I didn't realize this place was so busy." He gawked around.

I looked at Ana for a moment, and she nodded her head to me. "I don't think it is quite this busy every day. A hatch has begun." I leaned close to him conspiratorially.

"Oh no." He paled and hugged Loki a little closer. "Now what?"

"Now we get you into the DMRM and go from there. Thank you so much for coming, Jacob," Ana said.

"Don't mention it. I didn't want you to send security to drag me in kicking and screaming," he jested.

Ana tilted her head sideways and looked into the distance as if visualizing the scene. Then she motioned for us to follow her. Jacob looked at me with his eyes bulging from her response to his light-hearted sarcasm and blanched completely. He soon forgot about the potential threat to his freedom, though, as he oohed and awed at the splendid architecture and, finally, the DMRM.

"This is fantastic," he said and put Loki down.

This area was busier than before the alert went out. Ana took me aside, and we waited on a couple of chairs out of the way. A small group of Nekxus staff gathered around Jacob and gave him instructions and reassurances about his safety from dangerous radiation. He was so eager to cooperate that he put the goggles on before anyone had the chance to walk him in the machine.

"What if he has Darachnids?" I asked Ana.

"We are collecting as much data as possible; if he has an orange to red infection level, we learn something. We aren't certain if genetic, environmental, geographical, or unconsidered factors cause your resilience to Darachnids. If his outcome is like yours and Loki's, we widen our investigation to consider additional explanations."

"Red and orange?" I wondered.

"Nekxus has labelled infection levels according to how badly the swarm of Darachnids are infesting the individual. Red is the worst, with over eight thousand Darachnids."

"Eight thousand," I repeated and let out a long sigh. I didn't realize how many were there when Zeevax showed me the video. "How many are female?"

"Approximately sixty to seventy percent are female. The males mate with several females and die a couple of years afterwards—just after the eggs hatch. Four to six nymphs usually hatch, but we've seen up to ten in some cases," Ana said.

"So the current numbers are going through the roof," I said grimly.

"Yeah, scary, isn't it?" Ana strained her neck, looking at the scientists hovering around the control panel. She stood up when Jacob came out of the DMRM and handed the goggles to the young woman I recognized as Jennifer. The group reading the results were excited, scratching at their heads and remarking on how unbelievable his scan results were. Ana moved to join them, and the crowd moved aside to create an opening for her. She moved to the front and inspected it for herself. Loki and I walked toward Jacob.

"That was awesome, Kim." He turned his head back to admire the machinery. "I can't believe how fast it was."

"I know, right?" I jutted my chin toward the people, captivated by whatever they were looking at on the panel. "I think it's safe to say that your results may mean you aren't swarmed."

"Good, I don't want the little shits all over me anyway," he said low enough that only I could hear him.

Ana made her way back through the gathering of Nekxus employees to collect us. She was smiling a little. "Come on, let's get you to the CS so we can get a good look at your Companion—yours too, little fellow." She pulled a treat out of her pocket and tossed it to Loki, who obligingly grabbed it out of the air.

I laughed. "You're always equipped."

"Yes, there is more where that came from; I figured if Loki found the atmosphere upsetting, it would be good to have something to bribe him with," she said.

"I brought treats, too." I motioned to my doggy bag.

"Mhmm, but did you bring freeze-dried liver?" She gave me a sidelong glance.

We made our way to the exit, and Ana drove the four of us passed the Medicorium to another one with the strange architecture where she usually worked. I used my app to identify the name of the building as Aurora.

"Wow, look at that, Kim," Jacob exclaimed.

"I know it's amazing, right?"

"You got that right. Damn Ana, you work here?" he asked.

"Yes, every day. I forget how impressive it is the first time you see it," she said.

We waited for Loki to sniff around and potty. I picked it up with a poop bag and dumped it in the nearby receptacle.

"Even the garbage cans are fancy," Jacob said.

The garbage can resembled a robot—it wouldn't have shocked me if it got up and walked off after I dropped the bag in it.

Once we arrived at the CS lab, Ana explained the procedure to Jacob. He changed into the white jumpsuit and entered the glass cube. It was just as strange to watch the process from the outside as it was to partake in it. The metal claw came down, clamped overtop of the cube Jacob stood in, and we waited five minutes for the scan to complete.

I took the opportunity to ask Ana to explain the other colours describing the rate of infection. She told me that orange indicated between approximately five to eight thousand Darachnids, yellow was three to five thousand, green was one to three thousand, and blue was zero to one thousand. Blue was the code generally used for youth who hadn't reached sexual maturity or an individual who had just received treatment in the Pyramid.

"So, I'm blue." I looked down at Loki. "We're blue." He looked up, wagged his tail, then rolled onto his back for a belly rub.

"Actually, no, you're purple," Ana corrected.

"Purple?"

"That's right, Zeevax has created a special designation for an individual with no dark matter pollution *and* a healthy Companion. Children don't necessarily have healthy Companions. Like I said before, the Darachnids, for the most part, don't feed on children. We suspect the exotic matter the Darachnids feed on isn't created until an individual reaches maturity. Our lifestyles and toxic environment have weakened our Companions," Ana explained.

The clamp started to lift, and we could see Jacob standing still as per the instructions; then, the cube opened.

"You may exit," Zeevax's voice came out of nowhere.

Jacob waved to us and went to the changing room to put his street clothes back on.

"I keep forgetting Zeevax is here." I looked around for where the speaker was.

"Zeevax is always with us, right Zeevax?" she asked the air.

"Affirmative," the AI replied.

Together, we looked at Jacob's results. His Companion was different. It glowed yellow and hazy blue but with none of the sparkling or swirling mine had. Ana seemed slightly disappointed but still immersed herself in many possibilities she discussed with the other scientists working with her.

"Not like yours, is it?" Jacob asked.

"No, I still think yours is better than most. I saw the average Companion, and they were dull and reddish," I told him.

"Your Companion is in exceptional shape, Jacob," Ana reassured. "We think, however, that you have damage from Darachnids. Your condition might help us find the key to ridding ourselves of the pestilence. If you were infected—but not treated—that is fantastic news. We hope to learn how this occurred and replicate this phenomenon."

Ana's phone must have vibrated because she pulled it out of her pocket and stared at it with a puzzled look.

"What's the matter?" I asked.

"I'm not sure if anything is the matter. Dr. Jones was supposed to meet us here with your father, but she sent a message for us to meet her in an office on Aurora's main floor."

"I bet they want me to calm him down. I can imagine he is giving the doctor a hard time. His symptoms from Alzheimer's have become debilitating at times. He is having more frequent mood swings, delusions, and significant issues with his short-term memory," I said sadly. "We better go help her out; I doubt he remembers where he is and is probably upset."

"We'll have to postpone your examination, Loki." Ana scratched his neck.

We left the CS to take the elevator to an upper floor, where the doctor waited for us. Ana opened the door; I entered the room expecting to find my father throwing a fit or refusing to cooperate. Instead, two men dressed in full military uniforms were standing at attention beside a tiny woman with white hair who couldn't have been more than five feet tall.

"Hello, Kim. I'm Dr. Opal Jones." She walked toward me and held out her hand. I shook it and looked at the army guys standing silently, wondering how bad of an outburst my dad had. I suspected they had to sedate him because he wasn't there.

"Please have a seat." Dr. Jones motioned to the sofa.

Loki jumped up, and I sat, waiting for the doctor to explain. Ana stood by the door, probably impatient to return to her lab.

"I regret to inform you that your father took his own life this afternoon," she said regretfully.

"What did you just say?" I demanded.

"We went to the Doon Care Centre to pick Doug up and bring him here to Nekxus. When we entered his room, we found he was already dead. I'm very sorry for your loss," she said gently.

I sat there stunned for a moment. Jacob reached to put his arm around me, but I tensed and stood up.

"That can't be right; I just saw him." I felt dizzy. They must have gone to the wrong room, I rationalized. "Are you sure you got the right room? Maybe it was another senior. I don't believe it. Please, you need to check again," I pleaded. I looked frantically back and forth from the doctor to the soldiers. They all wore the same sad expression. My legs felt weak, and my knees gave out as I dropped back down on the couch and started to cry.

# CHAPTER 14
## Imperial Jade

**THE UNEXPECTED NEWS** of my father's death was physically painful. My head was pounding like a drum, my eyes were sore from crying, and I felt like someone had kicked me in the stomach. After a few minutes of sobbing and gasping for air, I blew my nose with tissue from the box on the table, took a sip from the bottle of water Ana handed me, and settled down.

"You're going to be okay, Kim," Jacob consoled me as he held my hand.

"I don't understand. What happened? How did he die?" I questioned Dr. Jones.

"I can only imagine how hard this is for you. Your father took his life by a method called a drop hanging. He tied his sheets to the toilet on the other side of the bathroom door and used a chair and his belt." She paused before continuing. "I hope it's a small consolation to you to know that he didn't suffer. His neck broke immediately, and death would have occurred instantly."

"Where is he?" My voice squeaked because I was trying not to sob again.

"We transferred his body to the Nekxus mortuary for the time being."

*His body...* The words solidified the image of my father's death in my mind. Ana's phone chimed; she sat beside me and gave me a sympathetic look.

"Kim, please listen to me. I know you've been through a lot, but I need to ask you something because Zeevax can't find anything in the system. Do you know what your father's wishes were? Did he have a legal will made up?" She shifted on the couch, visibly uncomfortable asking the question.

I looked up at the soldiers who were still standing silently at attention. "No, he didn't have a will. He talked about cremation and having his ashes spread in Lake Ontario," I answered, doubting it was legal but not caring.

Ana nodded thoughtfully before making her request. "We can still learn something from your father, but every second counts. Would you be willing to permit us to continue with the scheduled tests for your dad?"

I was stunned by her question. I'd completely lost track of myself from the tragic news and forgot that we were amidst a war trying to save humanity. Whether or not it was appropriate, I knew my dad well enough to know what he would have wanted. He was a patriot.

"Do it." I stood up and looked around the room for a moment. "Where's the washroom? I need to clean myself up and call my sister."

"This way." Dr. Jones directed me around the corner.

Once in the washroom, I vomited in the toilet, washed my face, and stared at my reflection in the mirror. *Are you in there?* I asked my Companion. My lips pursed immediately. I thought about my dad and how often he left us for some third-world country in the middle of armed conflict. He didn't know if he would ever come home and see my mother, sister, and me again. His bravery was legendary in my mind...and he *killed* himself. That bloody Alzheimer's, or maybe those inter-dimensional bugs—I needed an enemy to focus my rage.

"Are you okay? Can I come in?" Jacob asked from the other side of the washroom door.

"Come in." I was sure he was about to anyway.

The door swung open, and Jacob had tears in his eyes. He was such an empath; I was lucky to have him as a best friend.

"Ana and the doctor left to examine your dad. Are you sure you're all right with them doing that?"

"Yeah, I know he'd volunteer if he could. The only reason this happened is that stupid disease, or maybe he's infested with those life-sucking parasites," I snapped.

Jacob hugged me, and this time I controlled my tears. I had a duty to perform, and I needed to focus on that.

"Where's Loki?" I asked.

"Oh, he's with the soldiers. They are both still standing in the other room like statues. I asked them to watch Loki. I figured they might as well make themselves useful." He shrugged.

"I've got to get a hold of Julia."

We left the washroom to find Loki sitting on the couch with his fox, wagging his tail and looking at us. I looked at the two military men wondering why they were still there. "Do you guys need anything from me?"

"No, ma'am, we are here on behalf of Doug. Before he ended his life, he called a classified phone number requesting a favour," said the shorter soldier with the more decorated uniform.

"He wanted to ensure you and your sister received this letter." The taller soldier with a deep baritone voice reached into his pocket and handed me an envelope.

I took it and flipped it over. *To my precious daughters*, it read on the back flap.

"When did he give this to you?"

"He didn't. Chris and I showed up at the same time as Dr. Jones—the letter was on the bed. We've known your father for a long time; he recruited both of us into the service fifteen years ago. My name is Richard; we are here to help. If there's something you need, we'll get it done," Richard said.

"Thanks," I sniffed. I put it on the table for the time being. I needed to control my emotions.

"Ma'am, there's something else. When your father called the classified phone number, he mentioned something important to the captain on the line," Chris said.

"Your father said he had the quantum sample," Richard said.

"What does that mean?" I asked.

"We aren't exactly sure. We talked with one of the nurses working the days before Doug's death. He told us that last night Doug was furious that someone stole his rock; he was frantic and tore his room apart, looking for it," Richard said.

"Jesus Christ, he thought someone stole it?" I exclaimed, rubbing my head.

"Have you seen the meteor sample?" Chris asked.

"It's a rare piece of jadeite with fragments of an element not of this world. Your father and I received orders to retrieve it from a hostile territory overseas years ago, but the enemy captured us briefly. A search and rescue operation retrieved your father and me, but no one found the stone," Richard said.

"He gave me a strange green rock and told me to use the *meteor* to save myself. Please tell me he didn't kill himself because he couldn't remember giving me that fucking rock," I said.

"Kim, your dad was sick. Don't overthink it," Jacob interjected.

"Your friend is right; we believe his illness-related suffering is the reason for his premature death. He made a conscious decision to end his life before the disease could take over completely," Chris said.

"Doug was always very proud of you and your sister; he wouldn't have wanted you to see him as vulnerable," Richard said.

I couldn't speak. I just wanted my dad—even if it meant I had to remind him now and again who I was. After losing our mother, he was never quite the same, but the only thing that mattered was that he loved my sister and me. I sat on the couch and stared at my phone for a minute.

"I need to call my sister." I looked at Jacob for strength.

I tapped her name from my favourite contacts and took a deep breath. She answered right away. It sounded like she was on the beach. I told her I'd just discovered our father had ended his life. Julia didn't ask questions; she was silent on the other end of the line. Then she said Jeffery would book the next possible flight, and they'd be in touch as soon as they landed in Toronto. I put my phone down and opened the letter.

. . .

*Jules and Kimmy,*

*Know that your mother and I will always be with you. Nothing in this world has filled me with as much pride as being your father. You must do what is necessary to stop the total annihilation of life on this planet. My only regret is that your mother didn't get to see what strong, beautiful women you both turned out to be. Trust my men. They will lead you to the company.*

*Love, Dad*

It wasn't the ravings of a madman, but it didn't make much sense to me, either. I reread it, shook my head, and put it back in the envelope. Chris and Richard were still standing like a couple of toy soldiers waiting for me to do or say something. I scratched Loki's ears and looked into Jacob's sad eyes before returning my attention to my dad's army buddies.

"You want me to give you the rock, right?" I asked.

They both looked at each other for a moment, then Chris answered. "It belongs to the company. They will know what to do with it."

"Priya and Veronica are on their way," Zeevax announced.

Jacob twitched when Zeevax spoke out of the blue. I, on the other hand, was getting used to it. Chris and Richard gave me their contact info and assured me they would collect my father's belongings and start preparations for a funeral. Richard insisted that Nekxus was taking care of the arrangements.

"I'm going to stay with you," Jacob insisted.

"I was hoping you'd say that."

Ana re-entered the room, followed by two young women. "Kim, I'd like to introduce you to Veronica and Priya. They are the science officers assigned to study your household and personal habits. If you feel you can't cope right now, they'll wait until after the funeral."

"We are so sorry for your loss," Priya said.

"Truly," Veronica agreed.

"Thanks."

"It's up to you, Kim. The girls will stay with you for a couple of days and set up some equipment to collect data for our experts to analyze. Otherwise, we wait until you feel you can handle it." Ana had a tight-lipped expression, and I could see she was uncomfortable making the request.

"It's fine; I welcome the distraction. What will I tell Julia? They are flying in tomorrow or early the next day and will come straight to my house."

"Zeevax has expedited tickets for Jeffery, and he's purchased them already. They'll land tomorrow morning at ten," Ana said.

*My God, they move fast here.* My head was spinning; I looked down at Loki for stability then at Jacob. If they weren't here, I wouldn't be holding it together.

"Chris and I will meet your sister at the airport," Richard said.

Richard's statement surprised me, and I looked at Ana to see her reaction.

"They'll escort Julia, Jeffery, and your niece to your house. Nekxus will conclude the tests and autopsy on your father's body by the afternoon. When you and your sister are ready, you'll have an escort to Nekxus. Samuel, Ramesh, and I will explain the situation to Julia and her husband," Ana said.

"What's with the escorts?"

"I don't want you to be scared, but you should prepare yourself. We can't predict what the dangers that lie ahead are. Only that there are many of them," Ana said.

The door opened, and Benjamin the veterinarian poked his head into the increasingly crowded room. He looked at Ana, who put her index finger up in the air, signalling him to wait a moment.

"Kim, Benjamin wants to take Loki into the CS before you leave. I know it's unpleasant to think about sedating him, but I promise to be there the whole time. He'll receive a minimal dose and be running around within half an hour, then you can take him home." Ana searched my face for a response.

I bowed my head, resolved that I was in this war whether I liked it or not. I trusted Ana and silently handed her his leash.

"Thank you. We will be back soon." Ana fed Loki a piece of liver, and he followed her happily. *Poor Loki, he's not going to be so perky when Benjamin sticks him with a needle.*

Veronica and Priya excused themselves to gather the equipment they would bring to my house for their investigation. Chris and Richard said they'd wait for Jacob and me at the main entrance then escort us home.

"Why do we need escorts already?" Jacob asked once we were alone.

"Good question. Zeevax, why do Jacob and I need escorts right now?" I looked sideways at Jacob, and he rolled his eyes.

"Your safety has been assigned top priority. The Cosmic Saviours have gathered at the main entrance and are unwilling to move," Zeevax replied.

"That damn cult." Jacob spat the words with distaste.

"I'm going to call Matt, okay, Kim? I want to let him know that there has been a tragedy, and I won't be available to see him for a few days. I'll call work and let them know I need some time off," Jacob said.

While Jacob made his phone calls, I read Dad's letter again. It filled me with sadness, and I put it back in the envelope, vowing never to open it again.

"It's done. I'll go home, grab a few things, and stay in your art room across the hall from you. I can sleep on the day bed that's in there. If you don't mind me suggesting, you should put the Nekxus girls in the basement. That old pullout couch is comfy enough, I've slept on it many times, plus there's that little bathroom down there. They'll have to come upstairs if they want to shower, though." He paced the room, thinking out loud.

"That works, Julia and Jeff can have the guest room, and Sherry can sleep with me."

After a short while, Ana returned with Loki, who was still unconscious and snoring softly in her arms.

"And?" I inquired.

"His Companion is extremely healthy. Like you, I suspect he's avoided infection from the Darachnids," Ana said.

"Good," Jacob piped.

"I'm taking you back to Commune A, and I want you to drive straight home," Ana said.

"I'm going to get some personal things; I will stay with Kim for a few days," Jacob told her.

"Good idea," Ana said.

While Ana drove us back to the main building, I sat in the front with Loki on my lap. Before she pulled into the drop-off area, he woke up. He was a little dizzy but didn't seem the worse for wear. Chris and Richard were both standing on the curb, waiting for us.

"Richard is going to follow you home for your safety." Ana gave Loki a little pat on the head. "Please give him the imperial jade sample; he'll bring it back for inspection. Diego has already boarded a Nekxus jet and is on his way here to see it," Ana said.

"Okay," I said.

"Veronica and Priya should arrive at your house in approximately an hour, and I will pop my head in tonight to see if you need anything." Ana exhaled and looked at her phone. "I think that's everything; for now, any questions?"

"Imperial jade? I thought the meteor sample was called jadeite," Jacob asked.

"Different name, same stone. We haven't seen it. We hope it's the meteorite that Doug was supposed to retrieve years ago," Ana said.

Ana looked carefully at me, and I shrugged. For the moment, I had no questions. I wanted to go home and shower before the science officers showed up at my house.

"I'm so sorry for your loss." Ana hugged me and placed her hands on my cheeks, looking deep into my eyes. I don't know what she was looking for, but her expression changed, and she nodded with a determined look and left us to go back to work. Richard walked me to my car and got into a black sedan after instructing me to follow him.

I felt shocked driving to the exit. Police cruisers with their lights flashing and at least one hundred protesters crowded the area. I could see the cops set up barricades to keep the mob from traffic. Loki was in the back, lying sleepily with his fox, coming off the sedatives. I drove behind Richard and tried to ignore the hateful crowd.

They were more threatening this time, and I could hear them chanting, "Die Nekxus demons, die!" Fighting broke out between a group of men and the police, and some other combative demonstrators pushed on one of the police cruisers, trying to bounce it enough to flip over. This mob was getting out of control, but I could see military vehicles pulling into the complex. *Good*, I thought, because it was evident that the local police lost control of the situation.

The drive home was rough too. I witnessed two car accidents and almost got into one myself. People drove like maniacs, cutting each other off without signalling and screaming out their windows. I'd never seen anything like it and lost count of how often I heard a car horn or the screeching of tires. *Brace yourself—this is just the beginning*, I thought. *The uncivilized behaviour is about to get ferocious.*

When I pulled into my driveway, Loki seemed fully recovered, wagging his tail and happy to be home. I walked him around the side and opened the gate to let him off the leash so he could run around in the backyard. Richard had pulled to the side of the street in front of my house, got out, and talked to a man sitting in his car parked on the other side of the road. I unlocked the front door and left it open for Richard, who shook the other man's hand and made his way up to my porch carrying a metal briefcase.

"Tom will stay outside and watch over the two houses." Richard jutted his chin toward Ana's house to indicate hers too.

"He will be replaced in eight hours by another corporal. They'll rotate surveillance on the properties; someone will always be out front. If you need anything, dial 911. Zeevax has your phone programmed to alert our security team—they will come instantly," he assured.

"Thank you."

Richard waited in the foyer for me to get the stone for him. I grabbed it from the china cabinet where I had placed it in one of the drawers. I usually put things there I wanted to keep but hadn't decided where I wanted them to go yet. It was even heavier than I remembered; I held it up to the light to inspect the strange black webbed pattern deeply embedded inside, then brought it to Richard.

"It's freezing and heavier than it looks," I said, trying to hand it to him.

He opened the metal briefcase and held it towards me to put the rock inside without touching it. The interior had a soft black egg carton-shaped foam material. I placed the stone in the centre; Richard didn't seem interested in looking at it. He shut the case and locked it immediately, which made me wonder if the damn thing was radioactive and could cause Alzheimer's. My mind wandered, and thoughts of my dad carrying around a dangerously contaminated meteor rock only pissed me off.

"Thank you, Kim. I'll see you again soon." Richard left.

Loki was scratching the patio glass door, so I let him in and headed straight for my shower. I stood under the faucet with hot water running directly into my face. I washed with my favourite vanilla soap, breathing in the scent to clear my head. I found some casual and comfortable clothes to put on and checked my phone for messages.

Julia had sent a text saying they'd bought tickets and expected to arrive in the morning. Of course, I already knew that. I replied, *See you soon*. I didn't tell her about the soldiers meeting her at the airport. The truth was going to hit her soon enough. Let her thoughts be with our dad for the next few hours so she could grieve a little first.

"Hello?" Jacob's voice bellowed.

"I'm up here; I'll be there in a minute," I hollered back.

Back in front of the mirror, I inspected my appearance. I put my hair in a French braid and headed downstairs to see Jacob. He was in the kitchen with a bag of food, putting things away.

"I brought some stuff from home. I'm going to cook dinner for you. How do you feel about stir-fry?"

I sighed. "Anything will do, Jacob. I'm just so grateful that you are here. I don't know how much I'll eat, though."

"Once you smell my cooking, you may change your mind. My drive home was shit, by the way. Navigating through the mass of nutbags at the Nekxus entrance was bad; I saw cops dragging one guy off in cuffs after he pulled a knife on them. Then, some idiot cut me off then screamed out his window, telling *me* to watch where *I* was going. Not long after that, Chris almost ran over a bicycle. A woman lost her mind at the intersection for no apparent reason. She got off her bike and threw it in front of the oncoming traffic." Jacob shook his head.

"I wonder if the hatched larvae have something to do with it," I said.

"I don't know, but I sure hope that magic rock works. I don't want to drive anywhere right now. It's fucking bonkers out there."

Loki started to bark. I joined Jacob at the kitchen window.

"The science girls are here," Jacob said.

# CHAPTER 15
## *Funeral*

A DARK BLUE van pulled into the driveway.

"Where's your car?" I looked past Jacob, not seeing it anywhere.

"Oh, I had Chris drop me off. The driveway will get too crowded with your sister coming and the Nekxus staff here."

I put a pot of coffee on while he went outside to help Priya and Veronica. They unloaded and carried the equipment into the house. Most of what they brought with them was in large plastic suitcases. A couple machines on wheels resembled carpet cleaners. They used a dolly to bring in a yellow cylindrical horizontal tank about four feet tall with three little dishes that looked like mini satellites.

"Loki! Let them get set up." The little menace was torn between sniffing the instruments and getting affection from the new guests.

"Oh, he's such a little darling. I love that you didn't crop his ears or dock his tail." Priya giggled at Loki's kisses.

"Good luck; he's probably going to pester you. Let me know if any of this stuff is sensitive, so I know what to keep him away from." I gestured at the packed foyer.

"Don't worry, most of it will be in the basement where Jacob said we could set up. Thank you so much for accommodating us during this delicate time." Veronica said while taking off her shoes. "We'll do our best to be invisible."

"I'm brewing coffee. Cups are here, sugar there, and cream is in the fridge." I pointed at the cupboard and counter. "Please help yourself."

"Thanks, Kim," Priya said.

Jacob helped them move most of the sizeable equipment, except the yellow tank, into the basement. They moved my cocktail table to the side and positioned the yellow tank in the centre of the living room. Veronica told me it could detect ripples from gravitational waves if something moved nearby from the fourth dimension. She indicated that it would be a long shot for the machine to sense anything and assured me I needn't be concerned because the lasers inside the unit were not radioactive.

"Well, that's ugly." Jacob sat beside me on the couch, and we both stared at the unsightly apparatus.

"It hums."

"Mhmm, I hear it," he said.

Loki sat between my feet, looking at the gadget with his ears lifted and head tilting to the left.

"It's only temporary, Loki." I rubbed his chin.

Veronica planted sensors in the ground outside my house while Priya placed small grey cylinders in the bedrooms, bathrooms, and kitchen. Jacob and I sat on the couch with my laptop, emailing a few of my dad's friends, notifying them of his passing. I called my aunt Laurie and told her on the phone. As she was my father's only sister, I wanted to ensure I spoke to her personally.

After about two hours, Priya came up from the basement and poked her head into the living room. "We're all set up down here. Would you like to see it?"

Loki ran past her feet into the basement, taking advantage of the open door, and Jacob stood without saying anything and moved to follow.

"Sure," I said, closing my laptop.

"I don't know whether to be amazed or creeped out." Jacob stood with his hands on his hips.

Half of my basement had been turned into a recording studio—at least, it looked like one. Eight monitors displayed images around my house in infrared. The main screen seemed to graph and record a particular frequency with a timer. It put the state-of-the-art equipment I'd seen before to shame.

"I'm not even going to ask. I'll be upstairs if you need me." I turned and went back upstairs.

The doorbell went off before I made it to the landing, and Loki flew past my feet, barking on his way to the front door. I opened it to find Chris standing on the step with a container.

"I wanted to drop off Doug's belongings before your sister arrives tomorrow. Here's everything from the Doon Care Centre." Chris handed me a plastic tote, saluted, and returned to his car.

"That's all?" Jacob said.

"He was a minimalist," I replied. "It's common for soldiers."

"I'll leave you to it. I'm going to start dinner." He touched my nose lightly and went to the kitchen.

I opened the container, took each item out one at a time and placed it gingerly on the couch. There wasn't much: a few items of clothing, a wallet, shaving supplies, military dog tags, and a framed picture of my mother, Julia, and me at the beach. I placed the items carefully back in the container and put them aside for Julia, returning my attention to the emails.

Jacob called out when dinner was ready. The stir-fry was terrific. He made enough to take a couple of plates to the basement, and I could hear the girls expressing gratitude for being saved from ordering greasy pizza. After doing the dishes, we settled on the couch with the radio playing in the background, and Jacob listened to me reminisce about memories of my father.

I was about to get ready for bed, but someone rang the doorbell.

"Hi guys," I said to Ana and Andrei, who had come over to express condolences. I motioned for them to enter.

"We aren't staying; we just wanted to check on you," Ana said.

Andrei hugged me. "I'm so sorry to hear of your father's passing."

"Any news on the results of my father's exams?" I choked a little and thought maybe it was too early to ask.

Ana's face tightened, and her eyes flicked toward Andrei for a moment before answering. "It seems your father had a low concentration of Darachnids, but the interesting thing we discovered is…there were no larvae."

"I assumed they only fed off the living," Jacob said from behind me.

"True, but because time doesn't move at the same speed in the other dimension, it takes a few days before they all drop away from a host," Ana clarified.

"So does that mean he just acquired the Darachnids recently?" I asked.

"Perhaps…" Ana paused. "Companions take about forty-eight hours before they start to fade away when death to the body occurs, so we tested his. The results were similar to yours, Jacob." She turned to Jacob, then back to me. "Doug's Companion was relatively healthy. They will perform an autopsy tonight and prepare the body for viewing tomorrow evening for you and your sister's family."

"You folks don't waste any time, do you." Jacob raised an eyebrow.

"Time is a luxury we are running out of," Andrei said.

"Thank you, Ana," I said.

"Don't mention it. It's the least we can do under the circumstances. We're right next door if you need anything. Try to get some rest, and we'll talk tomorrow." Ana bent down to rub Loki's chin before leaving.

Andrei put his hand over his heart. "Have a good night."

"Goodnight." Jacob closed the door and turned to me. "You should try to get some sleep, Kim."

"I'm going to let Loki out back first."

I watched my pup as he ran around the yard sniffing at the equipment Veronica had set up earlier. Inwardly I groaned when I saw him lift his leg and relieve himself on one of the sensors. It was in the open where rain could get at it, so it was weatherproof. He trotted happily back to the door for me to let him in. "You had to pee on it, didn't you?" I mocked. I swear he was proud of it. "Come on, rascal, it's bedtime."

We retired to bed, and I realized how exhausted I was as soon as my head hit the pillow. I woke from an odd dream about my Companion.

I was standing knee-deep in water in the middle of a lake. My twin stood facing me, whom I knew—as one understands things in their dreams—was my Companion. My Companion didn't speak; she just looked at me with a deadpan expression. Then slowly, she lifted her arm and held out the imperial jade stone my father had given me. When I tried to take the green rock from her hand, it disintegrated into ash, and the wind scattered it onto the lake's surface. I asked her, *What's the matter?* She threw her head back and let out a blood-curdling scream that shocked me awake.

My phone displayed quarter after five. I wasn't going to sleep anymore, so I got up and went to the kitchen to turn on the brewer. In the quiet morning, the sound carried, and I could hear Priya and Veronica talking downstairs.

I cracked the basement door. "If you ladies want coffee, it's ready."

After a few minutes, they joined me in the kitchen. They'd slept a little, they assured me, but two sensors had gone off and woken them.

"Do you mind if I go into your bedroom and check on our equipment to confirm it's functioning properly?" Priya asked.

"Go ahead." I waved my hand towards the stairs. "Try not to wake Jacob; I think he was up late."

"Of course," she said and slipped up the stairs.

"The sensor in my bedroom went off?" I asked Veronica and sipped my coffee.

"It did. The one in the backyard went off first, then the one in your bedroom. It happened no more than fifteen minutes ago. The sensors recorded one of those quantum ripples I told you about," she said.

Priya returned down the stairs, looked at Veronica, and gave her a thumbs up. They sat in the kitchen with me for a while until they finished their coffees, then went back downstairs to their equipment. From listening to them talk, I learned the equipment was functioning correctly, and Zeevax calculated the possibilities of whether the ripple was random or from some unseen force.

"Good morning, sunshine," Jacob said, yawning.

"How did you sleep?" I poured coffee into a mug and handed it to him.

"Great, the daybed in your art room is amazing. I need to get one of those, and you?" he asked.

"I slept all right, considering," I trailed off, not wanting to brood. "I guess the sensors went off this morning. One in my bedroom and the other in the backyard right around the time I woke up from one of my weird dreams."

I put four pop tarts in the toaster for us.

"Maybe whatever set the sensors off woke you up," he suggested.

"Maybe."

We sat outside on the deck in our pyjamas before getting ready for my sister and her family. Around ten thirty, I heard a car out front, and Loki started barking. "They're here." I took a deep breath and went to the front door to greet them.

Jeffery grabbed their suitcases from the trunk, and I walked down the driveway to embrace my sister. Her eyes were red and swollen from crying, but she controlled her emotions.

"Auntie Kim," Sherry squealed, rushed over, and threw her arms around me. "I missed you. I'm sorry that Grandpa died."

"I am too, hun." I lifted her off her feet with a bear hug. Once I put her down, she immediately got on the front lawn and snuggled Loki.

Jacob helped Jeffery bring their luggage into the house, and I saw Richard wave at us before he drove away. Julia waved to him and gave me a stern look.

"What's going on, Kim? Soldiers were waiting for us when we got off the plane." She walked into the living room and pointed at the big yellow tank in the middle of the room. "What the hell is *that*?"

Things did not go as I had planned. I was supposed to mourn my dad with my sister and slowly prepare her to be introduced to Nekxus so that the experts could explain our perilous situation. Instead, I spilled my guts to her and Jeffery about everything except the incident at the restaurant. They listened speechlessly; Jeffery looked at Jacob occasionally, who would nod, corroborating my story. He also added his experience at Nekxus, including his CS and DMRM exams.

After an hour of unloading the last couple of days on my older sister and her husband, I went into the kitchen to grab a bottle of wine. Sherry was colouring on the kitchen table, and Loki curled up underneath her chair. I rustled her hair, kissed her forehead and went back into the living room to prepare for my sister's reaction. I looked at Jacob first, and his eyebrows lifted in response.

"Nekxus is a behemoth of a company. I know. They've poached a few engineers from the company I work at over the years. I wasn't aware of exactly what they did, being too busy with my projects," Jeffery said, rubbing his beard thoughtfully.

"Mom called them angels," Julia said, staring into her wineglass.

"Mom called who angels?" I asked, puzzled.

"She knew about the Companions. She said they were angels and heard their voices—I heard her and Dad talking about it. One day I asked her about it, and she told me we all have a guardian angel that never leaves us. She described it as a loving energy field that surrounded every living being." Julia fiddled with the cross around her neck.

"I didn't know that," I said.

"I wouldn't call them angels. The microbiome that Kim is talking about is a biological entity. I don't think you should assume it's evidence for some biblical mythological being, Jules," Jeffery said.

"Mythological? The Bible is not a work of fiction, *Jeff*. You can't just dismiss everything in the scriptures because they are at odds with your scientific knowledge. What about this hidden dimension? From what I understand, it's mostly unknown, right Kim?" Julia said.

"Anything is possible," I said, glaring at Jeffery.

"See?" Julia added.

I looked at Jeffery, thinking, *Leave it alone for now*. I'd heard it all before. Mom was a devout Catholic, and Dad was indifferent. Julia followed in Mom's footsteps in her beliefs while I studied philosophy with an open mind to all religions.

"I know you're upset about your father right now. I didn't mean to set you off," Jeffery said.

I looked at Jacob. "Loki needs to go for his walk now."

Jacob jumped up fast and headed directly to the porch to put his shoes on.

"Set me off?" Julia raged.

We exited the living room while Jeffery attempted to soothe his wife, which would take a few minutes, and I doubted having an audience helped. I thought about the performance the Nekxus girls were going to hear through the floor in the basement and decided they were on their own. Anger might help Julia cope more than the sadness and depression from losing a loved one.

"Let's take Loki for a walk," I said to Sherry.

Once outside, Jacob waved to the officer in the black sedan parked a few houses down. Sherry held Loki's leash, and the three of us enjoyed breathing in the fresh air.

"Julia and Mom always had a special bond over Mom's belief in Christianity, but I didn't know about the angels. One of the reasons Julia became a nurse was because Mom encouraged her to help people," I said quietly to Jacob.

"I see she hasn't managed to indoctrinate her husband yet." Jacob rolled his eyes.

"They have a lot in common, but religion isn't one of them. Jeff's an engineer and believes solely in science."

We returned after about twenty minutes to find Julia's eyes wet and Jeffery sitting with his arm around her. She had the letter our dad wrote in her hand.

"You can keep it," I said gently.

"Thank you. We're ready to go. Call your people. Jeff and I want to get checked for these insects in case they affect our behaviour," Julia said.

I opened the Nekxus app and tapped Ana's name. She responded after one ring.

"They're ready," I said.

"A van will be there in twenty-five minutes to pick you all up. I'll meet you at the entrance of Commune A. See you soon," Ana said.

"Okay." I hung up. "Nekxus is sending a van to pick us up in twenty-five minutes."

"I'll stay here with Loki and keep an eye on them." Jacob pointed to the floor.

"I appreciate it."

The driver of the shuttle van was another uniformed military officer. He took a weird route to the company, zigzagging through some side roads and avoiding the highway. When we arrived at the front gate, there were no protesters; the military had occupied the entire entrance and had it barricaded off with vehicles and tents. Soldiers were all over the place, guiding traffic and assembling fences with barbed wire.

"I feel like we're on the base again with all these green uniforms and canvas everywhere," Julia said, remembering a childhood as an army brat.

"It wasn't like this yesterday." I stretched to look at the troops.

Ana and Samuel were waiting at the main entrance for us. I immediately let them know that I'd already divulged everything I knew about Companions and the war against the dark matter infestation. Samuel answered a few questions that Jeffery had for him regarding some of the mechanisms the company used and the nuclear fusion reactor underground. Julia and Ana discussed the possibility of Companions being angels. Julia was pleased when Ana revealed that many of the pope's advisors had come to the same conclusion.

We first travelled to the Aurora building to the CS machine, where the scan revealed that Julia, Sherry, and Jeffery had Companions in average condition. Afterwards, we hastened to the DMRM. Once that examination was complete, we learned that Julia and Jeffery had quite the infestation, including larvae. Only eight years old, Sherry showed no signs of Darachnid presence—as expected from a child. Samuel made several calls expediting the Pyramid's availability and arranged for my sister and her husband to get a purification bath. I went with Ana and Sherry to a Nekxus children's facility, Commune P. It was a fully equipped childcare centre with daycare, a jungle room, arts and crafts, and goodies.

We had lunch at Commune P, where the Nekxus staff's children were allowed to enjoy a mini wonderland. While Sherry played, Ana explained that my father's funeral was arranged for later in the evening so we could say goodbye.

"Julia is going to snap. What about our aunt? Dad's sister should be able to attend. Can we put it off until tomorrow?" I asked.

"I can only imagine how difficult this is, Kim. The truth is that the military has forbidden any unnecessary civilians on the property due to the wave of violence that's already started. They're planning a series of lockdowns. Your father's procession is the only one being allowed. I imagine it will be the last one for a long time." She rubbed her arms self-consciously.

Ana left for a few hours and returned before Julia and Jeffery showed up and joined us.

"Mommy, Daddy, look at me, no hands," Sherry squealed when she saw them sit on the bench with us. She was hanging from her legs upside down on the monkey bars, swinging and waving at them.

"Wow, sweetie. That's cool," Jeffery called out to her.

"Kim, I know you aren't going to like this, but Samuel has insisted that we rush a small service for Dad in an hour," Julia said carefully.

"I heard."

We watched Sherry play before Jeffery told her it was time to go. This upset my little niece, and she attempted to bargain for more time by offering to do dishes for a week.

"We're going to say goodbye to Grandpa now," Julia said.

Ana walked with us to the van and excused herself to finish some work while we rode the shuttle to the back entrance of the Medicorium.

We pulled up to a little chapel with red and white roses at the entry. Twenty soldiers dressed in their officers' uniforms, including Chris and Richard, stood at attention on either side of the aisle. My dad was lying peacefully in an extravagant casket. He would have been annoyed if he'd seen it, knowing that the coffin would burn with his body. I was sure he would have considered it a waste, but it was beautiful.

We took turns saying goodbye, and the officiant asked if we wished to say something. I declined, but Julia spoke up. Her voice cracked as she quoted some Scripture from the Bible, and watching her repeatedly swallow and close her eyes as she spoke the words moved me to tears. I looked over to the soldiers, and although none of them had moved, Richard had a single tear running down his cheek.

Julia and I shook hands with each soldier as they took turns paying their respects to our father. Only a few words were exchanged here and there, but it felt powerful, and I believed that our dad would have approved of the simple ceremony. Jeffery and Sherry sat patiently, waiting for us to do one more walk by our father's body before we left.

"Regarding Doug's ashes, would one of you be taking them, or shall I have them divided into two cremation urns? You don't have to decide right now. I could reach out later," he assured us.

"You take Dad's ashes. I have Mom's," Julia decided.

The officiant looked at me, and I nodded. Outside, a vehicle was waiting to take us home, and my phone beeped while we were getting in. I looked to see I had a message from Ramesh.

"Who's that?" Julia asked.

"Oh, um, it's a scientist. He works in the same department as Ana," I said, dismissive because she raised her eyebrow at me.

"Is he expressing his condolences?" she asked.

I opened the NexChat app and read Ramesh's message. *Hi Kim, I'm very sorry for the loss of your father. Call me when it's convenient, I have some good news for you.*

## CHAPTER 16
## *Vaccine*

THE MAN DRIVING the van was the same one from earlier. I recognized his face before I read *John* on his name tag.

"Are the main roads busy, John?" I asked when I noticed he took the same back roads home.

"I'm not sure I'd describe them as busy, but instructions are to stay off the highways for the time being," he replied.

I detected a tone in his voice that implied he wasn't going to elaborate. I could see his eyes in the rear-view mirror from where I sat. In my mind, I posed the question to him—*The main roads aren't safe, are they?* His eyes moved, and he looked into the mirror directly at me, then squinted before returning his attention to the road. I reached for the grab handle above the door, worried about our welfare.

"Samuel has arranged for us to stay in a condo nearby. Nekxus has company-owned buildings with units blocked off for foreign staff visiting. They function as temporary housing for employees until they arrange for permanent accommodations," Julia said.

"You're kidding," I said.

"Not only that, Samuel asked Jeff to consider coming to work for Nekxus."

"Really?" I said, shocked.

"It's true," Jeffery confirmed. "Samuel spoke with Julia and me while we took turns getting purged of Darachnids inside the field warping generator. He wants to recruit me temporarily to assist with the maintenance of automation equipment. They need engineers, especially now that Nekxus is building new locations simultaneously worldwide."

"It would be so nice to have you all close by, especially you," I said and tweaked Sherry's nose.

"We'll stay with you tonight—they've sent someone to grab some stuff from our place in Timmins—and we'll go to the condo for a few weeks until we decide what we want to do. I'll take Sherry there tomorrow to check it out, and Samuel has invited Jeffery to participate in orientation with Zeevax." Julia gazed at Jeffery then glanced at Sherry, whose head was on my shoulder as she started to doze off.

We arrived home to find Jacob had a homemade lasagna in the oven. The savoury garlic fragrance and baked cheese filled the house. "Smells wonderful, Jacob."

"Prepare yourselves; I intend to shame your previous pasta experiences," Jacob teased.

"Excuse me for a moment; I'm going to call Ramesh. He said he had good news." I held my fingers up and crossed them for everyone to see.

"Ramesh, eh?" Jacob smirked.

I went upstairs to my bedroom for privacy and tapped his name from my Nekxus contact list. Ramesh answered right away.

"Hello Kim, I just want to start by saying how sorry I am for your loss," Ramesh spoke kindly.

"Thank you, Ramesh." Hearing his voice and saying his name made my heart rate go up.

"I cleared it with Samuel first because we shouldn't get carried away—I wanted to be the one to give you the good news. The classification for this project is level 4, but I argued that you submitted the artifact. I felt the company should keep you advised."

"The stone was of value, I take it?" I asked, feeling a swell of excitement for the possibility of this roller coaster ending soon.

"Yes, Diego arrived and determined with Zeevax's assistance that the missing element he was looking for was inside the stone. He's been labouring on this project for almost a decade and is prepared to move forward now that he has the missing piece of the puzzle. They're extracting the exotic matter to be put in a containment field as we speak," he said.

"That's great news; I hope it helps." I failed to comprehend the significance of what he was telling me. I only knew it would be a critical weapon in the war against Darachnids.

"I won't keep you; I'm sure your hands are full right now. Zeevax has indicated that we require a few more tests from you. Can you find time tomorrow to meet with me so I can bring you to the computer lab?" Ramesh asked.

"Sure, how about after lunch?"

"Sounds good. I'll send a car to pick you up at one o'clock."

"I'll be ready," I said.

"Take care, Kim." Ramesh hung up.

I went back downstairs to join the others, setting the table. We devoured the delicious lasagna and munched on the buttery garlic bread. Jacob made an overflowing dish, but by the time he portioned it out to everyone—including Loki and the guests in the basement—the pan was empty. I poured out glasses of an exceptional earthy Merlot I'd saved for special occasions and grape juice for Sherry.

"Are you going to tell us the good news or what?" Julia asked, sipping her wine.

I considered Ramesh's comment about security levels before answering. I decided he didn't say much, so I told them about the discovery of exotic matter in the stone specimen I'd handed to the company. Julia felt this news verified her belief that our dad's death had a divine purpose. Jeffery learned his lesson from their argument earlier and kept his mouth shut this time.

Over another bottle of wine, we discussed the plans for the next few days. Julia and Sherry would leave late in the morning to check out their temporary accommodations and determine what they'd need to acclimate. Jeffery would go for orientation to see how he felt about accepting the generous proposal from Nekxus, and Jacob would hang with Loki.

"Now that the company's getting ready to implement Project Arrow, I think we'll be out of your hair in a few days," Veronica said on her way to the kitchen with the dirty dishes from the basement.

"Are you allowed to talk about that?" I asked, surprised she brought it up.

"Zeevax notified Priya and me that you have been assigned clearance for it, so I assume so." She shrugged.

"Ramesh told me that the missing element was discovered in the jadeite sample and talked about a project, but I didn't know it was called Arrow," I admitted.

"I'm sure he'll explain everything to you tomorrow. Arrow is clever; it's pointy like a needle's delivery system." Veronica giggled and returned downstairs.

I took Sherry up to my bedroom and tucked her in. Loki curled beside her, and I snuck out of the bedroom to return to the others.

"Kim, I think I'm going to call Aunt Laurie tomorrow," Julia said.

"What are you going to tell her? When she finds out we had Dad's funeral without her, she will be furious with us."

"Yup, I'm going to lie to her. I want your consent first."

"What are you going to say?" I said, searching her face for clues.

"I think it's because I'm a nurse, but it occurred to me that we could say dad's body was under quarantine. The Public Health Department had his body cremated as a precaution against an outbreak," Julia suggested.

"What kind of outbreak? I told people he killed himself." It was a brilliant idea, I thought, except for that snag.

"I don't know; I'll say it's some rare painful form of hemorrhagic fever and that's why he took his life. With Aunt Laurie's paranoia of COVID, I'm sure she'll drop the subject quickly and accept that we aren't having a funeral." Julia was nervous, speaking rapidly, and her hands were flying around.

"Are you sure you want to lie to your aunt?" Jeffery asked.

"Jules is right. Aunt Laurie will be a headache if we don't tell her something. A contagion is perfect. You have my permission."

Our conversation changed to discuss the chances of Jeffery taking a job with Nekxus. They offered him double what he was getting in his current position. He clarified that money wasn't a factor when considering the career. His new knowledge of the fourth dimension and the opportunity to work with the latest sophisticated technology prepared him to pack up and move the family on short notice. Julia seemed sold on the idea because she wanted the annual Pyramid bath for the family that Nekxus included in the proposed employment contract for Jeffery.

Eventually, we all got tired and headed off to bed. Loki yawned and rolled over when I carefully crawled under the sheets; Sherry slept deeply. When I woke, I looked up to find she was wide-eyed over me.

"You okay, Aunty?" she asked with concern.

"Yeah, I'm fine. What's the matter, hun?"

"You were making funny noises and puffing." Her little hand was petting my head like she was soothing an animal.

"Ptah, you don't need to worry about me; Aunty sleeps weird." I tickled her, and her laughter had Loki joining in and licking her face, which caused more giggles.

"Let's go get breakfast." I squinted against the radiant sunlight creeping around the curtain and reflecting off my dresser mirror directly into my eyes.

---

The morning flew by as everyone scurried around—showering, eating, and preparing for the day; Jeffery left first. My house felt so alive; since the divorce last year, it was usually only Loki and me.

My ride showed up at precisely one o'clock. "See you later, Jacob," I called out and rubbed Loki's head. "You be a good boy."

"Let me know when you'll be home," Jacob said.

"Will do."

The driver who picked me up was different today. The van from yesterday came for Julia and Sherry earlier because they had their luggage from the trip to Mexico to take with them. A small blue electric car pulled up to the house for me, and I got into the passenger seat. The driver's name was Cynthia. I'd always had a fondness for large gaudy purses roomy enough to fit my laptop, so when I got into the passenger seat, I put my handbag in the back so Cynthia wouldn't feel crowded. We didn't get five minutes down the street before running into trouble.

"Turn left here," Zeevax's voice boomed out of the car speakers.

I could see why. A hundred meters in front of us, an ambulance and two police cruisers blocked the road. Three officers were dragging a half-naked man who was wrestling against the officers, screaming, "Fuck you, pigs!" Even though he was in handcuffs, they struggled to get him in their car. The paramedics were on the other side of the road, loading a stretcher with someone in a zipped-up body bag.

"Homicides have doubled in the last twenty-four hours," Cynthia told me flatly.

The side street we turned onto led us through an even sketchier-looking neighbourhood. I caught sight of a gang of marginalized people gathering around a fight between two girls that looked no more than eighteen years old. They were bleeding from exchanging blows, and tufts of hair were flying. The onlookers were cheering and shouting, "Kill her!" I felt nauseous.

"Are you sure the highway isn't a better route?" I asked.

"The highway is gridlocked," Zeevax answered.

"It seems everyone forgot how to drive," Cynthia complained.

We arrived at the main entrance of Nekxus, where soldiers who occupied the area ushered us through rapidly. Ramesh was waiting outside Commune A; I suspected he was tracking us from the app.

"Thanks for the ride." I waved at Cynthia; she nodded, then sped off.

"Nice to see you, Kim. Our shuttle's waiting; we'll head straight to the lab." Ramesh opened the auto-piloted car for me to get in.

"My God, what an ordeal it was getting here. I think the newly hatched Darachnids are messing people up. Dirtbags out there are out of control." I held my purse close to my body.

"I don't doubt it. The larvae devour more than an adult Darachnid will, putting people in a miserable state of mind," he said.

"So, tell me about Project Arrow."

"Oh, you know the project name?" Ramesh's eyebrow shot up in surprise.

"Veronica told me."

"Diego is leading the teams that are working on Project Arrow. They have synthesized a copied version of the exotic matter. The plan is to use our nanotechnology to deliver the material into the pineal, pituitary, adrenal, and hypothalamus glands." Ramesh ran his fingers through his hair and looked out the window before continuing. "The nanobots are being preprogrammed to transport distinct amounts of the synthetic sampling to each gland. Plenty of Nekxus staff volunteered to be test subjects for assessment to accelerate Project Arrow for mass distribution into the population."

"It will be injected using a needle?" I asked.

"Right. The plan is to announce the availability of a new COVID vaccination shot. The new shot will be the delivery system for Diego's synthetic version of the exotic matter. They expect this to act as a kind of bug repellent against the Darachnids," Ramesh said.

The car dropped us off. After the whirligig of an elevator ride and a walk through the hallway of Zeevax's artwork, we were back in the computer lab. In a room full of high-tech computer equipment, we listened to Billy rant about how irresponsible the company was for barging ahead with Project Arrow.

"Zeevax can program the nanomachines to do exactly what Diego wants them to do—that's not the problem. The problem is unpredictable particles from the fourth dimension. We don't know what they are capable of," Billy growled.

"I'm sure that Diego and his team have taken every precaution to safeguard the synthetic version of the particles so they will be harmless," Ramesh tried to reassure Billy.

"Zeevax, back me up," Billy grunted.

"Project Arrow has no information on the scale of long-term side effects," Zeevax said. "There are too many unknown variables regarding inter-dimensional particles and their behaviour. Testing has proven optimistic, but our test subjects have already experienced side effects—blurry vision, headaches, and abnormal heart rhythm, to name a few. The particles could interact with atoms from our dimension inside the subject's body on a subatomic level. Theoretically, the dark matter could be unstable and rip molecules apart from the quantum level inside the participant."

"You hear that? This bizarre substance could rip people apart from the inside out," Billy said, exasperated.

"What do you suggest?" Ramesh asked.

"Kim is the key. Zeevax's calculations reveal she is our best shot at neutralizing and maybe mending damage from the invaders," Billy said.

"What's Billy talking about, Zeevax?" Ramesh asked.

"We have yet to determine why Kim's Companion is in optimal health, but the absence of Darachnid infestation is not a coincidence. Sensors were set up all around the city, but only those close to Kim's house signalled gravitational ripples. Soil samples taken from the area showed no abnormalities. The recommendation is to reopen the Gamma Project—put Kim into the tank, and proceed with around-the-clock observation. This has the highest probability of successfully understanding the connection to her immunity to the parasite," Zeevax said.

*"Not a chance,"* Ramesh snapped.

"Hear Zeevax out, Ramesh," Billy insisted. "Kim, you wouldn't be in danger, especially if Diego's vaccine is as effective as everyone thinks it is."

"You just said it may not work and may even be dangerous," Ramesh said.

"Ah ha, and you agree. We wouldn't be having this discussion if you trusted Diego's shot. There would be no reason to fear for your new girlfriend's safety."

"That's not what I'm saying," Ramesh countered.

I listened to Ramesh and Billy without interrupting them for a few minutes. They circled around and around the same argument. Billy and his multi-billion-dollar baby Zeevax had calculated the risks too significant to give the general public an experimental shot with an army of nano-robots carrying unpredictable exotic matter into their bodies. Ramesh considered the Gamma Project inhumane and refused to entertain the idea of putting me in the tank near an assemblage of deeply infested animals. He completely ignored the fact that Billy called me his girlfriend. I let my mind wander, having reason to believe that Ramesh wasn't already in a relationship.

"Here you go." Ken handed me a soda while he chewed on a piece of black licorice. "They'll stop soon. Come with me; I want to show you something."

"Thank you." I cracked the can and took a swig. I didn't usually drink soda, so the sugar rush would probably make me shaky soon, but I welcomed the sweet, bubbly syrup anyway.

Ken led me to an adjacent room, away from the control centre for Zeevax. It was an office fully furnished with a desk, cabinets, and a round table surrounded by wing chairs. We sat in the comfy chairs away from the argument but still within earshot.

"Don't worry about those two. Ramesh and Billy squabble like this all the time." Ken sat back in the chair and crossed his legs, making himself comfortable. The chair seemed smaller with him in it. He was tall and looked like a young Jeff Goldblum.

"They are seriously going at it," I said.

Ken laughed, but I didn't see the humour. Billy was swearing loud enough that there was no doubt that the whole department could hear him. Ramesh's vocabulary wasn't as colourful as Billy's, but he held his own, justifying his reasoning in the quarrel just as vehemently.

"Everyone in this sector knows how Billy gets. He'll settle down any minute." Ken smiled and raised his soda can in a cheers gesture before finishing it.

"If you say so." I had my doubts, but Ken knew them better than I did, so I tried to ignore them.

"Zeevax, please display the postulation index for parasite eradication," Ken said.

"Displayed," Zeevax replied.

Above the round table, a hologram appeared with six three-dimensional graphs. Five were pitiful-looking things compared to the sixth one, which stood out like a lighthouse overlooking the sea. The diagrams featured images on top with titles, and I couldn't take my eyes off the face atop the giant one.

"You are looking at the theoretical solutions with the highest probability of success determined by the world's most intelligent AI system. Zeevax has calculated that our best course of action is reopening the Gamma Project and studying how you and your Companion cope with having the Darachnids thrust upon you. As admirable as it is to avoid the ugly and potentially dangerous situation, most of us in this lab agree that Zeevax is right," Ken said.

"No one has asked me, but I've already clarified that I want to help. I'm scared, of course, and I'm not being self-righteous either. If I can make a difference, I'll do it because I don't want to live in a world where violence and savagery are the mainstream," I said.

Ken chuckled. "Bold and full of courage, I like that. Unfortunately, it isn't up to you or me, but perhaps you could talk with Samuel. The company execs make all the important decisions. They think of Zeevax as a tool; they consult the AI system but make decisions based on their limited knowledge—*humans*." Ken rolled his eyes, evidently frustrated with the leadership.

"Zeevax thinks I'm the answer to saving us from the parasite," I said, leaning closer to the hologram to look at the virtual image of my head. My features looked robotic, and since I hadn't posed for the picture, Zeevax must have generated it independently.

A young woman with pigtails and a purple jumpsuit with white polka dots slipped into the room and sat in the chair beside Ken. She'd have had to walk right past Billy and Ramesh in the other area to get to us. Her presence didn't affect the guys because they didn't falter from their debate.

"Is that her?" she asked Ken.

"Yes, Suzy, this is Kim. Kim, this is Suzy." He waved his hand back and forth between us.

"Hi, Kim." She barely glanced my way with her full attention on Ken. "I don't know if you're aware, but when I got here, I saw a procession of mobile health units pulling into the back entrance towards the Medicorium." Suzy said it all in one breath, unmistakably a fast-talker.

Ken paled. "You're shitting me."

"I wish I was." Suzy gulped, snatched licorice from Ken's hand, and popped it in her mouth.

"They can't. It's too soon. There is no way they could get approval already. Nekxus isn't that reckless." Ken pressed his fingers to his temples.

Suzy looked like a cornered rabbit, her big eyes darting around the room as if searching for something. "I can't believe Zeevax allowed it," she exclaimed.

Ken shot her a look that indicated she'd said something she shouldn't have.

"It's not up to Zeevax," Ken warned.

Suzy's head bowed, and she stared at the floor. I expected Zeevax to speak up as I'd become accustomed to the AI's never-ending presence.

"Did you ask her?" Suzy spoke to Ken as if I wasn't still in the room.

"Kim is on board," he replied.

Suzy looked at me now thoughtfully with her finger on her lips. My phone vibrated in my pocket, and I could hear a choir of chirps, tones, and beeps around the department. The sound was familiar. Nekxus must have sent out an alert. I looked at my phone to read the broadcast. *Project Arrow – initiated.*

Billy's voice boomed from the next room. "It's too fucking late now anyway."

## CHAPTER 17
### *Youth*

BILLY'S FACE was flushed from breathing heavily when he stormed in and joined us. He plunked himself down in one of the wing chairs. Ramesh followed shortly after and regarded the holographic graphs above the coffee table for a few seconds before sitting beside me.

"I see Ken and Suzy have shown you the postulation index," Ramesh said disdainfully.

Suzy threw her hands in the air. "The hologram was here before I showed up—don't bring me into this."

"It's fine, Suzy; I'm not hiding anything from Kim." Ramesh turned to me. "Zeevax wants you to provide a sample of your bone marrow."

"Okay... I suppose it's going to sting, right?" I winced.

"Don't worry about any pain. Nekxus has painkillers that are so effective they will make you think you went in for a massage," Ken said.

"Zeevax requested we get a biopsy to look deeper into your biology. You have macrocytosis—your red blood cells are larger than normal. You also have a fast heartbeat," Billy said.

"I didn't know that. Is it serious?" I asked.

"Hard to say without further examination. Red blood cells carry oxygen; from what I understand, it could simply mean that you're borderline anemic. Nekxus is researching and logging everything about your health and lifestyle," Billy answered.

"If you thought you had any privacy, think again," Suzy said sarcastically.

"What was that other thing you found, Zeevax?" Billy sat back in his chair, his colour returning to normal.

"We discovered two infrequent non-coding DNA sequences in Kim's genome. One of the strands of DNA serves an unknown functional role that might decipher why Kim seems to have protection against attachment or feeding from the Darachnids. The other transposon regulates the enzyme responsible for bacteria tolerance. This special gene allows Kim's bacteria to flourish, which could help explain her exceptionally healthy microbiome. The mutation may be key to the human–Companion relationship," Zeevax responded.

Billy leered at Ramesh, and I sensed he was using his Companion to communicate. Ramesh tented his fingertips and gave Billy a brutal look in return.

"Zeevax, any records of similar noncoding DNA in your database?" Ramesh asked.

"Yes, samples of the same sequences are in the remains of human sacrifices from a Mayan temple in Chichén Itzá. Specifically, a priest chamber where all human remains have the same mutagen."

"Let me guess…the Alligator Chamber," Billy said.

"That is correct," Zeevax said.

"That's where Diego found his jadeite meteor sample with the tiny fraction of the exotic matter he's been so obsessed with for the past ten years. It was in the belly of an alligator near the secret chamber. The reptile had a few stones it had swallowed, probably so it could dive deeper. That's why the temple beside it was named the Alligator Chamber," Billy explained to the rest of us.

"That's interesting. I've spent months studying the classified Dark Codex found in that temple. They sacrificed members of one of the tribes to appease their God from the dream world—Puchi. The codex described a mysterious world overlapping ours, crawling with evil monsters that Puchi would unleash upon them if they didn't perform a monthly ritual. Approximately every thirty years—coinciding with

Saturn's orbit—they would also have a mass sacrifice of hundreds of tribespeople at once. The timeline corresponded to the Darachnid life-cycle. We presume the ritual was to counter-act the egg hatch somehow," Ken said thoughtfully.

It sounded morbidly absurd, but at the same time, these ancient Mayan priests were on to something. They knew too much about the fourth dimension, the Darachnids, and their life cycle. I was disturbed by hearing they targeted folks with the same rare noncoding DNA I had and was none too impressed with the god Puchi.

"Project Arrow has taken precedent, anyway, so I doubt Zeevax's index will mean anything. I hope for victory; then we can get on to the fun stuff like augmented reality," Suzy said and applied a lip balm.

"We all hope for the project's success; I'm concerned because Zeevax is concerned," Billy said pointedly.

Suzy turned to stare at Ramesh. "Kim has agreed to participate in the Gamma Project."

"Samuel hasn't expressed interest in the Gamma Project and will be focusing on Project Arrow right now. I'll take Kim to get the bone marrow sample; we'll hope for the best." Ramesh stood and looked down at me. "If you come with me, we'll go to the Medicorium."

We said goodbye to the group at the computer lab and headed to the exit.

"What exactly is noncoding DNA?" I asked once we were in the elevator.

"Picture a birthday cake. If DNA gives you the ingredients, then noncoding DNA tells you when the birthday is and how much cake to make. You may be familiar with the term *junk DNA*. We're learning that even what seems to be scrap has a purpose," Ramesh said.

"Fascinating," I said.

We found the Medicorium crowded with people and mobile units. Inside and out were line-ups of Nekxus staff getting their nanobot-infused shots. Ramesh escorted me to a reasonably vacant area compared to the rest of the medical centre and was kind enough to wait for me. Ken was right, I donated a sample of my bone marrow, and it was painless. The nurse applied the local anesthetic with a cotton ball, and I didn't feel the needle in my hipbone.

After the biopsy, we rode the shuttle back to Commune A, where we sat on the bench for a few minutes before ordering me a ride home.

"How many injections are being administered to start with?" I asked.

"Nekxus outlined this vaccination plan years ago. They've invested untold amounts of money in nanotechnology, medical equipment, and staff who were on call waiting for the go-ahead." Ramesh flipped through something on his phone. "If I were to guess, I'd say once they ramp it up to the general public, they'll be able to give out six or seven million doses daily."

"That's great news; will the Companions heal?"

"We don't know for sure. We hope the children can grow into adulthood without ever having to experience the invading parasite feeding off their glands. In this case, society will have a new mentally competent generation without the hindrance of sociopathic personalities lacking empathy," he said.

Ramesh reached into his pocket and handed me a box that looked like it held jewelry. I took it and looked up at him. *Are you giving me a present?* I framed the words in my mind as I looked into his eyes. He blinked twice, which I had come to realize meant *no*. Scolding myself internally for feeling disappointed, I turned the box over to inspect it.

"What's this?"

"Nekxus would like you to wear it at all times. This waterproof health monitor is called a Welxus; it will track your vitals twenty-four seven," Ramesh said.

I opened the box to find a stainless steel bracelet. I put it on and admired how stylish the simple braided design was. It was dainty, and unlike my smartwatch, it had no prominent components. According to the instructions, it only needed to be charged for an hour once a week.

"At least it's pretty," I said.

"So are you."

My heart raced, and I cursed myself for putting the bracelet on already—*Zeevax is probably recording an anomaly right now.* I smiled weakly at him and fiddled with my hair for a moment. Ramesh turned suddenly, and I saw the little blue electric car pull up with Cynthia behind the wheel.

"Lay low, and please try to stay close to home for the next few days. I'll be in touch with you soon." Ramesh opened the car door.

"Okay, thank you." I touched his arm lightly, and he smiled before backing away.

---

On the ride home, I clutched the seat and stayed quiet as Cynthia weaved in and out of side roads and alleys. Zeevax directed her, and although we took an extra fifteen minutes to get home, we only witnessed a couple of fender benders and one house fire. Cynthia explained that the alleys and side roads were safer because troublemakers had moved from shadowy neighbourhoods to the main roadways. I relaxed once she dropped me off at my house. Once inside, Loki carried one of Jacob's dirty socks and ran to maul me.

"What's this, baby? Thank you." I sat on the floor to take off my shoes and threw the sock to Jacob.

"I was listening to the news, and the Public Health Department just announced a new COVID vaccination against another dangerous variant. There's a hotline for people to make appointments around the clock. Military and mobile units are getting set up all over the city," Jacob said.

I put my shoes and purse away. "Did they? It's amazing how efficient Nekxus is."

"I figured it was something like that." He closed the app on his phone.

"Yeah, they've been sitting on Project Arrow for about a decade. Dad's rock sample provided the missing puzzle piece, and they have launched the planned *attack* on the invaders," I said dramatically.

"Too bad they didn't start before the hatching. The radio station also reported several assaults and a bunch of property damage. The main highway is gridlocked from multiple pileups as well." Jacob crossed his arms.

I exhaled. "It's fucking scary out there, Jacob."

Jacob described his day as uneventful. The science girls in the basement were so quiet that he had popped his head downstairs partway through the day to see if they were still there. Priya whispered to him that it was Veronica's turn to sleep—they took turns so one of them was always awake to check the readings. They watched to see whether the resonance fluctuations recorded were spontaneous or had a pattern.

I recounted my day to him, explaining that Project Arrow's nanotechnology was in the COVID vaccines coming out for the new variant. I also described the strange and creepy connection between my junk DNA and Mayan sacrifices.

"I would love to get my hands on that classified Mayan codex." Jacob rubbed his hands together as a fly does when it cleans itself.

"I figured you would. As soon as the guys talked about secret chambers, sacrifices, and rituals, I thought of you." I lightly punched him on the shoulder.

"You know what I like." He wiggled his eyebrows at me, making me laugh.

For dinner, we ate pizza paid for by Priya, who assured us she was using a Nekxus credit card. The pizza came almost an hour late.

"It's a jungle out there. People are acting all crazy tonight," the delivery driver told us. He looked like he'd seen a ghost and darted away like he was being chased by one.

"Poor kid," Priya said.

I closed the door while she took the pizza to the table. I insisted Veronica and Priya eat in the dining room with us since they provided the meal. I wolfed down three slices and listened to Jacob question the girls about the structure of the fabric of our reality.

"The three-dimensional flower of life pattern can describe the gravitational field of any object in our dimension. Zeevax has postulated that the laws that govern the particles in the hidden fourth dimension are quite different," Veronica said.

"We believe the wavelength of the most fundamental fragment of dark matter is longer and vibrates slower than those in our dimension. It hardly interacts with the electromagnetic field and is essentially *cold*," Priya said.

"Do you think there is intelligent life in the dark dimension?" Jacob asked.

Priya and Veronica looked at each other for a split second, and Veronica took a sip of her soda.

"Hard to say." Priya brushed her bangs out of her eyes. "Intelligent life has not been ruled out because we know so little about WIMPs. Usually, time is considered the fourth dimension; that's why the dark matter dimension is called the *hidden fourth dimension.*"

"I understand four dimensions. If I tell Kim to meet me at Bean Island Café, I can give her the location in three dimensions, but if I don't tell her the fourth—what time to meet me—my coffee will get cold while I wait for her to show up." Jacob winked at me, and the girls laughed. "Where *is* this hidden dimension?"

"It's right here." Veronica opened her arms wide. "The dark matter dimension is superimposed on ours. Visualize a holographic image on a two-dimensional baseball card. You can turn it slightly and see a three-dimensional image."

"So, if I could turn our world sideways, I could see the hidden dimension?" Jacob's eyes searched the room as if he was trying.

"Dark matter moves incredibly slow, and everything, including a stone in our world, is vibrating fast and hot within it," Veronica said.

"Kinda makes me think of the Chinese yin and yang. Hot versus cold and fast versus slow, all within each other," I said.

"Mathematically, it's much more complicated than that, but I see how you could make that connection." Veronica smiled at me like I was a child.

Jacob's phone rang, and he excused himself to take the call. I could hear that he was speaking with his new friend Matt. Veronica and Priya returned to work in the basement, and I took Loki out to the backyard. I dialled Julia's number for a video call to see how they made out in the Nekxus residence. She walked around the place holding her phone camera so I could look at the elegant condo.

"Holy crap, Jules, what a view," I said.

"I know it's beautiful. It overlooks Lake Ontario."

"So? Don't keep me waiting," I said.

"Jeffery has accepted the position for a one-year contract." Julia's white teeth gleamed on my screen.

"That's great," I said, delighted. "How are you holding up?" I asked, feeling sad suddenly, knowing that living here meant she could have seen our father more often if he was still alive.

"I'm holding up well enough, considering I miss Dad terribly. It's strange being here in Hamilton and not going to the Doon Care Center."

We talked briefly about him, then I chatted with Sherry, who showed me some pictures she'd coloured, which roused a desire in me to start another art project myself. After ending the call, I found Jacob waiting in the kitchen for me.

"I'm going home tomorrow if you think you'll be okay. Of course, I'll check in on you—and if you need anything, call me." Jacob cocked his head sideways, watching for my reaction.

"I'm good, thank you." I peered out the window to see the unmarked security vehicle parked on the street with two Nekxus officers watching the house.

---

The next few days were blissfully uneventful. Jacob left early in the morning before I woke and left a note with instructions to behave and call regularly. Veronica and Priya stayed for two more days but were almost invisible. I spent the first day reorganizing my spare room so I could start a new painting. It had been a while since I'd fostered my creative side. Now with the opportunity to relax, I played my favourite music and enjoyed focusing my mind on artistic expression. Mixing the colours to create a unique picture on a blank canvas made me feel like a magician. I found it to be therapeutic.

Loki woke me up on the third day by whining in my face. I opened my eyes to the usual sloppy kisses and a wagging tail. My phone showed I had slept two hours past when I usually got out of bed.

"Just let me get my robe on, and I'll let you out, sweetie."

I poured cereal into a bowl while watching him run around in the backyard. He was sniffing the packed grass where the sensors that Priya and Veronica removed the previous day had left indentations. They'd packed their gear last night when Nekxus reached out to them, saying they'd collected enough data at my place. I was to keep wearing the Welxus monitor that Ramesh gave me. He sent me several messages, checking how I was doing and informing me that the bone marrow tests didn't reveal anything special.

I was putting a load of laundry in the washer when the doorbell rang. Loki beat me to the entrance, and I opened the door to see Ana with unusually messy hair, looking like she hadn't slept.

"Jesus Christ, Ana, you look like shit; come in the house," I blurted.

"Thanks." She stepped inside and looked over her shoulder self-consciously at the security detail parked outside our houses.

"What's the matter?" I asked.

She flipped her shoes off and went to sit on my couch. Loki jumped on her lap, and she hugged him. "Oh, Kim, it's a fucking disaster." She ran her fingers through her hair.

I tensed; she was scaring me. "What happened?"

"Project Arrow. It's completely backfired."

I dropped into the chair across from her. "What do you mean it backfired?" I remembered Billy's warning. Images flash through my mind of people getting sick from radiation poisoning or torn apart from the inside out.

"At first, everything went as expected. The nanobots successfully inserted Project Arrows synthetic particles into the targeted glands. It was wonderful, and we celebrated. The Darachnids stopped feeding, and follow-up tests showed they had disappeared." Ana sniffed.

"Where'd they go?"

"We didn't know at first. We foolishly hoped they were poisoned and died." Ana put both her hands on her cheeks. "They didn't go far. Wherever they went, they had undergone a type of biological metamorphosis."

"Oh no."

"Zeevax concluded that the Darachnids and larvae were under stress from hunger. Initially, the synthetic particles repelled them, but they also provoked a physical and behavioural change. The people who received the Project Arrow injection came in to get rescanned. The Darachnids had reattached to them with bloated stylets and fed more aggressively. The transformed parasites behave like a single-minded swarm, hyper-focused on the pineal gland." Ana rubbed her head roughly, which tousled her hair so she looked crazed.

"I'm so sorry to hear that. I didn't know that would happen." I opened my arms wide with palms forward. I felt responsible because I was the one who gave the jadeite sample to the company.

"Of course you wouldn't know. Please don't blame yourself; this is above your head, even mine. I haven't told you the worst of it," she said.

"It gets worse?" I already felt sick to my stomach.

"Oh, Kim, I'm so upset. Project Arrow started with Nekxus staff, and after a few positive results, without hesitation, we moved forward. Sneaking it in the new COVID vaccine advertised to prevent infection from a new variant."

"I heard. How many people had the injection?" I asked warily.

"Over thirty million worldwide."

"Shit." I sat back in the chair and folded my arms across my chest.

A massive egg hatch just occurred, with multitudes of larvae feeding off the vertebrates on our planet, and Nekxus made the situation far worse. In their attempts to mitigate the insects' damage, they caused a chain reaction that would increase the devastation.

"They're feeding on children now. *My God*, Kim, it's the worst possible scenario that could've happened. Zeevax didn't foresee this outcome as even a possibility. Prepubescent children were presumed not to produce the type of particle the Darachnids consumed. The modification to their stylets has taught us a horrible lesson. No one is immune." Ana wiped a tear from her cheek.

I stood up, fuming, and paced around the room. I wished that my dad had never found that stupid piece of meteor rock. The nurse said he was looking for the cursed thing, I was sure it played a role in his death, and for all I knew, it was the reason for his Alzheimer's. On top of that, it created a more aggressive parasite that fed on what we hold most valuable, our youth. I looked at the bracelet on my wrist, wondering if Zeevax was registering my heart rate or if the AI was too busy calculating possible solutions to our catastrophe.

"Billy was right. He told Ramesh that Project Arrow was a bad idea. He wanted to move forward with the Gamma Project and put me in the tank. Zeevax suggested that was our best option," I said. My voice sounded manic.

"I know." Ana looked up at me with concerned eyes.

"I'm prepared to do it, Ana. Say the word," I insisted.

I looked into her eyes and pushed the thought, *It's going to be okay.* Ana closed her eyes and bowed her head into her hands.

"I'll let Samuel know. It's going to take another day at least for us to infest the animals with a higher concentration of the parasite," Ana said almost in a whisper. "I need to warn you that they want to expose you to the newly mutated Darachnids too."

"Makes sense. I don't have any children, but I am an aunt. I would do anything to protect my niece."

"I'm so heartbroken it's come to this," Ana said.

"As you said to me earlier, it's not your fault. This war includes all of us," I said.

# CHAPTER 18
## *The News*

ANA PULLED out her cell phone, tapped the screen, and put it to her ear.

"Hello, Samuel. Yes, I spoke with her. That's right; she's here with me now. Okay, I understand. I'll let her know; bye for now." Ana put her phone on the couch and looked at me somberly. "Samuel will gather a team to prep the animals and prepare the tank in Section F for the experiment."

I shivered at the thought of sitting in a tank surrounded by wildly insane animals who were locked up, suffering, and enraged. I reflected on my dad's words; they kept me focused when I felt stressed—*pain or balance*. I could almost hear his voice if I concentrated hard enough. Ana and I just stared at each other for about a minute.

"We might as well drink," I said, breaking the silence. I practically raced to the kitchen to find a bottle of alcohol. My hands trembled as I poured glasses of white wine into cheerful glasses with purple grapes and green leaves. I'd painted them a while back when I was bored. I brought one out to Ana, who immediately swallowed half of it in one gulp.

"Samuel is incredibly discouraged right now, and poor Diego is beside himself with guilt. The atmosphere was dreary at our last meeting when the update came in. Project Arrow has come to a grinding halt while Nekxus examines what happened," Ana said.

She left not long after her glass of wine to call Aleksander to see how he was doing at the university. She was worried about reports that the school had to increase security in residences. Allegedly too many parties broke out into violence. She hugged me and said to take it easy until someone reached out to notify me when the Gamma Project was set.

I called Jacob.

"Hey stranger, I haven't heard from you in a few days. I was beginning to worry," he said.

"I've started another painting."

"What the hell is the matter with you?" Jacob said abruptly.

"What do you mean? I shouldn't paint?" I asked, confused by his reaction.

"Get to the point. I can hear it in your voice; you're upset. Is Loki okay?" he asked.

"He's fine."

"Thank God. What is it?" Jacob breathed a sigh of relief because, next to me, no one loved Loki more than he did.

"I'm going to need another favour. Can you come by tomorrow afternoon and stay for a night or two?" I asked.

"Of course." He paused, waiting for me to continue.

"It's Project Arrow," I said.

"How bad is it?"

"It's a disaster. They want to put me in the Gamma Project with the animals."

"Shit. Okay, I'll go to work and cough up a storm, so my boss will think I have COVID. I'll see you tomorrow at lunch," he assured.

"Thanks, Jacob, you're the best."

"Don't forget it. Kiss Loki for me." He made some smooching noises and ended the call.

The evening was quiet. I suspected Jeffery hadn't heard of what Nekxus was asking from me, or he would've told Julia, and she'd have called me by now. I decided not to say anything to her yet; I didn't need the argument. Instead, I finished my painting, cleaned up, ran a hot bubble bath, and went to bed.

I had trouble falling asleep; visions of animals snarling and ripping each other to pieces filled my head and made me anxious. I picked a novel randomly from my bookshelf and tried to read it with Loki snuggled at my feet. I hoped a fiction novel would distract me.

I fell asleep eventually because I woke up to my phone going off. It was the NexChat app; I saw a message from Billy. The icon for him was a picture of his tattooed arm, flexed to show his bicep. *Classy*, I thought wryly.

*Hi Kim, your Welxus just sent off a warning, and I wondered if something happened — Billy.*

I yawned and looked suspiciously at the shiny bracelet responsible for disrupting my sleep.

*Hey Billy, I didn't notice. I was sleeping*, I typed.

*Weird… Sorry to wake you.*

It was a few minutes after three, so I flipped my pillow over to put my head on the side I didn't drool on and passed out again.

When I opened my eyes, the sun was scattering warm golden light into my bedroom, giving the impression that it would be a beautiful day. An hour later, watching the morning news, that fantasy was crushed.

The international breaking stories described the violence erupting in various major cities. Noticeably, crime skyrocketed across all demographics. North America had mapped shootings spread across the continent so sporadically that it looked like they could have been painting splashes. Homicides in gated communities, assaults in churches, robberies in nursing homes, traffic offences in front of elementary schools…and the list went on.

One recurring topic that concerned me was that riots erupted in penitentiaries worldwide. The convicts had spontaneously aligned themselves to a common goal—*escape*. The television programs seemed saturated with journalists and camera crews showing videos of prisons on fire. The felons were burning everything and killing each other and the guards. It filled me with terror to watch. Eventually, Loki interrupted my trance by whining to go outside.

"Okay, buddy, off you go," I told him as I opened the patio door.

I felt contrite, but I was too scared to take him for a walk. I hadn't seen any violence in my neighbourhood yet, but I heard sirens a few times, so it was only a matter of time. I messaged my sister, told her to get delivery if she needed any food, and directed her not to take Sherry to the park or anything. She responded that they had security in their building and that Jeffery had already put her and Sherry on *house arrest*, as she put it.

Shortly after noon, Jacob showed up via taxi. Usually, he was clean-cut and sharply dressed. He wore a black T-shirt with ripped blue jeans, which were out of character for him, and it looked like he hadn't shaved for a few days.

"Hey, doll, how are you holding up?" he asked.

"Well, you know. Not too bad, considering it's *the apocalypse*," I said sarcastically.

"Tell me about it. I didn't have to pretend to be sick last night. A brawl broke out, and a woman died. It was tragic—she got trampled by a stampede of unhinged lunatics. The bar is a crime scene and closed, pending investigation." He closed his eyes and curled his lips in disgust.

"I can't believe it, Jacob. Don't people recognize how outrageous their behaviour is? I mean, what do they think is going on?" I asked.

"I don't know, but the cabbie who drove me here wasn't shy about stating his opinion. He thinks the government is responsible. He suspects vaccinations have made people violent, and that's why we have the pandemic lockdown."

I could see how someone could come to that conclusion. It wasn't that far from the truth after Project Arrow. We sat in the living room and watched the local news for a while. Reports that crime was soaring were coming in from all over the city. There seemed to be a domino effect—people were fighting back, which resulted in more injuries from assaults. The hospitals were overwhelmed, and the police department released a statement asking people to go out only if necessary. They didn't have the workforce to handle the public disorder.

"I'm going to order groceries from the online delivery service. I don't know how long before I dare to go shopping," I said after shutting off the news.

"I'll pay for half; let's get a list together." Jacob grabbed a pen and paper from the kitchen.

We made a grocery list and ordered from the closest store, hoping they wouldn't be too busy. I was sure many people had the same idea. The app notified me an hour later when the bags arrived. We brought them into the kitchen and found some dented cans, squished bread, bruised apples, and broken boxes. The frozen stuff was still cold, so I checked off *satisfied* in the comment section, hoping not to anger a passive-aggressive employee. We cooked dinner together and were just about to sit down at the table to eat when Loki started growling.

"What's the matter?" Jacob's eyebrows furrowed as he looked at Loki.

Loki rushed to the front door, growling and barking up a storm. I dropped my fork out of surprise, and it landed on the floor with a piece of parmesan chicken. Loki ignored it and stood on his hind legs against the front door, sounding ferocious for a wee thing.

"Do you hear that?" I asked Jacob.

He stood up and went to the kitchen window, and I followed. Someone was screaming threats and swearing like an idiot.

"Cosmic Saviours are united against you, demon scum," a fanatic yelled at my house. He was being held face down in the grass on my front lawn by the Nekxus security guards.

"Holy shit, the cult knows where I live?" I trembled and rushed to the front door to pick Loki up.

"I'm on hold. Can you believe it? I call 911, and they've got me on hold," Jacob growled on his phone. He grabbed my phone off the counter and used it to video record the scene on my front lawn with his free hand.

Loki was barking and shaking in my arms, and I tried to soothe him while simultaneously watching the commotion. Two Nekxus security officers put zip ties on the perpetrator's hands and feet. An unzipped black duffle bag sat on the grass, a baseball bat handle peeking out of it. I was angry and fearful at the same time, as well as grateful for the Nekxus security detail.

"Are you *fucking* kidding me?" Jacob roared. "The line disconnected." He redialed and rolled his eyes with his jaw clenched, which told me he was on hold again.

A military vehicle pulled up to the curb. We watched a couple of soldiers in uniform jump out of the truck and throw the offender in the back before driving away. Jacob stopped recording and ended the call to the operator. We went to the front door to talk to security.

"You folks okay?" The officer picked up the black bag and a few Cosmic Saviours flyers that had fallen out of it.

"We're fine," I said, hugging Loki now that he'd calmed down.

"Someone in the Cosmic Saviours must have recorded your license plate number when you drove by the protest last week. Zeevax found the cult member who hacked the Ministry of Transportation and stole your personal information. Your identity is compromised. For your safety, we need to move you to a more secure location," the Nekxus officer said.

"Where?" I asked, shocked.

"Head office wants us to take you both to Nekxus housing. We're preparing a two-bedroom down the hall, on the same floor as your sister. We'll remain stationed here to watch the properties, but you'll be safer in the building with a controlled entrance."

Two blue vans came up the street; one pulled into Ana's driveway and the other into mine. I realized they were moving her and Andrei as well. Jacob and I rushed around, filling suitcases, totes, bags of Loki's stuff, and a cooler with the groceries. We loaded the van within the hour. Andrei finished packing the van that showed up for them before us, and he waved before driving away behind the vehicle in his work truck.

"I want to bring my new painting," I said as we collected the last tote.

"It's dry?" Jacob asked.

"Yes."

"I'll get it." He dashed upstairs to the art room to grab it.

He had thrown a sheet over it for protection. We loaded the essentials I thought I'd need, including some of Jacob's clothes that he kept at my place. I locked my door and felt sad, wondering when I would return. Loki rode on my lap; it took half an hour to get to the modern condominium taking back roads.

It was around twenty floors, with one side facing the lake. There was a gated entry with a pass to get in, and the balconies were black with frosted glass for privacy. Parking was underground; the driver helped us carry the stuff to the elevator and gave me a keycard for unit 64. We went to the sixth floor and unloaded my things into the two-bedroom condo. Loki ran around sniffing everything while Jacob put the groceries away. I told him I'd be right back and called Julia.

"Hi, Kimmy," she answered.

"Hi, what unit are you in?" I asked from the hallway.

"Sixty-eight, why?" she said.

I knocked on her door and hung up the phone. She opened the door and laughed for a moment until she saw the concerned look on my face. She shuffled me inside, and after I hugged my niece, I told her about the cult member who showed up on my property.

"Good God, Kim, that's awful," Julia said, exasperated. "I'm so glad you're here, in any case. Is Jacob with you?"

"He's in my unit with Loki."

"Loki's here." Sherry jumped up. "Where is he?" She showed more excitement to hear my dog was nearby than she was to see me.

"Come on," I told her.

Julia reached for her phone and came along.

"Loki," Sherry squealed and bent down with her arms open when I opened the door. He ran at her full tilt and knocked her on her butt. Jeffery had updated Julia about the perilous situation with the downfall of Project Arrow. Julia wasn't aware of the Gamma Project, and Jacob took Sherry to the kitchen to have a snack of peanut butter cookies dipped in warm milk while I explained it to my sister.

"I don't know, Kim, that sounds like a bad idea," Julia said.

"It's a terrible idea. But the world's most sophisticated AI has a graph with an image of my head on it that says this is our best chance against these invaders. I'd take a different stance if it were just the *human* committee, but Zeevax is certain this is the way. I feel I can help —I want to help," I said.

"What if they used Loki instead?" Julia said thoughtfully.

"Excuse me?" I snapped. "I mean, no, not a chance in hell."

"Well, why should I feel comfortable with my baby sister going in there if you don't even trust putting your dog in there?" she asked, her palms forward.

"I knew you'd feel this way. I didn't even want to tell you," I said, frustrated.

"Am I wrong?" Julia asked.

"Yes, you are. Loki is a dog, so he can't give consent. I can. He would be traumatized, but I understand why I'm doing this. I may not have a child, but I love Sherry like my own, and Loki is like a child to me. I'm the one with the rare genetic makeup, not him."

I was too loud. I heard Sherry ask Jacob if I was mad. I sat down to try to control my breathing. Julia looked at me with sad eyes, and I knew I'd driven my point home.

"I would do it if they asked me," she said and wiped a tear from her eye.

"Don't be upset, Jules. We must stay focused and compartmentalize our emotions the way Dad taught us."

Julia sighed. "We aren't soldiers, Kim."

"Neither were soldiers...*until they were*. Turn the news on, and you will see we're at war."

"Popcorn, anyone?" Jacob called out.

That was his telling us to keep it down because Sherry was listening. I gave her a half-hearted smile and went into the kitchen to explore the cupboards and keep my niece from getting concerned. We made microwave popcorn, sat together and watched a comedy movie.

Julia and Sherry returned to their unit when Jeffery called. He panicked when he found his wife and daughter weren't there. He poked his head in and spoke with me briefly; he knew what the company asked me to do and wanted me to know he'd be nearby in the complex if I needed anything.

On the fridge was a note that some green space on the roof was accessible with the condo key cards for fresh air and pet owners. Jacob and I took Loki up the elevator to check it out before bed. We were taken aback by the fantastic landscape. A solid plexiglass fence surrounded the roof with reinforced beams five feet high. Grass and small trees were growing, and there was a fenced-off area with a dog sign. There was a poop station with baggies and a little fountain with water cycling for them to drink. Loki loved it. We stayed for about half an hour before going back inside.

In the condo, we turned on the news again to find things were spiralling out of control. Some countries declared civil war, and governments deployed armed military forces all over the globe. The cause of crime couldn't be found, reporters claimed. Typically drugs, politics, poverty, or religion were a catalyst, but this was without reason or warning. They were blaming COVID.

We turned off the television and talked about Jacob's new love interest, Matt.

"He's a nice guy, but starting a relationship with someone when I must lie all the time sucks. I signed the non-disclosure agreement with Nekxus. Even if I did tell Matt the truth about the shitstorm we're in, he might figure I'm crazy. Maybe that creepy AI program would know I blabbed and send out the mercenaries after me," he said sardonically.

"That does suck," I said.

"It's getting late, and you should get some rest. They're going to come for you anytime now." Jacob slumped his shoulders, resolved that things were out of our hands.

"All right," I said.

The rooms were identical, with ensuite bathrooms. I washed up and climbed into bed. Loki had made himself comfortable already, as it was past his bedtime. I put my phone on the charger and crawled into bed.

---

I woke soaked in sweat and gasping for air. A nightmare where a Mayan priest sacrificed me by throwing me into some godforsaken fire pit freaked me out. The priest wore a black cloak that covered his face, but I heard his voice. Of course, he spoke English because it was a dream and not a real Mayan priest. *"You come from the sixth dimension of sage."* I pushed the ridiculous subconscious thoughts out of my mind, got up and slurped running water from the tap. I would have drunk toilet water if I had to; I was incredibly thirsty.

I showered and dressed before Loki started whining to pee. I let him out on the sizeable balcony where Jacob had placed the pooch pad so I could make breakfast. He joined me; this time, he was freshly shaven and wearing a collared salmon shirt with a nice pair of athletic pants. I was pleased to see he was looking more like himself.

"I think we'll keep the television off today," he said.

"Agreed."

We ate breakfast on the balcony and admired the view of the enormous body of water. It looked like an ocean, with lake freighters off in the distance, probably coming from St. Lawrence Seaway. I did the dishes while Jacob talked to someone on his cell.

My phone was on the counter when it went off. I stared at it until Jacob poked his head around the corner with wide, questioning eyes. The name displayed was Samuel's.

"Hello," I said.

"Good morning, Kim; I hope you're doing well," Samuel said.

"Well enough, I suppose," I said, feeling my voice quiver.

"We have everything prepared here. When you're ready, say the word, and I will send Ramesh and a security team to pick you up. Ramesh has insisted he be present for the Gamma Project as a representative for your welfare. I could assign Ana if that makes you more comfortable; it's up to you," he said.

Samuel's voice was authoritative but kind; he had the qualities of a strong leader. I regarded him highly, as did everyone else I witnessed in his presence. If he felt Ramesh held my best interests, I trusted that he did too.

"I'm comfortable with Ramesh, thank you. I'll be ready if you give me an hour," I said.

"Very good." Samuel ended the call.

Jacob was standing in the doorway, having hung up on his call to eavesdrop on me. He let out a long exhale when I put the phone down, and I realized he was holding his breath.

"You got this," he said and clapped his hands together hard enough that it startled me, and I jumped.

## CHAPTER 19
## *The Restaurant*

**ONE HOUR PASSED QUICKLY.** I drank water and sat with Loki on my lap, listening to Jacob lecture me on following instructions and keeping him in the loop. When the security team showed up, I was pleased to see it was Rick and Chris, my father's army buddies.

"Take care of her," Jacob said to them, then turned and wagged his finger at me. "You, little missy, don't be a hero. If something is too much—*say something*. None of that internalizing bullshit."

"I promise." I blew him a kiss and left with my bodyguards.

I felt like an imposter because I was treated like a celebrity or an ambassador. The entourage for my protection included a black Jeep in front of our vehicle and another behind. I reminded myself that it had everything to do with their science project and nothing to do with my spectacular accomplishments.

"We were debriefed about the tragic results of Project Arrow and the reinstatement of the Gamma Project yesterday," Rick said. "Our mission is solely your protection."

"Unless Project Gamma fails, I'm sure any value assigned to my well-being will depreciate." I snorted.

"Not in our eyes," Chris said as he looked into the driver's rear-view mirror to give me a slight nod.

"Thanks." I gazed out the window noting a few mysterious plumes of smoke billowing from distant areas of the city.

The main entrance was encompassed by military personnel. I didn't see anyone wearing civilian clothes, not even at the gate. The two Jeeps escorting us didn't enter the complex. They just pulled off and continued to some other destination. We arrived at the familiar DMRM revolving doors to find Ramesh waiting outside.

"Hello, Kim," he said, reaching for my hand to help me out of the sedan.

"Nice to see you," I said.

"I wish it were under better circumstances." He looked at Rick and Chris.

The four of us entered the more oversized elevator that would take us to level 161, where Sector F was. This elevator moved at a slower pace which Ramesh explained was purposeful to decrease the anxiety of animals travelling in it. We had to walk at least a hundred metres around a dome section. I presumed that was where they pit the animals against each other from the video Ramesh showed me. I couldn't tell for sure because it was dark, and I'd started to shake from fear, so I didn't push to find out.

I was mindful of what was lurking in the covered containment units on the other side of the stadium-sized area. The growling and snarling echoed in the grandiose Section F. The sounds were sharp enough that I felt them penetrate my bones. When we got to the control centre, Samuel was waiting with a group of scientists and armed forces personnel, watching the containment units warily. The temperature was frigid, so I rubbed my arms to increase circulation. Samuel noticed and gestured to his colleague, who disappeared for a few seconds and returned with a warm lab jacket for me to wear.

"Hi," I said meekly, searching the crowd for a recognizable face.

"Hello Kim, I'm sorry Ana isn't here. She was, but she had a bit of an emotional breakdown, so I asked her to watch from a remote location," Samuel said apologetically.

I tried to hide my disappointment, but I couldn't blame her. I jerked suddenly when a ferocious roar came from one of the distant containers. Whatever it was, it set off an orchestra of increasingly freakish animal noises in response, reminding me of slobbery grunts and howling. The hum of large fans didn't help ventilate; the smell was atrocious.

"Here you go, Kim," a poker-faced military-dressed woman handed me a canvas basket. I peered inside to see a tablet, a water bottle and a pair of headphones.

"There's no internet down here, so we had Zeevax prepare a couple of movies and a few audiobooks to take your mind off your surroundings," Ramesh said.

"Zeevax used your digital history to determine the best diversion for you," Samuel added.

"How long will I be in the tank?" I asked.

"Four hours," Samuel answered.

Ramesh showed me how to use the tablet and assured me that the noise-cancelling headphones were top of the line. He explained that I shouldn't hear the commotion if I kept the volume over thirty. When he finished, the woman who gave me the basket walked me to a bathroom nearby to use the facilities before the trial started.

The tank, positioned in the middle, had nine compartments surrounding it, at most five feet away. The rest of the onlookers would stay thirty-five feet away; otherwise, the Darachnids may sail toward them. Five feet, I was told, was the sweet spot. Ramesh walked me along a pathway of taped arrows on the concrete floor. The taped pointers were blue, then there were orange ones; that's where he stopped.

"Maxine is an automaton that will walk you to the tank," Ramesh said.

I looked at the little robot respectfully. Maxine was a three-and-a-half-foot-tall silver humanoid. I suspected they used biomechanic machines if they were moving these containers with madly infested animals around.

"Thanks, Ramesh. I'll see you in a few hours?" I asked, uncertain.

"I'll be right here the whole time," he said, taking my hand in both hands for a moment.

"Thank you." I smiled melancholically at him. "Okay, Maxine, lead the way."

"Come with me," Maxine said in a mechanical, electronic voice.

I followed Maxine along the orange arrows taped on the floor. I could've walked by myself, but I presumed Maxine was escorting me so I wouldn't feel so alone. I realized it wasn't a tank when we got to our destination. It was more of a chamber surrounded by the cries of terrorized beasts. Maxine pressed a button, and the door slid sideways, opening to a grey room boasting a black lounge chair, a little side table, and a soft yellow lamp. The decor was out of place, like something from *The Twilight Zone*.

The door slid closed immediately after I entered, and I put the headphones on and hit play on the movie I'd already selected. As the soundtrack played, I breathed a huge sigh of relief that I couldn't hear anything but the movie. I sat down in the soft chair and made myself as comfortable as possible under the circumstances. Above me, I noticed a red light flashing beside a camera, so I waved at it ungracefully and pretended I was interested in the movie.

I watched two movies and was in the middle of a mystery audiobook when Maxine came in to get me. The whole experience was relatively uneventful. I knew what was happening around me, but I calmed down while watching the adventure movies. I gathered the things I brought in and followed Maxine to where Ramesh waited. When I took off the headphones, I was reminded of the horror they had been listening to for the past four hours.

"How are you feeling?" Ramesh asked.

"I'm okay. How long do I have to stay here?" I asked, eager to get the hell out of there.

"Let's go. We need to see if the Darachnids could attach to you and your Companion," he answered.

Samuel, Rick, Chris, and three other scientists came with Ramesh and me. We took the monster-sized elevator back to a section where we transferred to the smaller elevator that took us to the DMRM. I went into the scanner with the dark goggles and came out shortly after, looking at Samuel expectantly to see the verdict.

"You are suitably infected with parasites," Samuel confirmed. "We'll give it fifteen hours, and you'll go into the DMRM again, then the Pyramid for the purification bath. After that, we'll begin reinfection in the tank. Rick and Chris will stay with you until the night shift and resume accompanying you tomorrow."

"I'll stay with you for the next two hours; you can keep me apprised of physical sensations or emotional changes you may experience. The Welxus will keep Zeevax up to date on any biological differences," Ramesh said.

"So far, I don't feel anything," I said honestly.

"We can go to the lounge and grab a bite to eat, and I'll monitor your condition. The Darachnids will be delving into a feeding state right now," he said.

"Well, that made me hungry." I rolled my eyes sarcastically.

Chris snorted at my comment. I used affiliative humour often because it helped me and the people around me cope better. We went to the lounge at Commune A to find Ana holding a table for us.

"I'm sorry I wasn't there for you, Kim. I'm so ashamed of myself. I'm usually very professional, but this time I cried. I think the last few weeks have gotten to me," Ana said.

"Oh, please don't mention it. I understand; it was bloody horrifying. I'm going to put the headphones on earlier tomorrow. It was awful to hear those creatures screaming in anguish," I said.

We sat and drank tea with scones, and Ramesh talked about how the strange subatomic particles in the jadeite sample travelled backward through time, allowing them to cross over into the fourth dimension of dark matter. This explained why they repelled the Darachnids, but the synthetic version from Project Arrow wasn't a perfect replication, nor could it be—that's why it failed. Ana's phone started to vibrate, interrupting Ramesh's story. Rick looked almost relieved; I don't think he understood much of what Ramesh said.

"Hey babe," Ana said and continued the conversation in Russian.

I knew it was Andrei. It was weird that she stood up, started talking faster, and walked away. I worried that something was wrong with Aleksander. Ramesh continued talking, but I was straining to hear what Ana was saying and watching her body language. She kept peeking over and looking at me. Finally, she hung up and returned to the table but didn't sit.

"Andrei just called; there's another crisis. He's at the emergency department in the hospital—it's Di," she said with concern.

"Di? I haven't spoken with him because he thinks I'm in Mexico on vacation. What happened?" I questioned.

"He's been beaten badly, and there was an explosion at The Jade Castle. It was consumed by flames when Andrei arrived."

I stood up with my heart racing. "I need to go," I blurted. "Can you take me to the hospital, please?" I turned and looked at Chris.

Chris and Rick stood instantly, and Rick motioned for me to wait. He walked off for privacy and made a phone call to what I guessed were his superiors. Feeling nauseous and guilty, I started to pace. Since the incident at the restaurant, I missed Di, but I had yet to reach out because I was maintaining the precept that I was in Mexico. If Di were in the hospital, then Jing would be frantic, which was terrible for her pregnancy.

"A detail is on its way to meet us at the gate, and safety arrangements are being implemented at the hospital's service entrance," Rick said.

"A hospital is a dangerous place right now; they are overcrowded and understaffed. Are you sure you want to go there?" Ramesh asked.

"Yes," I said, not wanting to get into details with him, so I looked at Ana for support.

"Andrei is there. I'll have him stay with Di until you arrive," she said.

"Then I'm going with you," Ramesh said decidedly.

The four of us left Ana in the lounge, where she was talking on her phone, to venture out and see Di. I was feeling hopeless and having trouble concentrating. Pessimism was not one of my usual qualities, and I wondered if the Darachnids feasting all over me had something to do with it.

"How are you feeling?" Ramesh asked once we got in and buckled our seatbelts in the back of Chris's sedan.

"Heavy," I answered without thinking.

Ramesh seemed upset but tried to control it, probably to keep me from worrying even more than I was already. More images of the end times flashed through my mind. Chris and Rick kept the radio off

*—probably a good thing*, as the news likely would have amplified the negativity we were all experiencing. The two jeeps were waiting at the exit to escort us, and we drove to the hospital.

On our route, military barricades were going up in sporadic areas to redirect traffic to keep people apart. I wondered how long until the government declared martial law, or perhaps they had already.

The ride was grim, and the blackish mixture of smoke rising had increased since my trip earlier to the company. I wondered how many buildings were on fire from arson.

When we got to the hospital, we pulled into the maintenance service entrance. The soldiers in the jeeps parked and got out. Two of them stayed at the back entrance guarding it, and the other two went into the hospital ahead of us.

We took the stairs, which made me realize how badly I was out of shape. I struggled to keep pace with the men, almost out of breath when we got to the eighth floor. When we got to Di's room, I was grateful to see Andrei inside, sitting with Jing.

"Kim," Jing exclaimed and came over to hug me. "Thank you for coming. I tried calling, but your number kept going to voicemail. Andrei reached out to Ana to track you down. I thought you were still in Mexico."

I put my arms around her as I failed to think of something comforting to say. I looked over her shoulder at Di, whose head was bandaged, his right arm and ankles in casts. His eyes were puffy and purple from bruising, and his bottom lip was split open. I held back the urge to be sick.

"Di, Kim's here," Jing said, wiping tears away.

Di moved his head a little, trying to look at me, but I could see he winced in pain, so I hurried around the bed to get closer.

"Di, I'm so sorry this happened." I reached out and held his hand.

"Jing, can you call my mother now? Just outside the room so she doesn't hear us talking," he asked.

Jing stood slowly, holding her back, sore from the pregnancy, said something in Chinese to Di, and left the room.

"Is she gone?" Di asked.

"Yes," I answered.

"I waited until you got here to ask her to call my mother so we could talk privately," Di said with a raspy voice, his words slurring, most likely from his intravenous drugs.

Ramesh and the officers waited outside; it was just Andrei and me in the room with him. "What happened?" I asked.

Di confirmed my worst suspicion. He was alone at the restaurant early in the morning—a workaholic that he was—going over diagrams of the renovations. Suddenly, someone smashed the glass door at the entrance, and three men flew in. One of them introduced himself as Ryan's brother Tony, Di explained. Apparently, the dead guys Andrei and I buried up north had told Tony about their plans to rob the place. After a while, Tony suspected something had happened, so he came to the restaurant looking for answers with the intent to burn it down. Upon finding Di there, Tony had his buddies hold Di while he beat and interrogated him on his brother's whereabouts.

"I never told them what happened. I knew they wouldn't let me go alive when they broke both of my ankles. I wasn't going to jeopardize either of you," Di said.

I was furious. I bit back the urge to start cursing. "How did you get away?" I asked in the calmest voice I could muster.

"I didn't. They set fire to my kitchen…" He paused, choked up, recalling the event before continuing. "They were merciless and told me I was going to burn with my restaurant and hit me a few more times, then some soldiers showed up." He swallowed. "The army guys saved my life. Someone must have called the authorities because the fire was moving fast through all the construction materials in the kitchen."

"Motherfuckers." I growled the word, and Andrei gave me a look, so I shut my mouth.

"When I arrived, the medics were loading Di in the ambulance, and Jade Castle was already up in flames. The paramedics said the fire department had every truck putting out fires all over the city on other calls. I didn't see any soldiers." Andrei's posture tensed.

"The medic said the army had apprehended the men responsible and left shortly after the ambulance arrived," Di said.

Jing returned after calling Di's mother and spoke to Di.

"I'm going to see if I can salvage anything at The Castle. I'll give you my cell phone number, Jing, and you call me if you need anything. I'll be in touch," Andrei said, his lips pressed into a thin line.

"I didn't realize you were back from Mexico, but I should have known your vacation would've been cut short with the world unexpectedly going insane," Jing said sadly.

"It's a war zone out there," I said, purposefully avoiding the topic of my trip.

"Who's the guy with you?" Jing asked, looking over towards the door. "I noticed he has some security guys with him."

I assumed she meant Ramesh; he was sitting in the waiting area with Rick and Chris. The other two soldiers were down the hall near the exit. I had to figure out what to say, so I lied.

"Ramesh is my new boyfriend. He works for Nekxus and holds a significant position on some classified projects; he came with me here. The security detail is for him." I stared into her eyes, willing her to believe my story.

"That's nice of him," Jing said, gazing longingly at her husband.

Di had fallen asleep, and Jing didn't want to leave his side. I stayed with her for a while and kept her company, but the nurses gave Ramesh and the soldiers a hard time. The floor was crowded, and the security team questioned everyone who came and went. I told Jing that my sister was in town for a while and gave her Julia's number in case she couldn't get a hold of me. Jing thanked me and said that some people from work called asking to visit Di, so she had plenty of friends available if she needed anything. I said goodbye to her and left without waking Di; he needed rest to heal.

"I'm ready to go," I told Ramesh, who was texting someone when I came out in the hallway.

We left the same way we came. Rick explained that they were going to drop me off at the condo.

"How do you feel?" Ramesh asked.

"I'm livid. I can't imagine it has anything to do with these bugs crawling through me. I'm just upset about Di."

"I'm sure. Billy messaged while you were in with your friends. It seems that Zeevax has been monitoring your home and workplace.

When the fire alarm in the restaurant went off, Zeevax accessed the security cameras in the area and sent the subcontracted military guys to rescue your friend."

"Seriously?" I exclaimed.

"Yes, and Billy said wherever the soldiers took the thugs, it wasn't the local prison. So you needn't worry about them returning anytime soon," he said.

"Thank God, Zeevax saved Di's life. Do you think you could do me a favour, Chris?" I asked.

"Name it," Chris said.

"Could we drive by The Jade Castle before you drop me off at the condo so I can look at the damage?" I hoped it wouldn't be too inconvenient, as their priorities and mine weren't necessarily aligned.

Chris pushed a button on the steering wheel and spoke to the other vehicles driving with us, indicating we were taking a slight detour.

The drive by The Jade Castle was devastating. I saw complete ruin. There was a hole where the building was; all I could make out was a couple of I-beams; you'd never know what stood there before. The fire department hadn't even shown up; the ground still smouldered. We didn't stay long; there wasn't much to see anyway.

"Try to get some rest tonight, and if you need anything, message me," Ramesh said when we pulled up to the condo.

"I'll try. Won't these parasites crawl onto my dog and Jacob?" I asked, thinking about the five-foot rule.

"A few may detach and move towards another host, but I doubt it. You don't have enough to be crowded; with an abundant food source in you, they have no reason to exert themselves," he answered.

I looked up at the sky after hearing thunder. A storm was building, and I thought I might as well get inside before I got soaked. Ramesh got out of the car to walk me to the front door, and I waved goodbye to Rick and Chris.

"Will I see you tomorrow?" I asked Ramesh, feeling myself biting my lip hopefully.

"Yes, I'll be here every step of the way." He opened the door and gave me a determined look and a gentle smile before walking away.

# CHAPTER 20

*Apnea*

"HOW ARE YOU FEELING? I've been worried," Jacob said while moving aside as Loki barrelled toward me.

"Shitty—Di's in the hospital," I said gloomily while taking off my shoes.

"Loki, drop it," Jacob commanded to the little thief who ran off with one of my sneakers. "What do you mean? Is he okay?"

"Not really; you remember the gunman and the other bastard with the knife Andrei and Di killed in the restaurant?"

"The ones you and Andrei buried up north. Yeah, of course; how could I forget." Jacob followed me into the living room, where I sat down.

"The one guy's brother came with a couple of thugs, and they beat Di within an inch of his life and burned down the restaurant." I wiped tears from my cheeks.

"Holy shit," he exclaimed. "This is bad. I'm so sorry for him and his wife."

Jacob had met them a few times over the years and was fond of Di's wife, especially because she was such a kind person. I told him about Di's injuries and described the gaping hole in the ground where the restaurant used to be.

"It's so depressing. I mean, not only will he be out of commission with his injuries, but the restaurant was becoming what he always dreamed of." Jacob shook his head regretfully. "What about the experiment? Was it put off, or did you go in?"

"It was simultaneously awful and unremarkable," I said.

I spent another half hour talking to Jacob about the sound of the animal uproariousness and the future plans to repeat the process.

"So, you are infested now?" Jacob sat back a little as if to distance himself from me.

"Yeah, with both types. Not enough that they would bother expending the energy to detach and reattach to another host, apparently," I said, scratching my head at the thought.

I stood up and thought better of trusting the company one hundred percent.

"Maybe keep five feet away from me and sleep with Loki tonight, just in case. Give me a second." I put my index finger up in the air.

"I can do that." Jacob rubbed the scruff of Loki's neck.

I video-called my sister.

"Hey, Jules," I said.

"Kim, how did it go?" she asked anxiously.

"Fine. I was hoping you could keep your distance from me for now. The scientists assured me the Darachnids should stay attached to me, but…" I hesitated.

She finished my sentence. "But they've been one hundred percent wrong before. I get it. We shouldn't take any chances."

"That's right, the Darachnids are now feeding off me, including ones that have undergone mutation. I don't want Sherry anywhere near me until we sort this out."

"Understood. I hope this works," she said.

I told Julia roughly about Di's getting assaulted and the fire at Jade Castle. She was horrified but not shocked after watching the news for the last few days. She promised that if Jing called her for anything, she would get the message to me straight away. It'd be hard to predict when I'd be able to get calls on my phone while participating in the experiment.

Jacob made homemade macaroni and cheese. "Dinner's ready."

"Smells great," I said appreciatively.

I didn't eat much during the day, but now I was getting an appetite. We sat at the far ends of the table, away from each other, taking extra precautions, but Loki kept hovering around me. I hoped that the bugs stayed with me or, even better, the rotters could die off.

"Do you feel any different?" Jacob asked in between forkfuls of mozzarella-coated noodles.

"I'm not sure," I answered. "I feel kind of heavy. It's like my muscles are all weaker, or I'm underwater."

"You look depressed," he said, squinting at me.

"That's because I am. My friend, *my boss*, is in brutal condition at the hospital, and the restaurant I work at has burned to the ground. My father died, and I'm covered in shitty little mongrels eating up my happiness." I snivelled and stabbed my fork into my macaroni.

"Mhmm, it's affecting you." Jacob forcefully exhaled between pursed lips.

I did the dishes while Jacob took Loki on the roof to get some fresh air. Afterward, I stood on the spacious balcony and looked at the water. I could hear sirens all over the city. That and the fact that it started to rain might have been a turn-off because Loki and Jacob didn't stay long on the roof.

When they returned, he put the news on the television. Neither of us could help ourselves from watching the horror unfold. The United States imposed martial law. In Canada, the government invoked the War Measures Act and the Emergencies Act for the second time since the pandemic. Both countries had a seven o'clock curfew, and kids were back to online learning. Lockdowns and stay-at-home orders started up again all over the globe. Most news reports were conspiracy-based, blaming people's atrocious behaviour toward each other on the vaccine's side effects.

"That painting is one of your best," Jacob said, returning from the bathroom. He stood in front of my latest work, ignoring the news.

"I painted it from memory. In Commune A, there was an artifact in a glass case titled *Gilded Mummified Scara*—it was stunning. The emerald-encrusted wings of the beetle, gilded in gold, held a giant ruby," I said.

Jacob frowned. "It's no wonder that you are painting bugs now."

"I had the urge to paint after seeing my niece's colouring. I sat staring at a blank canvas. After some time, I asked my Companion, *What do you want me to paint?* The image of the artifact popped into my head. The more I tried to ignore it, the more persistent it was." I shrugged. "So, I painted it."

"It must mean something to your Companion for you to send me back in the house to grab it when we were *running for our lives*." Jacob suppressed a laugh.

"No doubt," I agreed.

I made an apple cinnamon tea with honey and ran myself a bubble bath. Jacob took Loki out to pee on the puppy grass on the balcony then to bed. Relaxing in hot water, I found a little solace from the day; it made me sleepy. I dried off and brushed my teeth. Looking in the mirror, I noticed dark circles forming under my eyes, so I moisturized my skin and crawled under the blankets.

It didn't take long for me to sleep. Once again, I woke convulsing and fighting for breath. This time I had an unpleasant dream of vermin.

In the dream, rats, mice, and squirrels were everywhere. They crawled through the city and into homes by chewing their way through the walls. The rats started attacking me, and the mice and squirrels followed suit, suffocating me. Snakes slithered up through the sewers from underground by the hordes and consumed the critters. That's when I awoke.

It was four in the morning, but I couldn't fall back asleep. I went to bed early, so I resolved to get up and prepare for round two of the Gamma Project.

Ramesh messaged early and asked if I'd be available to come an hour earlier. I responded to Ramesh that I was ready whenever. After saying goodbye to Jacob and Loki, I headed to the lobby to find Chris waiting for me. This time they picked me up in an armoured vehicle instead of a sedan. I admired the custom exterior with high suspension that made it suitable for almost any terrain.

"This is quite a beast, isn't it?"

"She sure is. Now that the prime minister has implemented the War

Measures Act, we get to bring out the good toys," Rick said, patting the hood fondly before opening the door for me.

We drove to Nekxus on the main highway. It was so dead that it was eerie. At least people were staying off the roads. I saw more military than civilian vehicles on our route, which might have explained why there was no traffic. I looked in the sky to see quite a few black helicopters buzzing around.

The stay-at-home order made it easy to control people, although I did witness one pickup truck driver arguing foolishly with a couple of soldiers; otherwise, nothing.

Ramesh was waiting at the entrance for me. Chris and Rick said they would see me later and be close if I needed them. "Good morning," I said.

"Is it? How are you feeling? You look well," Ramesh bumbled.

"Not bad; I was feeling heavy yesterday, but I think seeing Di in the hospital had a lot to do with it," I said.

"We don't want to count anything out. Zeevax can find the strangest things from data that we wouldn't look twice at." Ramesh directed me to one of the smaller escalators, which took us to a private room furnished with modern sofas and chairs.

*Did he bring me to a shrink's office?* The colours were warm browns, and soothing instrumental music played in the background.

"I'm going to talk to a psychiatrist?" I questioned, looking around for the doctor.

Ramesh gave me an amused look. "No, I thought you might like to come here and relax a bit away from the militaristic atmosphere before we continue with the project."

"Oh, it doesn't bother me at all. You know I grew up on a military base, right?" I asked.

"I did read about it."

"I'm a bonafide army brat." I saluted comically at him.

"That must explain your courage," he said, holding my gaze a little longer than expected.

"It's not courage; it's resilience," I corrected. "We all have to adapt to change."

"That's the explanation of a philosophy major," Ramesh said.

"There was something I keep forgetting to mention. I don't know if it matters, but it keeps happening. I think I have sleep apnea," I said as the thought struck me suddenly.

"Zeevax, do Kim's files indicate any record of sleep apnea?" Ramesh asked.

"There are no records of sleep apnea. Further tests would be required to confirm this condition," Zeevax responded.

"What makes you think you have apnea?" Ramesh asked.

"I wake up gasping for air, usually during some bizarre nightmare."

"Zeevax, should we test for sleep apnea?" Ramesh inquired.

"Yes, I will arrange for nocturnal polysomnography. The Wekxus had logged some strange readings during Kim's sleep cycle, and apnea could be the cause," Zeevax replied.

"I shouldn't have said anything," I grunted and sat back in my seat.

Ramesh chuckled. "It's not so bad. The Medicorium has charming little rooms set up for sleep studies."

"Let me guess, state-of-the-art equipment?" I asked, raising my eyebrow at him.

"That's right, no tubes up your nose or anything like that. They'll monitor your heart, lungs, brain activity, and blood oxygen levels while you sleep inside a specialized capsule. You'll have a great sleep." Ramesh gave me a warm, reassuring smile.

"It sounds like you've had experience," I said.

"Many of us here at Nekxus have participated in sleep studies," he said.

We sipped herbal tea, and Ramesh showed me some of my medical records on a tablet. Time flew by, and we made our way to the DMRM. Soldiers were spread out around the complex, stationed near the entrances and elevators.

"Good morning, Kim; I want to introduce you to Diego." Samuel walked towards us with a slender middle-aged man I recognized from the display monitor from the boardroom days ago.

Diego reached out to shake my hand. "Hello, Kim."

"Hi," I said, clasping his hand and giving a firm shake, noting that his palms were warm and sweaty.

"I wanted to meet you personally and express my gratitude for all you're doing to help Nekxus battle against these dark forces," he said.

"Nekxus has been very accommodating; I am glad to be of service," I said.

He didn't mention the meteor sample of exotic matter, and I sure wasn't going to bring it up. I was promptly ushered to the DMRM so we could get going on the Gamma Project. This scan was like lightning compared to the Pyramid, which would take three hours. Then to the awful tank, which would take four.

There was a buzz of discussion amongst the scientists, and a few raised eyebrows when I came out. Ramesh hurried from the monitoring platform over to talk to me.

"It's amazing; you're clear," he said.

"You need to get Jacob and Loki in here immediately," I exclaimed.

My heartbeat raced, and I felt panicky. Where the hell did they go if the damn bugs weren't attached to me anymore?

"Zeevax has already dispatched a team to retrieve them, and Samuel is on the phone with Jacob right now," Ramesh assured.

Hearing his words, I calmed down but still felt apprehension. I looked at Ramesh and phrased the question in my mind: *What if I am cursed?* First, the failed Project Arrow, with *my* contributed sample and *my* immunity to the dark matter creatures, potentially put those I loved at risk.

"You aren't cursed," Ramesh said, putting his hand on my shoulder.

"You heard me," I gasped.

"What do you mean?"

"I asked you, *What if I'm cursed?* And you answered," I said.

"Oh, I didn't hear your words; I just read your face," Ramesh said. "Your Companion would have expressed your words to mine, in any case. Interesting it was able to pick up the exact phrase."

Samuel and Diego walked over to join us.

"Jacob will come in with your dog for a DMRM scan, just in case. We don't expect that the Darachnids have infected them, but we aren't going to take any chances," Samuel said.

"I'm worried," I said. I looked toward the pod and imagined Jacob and Loki inside.

"We hope that you and your Companion radiate harmful particles that are toxic to the Darachnids," Diego said thoughtfully.

"Same here," I said.

Samuel, Ramesh, and a couple of scientists led me directly to the Gamma tank for *reinfection*. There was no need for a Pyramid bath. Samuel expressed concern about this unexpected outcome because, although it was good that the Darachnids were gone, it was unknown why. Therefore, the test might give them a different answer than they sought. The Gamma Project included purification in the Pyramid and reinfection. In my unique circumstance, one stage of the equation was omitted. No one could say for sure what that meant for the experiment; we'd have to continue testing to see if the results would be reproduced.

Once in Section F, I put on the headphones as soon as they were handed to me by a soldier and tilted my head apologetically toward Ramesh. I was getting polluted with Darachnids, but he would have to spend the next four hours hearing the grisly tortured cries of the wretched creatures in their containment units. I didn't ask why, but no one else seemed to have earplugs.

Maxine was waiting for me, and I followed the android to the chamber and sat in the chair to finish reading the novel I'd started the previous day. I worried the Darachnids crossed the hall during the night and infected little Sherry. I couldn't sit still, shifting around in the chair the whole time. I hated feeling so helpless. Maxine reappeared, and I knew the four hours were up. I felt anxious when I saw Ramesh waiting for me because Samuel was beside him.

I took off the headphone and winced when I heard the animal screams. "Jacob and Loki—how are they?"

"Jacob and your dog are clear. They have nothing," Samuel said, looking puzzled.

"What does that mean?" I practically had to yell the words to him to be able to hear my voice over the howling behind me.

"Let's get out of here," Ramesh said.

Once we entered the elevator, Samuel answered my question. "We don't know what it means exactly. Zeevax has theorized that you are terminating the Darachnids somehow," he said, his voice conveying his hope.

"Great, let's figure out how to kill them all," I said bitterly.

"That's the plan," Samuel said.

"Zeevax is convinced that your apnea has something to do with your ability to ward off the parasite and has given us instructions to surround the sleep capsule with sensors similar to the ones we placed at your residence," Samuel said.

"Between the rare genomes we found in your DNA and the curious readings we've collected at night from the Welxus, there must be an answer," Zeevax interjected.

"Jacob and Loki are waiting to visit with you at the lounge before they return to your condo," Ramesh said.

We went to the DMRM and confirmed I was indeed infected with Darachnids again, but less so than before. It was a fractional amount, but I was assured that the infestation consistently increased in the previous Gamma Project experiment.

Samuel told me that if I needed anything, make a request. If no one was around, I could ask Zeevax, and they would do their best to accommodate me. He thanked me for my continued cooperation and left for a conference call.

Ramesh accompanied me to Commune A, and Loki almost lost his mind when he saw me. It drew the attention of everyone around. Jacob held tight to Loki's leash, and he whined and moaned until I got close enough for physical contact. Ana was with them; she looked stressed but better than the last time I'd seen her.

"Hey guys," I said, sitting down, trying to dodge the continuous face-licking from Loki, who eventually settled on my lap.

"Loki and I have been getting first-class treatment since I got the call that scared the shit out of me." Jacob's eyes bulged then he wrinkled his nose.

"I can relate; I dreaded thinking I did more harm than good again." I ran my fingers through my hair. "Have you heard anything from Andrei about Di?" I asked, looking over to Ana.

"Yes, he's in stable condition," she said. "Andrei dropped in there this morning and had to wait an hour to see Di before there was a line-up of friends eager to see him."

That was no surprise to hear. Di was a fantastic person. As an employer, he was kind and fair. If I hadn't seen him cut Jimmy's throat with my own eyes, I never would have believed he did it. I'm sure this pestilence had something to do with his reaction. His instincts were correct. However, they weren't just going to let us go.

"It looks like I'll be sleeping in the Medicorium tonight. I'm finally going to get that sleep apnea checked out." I winked at Jacob.

"Now I want to sleep there too. Maybe your fucking nightmares are so scary that they frighten the parasites to death," Jacob joked. "Loki and I will survive. You folks need to figure this shit out. I want my best friend back." He directed his attention toward Ramesh, who hadn't said anything. "I'm Jacob, by the way." He reached out to shake Ramesh's hand.

"Nice to meet you." Ramesh took it and smiled.

"I'm sorry, guys, I'm so rude." I shrank in my chair.

"Oh, shut up, Kim; you are preoccupied with the end of times; no one thinks you're rude. Especially not with me around," Jacob jested.

Ana grinned. Seeing her face relax after being so wound up was good; she left after a short time. Ramesh, Jacob and I had dinner together. Jacob was going to leave, but Ramesh insisted he stay so I could spend more time with him and Loki.

"So, Ramesh, what do you think? Do aliens from outer space exist?" Jacob asked Ramesh, which caused me to spit out my drink, stunned.

"Certainly," Ramesh answered and handed me a napkin.

I looked at Ramesh apologetically, but Jacob continued.

"I think they must come from this strange hidden dimension. If there are little fucking bugs, what else lives there? Area 51 supposedly has a crashed ship from 1947. Does Nekxus know about that?" Jacob stared at Ramesh, searching for answers.

"If they do, it's above my clearance level." Ramesh shrugged casually.

He handled Jacob like a pro, eventually winning him over. When we walked Jacob to the exit, I snuggled Loki and told him to behave, and Jacob told me the same. Then he poked me in the ribcage and whispered, "I like him."

"So do I."

Ramesh and I hung out in the lounge for a while then went to the Medicorium, where the doctors had prepared a sleep lab for me. I was a little creeped out but also impressed that they had a suitcase waiting with some of my belongings, including my pyjamas.

"It was for your safety and efficiency that Nekxus sent a couple officers to gather a few of your belongings," Ramesh explained before I had the chance to ask him.

"Who made a list?" I asked, thinking it must have been Ana.

"Zeevax," Ramesh answered.

# CHAPTER 21
## *Scarab*

"IF I WASN'T IMPRESSED before, I sure am now. Zeevax thought of everything," I said, rifling through the bag with my belongings.

Ramesh showed me the sleep capsule. *Lucky for me, I'm not claustrophobic*, I thought, seeing it was a couple of metres long and around a metre and a half wide within another room. At least there was a sink and toilet in there. That would provide a little privacy for me if I got up to stretch or use the bathroom. Inside the oval capsule were control dials for temperature, music, and light. Relaxing symphonies, nature recordings, or white noise were the three selections. One of the nurses, who introduced herself as Tiana, showed me a panic button. She'd be monitoring the cameras, along with Zeevax.

"I'm surprised to see dials and buttons. Everything else here is so high-tech. No touch screen or voice activation?"

"Sorry, but the electronics in these sensors are quite sensitive, recalibrated to detect gravitational waves and quantum fluctuations," Ramesh said.

He pointed around the room at the parabolic disc-shaped bowls wired to clunky equipment that looked like stuff out of *Star Wars*.

"I'm kidding. It's refreshing to see the buttons around all these sophisticated gadgets. Don't apologize." I smiled. "How long do you work anyway? It's getting late; when does your shift finish?"

"Oh, I'm finished. We make our own hours usually, and I'm on call when needed. It's my job right now to help keep you content enough to continue participating voluntarily…" He faltered.

"What would happen if I didn't volunteer?"

At first, Ramesh didn't answer. His face contorted into confusion as if he was struggling to find the words. His eyes flicked upwards, then he held my gaze. *Zeevax is listening.* The words formed in my mind, and I was convinced Ramesh was using his Companion to interact. I realized he didn't want to answer. That told me enough.

"It's very generous of you to offer your assistance," Ramesh said a little too formally.

I decided to get him off the hook. "It's the right thing to do."

"If you think you're good here, I'll go home and get some rest and be here early tomorrow morning to see how things went," he said.

"As good as it gets under the circumstances," I said.

"Sleep well, Kim." He lightly brushed my hair off my cheek, which caused my heart to flutter.

"You too," I said, feeling idiotic for blushing again.

He closed the door behind him, and I looked around the small room crowded with mechanical devices and the sleeping vessel. I felt alone. Each passing day got weirder and weirder, I reflected. Self-pity was not a redeeming quality, so I tried not to feel anxious about my life's bizarre turn. I had to bend down to crawl into the pint-sized container to sleep.

I put the light as dim as possible without shutting it off and turned the temperature dial to point to cool. The classical music seemed relaxing enough, and I lay on my back, trying not to think. That was useless; my mind raced in circles. *What could be so different about me that I drive away this foreign parasite?*

Something magical was happening, and of course, like in every fairy tale, a monster in the dark feeds off of the good leaving evil in its wake. Had Companions influenced history's famous storytellers and myths? This dark creature had been plaguing us for centuries, and I suspected the Darachnids could be held responsible for many terrible events.

I woke up twice during the night but had little trouble falling asleep again. The capsule was relatively comfortable. Eventually, I got up and brushed my teeth. After dressing, I gathered my bag and opened the door to find the nurse. Tiana was sitting across the hall behind a control panel and waved for me to come over.

"Good morning, Kim; come check out your sleep study results," she said. "Your apnea-hypopnea index is severe. The average number of respiratory events was over thirty per hour. Your sleep cycle is fragmented, and your apnea worsens during REM sleep. You stopped breathing for over two minutes at one time during the night. I almost woke you up, but you resumed breathing."

"Two minutes!" I exclaimed. "I can't even hold my breath underwater for thirty seconds."

"Your fight or flight response was triggered, your legs jerked, and you started breathing again. It's very stressful for your heart." Tiana put her hand on her chest, emphasizing. "Get that addressed as soon as possible, whenever they finish with you." She jutted her chin towards the sensory equipment.

"Ramesh is on his way," Zeevax stated.

"Okay, great, I was just about to ask." I looked at Tiana, who tilted her head and gave me a tight smile when Zeevax spoke.

She showed me the four stages of my sleep cycle in charts. She explained that I fell asleep fast, spending next to no time in the first stage of sleep. I spent about half of my night in the REM stage, which was above average.

"You see here." She pointed at the monitor to a bunch of wavy lines. "The sleep spindles are all over the place, and over here, it almost looks like you had a seizure similar to epilepsy."

Tiana pointed to a few areas on the screen, but to me, they just looked like strange patterns of wavy lines. She changed the view to show the chart in three dimensions, making it look neat but no more relevant to me than before.

"Good morning," Ramesh said, startling me. I was too preoccupied with the animated graphs to hear him come up behind us.

"Morning," I said, smiling.

I must have said it a little too cheerfully because I saw Tiana's eyebrows raise for a second, then she smirked at me.

"How did you sleep?"

"Fine—check out my chart." I stood aside so he could take a closer look.

Ramesh asked Tiana a couple of questions about what they were looking at, and they talked a little bit about brain waves and temporal lobe epilepsy.

"Kim and Ramesh, Samuel requests your presence in the boardroom," Zeevax interrupted.

"We better go," Ramesh said.

"Thank you, Tiana. It was nice meeting you," I said.

"Likewise."

Ramesh picked up my overnight bag up and carried it for me. A shuttle was waiting for us outside. The military personnel patrolled the grounds in pairs; I had the familiar sensation that I was back on the army base again, where I used to watch the recruits practising their foot drills everywhere. When we entered Commune A, Ana was waiting at the bottom of the escalator, waving anxiously at us.

"Hey, is everything okay?" I asked.

"Well, the world is falling apart, but other than that, I'd say so," she said sarcastically.

She stepped on the escalator ahead of me, and Ramesh followed behind us.

"Who's waiting for us, Ana?" Ramesh asked in a severe tone.

"Everyone," she answered.

"Did they find something helpful?" I asked.

"I don't know. Zeevax told me it was priority one, and Samuel requested all senior staff and you. I wanted to wait for you so we could go in together. It must be overwhelming enough for you," she said, looking at me with concern.

I shrugged. It could be a good thing. I wasn't staff, let alone senior team, so hopefully, the Nekxus geniuses discovered how my Companion and I repelled the Darachnids. Ramesh didn't share my optimism; he was biting his nails. He stopped when he saw me watching, wrinkled his nose, and smirked at me.

When we entered the boardroom, we found it packed. This time a few high-ranking military officers stood with the Nekxus personnel.

"Good, you're all here; we can get started," Samuel said. "I've already brought Captain Gordon and Colonel Anderson up to speed with your unique capability Kim; they are here to observe and contribute their tactical expertise." Samuel held his arm towards two decorated officers, then looked at the slate grey wall behind him. "Zeevax has analyzed all the data and come up with a plan—Zeevax, please display the eradication strategy."

The wall lit up like a screen at a movie theatre. Segments of the wall on the left showed video feeds of awful active global atrocities. Riots and fires were breaking out everywhere. The world was plunging into desolation. I made eye contact with Rick across the room, who gave me brief eye contact before he looked back toward Samuel.

"As you all know, we've started the Gamma Project, and Kim has evaded full contamination of the Darachnids. We don't know how she's doing this yet, but some discoveries have brought us here today, so we can decide how to proceed. For those who don't know, this is my assistant Beth; she will take it from here." Samuel walked to the window and folded his arms across his chest.

Beth may have been the shortest person in the room, but she commanded everyone's attention when she started speaking. Her voice was gravelly, and she looked around the room with a piercing gaze. She gave me the creeps.

"Kim participated in a sleep study last night to check for apnea and other peculiar readings. We had the physics team set up the room she stayed in with our most sensitive quantum and gravitational detection sensors in hopes of picking something up." Beth turned around and pointed to an image that resembled infrared. "You see this here?" she asked rhetorically and continued without waiting for anyone to answer. "The mass set off our sensors, and the blurry object came from underground at the precise moment Kim's sleep apnea caused her fight or flight response to kick in." Beth used her hands to make a cup around the glowing area. "Zeevax has created a computer-simulated scene of what occurred. Zeevax, please play simulation Ground One."

"Rendered," Zeevax responded.

Everyone was quiet as Zeevax projected the computer-simulated video. I recognized the room's shape and pod; otherwise, I had the impression we were watching a video game play out. A slightly transparent person represented me, the bones and organs visible. Black bugs were nestled inside the body like grapes on a vine. We watched as the character crawled into the sleeping vessel and lay down.

"Fast forward to the event," Beth said.

Watching my bug-infested avatar flopping around like a fish out of water inside the little pod was strange. I looked around the room. Everyone was watching the screen intently.

"Slowing down," Zeevax said.

"Please explain to us what you suspect is happening, Zeevax," Beth said.

The avatar lay perfectly still for a long time. Then a glowing light radiating from the centre of its head started to pulse—waves resembling water ripples radiated outward from the body in all directions. The solid objects didn't hinder it. It went through the ceiling and the floor without interruption. At first, the waves were red and long, then they shortened and turned yellow.

"You can see Kim has stopped breathing, and her heart is in distress. This caused a reaction between her body and the Companion. Communication of distress is believed to trigger the creation of a signal. The frequency this signal produces radiates into the fourth dimension. Here you can see the mass coming up from the earth underneath her," Zeevax said.

We watched as a substantial fuzzy blob of green light came from underneath the avatar and shrunk as it got closer. It was like the image at an optometrist's office when they changed the lens, and the picture got sharper. The green mass shrunk until it was a darker shade of green and enveloped the body. Then the avatar twitched and gasped for air before rolling over and fluffing the pillow. The black bugs faded until only the green glow pulsed then slowly descended and faded back down to the ground from which they came.

"The Darachnids have been consumed by the mysterious life form we have yet to identify," Beth said.

This revelation caused a stir. The deadly quiet room was suddenly filled with unintelligible babbling, and everyone began to talk at once. I witnessed looks of shock, and people glanced at me as they discussed this discovery. I could hear tidbits of the conversations like *is it another organism?* and *what does this mean?*

"After reviewing the new data combined with centuries of information on the fourth dimension—there is a highly probable theory. A species of carnivorous Scarabaeidae inhabits the hidden dimension. Theoretically, the beetle is vibration sensitive. Kim's Companion, under life-threatening duress, sets off a substrate-borne vibration into the fourth dimension on a low frequency that alerts a swarm of predatory beetles that feed on the Darachnids," Zeevax stated.

"As you all know, Zeevax has access to enormous amounts of information and uses quantum computing to postulate the scenario you watched in the simulation. We are very confident that the accuracy of this rundown is likely," Beth added.

"Wow, that's crazy," I said to Ana in a hushed tone.

"This is the first I'm seeing of this," Ana said thoughtfully.

"We need to confirm Zeevax's assessment." Samuel stepped forward, and Beth took a chair and sat.

"How?" Colonel Anderson asked.

"Zeevax has suggested we set up a sleep experiment in the DMRM and have Kim sleep in there in the hopes that her apnea causes the same reaction. We need to put her through reinfection, of course." Samuel looked at me.

I wasn't a big fan of being spoken of in the third person, but I could see it made sense in a room full of people who didn't know me.

"The DMRM goes so quick, though. How will you time it to get a good view of what's going with these creatures in the dark dimension?" Colonel Anderson asked.

"Zeevax had calculated the timing between the length of time Kim stopped breathing to when she sent out the signal; the event happens shortly after, and we have sensors to ensure a ripple is recorded before turning the DMRM on," Samuel said.

"Do it," the colonel said. "Keep me updated, Samuel." The colonel nodded at Samuel and strode out of the boardroom, followed by Captain Gordon, who made no eye contact with anyone.

"I don't like him," Ramesh said to Ana.

"He does seem impolite," she commented.

"Is he the one in charge here?" I asked.

"Hard to say; he's in charge of something. I've never seen Samuel answer like that to anyone," Ana said.

I looked over to see Rick watching Samuel give instructions to a small group of scientists on how to set up the room so I'd feel comfortable enough to sleep. I had an uneasy feeling from the chilly quality the colonel gave off. *Am I in danger?* I asked Rick in my head. Getting answers this way was unreliable, but I learned it was effective when the question couldn't be asked outright.

Rick turned his head, pressed his lips into a thin line, and held eye contact with me until I blinked. My mouth went dry, and I looked away.

"Excuse me for a minute," Ana said, walking purposefully across the room to join Samuel.

"I need to use the washroom; be right back," I told Ramesh.

"I'll wait here," he said.

I went to the washroom, making eye contact with Beth. Her small eyes were close together, considering the size of her face, which reminded me of a wolf. I smiled at her awkwardly, something I occasionally did when I was nervous, and she looked away as if it made her uncomfortable.

In the washroom, I stood in front of the mirror and looked into my reflection to find my skin looked ashen. *What the hell have we gotten ourselves into?* I asked myself. A toilet flushed, so I turned the tap on to splash water on my face.

"I don't envy you, but I can say you've earned respect," a young woman dressed in an officer's uniform said.

"I appreciate that, thank you," I said.

"I wish you good luck, Kim. We're all counting on you," she said, leaving me dumbfounded.

Her words had a profound effect on how I was feeling. I never imagined being counted on for anything other than perhaps Loki's dinner. This was surreal. My parents always told my sister and me that life would take unexpected turns and that we needed to learn to adapt. I felt like Nekxus was doing all the heavy lifting, but I had the sneaking suspicion that was about to change. I took a deep breath and exhaled slowly to gain control of my paranoid thoughts before rejoining the others.

I strolled casually to the window where Ramesh was now sitting. I could hear a little of what Ana and Samuel discussed about the plans Zeevax had displayed. Rick was whispering with Ramesh and looking out the window.

"How are you, Rick?" I asked.

"Fine. I'll leave you two for now. I've got to join the captain. If you need *anything*, message me—Ramesh has my direct line." Rick saluted us and left the boardroom.

"That was weird? Or maybe I'm crazy?" I asked Ramesh.

"According to your psychological evaluation, Zeevax determined that you are sane," Ramesh said flatly.

I felt my jaw drop, quickly closed my mouth, and stared at him. Slowly the corners of his lips turned upright until his teeth gleamed bright white through a full-blown smile. Then he winked at me.

"Christ, I thought you were serious," I slapped his leg lightly, smiling back at him.

"It's true. I considered telling you that your analysis showed that you were certifiable, but I figured you might not see the humour." He chuckled and opened his arms.

"Oh, I didn't realize you were a comedian," I said, grinning and shaking my head.

I looked out the window and immediately noticed what they were looking at. From this higher floor, we could see the military presence had doubled or even tripled since the previous day. Armed soldiers were everywhere. Most of the green space at Nekxus was covered in canvas military tents and equipment. The only thing I didn't see were tanks—yet, I thought to myself. Ana walked toward us.

"Chris will escort you both to Sector F for recontamination," Ana said.

"Recontamination is a horrid word for the dreadful procedure," I said.

"I know, Kim. Believe me; No one's happy about it. If it makes you feel better, Samuel has promised that if and when we come up with a workable solution, he will find time to put all the participating animals in the Pyramid then into a medical rehabilitation program. The American Nekxus office excels at formulating effective drugs for treating most conditions."

"I'm praying to whatever God is listening; you brainiacs, find a way to overcome this," I said sarcastically.

"I am, too," she agreed.

Chris came over to join us, carrying a weapon. I doubted the Cosmic Saviours would get anywhere near the complex, but perhaps his concern ran beyond the cult. I hadn't checked the news yet but felt it was better to keep concentrating on what Nekxus asked of me so they could find ammunition in this war against the invasive dark matter. Interestingly, the solution seemed to lie in the hidden dimension itself.

"Ready?" Chris asked.

"I am." I looked at Ana.

"I will meet you at the DMRM this afternoon," she said, chewing on her lip.

"I'll stay with you." Ramesh put his hand on the centre of my back to usher me.

"See you soon," Ana said, sighing.

I followed Chris out of the boardroom. I glanced at Samuel, who raised his head to look at me, then bowed it to go back to whatever they were discussing in the circle of experts. We didn't say much on the way to level 161. The presence of the military didn't intimidate me; if anything, I found it reassuring. Of course, what concerned me was the purpose of their occupation of the Nekxus property.

"Are military setting up like this at all of the Nekxus locations around the globe?" I asked Chris.

"Yes, one-third of the international military units belong to a matrix organization that controls the planetary defence systems. Nekxus is a member of the organization for reasons I'm sure are obvious to you," Chris said.

"Military has the armoury, but Nekxus rules technologically," I said.

"You got it," Chris said. "We can help with the chaos here in our world, but when it comes to other dimensions and stuff like that, Nekxus is the front line of defence." Chris put his hands up in surrender.

Ramesh stood a little straighter at Chris's comment to indicate he took his role in this war very seriously. We arrived at Section F, and one of the scientists was kind enough to hand me the headphones immediately when we got off the elevator to spare me a few extra minutes of the anguished cries from the creatures. Maxine was waiting for me, and I followed the droid to go for another round of Darachnid infestation.

# CHAPTER 22
## *Debate*

I PUT on the movie *Troy* and watched the Trojans and Greeks fight. I tried to focus on the ancient battle and ignore my surroundings. The film was over three hours long, but I had a little more time to kill before Maxine came to retrieve me, so I played an audiobook and focused on trying to solve a whodunnit. Finally, Maxine came in, and I followed the robot to where Ramesh was waiting.

He looked stressed and needed a shave. We headed directly for the exit, where I handed the headphones to Ramesh, he set them on a stand, then we left for the DMRM. Ana looked busy speaking with a couple of scientists when we arrived.

"There you are," she said and walked towards us.

"Let's get this over with," I said, eager to return to the lounge; my fascination with their modern technology had waned.

Ramesh flinched, and I regretted my curtness. Ana walked me to the machine this time and handed me the goggles. After the scan, she confirmed both variations of the Darachnids were inside me.

"Let's have lunch, Kim; Ramesh has a meeting," Ana said.

"Sure," I said, looking at Ramesh.

"I'll catch up later," he said.

On the shuttle back to the main building, Ana went over the plan to have me sleep in the DMRM. While I slept, Zeevax would monitor my breathing until it stopped, then Zeevax would have the DMRM record the presence of the theoretical Scaraboids from the fourth dimension coming to feed on the Darachnoids. It seemed simple enough.

"You have a couple of bouts of apnea per night, and once the DMRM gets confirmation of the Scaraboids, the plan is to wake you and move you to the CS for the rest of the night. Getting a recording of your Companion's distress signal is the ultimate goal," Ana said.

"Hopefully, I'll be able to fall back asleep. Will my Companion even signal after the Scaraboids already ate all the Darachnids?"

"Zeevax and the scientists whose authority it is to study the data have concluded that your Companion will signal when it feels threatened. It doesn't matter whether or not the Darachnid parasite is present," she said.

"I hope you're right," I said.

"Video footage of the Scaraboids feeding on the Darachnids is important. That's why you must get the DMRM scan first—so the scientists have all the information needed to weaponize the beetles."

That made sense to me. "Aren't you eating?" I asked.

"I'm not hungry right now," Ana said with a forced smile.

I was suspicious of her not eating. Ana's appetite matched mine, and I'd never seen her refuse to eat anything. *Is there something you aren't telling me?* I thought as I stared at her while she looked out the window. Ana avoided making direct eye contact with me, picked at her clothing nervously, and swallowed hard. I knew she felt stressed with all that was happening, so I chalked it up to anxiety.

"Have you heard any news about Di? I was going to phone Jing. I doubt they'll let me out of here to visit right now," I asked.

"Andrei was there yesterday, and he said Di was improving." She crossed her legs and leaned forward towards me with her elbows on the table. "For the time being, you must stay here; too much is at stake."

I suspected as much. There was no way to beat around the bush. They weren't asking much from me anyway, so I didn't dare complain. People were killing each other because they were suffering from this dark affliction. The lounge was crowded compared to the first time I was here—people dressed in plain clothes mixed with others in uniforms. The atmosphere was noisy with nervous chatter.

"Is there somewhere private I could go to make a couple of phone calls?" I asked Ana.

"Certainly, let's get out of here." She stood and motioned for me to follow her.

We went down the gigantic escalator and around the main lobby behind the moving stairways. Ana palmed a scanner, and the door marked as L-8 opened to a small private lounge area. It was one of twenty. She informed me as I glanced down the hallway to see rows of doors.

"I'm letting Ramesh know where we are," she said, tapping her phone.

Ramesh joined us only a short time after I called Jing. He was carrying a leather briefcase with an expression I couldn't quite recognize. It looked a little like anguish, but I wasn't sure.

I called Jacob while Ana and Ramesh sat on the couch, discussing the machine the Nekxus engineers set up for the CS. Most of what they said was technical, and I wouldn't have understood it anyway. I video-called Jacob so he could point the camera toward Loki. I whistled and cooed on the phone to my little fur baby. My heart ached as I watched his head turn sideways and bob around, searching for me with his tail wagging. I assured Jacob I was being treated well before ending the call.

"I'm going to call my sister now," I said to them so I didn't appear rude being on the phone.

Neither of them seemed to notice me anyway. They were both absorbed in some crazy-looking diagram Ramesh had pulled out of the briefcase to show Ana. I shrugged, sat in the corner chair, video-called my sister and explained I'd be here at least one more night, then gabbed with my niece for.

"I need to see this for myself. Those fools will wreck my machine if they aren't careful." Ana stood abruptly, sounding pissed.

"I know." Ramesh let out a sigh.

"I apologize for running off again, Kim. Ramesh will be here for you. I must go ensure those mechanical guys don't break the CS scanner. They have no idea how delicate some of the electronic components are," she said.

"It's okay," I said, trying to sound disappointed even though I didn't mind being alone with Ramesh.

At my insistence, we went for a walk around the complex to get some fresh air. Ramesh assured me there were no rules prohibiting it even though the army had stationed themselves around the property. He talked about his work at the Nekxus branch in India, before transferring here to Ontario and about missing his family. Since I was like one of the Nekxus *science projects*, I didn't need to talk about *my life*. I was fully aware that he'd already studied it thoroughly.

We had dinner in the private room and conversed about anything except current events. Time flew by, and before long, it was time to head to the DMRM. Chris showed up to collect me, and I said goodnight to Ramesh. Beth was waiting for our arrival at the DMRM, and I tried not to cringe upon seeing her.

"Hello, Kim," she said crisply.

"Hi," I said, looking over her shoulder for Samuel.

"Samuel is predisposed; *I* will show you to the chamber."

I speculated that Beth was good at reading my thoughts. I followed her as she waded through a group gathered around the entrance, down to the machine entrance. Inside they had set up an all-black canopy bed, reminding me of something out of a gothic magazine.

"This should be adequate, there's a change of clothes in the washroom for you, and I took the liberty of stacking a couple of books for you to relax. Sorry, but no electronic devices in here." Beth held her hand out, and I handed her my phone.

I shifted the curtain aside to peek at the bed with black pillows and sheets. After my mother died, I wanted my bedroom decorated like this, all in black, and my dad refused to allow it. Now, I could see why —it was depressing. Five books were sitting on the bed, and I noted they were all mystery novels by the same author I'd already been reading. One of them was the same book, and I picked it up.

"Thanks," I said, putting the book on top of the others. "I can pick up where I left off."

"That's what I figured," she said smugly.

I used the private washroom to brush my teeth and change into flannel pyjamas with the Nekxus logo. I walked from the bathroom to the DMRM; it was uncannily quiet. I peeked around, and there was still a couple of dozen personnel, but none looked my way, nor did they talk to each other. I was sure they had instructions to keep it down so I could rest. *Pretend you're in a crowded campground*, I told myself, and went into the dimly lit machine to read. The bed was comfortable, as were all the furnishings at the company. I read for a while, fantasizing about going home the next day, thinking about Jacob and Loki, and eventually dozed off.

---

"Kim, wake up." Beth's gravelly voice jerked me out of my blissful stupor.

I opened my eyes to find the curtain pulled back, the room lit up like Christmas, and the grinch Beth standing over me. "I'm getting up." I yawned. "Did it work?"

"Yes, yes, it went very well. Now come, we must get you to the CS right away," Beth said unceremoniously, thrusting her hand under my elbow to lead me to the exit.

She walked me to the waiting shuttle with a soldier I recognized from the boardroom. Once we arrived at the CS, I searched for Ana.

"Ana and Ramesh are not here," Beth said, again noticing me strain my neck to browse the unfamiliar faces. "I sent them home—they're both exhausted. I don't know why they insist on coddling you while we struggle for survival. This isn't a sanctuary retreat."

I was taken aback by her sharp words, but I could see her point. "I'm here of my own free will, and I understand this is serious," I said, defensive.

"Do you, though?" she snipped.

The soldier with us gave her a look, and she turned red but went quiet.

"I'll take you the rest of the way," he said.

Beth looked like she was about to protest but decided not to and walked away. The soldier gave me a small smile and gestured his arm out with his hand open as if to say *After you*. I took a deep breath and walked toward the washroom to change into the white linen material necessary to wear in the CS scanner.

"The thing up there should make it dark enough for you." The soldier pointed to the claw above the glass cube.

I saw a dome overtop the claw, and the cube had transparent plastic cables with lights I guessed were a type of fibre optic I'd never seen before. The only decor was a white mattress and blankets made from the same linen I was wearing.

"Yeah, once it comes down overtop the cube, it will make a difference," I said hopefully.

"I'll take your Welxus. You can't wear it in this machine," he said, holding out his hand.

"How will they know when to scan?" I handed him the bracelet.

"From what I understand, it will be running the whole time." He shrugged and marched off.

I stepped into the cube, the door shut behind me, and the claw covered with a dome made from metal and polymer panels descended overtop. The machine hummed, and I lay down on the mattress. It was harder to relax here. I tossed and turned for a few hours before hearing a familiar voice.

"Come on out, Kim," Chris said.

I blinked up at Chris, trying to read his poker-faced expression. He stared back at me, and I saw a flicker of sadness. "Please tell me it worked." I stretched and stood up.

Chris sighed and shook his head from side to side. "They're waiting for us."

I got up and headed to the bathroom to change out of the jumpsuit. I felt shitty. I slept like crap, and my nerves felt raw. I washed my hands, splashed water on my face, and looked at the bags under my eyes. I recognized the expression on my face; it just looked unfamiliar. It was fear.

I was afraid, and I'd been that way a while now. Everyone around me was scared, except maybe the army guys. Their military training gave them an advantage. Being in mortal danger was something they had ingrained into them, according to what my dad used to say. I gathered my wits and came out of the bathroom to follow Chris.

"Who's waiting for us?" I asked.

"Samuel, Colonel Anderson, and your friends," Chris answered politely.

"So, the scan didn't work. Now what?"

"I don't know, but they are arguing about it in the main boardroom," he said.

When we got there, I realized he was understating the argument. A few yards down the hallway, I could hear the raised voices. When we walked into the room, we witnessed full-blown shouting. I was shocked to find Ramesh and Ana in the middle of it.

"I don't give a damn. Find another way!" Ramesh barked.

"Please calm down, Ramesh; we'll take every precaution," Samuel said.

"*Bullshit!* You plan on waterboarding her," Ana roared. "What kind of bloody precautions are there for that, Samuel?" Ana's voice was manic, and she started cursing in Russian.

I started to shake. I couldn't have heard that correctly. Ana swung around angry, as if she was going to storm out of the room, then saw me. We made eye contact, and her eyes flooded with tears. She rushed over to me and put her hands on my shoulders.

"I won't let them do it!"

I just stared at her, speechless. I was stunned and confused.

Samuel marched over to cut in front of Ana to explain. "Zeevax recorded excellent footage of the Scaraboids. They are fantastic. We aren't sure how they can move so quickly, but they have a glorious set of exotic wings that move them through the ether in the fourth dimension," Samuel began.

"Whatever, Samuel, get to the point," Ramesh snapped.

I looked around the room and counted only nine people, including the colonel. He was staring right through me.

"Your Companion radiates a cyclic pattern of vibrations that travel into the fourth dimension, but you start breathing before the machine can get a full recording. Our equipment isn't sensitive enough to get the full signal," Samuel said gently.

"Get better equipment," Ramesh said.

"Did she say waterboard?" I interrupted, looking into Samuel's eyes and pointing at Ana.

"Zeevax has concluded that the only way to get a full reading is to put you in extreme duress. Your Companion has to believe it's going to die." Samuel exhaled.

"That sadistic AI has no empathy or respect for human life," Ramesh growled.

"Did she say waterboard?" I repeated with my voice raised, shaking.

"Find another way," Ramesh said as he positioned himself between Samuel and me, and I had only a view of the back of his head.

"Zeevax, please explain the scenario again," Beth said from behind the men where I couldn't see her.

"To collect the full signal amplified through the calcite micro-crystals in Kim's pineal gland into the fourth dimension, she must experience more extreme distress. Infestation is irrelevant. The Mayan Dark Codex chronicled that victims were sacrificed slowly by taking the heart out of their chest while still alive. The slaughter of tribespeople with the same rare non-coding DNA in this way was successful in getting their Companions to *scream*. The Scaraboids would come to feed in great numbers and cleanse the priests and those nearby of the Darachnid affliction." Zeevax played a holographic film for us all to watch the heinous act.

"You want to *rip my fucking heart out?*" I gasped.

"Controlled suffocation should be sufficient in causing the fear required to trigger the Companion to scream," Zeevax corrected.

*Controlled suffocation*—the words echoed in my head. I felt Ana slip her hand into mine, squeezing it and holding on tight.

"The severity of consequences based on the level of risk to Kim's safety is acceptable," Captain Gordon said.

I felt my eyebrows shoot up my forehead, wondering what the hell he meant by that. Suddenly the colonel stiffened and walked toward me. Samuel and Ramesh moved aside.

"That's enough; come with me," Colonel Anderson said.

He was intimidating, and I looked around, and everyone's head bowed in surrender to this man's authority. Even Ana reluctantly released my hand. I followed the colonel to an area I had overlooked before. Behind one of the beautiful Egyptian statues was a doorway that led to another section. Once inside, Colonel Anderson sat on a black leather couch and motioned for me to sit in a chair across from him.

"I want to show you something," he said to me. "Zeevax, please display my personal file, Projection One."

The back wall lit up with the current news. Then the screen changed to other pictures of what I guessed was the Middle East that had broken out into war. I watched horrendous acts with bombs exploding in buildings, churches, and schools.

"The footage you are looking at belongs to armed forces, some of it ours, some of it our allies," he said, pointing at the atrocities in front of us. "You see, in China, they have locked people in their homes and are shooting anyone who tries to escape. Terrorist groups have mobilized, taking advantage of the global uproar by kidnapping ambassadors, blowing up gas lines, and even committing genocide in some parts of the world. We don't have the human resources to stop any of this." He waved his hand at the images. "The Americans have started shooting each other in the streets, and many police officers have stopped showing up to work. We didn't foresee this chain reaction of events occurring so rapidly. We can't even keep the Darachnids off our people, and they're turning on each other now too."

Colonel Anderson stopped talking, and I watched the video feed of our planet gone to hell. I saw horrible things and had to look away. "I didn't realize..." I stuttered.

"You've been purposefully sheltered for two reasons. First, based on your psych exam, Zeevax concluded you would volunteer if we elicited your cooperation but kept you insulated. Second, we didn't know how your exposure to the brutality of what's going on out there would affect your test results, and we needed a baseline for accuracy," he said.

"So what are you asking from me?" I asked.

He raised his eyebrows slightly then tilted his head to the left. "I'm not asking you anything. I'm giving you the courtesy and respect I wouldn't bother giving most people because of who your father was. You're not a volunteer. We're moving forward with Zeevax's recommendation to put you in a situation to elicit the results we require," he said flatly.

I was shocked. I honestly thought I had been a willing participant, but I could see now that I never really had a choice. As long as it wasn't too demanding, I was pleased to volunteer the way a blood donor would. This colonel just told me I was getting tortured regardless of whether I agreed to it.

"Ana said waterboard. Can't you guys scare me or drug me or something?" I pleaded.

"You'd know you weren't in danger," he answered.

"Are you going to kill me?" I asked, feeling a tear run down my cheek.

He looked surprised. "No, the chances of your death from this are minimal."

"What's the difference then? I mean, if I know you aren't going to kill me, will it still work?"

"Oh, it will work all right. The bravest soldiers I've known, including your father, have undergone waterboarding. Volunteers at first, the brave lasted only around fifteen seconds before they were begging for their lives and threatening to kill the tormentor." He scoffed.

"I see," I said.

I forced my eyes to look back at the screen, and as the explosions and shootings continued, I realized every second meant another life. I took a deep breath and looked back at the colonel, who was staring at me intently. I could feel his Companion probing my mind, and he nodded and stood. Without saying a word, I followed him to the main boardroom, where the others were waiting for us. The colonel didn't have to explain anything; everyone seemed aware of the situation.

"I will be the one to do it," Rick said directly to me.

"You bastard," Ana hissed, her lips quivering.

Chris crossed his arms. "He'll do his best to keep her safe."

"She's not safe no matter who does it," Ramesh said.

"Better than a stranger," I said to Ana.

She hugged me tightly, and I felt my knees go weak. I hadn't even eaten breakfast yet, but I was sure they knew that. *Better I don't puke all over the place during the abuse.* I wasn't brave; I was terrified, and there was nowhere to run. Ana didn't want to release me, but the captain cleared his throat, which cued Samuel.

"Okay, Ana, let her go." Samuel pulled Ana away from me.

"I'm going with you," Ramesh said.

## CHAPTER 23
### *Broadcast*

**RAMESH AND SAMUEL** started to argue about whether or not Ramesh could be present during my torture. It was a short-lived fight because Colonel Anderson forbade it. I looked at Ramesh before leaving with the colonel, Captain Gordon, Rick, and Chris. He had an agonizing look, his eyes full of pain. I could hear Ana sobbing in the background as I walked out. Rick walked beside me, and the captain was behind us. *So much for making a run for it*, I thought bleakly.

"I'm scared." I looked up at Rick for reassurance.

"You should be," he said, clenching his jaw.

Everything started to spin, and I felt lightheaded. I looked around for something to ground myself then down at my feet. *One…two… three…four…* I counted my steps to the CS scanner. When we were in the shuttle, I lifted my toes inside my shoes to tap every time we passed a pedestrian. The urge to keep a beat seemed like the only thing that kept me from crying and fainting. *You are not going to die*, I promised myself.

"Did you waterboard my dad?" I asked Rick tentatively, not quite sure I wanted the answer.

"Nope—he did it to me." He must have seen the horror on my face because he answered my thoughts. "Don't worry; I'm not looking for revenge. Your father trained me. He first taught me that to understand something, you must experience it yourself."

"Any advice for me?"

"No," he said.

When the elevator door opened to level 83, soldiers and only three scientists populated the lab. A female soldier escorted me to the washroom to change into the white jumpsuit. When I started putting it on, I saw the sleeves were ridiculously long. Confused, I slipped my arms into them and attempted to bunch them up.

"Nuh-uh," the officer said as she reached out, took the ends of the long sleeves, and wrapped them around my back to tie them.

*Oh, Jesus, it's a fucking straight jacket,* I realized. After dressing, she walked me to the cube, and Rick was already waiting for me beside a narrow transparent polymer table with white cords. He was wearing a white jumper and standing near a large container full of water with a bucket and towels.

"I can't do this," I cried.

Rick and the female officer grabbed me by the arms and forced me into the cube. I struggled but not with all my might; when they got me to the table, I knew there was no winning. Rick held me down, and the woman tied straps around my legs, hips, chest, and finally over my head, covering my eyes. I was snivelling and sobbing shamelessly. I heard the door close, and part of me wanted to get a hold of myself to be brave, but almost as soon as the thought occurred, I felt a wet rag cover my mouth and nose.

I lost it. I struggled and wiggled to no avail while trying to scream as the table inclined and the blood rushed to my head. I felt the cool water pour over the towel covering my mouth. I held my breath and listened to the humming of the dome as it lowered over the cube. Rick caught me by surprise. The world spun around me as reality blurred. I couldn't hold my breath any longer and tried to inhale. Instead of air, water filled my nose and mouth until it trickled down towards my lungs, which desperately sought oxygen.

My whole body convulsed as I struggled to breathe, but the water choked and burned me. *It burns*—the words cried out to an empty void in my head. I gagged and gurgled—I was struck with terror at the realization that I was drowning. The stinging was so intense that I felt nothing except pain.

I tried hard to think of my dog or my family but couldn't summon their images. Everything was black. *I'm dying.* My ears rang so loud that it felt like a siren inside my head. Water kept coming, and my lungs were on fire. The sharp pain felt like a jagged cheese grater scraping the soft tissue in my chest as more fluid leaked into my lungs. Oxygen deprivation and agonizing pain had me wavering in and out of consciousness.

The towel lifted off my face, and I coughed and spat water or blood everywhere I couldn't tell. Convulsing as I fought for air, I wheezed and struggled to breathe.

Desperation I didn't know existed set in. I tried to speak and beg for Rick to stop, but the soaked towel lowered over my face again, and I experienced more hell. I would do anything to make it stop.

I needed oxygen; it was the only thing that mattered. *Please let me go.* My mind was foggy, and every muscle in my body hurt. It felt like shredded glass mixed with the water that filled my respiratory tract. The searing pain only increased. I would rather die than continue this torture, but it kept going. A mental haze of misery surrounded me as I sucked in more water.

Then the towel lifted once more. I choked, heaved, and pissed myself. I was too scared to feel humiliated. I wanted to negotiate, but I couldn't talk, only gasp in morsels of air. The towel came down again; it jolted me even though I knew it was coming. The pain was more brutal than before until everything faded.

I tried to open my eyes, but my eyelids were too heavy, and I felt dazed. *Help me.* I could hear voices, but it wasn't clear what they were saying. I thought I heard *She's coming around.* I tried to speak, but my mouth felt sluggish. I breathed in slowly, and although my chest ached, air filled my lungs. Soreness aside, I was eternally grateful for fresh oxygen.

"Kim, can you hear me?" a stranger asked.

I felt arms moving me, then a sense of weightlessness as they lifted me. I flinched before opening my eyes. The olive green bodies around me meant that either I wasn't in the cube or others were in it with me.

*God, please let it be over,* I prayed. My chest was bare, covered with little stickers; a blanket was placed on top of me. Arms lowered me to a softer surface, and soldiers carried me out of the CS floor and into the elevator.

"You're all right, Kim; we are taking you to the Medicorium now," one of them said.

I tried to ask his name but couldn't formulate the words. I focused on the laborious task of breathing while I listened to the beautiful sounds of life humming around me. I tried to lift my arm to touch my face, but my chest hurt.

"Just take it easy, Kim; we'll be there soon," someone behind me said.

They loaded me into a military ambulance and drove me the short distance to the Medicorium. As two officers unloaded me from the vehicle, I became reoriented and alert.

"Did it work?" I rasped.

I felt a hand rest on my shoulder, and an unfamiliar face leaned to look into my eyes. A young man nodded slightly. "Yes, ma'am, they got the recording."

Relief overcame me, and tears filled my eyes. I was crying out of gratitude for so many reasons. Mainly, I dreaded undergoing more torture.

"Kim, are you okay?" Ramesh's yelled from a distance, his voice filled with panic.

He was waiting for me at the clinic entrance. I was so happy to see him that I sat up, and they lowered me into a wheelchair. I felt like I could walk, but my legs were wobbly.

"Ramesh," I said weakly, smiling at him.

Ramesh took control of the wheelchair and ushered me inside.

"Bring her in here. Kim, I'm Dr. Han; let's take a look at you," a man wearing a white lab coat with thick glasses said.

Dr. Han examined me while Ramesh waited outside the room. The white jumpsuit was cut open. The doctor told me that my heart had stopped, the soldiers performed CPR, and they shocked me once with a defibrillator. My body vibrated with the remnants of fear as the doctor listed the physical trauma. He gave me an injection of antibiotics in case the respiratory tissue damage got infected. My larynx had suffered an injury, and I had a cracked rib. He also noted a few bruises from struggling against the ropes used to tie me down.

"I want to keep you here for at least a day for observation. We'll get some x-rays tomorrow. Your body will heal before your mind," Dr. Han handed me a robe.

"I need to clean up," I whispered. Chills ran up my spine when I realized I would have to get wet to shower or bathe.

"I'll get a nurse to help," he said and left.

I sat on the edge of the bed with the robe wrapped around me, disgusted. I wanted to shower, but the image of the water pouring on my body made me cringe. Images of death flashed through my head.

"Hey, hun, how are you doing?" Tiana said as she entered the room with a look of concern.

I tried to give her a slight grin, flipped my palms up, and did my best to hold back tears. Her familiar face made me emotional, and I appreciated that she was the nurse the doctor sent to help.

"Let's get you cleaned up, eh? I see Ramesh is outside impatiently waiting to see you. I've brought you some clothes; they are yours. Ana had them delivered a few minutes ago," Tiana said gently.

"Thank you," I said, my voice hoarse.

She took me into the bathroom equipped with a shower and a walk-in tub. "Take your pick," she said and put the clothes with towels on a bench against the wall.

I pointed at the walk-in tub. She waited for me to undress and climb in before she turned the water on. The warm water was comforting, and I was unequivocally grateful that it felt nice against my skin. Part of me suspected it would burn from having some PTSD against water, but this was good. Tiana turned the tap off halfway, and I washed with a bar of soap and leaned back so my hair would fall into the attached basin where she carefully lathered it, meticulously avoiding getting any water on my face.

I dried off and got dressed in the sweatsuit Ana selected for me. *Wise woman*, I reflected. I was sore all over, and unrestrictive clothing was the smartest choice.

"You up for visitors?" Tiana asked after I sat down.

"Please," I said.

She handed me a necklace with a panic button, put the Welxus bracelet back on my wrist, smiled, and told me to push the button for anything and someone would be there in a few seconds. She opened the door to leave, and before it could close behind her, Ana flew into the room with Ramesh on her heels.

"Oh, Kim, I've been so worried. How are you?" Ana gently asked as she circled me, inspecting my body and touching my hair.

"Been better," I said carefully so as not to strain my throat.

Ramesh stood there staring at me with his lips in a tight thin line. I looked into his eyes, trying hard not to let the tears overtake me again. My mind flashed to think of my father and what he would think. I took a deep breath and tried to smile assuredly at him.

"I'm going to be fine," I said hoarsely with a little more confidence than I felt.

Ramesh sat beside me on the bed and held my hand. I looked at Ana, whose eyebrows shot up before she started pacing around the room.

"Zeevax has collected the entire signal from your Companion and then some. They're cleaning that godforsaken equipment out of the CS department and rushing to customize and fabricate an audio amplifier to recreate it," Ana said, her voice trembling.

"It'd better work." Ramesh gave my hand a soft squeeze.

"I believe it'll work; it must. Zeevax, what's the probability of success for Broadcast Vanquish?" Ana asked.

"The probability of a favourable outcome from Broadcast Vanquish is eighty-nine percent," Zeevax answered.

That sounded good to me. In university, that would qualify as an A. We couldn't afford another failure. I was apprehensive about being too optimistic after Project Arrow's devastating lack of success. I heard my stomach groan and wondered if it was safe to eat or drink.

"Zeevax, please have someone bring Kim some soup, please," Ana said, looking towards my belly.

"Thanks. Tell me about Broadcast Vanquish," I requested softly, preferring to listen and not talk or think about what I just went through.

"Zeevax—" she started, but I put my hand up and motioned for her to stop, wincing a little. *Next time use your right arm*, I reminded myself. The cracked rib was on my left side.

"I'd rather hear it from you guys." I looked back and forth between them.

I appreciated Zeevax's thorough explanations, but the AI's clinical description didn't distract me from the pain. Hearing my friends' voices and watching their movements and facial expressions made me feel better. Ana gave me a reassuring smile and tilted her head to Ramesh.

"They are creating a replica of the signal your Companion emitted. Now that cellular company carriers use 5G networks, Zeevax can use people's cell phones to create a reciprocating signal that fluctuates between extremely low and high frequencies." Ramesh pulled his cell phone out of his pocket and held it in the air. "Zeevax will take control of these and temporarily increase the radiation output, pushing the pulse into the fourth dimension, mimicking what we call your *Companion scream*. This will be sent instantaneously worldwide in three or four bursts over two days. The fact that people carry their cell phones around in their pockets makes it ideal for reaching the masses," Ramesh explained.

"What about third-world countries and remote, isolated areas?" I asked, speaking slowly because my throat felt raw.

"Radio networks, antennas for data transfer, Bluetooth, wireless game consoles, speakers, and televisions will also work. The military will have to deal with logistics in the remote areas," he answered.

The door opened, and a Nekxus employee carrying a dinner tray set it at the side table beside a chair. Ramesh stood up and offered to help me cross the room to the chair, but I found my footing just fine. He lifted the cover, and underneath was a divine-smelling butternut squash soup—my favourite. I guessed the company knew what I liked from my file.

I sat down and sipped the warm creamy soup tediously; it was delicious—maybe even the best thing I'd ever tasted. I'd almost finished the soup when there was a knock at the door before it creaked open.

"Loki," I rasped joyfully.

Forgetting the pain momentarily, I bent down and suffered the consequences as my fur baby ran to me and hopped up and down like a little maniac.

"What the *fuck* did they do to you?" Jacob growled upon seeing me. "You were supposed to keep her *safe*, dickhead." Jacob had a fistful of Ramesh's shirt in his grip, glaring him in the eye.

"Jacob, stop," I protested while struggling to settle Loki down.

Ana came and kneeled to pet Loki beside me, and Jacob let Ramesh go. Ramesh didn't even flinch or argue. He looked resolved not to fight. Jacob turned away from him and stared at Ana now.

"Is someone going to explain?" He stood with his hands on his hips.

No one spoke. I massaged Loki's ears and looked up at him. He stared back and blinked a few times, then sat in the chair beside me and slumped his shoulders.

"They tried to stop it," I breathed.

"I didn't know they were going to put you in the tank *with the animals*," he grumbled.

"What? Animals didn't do this," I said, confused.

Jacob didn't know. I thought he was here because someone from the company told him what had happened in the cube.

"I'll explain, Jacob," Ana said.

Ana described the events that led up to the decision for me to be waterboarded and let him in on the fact that *none of us* were volunteers, to begin with, in any event. She told him she wasn't aware of the actual chain of command. The military started to actively take control of proceedings after the failure of Project Arrow and not just reside in the background. They were protecting their interests.

"So this signal will broadcast out into the world and ring the dinner bell for these Scarab beetles to come feast on the little Darachnid shit-eaters?" Jacob scratched his head and scowled.

"Yes, according to Zeevax," Ana said.

"No offence Zeevax, but I'm not that confident," Jacob said.

"No offence taken," Zeevax responded.

Jacob's face went red; he didn't realize Zeevax was listening and didn't expect an answer from the AI. He rolled his eyes then looked around for cameras. At least, that's what I suspected he was looking for, knowing how paranoid Jacob could be. I turned my attention to Loki; I was incredibly grateful to have him here.

"Who brought you two here?" I asked carefully.

"Rick showed up at the condo and said you were staying overnight in the clinic for observation. He said he wanted me to bring your dog for emotional support and that you were fine." Jacob scoffed.

"Rick," Ramesh spat.

"Yeah, Rick, you don't like him?" Jacob raised an eyebrow at Ramesh.

"He's the one who waterboarded Kim." Ramesh stared Jacob in the face, but his lip quivered.

"That *motherfucker*," Jacob roared. "I'm going to break his nose next time I see him."

"Not if I break it first," Ramesh said, nodding.

"Stop it," I said weakly, raising my hand. "Rick worked for my dad and wanted to carry it out properly. My dad was the one who taught him."

Jacob's jaw dropped, and he just stood there with a ridiculous look. I would have laughed at him if the circumstances weren't so brutal.

"I watched," Ramesh said.

"What?" Ana gaped.

"I did; I went to see Billy and had him hack into the security feed in the CS," Ramesh said, his eyes softening as he looked at me.

"I can't believe you watched and didn't tell me," Ana said.

"You wouldn't want to see it, Ana. It was bad." Ramesh said.

"I want to see," Jacob said.

"The military had Zeevax erase all recordings afterwards; it's gone," Ramesh said, pursing his lips.

"Shit, I wanted to see it too," I said.

"No, you don't," Ramesh assured.

"I don't want to see it." Ana shut her eyes tight.

Her phone went off, and she answered it to talk to Aleksander. We all heard part of the conversation; he and his girlfriend were now moving into the condo with her and Andrei.

"Samuel is requesting the presence of security level 4 and up in the main boardroom in Commune A," Zeevax said.

"That's us," Ana said, looking at Ramesh. "Let's hope it's good news."

She handed me my cell phone and kissed my cheek. I didn't realize she had it on her. Ramesh looked at Jacob, who frowned back at him, then at me and smiled before leaving with Ana. Jacob sat beside me; he'd been standing and shifting his weight around the whole time Ana and Ramesh were there.

"The bathroom is right over there." I pointed.

"Thank you," Jacob said.

Loki insisted on sitting on my lap. Thankfully he only weighed around four kilograms. He was licking my hand as I petted his smooth fur and tried to sit comfortably. I held the empty soup bowl and let him slurp up what was left, even though it wasn't much.

"I would ask why you didn't call me, but I saw Ana had your phone," Jacob said when he came out of the bathroom.

"Don't blame them; it wasn't their fault," I said.

"I'm so angry. Who's to blame?" He sighed because he knew the answer.

"No one." Truthfully the whole world was in a murderous rage. Not because people were terrible but because they were afflicted. "If I were in their shoes, I would have done the same thing," I said.

"What about Rick?"

I sat back in my chair. "I tried to get away," I said, embarrassed.

"Good," he cheered. "Fuck them."

"Didn't do me any good."

"At least you still have your sense of humour. Heads would be rolling around here if they killed that part of you," he said.

His threats were empty, and we both knew it, but it felt good to let it out.

A nurse popped her head in and looked at Jacob. "Do you want a cot?"

"You bet I do; I'm not leaving this place without her," he answered.

## CHAPTER 24

*Feast*

JACOB STAYED OVERNIGHT in the hospital room, positioning his cot between me and the door as if he were concerned that someone might sneak past him and snatch me. Loki slept curled up behind me with his head on my pillow. Usually, I wouldn't allow him to sleep anywhere but my feet, but I welcomed his presence this time. Ramesh and Ana didn't return to the room.

In the morning, a food service worker knocked on the door with some breakfast. I carefully swallowed Cream of Wheat while Jacob took Loki outside to pee. He returned and ate a couple of bagels while Loki eagerly ate a bowl of meat the staff had prepared for him. I sipped the coffee after letting it cool, then spilled it on myself when someone tapped on the door before opening it.

"Good morning; how are you feeling today?" Dr. Han asked.

"Pretty sore, but not too bad," I answered, wiping the mess unsuccessfully with a napkin.

He examined me briefly. "I see you are moving around pretty well. I don't think we'll need to give you any x-rays after all," he said. "Take two of these as needed and use an ice pack to reduce the swelling on your ribs and bruises for the first few days." He handed me a bottle of pills.

"Okay, what are these?"

"Strong ibuprofen," he answered. "Try not to exert yourself, and I'll have a nurse come check on you for the next few mornings around ten. Keep that with you for now." He pointed at the panic button I wore around my neck.

"I can go home?" I asked, feeling delighted at the prospect of getting out of there.

"Not home, but back to your assigned Nekxus quarters for the time being. I'm sure someone will reach out to you soon." He smiled and left.

"So?" Jacob asked, returning to the room after the doctor left.

"He said I can go," I said.

"Thank God." He folded up the cot and gathered Loki's leash and toys.

I checked my phone, which had the ringer off, to find a couple of messages from Julia and one from Jing. I read Jing's text first to see if there was an update on Di's health.

"Jing said Di's doing well, and the doctor will send him home soon," I told Jacob.

"Will he be safe?"

"I don't know; they live in a nice condo in a remote area of town, so I hope so," I said tentatively.

"Should we just go?" Jacob asked after collecting all of our things.

I shrugged. "I guess so."

Jacob opened the door and stiffened when we walked out to find Chris and another soldier waiting for us.

"Samuel wants to see you before we take you to your accommodations," Chris said.

"Where's Rick?" I asked.

"Who cares." Jacob turned and scowled at me.

"I want to see him."

"Sorry, he's not available right now," Chris said.

We sauntered behind Chris and the other soldier who escorted us back to the boardroom in Commune A. My body ached. During the shuttle ride I noticed that the military presence had lessened, and some of the tents were removed. When we arrived at the boardroom, Chris and the other soldier stayed in the hallway. The boardroom felt empty as Samuel, Beth, Fischer, and Ana were the only ones inside. I was a little disappointed not to see Ramesh.

"Sit here, Kim." Ana pulled a chair as my breathing was noticeably laboured.

"Thank you," I said.

I looked at Ana's face and focused my thoughts on asking her, *Is the signal going to work?* She took a deep breath, let out a long exhale, and nodded with a hint of a smile. Jacob pulled a chair beside me and sat down with Loki on his lap. I looked at Beth, who stared blankly at me. *She must be an excellent poker player.*

"How are you feeling, Kim?" Samuel asked.

"I'm okay," I said.

"She's in pain," Jacob blurted.

"Yes, I should think so." Samuel nodded calmly. "I wanted to apprise you of the status of what the higher-ups have called Broadcast Vanquish."

I sat back in my chair, wincing as I tried to find a more comfortable position.

"I'll jump in so that you can go home and recuperate; I know you've had a trying time recently," Fischer said.

Jacob snorted, and I reached over and put my hand on his arm to quiet him.

"Zeevax, display the debriefing I prepared for Kim," Fischer said, ignoring Jacob's admonishing behaviour.

Zeevax's familiar hologram appeared in the middle of the room above the conference table. The Earth, around three feet in diameter, turned slowly in front of us.

"I've simplified this file to break down the progress of the trials for you." Fischer opened his arms wide for emphasis. "The yellow areas are where we have sent out the first broadcasts. We tested the recipients shortly afterwards and found no Darachnids present."

He paced back and forth as he talked. The Earth spun around so we could see at least fifty yellow dots evenly spaced geographically around the globe. The yellow dots disappeared, and fewer green dots appeared in their place.

"These green areas you are now looking at are where Nekxus has operational DMRMs capable of recording Darachnids. We set up experiments and broadcast the signal to the test subjects inside the Nekxus DMRM locations. What we witnessed was better than we could have hoped." Fischer continued. "The Scaraboids came from below the ground and consumed all the Darachnids within approximately twenty-five feet."

"It's been one hundred percent effective," Ana said proudly.

"They come from the ground?" Jacob asked.

"We think that the centre of the Earth—the core—where gravity isn't as strong due to the surrounding masses counteracting one another, is where the Scaraboids nest. Zeevax has postulated that they have been dormant due to their lack of food sources. Without the Companions emitting the specific vibrational frequency—*the scream*—they wouldn't know where the Darachnids are. They don't have eyes," Fischer said.

"That's great news," I said.

"Indeed," Fischer agreed.

"Where do they go once they've feasted?" Jacob asked.

"Back toward the core, although there were a couple of instances where the Scaraboids kept flying upward, perhaps seeking more Darachnids; we don't know. The company plans to build deep underground to see if they can detect what's going on there," Fischer said, distracted.

Samuel cleared his throat, and Fischer's eyes flickered toward him.

"Anyhow, Nekxus has contacted various governments and cellular carriers. We plan to send out the signal as soon as possible. It will piggyback a global pandemic alert that we've created to mask the loud noise it makes," Fischer finished.

"Pandemic alert?" I asked.

"Yes, an audio signal will create waves, and we are using those sound waves to amplify the frequency to radiate outward as far as possible from the source. The source will be cell phones, television, radio, and other electronic devices. It will sound similar to the Amber Alert that Canada uses. The first one will be a *test*—that's what the news is telling people right now. Zeevax has taken control of the social media platforms to prepare folks for the alert as well—it will be loud." Fischer pulled his cell phone out of his pocket and put it on the table. "Zeevax, please send Broadcast Vanquish to my cell phone now."

Suddenly his cell phone vibrated and started to shriek an ear-splitting set of beeps and grating clicks with the volume on full blast. Loki barked and growled at the phone, seemingly offended by the jarring high frequency. Everyone around the room had irritated facial expressions and covered their ears. Jacob suffered through it and covered Loki's ears instead.

It reminded me of the awful noise dial-up telephone internet used to make mixed with our usual Amber Alert but amplified. When the noise stopped, I noticed the phone vibrate for a few seconds afterward.

"Right now, this room is filling with Scaraboids who will devour any Darachnids that may be present," Fischer stated. "There's an increase of radiation emitting from the phone, which is why I put it on the table. You'll receive a notification of the time broadcasts very soon so that you can put your cell phone on a table or somewhere away from your body. The mobile devices will heat up, and in some cases, the batteries will melt." He opened his arms helplessly.

"We've created a substantial fund that governments can tap into when the inevitable lawsuits pour in from disgruntled citizens," Beth added.

"What about cancer?" Jacob asked.

"Minimal risk, especially when you consider the state of the world. People are killing each other. We need to take action now," Beth answered snidely.

She shot a cold stare at Jacob, making me wonder if she were a human or one of the Nekxus androids wearing a human suit. Her head turned, and she turned her glare toward me. *Human*, I thought—her Companion was probably fine-tuned to pick up any thoughts projected toward her. I shuddered and turned my attention to Samuel.

"Do you have any more questions?" Samuel asked, looking between Jacob and me.

"Nope, I'm ready to go," Jacob replied and looked at me, widening his eyes a little as if to say, *Let's get the hell out of here.*

"No," I answered.

"We have plenty of work to do; I'll be in touch," Samuel said before turning to look at a tablet Beth was holding in front of him, probably with some new update.

Ana, Chris, and the other soldier walked us to the exit, where an armoured car was waiting to take us back to the Nekxus condo.

"I'll drop in later tonight to check in, okay?" she said as Jacob, Loki, and I got into the vehicle.

"See you later," I said.

Jacob and I sat in the back of the vehicle, and I couldn't help but gaze out the window for the ride home as I looked for some indication of what was happening in Hamilton. I didn't see much, thankfully. It looked like, for the time being, the military had a good handle on the lockdown. The streets were almost bare.

---

Once we got back to the condo, I breathed a long sigh of relief. I was so grateful to be out of the Nekxus complex. I missed privacy, even if it was an illusion. I knew Zeevax was keeping tabs on me, but at least I could relax without waiting for someone to barge in and request another test or worse...

I had just sat down on the couch, and there was a knock at the door.

"For Christ's sake," Jacob groaned. Before I could stand, he put his hand up to stop me. "I'll get it."

"It could be Julia, so don't bite their head off before you know who it is," I said, noticing Loki wasn't barking, just wagging his tail and whimpering.

"Right," he said and went off to answer the door.

Sure enough, it was Julia, Jeffery, and Sherry. Jacob let them in, and I could hear the familiar sound of my niece giggling with delight as she and Loki mauled each other. Julia and Jeffery came into the living room. My sister gasped when she saw me.

"Kimmy, what happened to you?" Julia exclaimed.

"I've had a rough couple of days." I tried to smile, but seeing her made the tears well in my eyes.

"Hey Sherry, you want to come with me up to the roof so Loki can go pee? He hasn't been out in a while," Jacob asked.

"Sure, can I, Mommy?" Sherry pleaded.

"You better tell them, or I will," Jacob said, leaning close to me so Sherry couldn't hear him, but Julia and Jeffery could.

Julia looked me up and down then to Jacob, who wore a no-nonsense expression. "Sure you can, honey—listen to Jacob, and don't mess around."

Jacob grabbed Loki's leash and the ball, then left with Sherry for the green roof space. I looked at my sister then at my brother-in-law Jeffery. I noticed his arms and legs crossed, and he couldn't hold eye contact with me. *You knew!*—I focused the words toward him, feeling shocked. He looked at me briefly and opened and closed his mouth, making a silent yup. I turned my gaze to Julia and asked, *Did you know too?* She blinked a few times and kept looking me up and down as if trying to figure something out. She didn't know anything.

"Maybe Jeff here can explain it," I said, squinting at him accusingly.

"What? What's she talking about, hun?" Julia said, turning to look at her husband.

He put his hands up defensively. "I didn't know until afterward. They tasked me with assisting the fabrication of a piece of machinery to be lowered overtop of the CS cube to collect data." Jeffery looked fearfully at Julia. "I asked one of the head engineers why we had to make those adjustments after the night you slept in there," he said, looking at me. "He told me it didn't work the way they hoped. One of the other guys I was working with overheard us. He was friends with one of the soldiers on guard duty when it happened."

"When what happened?" Julia asked him. Her face was red, and her voice sounded angry.

"He said his buddy told him they waterboarded Kim in the cube to collect some signal. I didn't know if he was bullshitting me, so I didn't want to say anything to worry you—especially if it wasn't true," he admitted.

"*Waterboarded?*" She drew in a breath. "What are you talking about? Like the barbaric hazing rituals in the military?"

"Yeah, like that," I sniffed.

I took my time explaining to Julia and Jeffery how the events led up to the eventual torturing of my Companion and me. I related that they had to do it to obtain a complete recording of the signal that acted like a beacon attracting the Scaraboids to feast on the Darachnids. Julia got up and sat beside me halfway through the conversation to offer emotional support as I fought to hold back the tears as I described how it felt.

"They could have killed you," Julia said, fuming. "I can't believe there wasn't another way."

"The military didn't have patience for any more research. The planet is plunging into violence. The colonel in charge showed me footage of what is happening in many parts of the world. It was necessary," I conceded.

"I'm not happy about this at all." Julia stood up, strode over to the window, and looked out over Lake Ontario off into the distance. "I'm not sure you should consider working for Nekxus, Jeff."

"It wasn't the company's decision. They are a member of a larger organization which seems to be run by a militant authority. Like me, they had no choice. Ana and Ramesh tried to stop it but were powerless," I said, remembering.

Jacob returned with Sherry and Loki at that point of the conversation, and we all went quiet.

"What happened, Aunt Kimmy?" Sherry asked as she sat beside me, noticing a couple of bruises.

"Oh, I had a little car accident the other day, but I'm fine now," I lied.

"I'm glad you are okay." She hugged me. "I'm going to make you a get-well card," she said and jumped up to go to the kitchen table where my pencil crayons were.

"Good one," Jacob said, approving my fib.

They decided to stay with us for the evening. Julia and Jacob prepared dinner while Jeffery and I sat watching the news. We watched the prime minister come out and announce that the lockdowns were necessary for a new virulent strain of COVID that had mutated once again, and people were dying worldwide from it. The mortality rate had skyrocketed.

"Looks like you're not the only one good at lying," Jacob said, peeking his head out from the kitchen where he prepared herbal tea.

"For all we know, he believes what he's saying. Over the last couple of days, I got the impression that the politicians were pretty ignorant of the facts. I think Nekxus prefers to keep them that way. Politicians don't have the same motivations as private corporations or the military. They crave power and get it through popularity contests and deceit. A lot of them have suffered through the plague of Darachnids and have psychopathic personalities," Jeffery said.

"You can tell he doesn't like politics," Julia said, rolling her eyes as she handed me a cup of lukewarm tea with honey.

We ate a variation of shepherd's pie my mother used to make for us for supper. It was smooth to swallow—blended yellow and sweet potatoes on top of creamed corn mixed in with the ground turkey. It smelled almost as delicious as it tasted. Shortly after dinner, while cleaning up, someone knocked on the door. Jacob answered it while I sat on the couch admiring the beautiful card Sherry had made for me. Ana and Andrei entered.

"Hey, everyone. We wanted to join you; Broadcast Vanquish is going to transmit in ten or fifteen minutes," Ana said.

"Where is Aleksander?" I asked.

"He's right behind us; he and his girlfriend Sam are just feeding her cat," Ana said, shaking her head.

"Cat?" I said, smiling.

"Oh yes, Bootsie—the princess," Ana said, snickering.

When Aleksander and Sam showed up a few minutes later, we all gathered around the television, leaving our cell phones in the kitchen underneath the sink. It was Jacob's suggestion, and Ana concurred. The noise would be irritating enough coming from the TV, let alone all eight of our cell phones going off simultaneously. If any of us had the Darachnids parasites within us, we wouldn't have them for long. Ana counted down on her watch, and we all sat silently in anticipation as if it were New Year. Sherry sat in front of me on the floor with Loki, and when Ana said, "Three, two, one," I covered Sherry's ears and braced myself.

I saw Aleksander mouth the words *Holy shit*, but I definitely couldn't hear him. Sherry held Loki close and covered him in a blanket I'd provided before the broadcast went off. Everyone around the room wore irritated expressions, and most covered their ears. Jacob suffered through it again, and Jeffery looked like he was straining to understand the sound.

The TV screen was flashing red and yellow with white writing.

*PANDEMIC ALERT – This is a global pandemic warning.*
*Effective immediately, lockdowns have commenced for everyone, including essential workers.*
*Stay in your homes and avoid gathering. This contagion is deadly; more instructions will follow.*

"What a gross noise, Aunty," Sherry said when it stopped.

"It was very unpleasant, wasn't it," I said, reflecting on how much more unpleasant it was obtaining the signal in the first place.

Jacob retrieved everyone's cell phones from the kitchen and put them on the coffee table. Ana explained that they would broadcast three more alerts twelve hours apart. Random testing in the DMRMs worldwide will hopefully confirm that the Darachnid infestation has terminated. Julia crossed her fingers, held them up in the air, and prayed for all of us.

Andrei sat beside me before they left and told me a story about his Russian military waterboarding experiences. Not only had he undergone the torture on more than one occasion, but he was also responsible for performing it on a couple of his comrades and a prisoner of war.

"You will never forget, but it is a good reminder that life is precious and fragile. Cherish every moment and remember that wolves are always circling, so don't act like a rabbit." Andrei rustled my hair and left with Ana, Aleksander, and his new girlfriend Sam.

"What does that mean?" Jacob asked with a puzzled-looking expression on his face.

"I don't know. Military people say some strange things, right Jules?" I said.

"They sure do. I used to ask Dad where he was going, and he'd always answered, *Overseas in a blood vessel*." She shrugged.

Julia and Jeffery stayed for a while until Sherry started to yawn. They retired for the night, with Julia promising to come in the morning before the company nurse at ten. She wanted to be here to get a thorough update on my health.

After everyone left, Jacob turned the news on, and we watched as the local reporter griped about the new pandemic alert. She called it redundant and said it was too late to send out a ridiculously loud alert for a pandemic lockdown that was already underway. The reporter also described complaints that the new broadcast had caused some phone batteries to melt. The noise was so shocking that there were car accidents because people were caught off guard by the shrieking noise from their pockets.

"If they only knew how grateful they should be for that alert," Jacob scoffed.

We turned off the news and put on the movie *Groundhog Day* to settle and relax before bed.

## CHAPTER 25
### *Anchor*

THE NEXT BROADCAST woke me up at seven in the morning. I'd anticipated it and left my phone in the kitchen, but the noise blared through the walls. Loki jumped off the bed and started to whine, so I threw on my bathrobe and took him out on the balcony to use the puppy pad. I had time to shower and eat oatmeal before Julia and the nurse showed up.

While the nurse examined me, Jacob took Loki and Sherry to the roof to play. My sister, who was also a nurse, seemed satisfied with the Nekxus nurse's assessment of my health and put a pot of coffee on when she left.

"What did the nurse say?" Jacob asked.

Sherry followed Jacob into the room, carrying Loki like a baby. She dressed Loki in one of her doll dresses. The poor little guy had a humiliated look on his face. As soon as she put him down, he slipped out of it and ran from her. She squeaked with delight and chased him around the condo with the pink lace dress held up in the air, waving it like a flag.

"Awe, poor Loki," Julia said, shaking her head. "Don't be upset when he rips it apart."

Sherry stopped and thought about her mom's words then put the dress on the counter in favour of a dog biscuit. Loki responded enthusiastically to the new offering and came running back to her.

My phone chimed, and I checked it to find that Ramesh had messaged me on NexChat. He wanted to know if it was all right to stop by in the afternoon.

*See you soon*, I responded. I reread it after it was sent and felt silly, wondering if I sounded too anxious.

"Ramesh is going to stop by this afternoon," I said.

"Is he now?" Jacob smirked.

"Sherry and I have this afternoon planned anyway. We are making crispy rice squares and working on a one-thousand-word puzzle that's not going to complete itself," Julia said, winking at Jacob.

"Well, I'm staying put. Just in case the company tries to use Ramesh as bait to abduct you or something," Jacob said, crossing his arms.

I rolled my eyes.

"If you find it crowded, Jacob, you're welcome to join us. Sherry and I wouldn't mind a little help with the puzzle," Julia said, giving me a sidelong look.

I went into the bathroom to put on a little makeup and used the straightener on my hair, then Jacob and I watched the news updates. Reports of the pandemic alert were coming in worldwide, indicating that the broadcast was working. It was the first of its kind in that no other signal had ever before been transmitted internationally like this. Of course, the grievances were numerous—and so were the conspiracies. Loki barked, startling me, and Jacob jumped up to get the door.

"I can get it, Jacob," I said.

"All right, all right." He threw his hands in the air. "I just don't want you exerting yourself."

Jacob hushed Loki while I opened the door. Ramesh handed me a bouquet of gorgeous orange and yellow carnations and brought a box of cinnamon rolls. I immediately blushed and moved aside to let him in.

"Wow, these are beautiful, thank you," I said.

"It's my pleasure," he said.

"Hey there, Ramesh, do I smell cinnamon buns?" Jacob said, straining to see around me.

"I brought a dozen. I hope you can eat these," Ramesh said with concern.

"Yes, I can."

I smiled and led him to the kitchen, where I searched for something to put the flowers in. My vases were still at the house, but I found a juice jug that would work fine.

"Don't worry; if she can't eat them, they won't go to waste." Jacob laughed, put three buns on a plate, walked to the front door, and put on his shoes. "I'm off to help your sister and Sherry with their project. Message if you need anything. See you, Ramesh," Jacob said before leaving.

I didn't realize he was going to leave, but he must have understood that Ramesh had no malicious intent when he saw the baked goods and flowers. Ramesh helped me fill the vase with water and put the carnations in it before we went to the living room to sit down.

"I wanted to start by saying how sorry I am for your pain and suffering. I feel ashamed I couldn't do more to stop it. I wish we could have found a better way to obtain what we needed," Ramesh said, regret in his voice.

"Please don't apologize. It wasn't your fault, and it's not lost on me that I am still alive," I said.

"You've been through so much—the violence you suffered at your workplace, your father's passing, and now the torture you had to endure so we could extract your Companions cry." He ran his fingers through his hair and tightened his lips. "It makes me angry and sad to think about it."

"You know about what happened at the restaurant?" I asked, shocked.

I hadn't thought of it, but Ana would have had to tell them everything, including the homicides.

All this started at the restaurant when my Companion echoed Andrei's voice in my head during our attack. That single event sparked a chain that led up to this point.

"I didn't realize you weren't aware that I knew. I would have told you sooner," he said, confused.

"Other than Samuel, I wasn't sure whom Ana told. It was a messed-up situation," I said.

"I can only imagine. So many people have suffered from this dark matter plague of Darachnids for so long that it's turned people into monsters."

We talked briefly about how well the pandemic alert was working for Broadcast Vanquish. Loki sat at Ramesh's feet, enjoying the attention as he scratched the pup's ears.

"I was hoping if all goes well and the world gets back to normal, I could take you out for dinner at my favourite Indian restaurant," he said.

"Are you asking me on a date?" I said, grinning.

"Yes, ma'am," he said, bowing his head politely.

"I would be honoured; I love Indian cuisine," I said. "Armageddon will have to wait now that we have a date. Nekxus better get their act together and put the fourth dimension back in its place," I joked.

Ramesh laughed, and we enjoyed each other's company for a while before he excused himself to return to work. He promised to call me later and kissed my cheek on his way out.

"What do you think, Loki? Do you like him?" I asked.

He wagged his tail and looked up at me.

"Yeah, I do too."

I went into the kitchen, put one of the cinnamon buns in the microwave, and poured a glass of milk. I gave Loki a bully stick to chew on and sat down to enjoy the delicious baked goody.

---

A few days passed, and the broadcast stopped going off every twelve hours. Ana told me it was working. The military was still setting up equipment in some remote and poor areas of the world to reach the people and animals who didn't have access to electronics. It would take a long time to ensure the extermination of Darachnids.

I talked to Di on a video chat, and he looked much better. He'd be in casts for a few more weeks, but otherwise, he was fortunate—no severe internal damage. His face was still bruised but not nearly as swollen, and Jing's pregnancy was coming along well.

He told me he received an expedited payment from the insurance company for the restaurant. Di was enthusiastically redrawing plans to rebuild an even more luxurious place now that he was doing it from the ground up. Ana told me Nekxus had intervened with the insurance company and tripled the payment out of goodwill. Di would never know.

Ramesh visited daily, and we talked about what other dark matter creatures could be lurking in the hidden dimension. His main concern was the health of people's Companions, and he expressed the opinion that the fourth dimension could be crawling with exotic species as long as they weren't parasitic toward life in our world. We were together when Samuel messaged and requested a meeting. I felt a pang of fear and immediately asked Ramesh if he knew why Samuel wanted to see me. Ramesh said he'd be coming with me, and I shouldn't worry, but I would have to wait for Samuel to explain.

"I've got a meeting with Samuel; I shouldn't be too long," I told Jacob.

"I'm coming," he said.

"It's okay, Ramesh and Ana will be there, and I'd prefer you stay here with Loki and calm my sister down in case she comes over and finds me gone," I said.

"Yeah, right; if she comes here, I'm going to tell her that you refused to take me, and I'm going to sit back and enjoy it when you return, and she gives you shit. If you don't come back within four hours, I'm sending out a war party," Jacob said, holding his fist up in the air towards Ramesh as a promise.

I laughed. "I'm hoping this is the end of this nightmare."

We both looked toward Ramesh, who was tight-lipped but nodded slightly toward Jacob to let him know he got his point.

"Amen to that," Jacob said.

Ramesh drove us to the Nekxus complex, and I was pleased to see a few civilian vehicles around, a pedestrian, and a couple of open signs on small business doors. What I didn't see was also encouraging: no military vehicles, no smoke rising in the distance from burning buildings, and no brawls in the streets.

The Nekxus parking lot had fewer military vehicles as well. Ramesh parked the car near the front, and we went through security up the grand escalator toward the boardroom. I felt a little nervous when we got there, remembering what happened to me, but it faded as I could hear friendly chatter in the background from staff members who were in uplifted moods.

I did my best to compartmentalize the trauma into the past. Upon entering the boardroom, I was grateful to see that Samuel and Ana were the only ones inside.

"Nice to see you, Kim; please have a seat," Samuel said.

Ana smiled at me, and I sat down beside her.

"I wanted to thank you personally for contributing to our fight for humanity against the Darachnid infestation. I'm excited to give you the good news regarding the status of this war now that we've managed to reach most of the human population. There are ongoing efforts to eliminate Darachnids from all vertebrates on the planet. Zeevax, please tell Kim the predicted outcome of the Broadcast Vanquish," Samuel said.

"In approximately five weeks, Scaraboids should consume ninety-nine percent of the Darachnids," Zeevax answered.

"That's wonderful news," I exclaimed.

I looked to Ramesh, who smiled knowingly, and Ana nodded, grinning.

"We are all very pleased. As we look to the future, we still have plenty of work ahead of us. There are a few easy fixes, like replacing cell phones damaged from the broadcast and removing the lockdowns in stages until society returns to normal. Healing people's Companions will be far more difficult, but it is one of the top priorities—which brings me to another subject. As you have been made aware, Nekxus has covered the insurance for your friend Di's loss of The Jade Castle," he said.

"Yes, I forgot to thank you. From what I understand, it was a generous payout. I'm so happy that Di's spirits are well, and he's already making plans to rebuild," I said.

"That's good to hear. One of the reasons I asked to meet with you is to extend an offer in person. Zeevax has confirmed that you would be an excellent candidate for an apprenticeship program at our university in Germany, where we'd like to send you. We feel you would do best in the CS department, where you could study and understand everything we know about Companion's microbiome." Samuel handed a tablet to me.

"This is a contract?" I asked.

Samuel nodded. "We offer incomparable expense accounts, benefits packages, salary, and retirement plans. I believe you would enjoy our education program, Kim. Do you think that working for Nekxus would be something you would be interested in?"

"Wow, I didn't expect this," I said, playing with my hair absentmindedly.

I first looked at Ana, who had an expectant look. I thought about how hopeful I felt when Samuel offered Jeffery a position with the company. Then I turned to look at Ramesh. He'd already helped me understand so much about Companions, but the science eluded me. I couldn't imagine anyone saying no to such an incredible opportunity. I was still paying off my student loan from the school, and Nekxus offered to pay for my education in the future.

"Can I take Loki to Germany with me?" I asked.

"Of course, you can take your dog with you. There are doggy daycares at all of our Nekxus locations for staff and students, including at the university," Samuel said.

"Well, then, yes, I'm very interested," I said.

"Wonderful, take your time going over the contract. Zeevax, please show Kim the apprenticeship offer we've prepared for her," Samuel said.

The section of the table in front of me lit up with the program for me to read. Ana excused herself to converse with Samuel, and Ramesh moved to sit beside me to answer any questions. The first thing I noticed on the tablet was that the offer started two weeks from now.

I would have to pack and figure out what to do with the house and break the news to Di that I wouldn't be returning to work for him. He'd be disappointed, but by the time he got things up and running again, I was sure he wouldn't have trouble deciding who would fill my position. I had a few recommendations in mind from the staff he had already employed.

Looking over the document, it appeared that I would alternate between spending six weeks in Germany and returning to Hamilton to do on-site training for three weeks until graduation in eighteen months.

"It looks good to me." I looked at Ramesh expectantly.

"I agree; everything looks in order. You can take some time to think it over if you'd want to. Don't rush your decision," he said.

I placed my thumb on the screen and scanned my print. "There, it's done. I'll never see another opportunity like this, and I've always regretted taking philosophy. It was fascinating but utterly useless in helping me build a career."

"I am happy you decided to take the apprenticeship. Samuel told Ana and me that an offer was in the works for you. Ultimately, you'd be working in the same department as us. He wanted to make sure we felt you would be a good fit for the CS department," Ramesh said.

Ana returned and stared at the table with a confused expression. "Did you read the offer yet?"

"Yes, I signed it already," I said proudly. "I am looking forward to getting started."

"That's great, Kim; I'm thrilled you will be joining our team," she said, beaming. "By the way, I wanted to let you know I checked with Samuel, and he assured me that the animals from the Gamma Project are doing well in the rehabilitation program. We purged them of the Darachnids by using your signal to call the Scaraboids instead of the tedious task of Pyramid baths for every creature."

"So, what will the Scaraboids eat now?" I asked as the thought occurred to me.

"We don't know for sure, but further study will occur deep underground. Zeevax has analyzed their anatomy and thinks they will hibernate in a dormant state in their dimension," she said.

"One more thing," Ana said reluctantly.

I knew it was too good to be true. I could hear the hesitation in her voice and see the fear in her eyes. *Here comes the catch*, I thought to myself.

"Rick is waiting in the hallway to speak with you. You don't have to talk to him; I can send him away," she said confidently.

"Rick? Don't send him away; I want to see him," I assured.

That's why she looked scared. The offer wasn't too good to be perfect after all. She was just worried about my emotional well-being from being confronted by my torturer.

"Are you sure?" Ramesh looked doubtful as he stood up and looked toward the hallway.

"Absolutely," I said. "Send Rick in."

Ramesh walked to the door, and instead of calling Rick in, he stepped out into the hallway and the door shut behind him. I looked at Ana, a little worried, but I felt my hands tremble in anticipation, so I dared not stand in case my knees gave out. I didn't expect to feel so nervous. It was probably only a minute or two before both men entered the room together, but it felt like a long time. I looked at Rick's face warily, unsure of what I felt.

"I'm glad to see you're doing well," Rick said as a sigh escaped him. "Do you mind if I sit down?"

I couldn't find my voice yet, and I stared at him and bobbed my head up and down until he spoke again. He pulled a chair across from me, and Ramesh returned to my side and sat down with us. Ana stood with her arms folded protectively across her chest, swaying side to side with her eyes narrowed on Rick.

"I'm not here to ask your forgiveness; I don't need it. I am here because *you* need closure. If you need to see a monster before you, *so be it*. I don't regret what I did; in this case, we were able to make a positive impact on the world. As soldiers, we go through things like this for hardcore training. We usually try to prepare our troops by giving them basic tools to handle physical, emotional, and mental abuse. I can promise that you are not alone and that no one can fully prepare their bodies for that kind of punishment," Rick said.

"I believe it," I said.

"If there is anything you want to say to me, I promise you won't hurt my feelings. Speak your mind, Kim."

I didn't expect the conversation to go this way. I wanted the opportunity to forgive Rick and tell him how I understood that what he did was necessary for the greater good. I didn't want him to feel guilty. There he was, telling me to give him shit because he could take it. Not only did he not feel guilty, but he wasn't going to apologize.

I shrugged. "I can't stay angry."

"Maybe you should enlist; you would make an excellent soldier," Rick said, pursing his lips in approval.

I snorted. "No, I don't think I'm going to show up at a recruiting office anytime soon."

"If you change your mind, use me as a reference. They'll fast-track you past the waiting list," he said.

"Thanks, I'll keep it in mind," I said, knowing full well that wasn't going to happen.

Rick stood up and saluted me before turning and leaving the room.

"Well, that was rude." Ana frowned.

"He showed me respect. I'm good with that," I said.

"Well, I'm not. Rick should have at least apologized," Ramesh said.

"He isn't sorry; he'd be lying if he apologized. Insincerity isn't going to help. I think it's better this way," I said.

"You should have at least slapped him." Ana scoffed.

I laughed. "We have to let it go."

---

After a couple of months, Loki and I returned from Germany for a few weeks to get practical experience in the CS department. It was nice to stay in my house, if only for a little while. Jacob had moved in permanently, and his boyfriend Matt often stayed there. I was happy to see their relationship blooming.

Ramesh and I were getting along fabulously. It was my twenty-seventh birthday, and we celebrated it by going out on his sailboat to spread my dad's ashes and have a picnic. It was a beautiful day and not too chilly for the early fall season.

"Loki love's this boat—look at him," I said.

Loki stood on the bow looking out over the water while Ramesh dropped the anchor.

"Good thing, too; I was worried he may experience seasickness. The waves in Lake Ontario can get bumpy." Ramesh smiled.

I set out the picnic basket, and he uncorked the wine bottle. Loki's attention was back on us when he smelled the meat and cheese after I opened the containers. Ramesh poured us glasses of a local sparkling Riesling, and we kissed then clinked glasses.

I had just finished swallowing my sip when I heard both phones go off. I ignored mine, but Ramesh looked at his screen and hit answer, putting the phone down in front of us on speaker. I rolled my eyes at him and chuckled.

"Ramesh, I see Kim is with you?" Samuel asked.

"Yes, we're both here. Is everything okay?" He looked at me, and we stared at each other, waiting for an answer.

"I need you both to come in, I see you're out on the lake; sorry about that, but a few of our new sensors went off in Antarctica. Nekxus is calling all hands on deck for this," Samuel said, his tone severe.

"You're kidding?" Ramesh said.

"Is it the Darachnids?" I asked.

"We don't think so. Something from the dark matter is moving, and it's *massive*. I'll see you when you get back." He ended the call.

"I'll be damned if we let this spread go to waste. Let's eat up first," Ramesh said.

THE END

# Acknowledgments

I want to express gratitude to my beta readers: Susan, Sylvia and Leanne, whose observations and feedback helped me improve my work. I value the input you all have given me.

I would also like to thank my editor *KristenCorrects* for thoroughly reviewing my manuscript and fine-tuning it with professional expertise.

I am very grateful to *Krystal Penney*, the graphic designer who created the surreal book cover that exceeded my visual expectations.

Last but not least, I wish to thank my family: Alexander & Jana, who volunteered to read each chapter as I wrote it, providing inspiring sentiments throughout this book and Curtis, who patiently listened to me brainstorm during our walks.

———

Your support and kindness mean the world to me.

# About the Author

Jody Swannell is a Canadian author residing in Waterloo, Ontario. Moving frequently in the past - she loves to explore and gain new experiences.

Her writing style is contemporary fiction under a few different genres; this is her first sci-fi novel.

Her goal is to keep readers eagerly turning pages while trying to guess what happens next, occasionally adding a splash of romance here and there to spice things up.

*Also by Jody Swannell*

Wrath of a Sister

Magic Passage

Manufactured by Amazon.ca
Bolton, ON